THE
HUNT CLUB

ALSO BY JOHN LESCROART

THE
HUNT CLUB

JOHN LESCROART

DUTTON

DUTTON
Published by Penguin Group (USA) Inc.
375 Hudson Street, New York, New York 10014, U.S.A.
Penguin Group (Canada), 90 Eglinton Avenue East, Suite 700, Toronto, Ontario M4P 2Y3, Canada
(a division of Pearson Penguin Canada Inc.); Penguin Books Ltd, 80 Strand, London WC2R 0RL,
England; Penguin Ireland, 25 St Stephen's Green, Dublin 2, Ireland (a division of Penguin Books Ltd);
Penguin Group (Australia), 250 Camberwell Road, Camberwell, Victoria 3124, Australia (a division
of Pearson Australia Group Pty Ltd); Penguin Books India Pvt Ltd, 11 Community Centre, Panchsheel
Park, New Delhi 110 017, India; Penguin Group (NZ), cnr Airborne and Rosedale Roads, Albany,
Auckland 1310, New Zealand (a division of Pearson New Zealand Ltd); Penguin Books
(South Africa) (Pty) Ltd, 24 Sturdee Avenue, Rosebank, Johannesburg 2196, South Africa

Penguin Books Ltd, Registered Offices: 80 Strand, London WC2R 0RL, England

Published by Dutton, a member of Penguin Group (USA) Inc.

ISBN 0-525-94914-3

Printed in the United States of America
Set in Salon
Designed by Leonard Telesca

PUBLISHER'S NOTE
This book is a work of fiction. Names, characters, places, and incidents either are the product of the
author's imagination or are used fictitiously, and any resemblance to actual persons, living or dead,
business establishments, events, or locales is entirely coincidental.

To Justine Rose Lescroart,
daughter of my heart

THE
HUNT CLUB

"You think you know yourself until things start happening, until you lose the insulation of normality."

—Robert Wilson, *A Small Death in Lisbon*

That was then . . .

1 / (1992)

From the outside, the large four-story San Francisco apartment building on Twenty-second Avenue near Balboa in the Richmond District was well kept up, but I had seen that before when I'd been called on complaints, and by itself it meant nothing. This building probably had forty units, each one a self-contained and discrete universe inhabited by singles, doubles, students, old folks, happy and unhappy, married and unmarried, gay and straight couples, with or without children.

On this cold and dreary morning, the mandated call had come from Cabrillo Elementary, where the kids were in sixth and fourth grade, respectively. Both of them had been absent the entire previous week of school, and no parent had called the office with an excuse. When the school's attendance officer had phoned the Dades' home for the first time last Wednesday, she'd left a message that no one returned. On Friday, she called again and talked to Tammy, the sixth grader, who said everybody had the flu, that was all. No, her mother was too sick and sleeping and couldn't come to the phone. Tammy thought that she and her brother would probably be better by Monday and she'd bring a note from her mother or the doctor. Somebody, anyway. Monday, they didn't make it, though, and the attendance officer had called Child Protective Services to check out what might really be going on. She noted on the complaint that both children appeared to be undernourished and poorly clothed.

Now it was Tuesday morning, a little before 10:00. My partner for the call, my favorite partner in CPS, for that matter, named Bettina Keck, stood with me—Wyatt Hunt—outside the building after the first few rings from the button in the lobby went unanswered.

"Why am I not believing nobody's home?" Bettina said.

It was freezing standing there and I had already had enough waiting. I was going down the list of residents' namecards, pressing each button one after the other. "I hate when they make us do this. If anyone answers, you up for talking?"

"Why me?"

"You're smarter? Wait, no, that can't be it."

"Funnier, too," she said. And as if on cue, a squawk came out of the box, the voice of an elderly woman. "Who's down there?"

Bettina leaned close to the speaker. "FedEx delivery."

"See?" I said. "Brilliant."

Bettina shushed me and we heard, "I didn't order anything."

"What apartment are you?"

"Eight."

My finger went to the namecard for Bettina to read. She got it without missing a beat. "You're Mrs. Craft?"

"I am."

"Well, you've got to sign for your delivery."

"What is it?"

"Right now, ma'am, it's a brown box. If you don't want it, I'll just have it sent back."

"To where?"

"Let me see. It looks like a jewelry store. Maybe you won a prize."

A pause. Then, "Oh, all right."

And the door buzzed, letting us into the building.

"You might be smarter at that," I said, holding the door for my partner.

"No might about it." She smiled at me. "Best part of the job."

We took the stairs, through a door just inside the entrance, and came out on the third floor. The Dade residence was number 22, down the hallway on our left, and we stood in front of its door, listening to the television playing inside. Bettina nodded and I knocked. Immediately, the TV sound diminished. I knocked again. And again. "Whoever just turned down the television," I said in a loud and authoritative tone, "open the door, please."

Finally, a young girl's voice, thin and timid: "Who is it?"

"Child Protective Services," Bettina said softly. "Open up, please."

"I'm not allowed."

"You're not allowed *not* to, honey. Is that Tammy?"

After a hesitation, the voice asked, "How do you know that?"

"Your school called us to check on you. They're worried about you and your brother. You've missed a lot of days."

"We've been sick."

"That's what they said."

"We'd just like to make sure you're okay," I put in.

"We might still be contagious."

"We'll take that chance, Tammy," Bettina said. "We're not allowed to go away until we see you."

"If you don't let us in," I added, "we may have to come back with the police. You don't want that, do you?"

"You don't need to call the police," Tammy said. "We haven't done anything wrong."

Effortlessly tag-teaming with me, Bettina spoke. "Nobody's saying you did, honey. We just want to make sure everything's okay in there. Is your brother with you?"

"He's okay, except he's still sick."

"How about your mom? Is she there with you? Or your dad?"

"We don't have a dad."

"Okay, your mom, then."

"She's sleeping. She doesn't feel good, either. She's got the flu, too."

"Tammy," keeping a rising sense of concern out of my voice, "we need to come in right now. Please, open the door."

A couple of seconds more and we heard the lock turn, and there she was. Remarkably composed and reasonably well dressed, I thought immediately, for a girl who was clearly starving to death.

Bettina went down on one knee. I heard her asking, "Tammy, honey, have you had anything to eat lately?" while I opened the door and passed behind them, half-hearing the young girl's response: "Some bread."

In the living room in front of the television set, an emaciated young boy sat under a pile of blankets, staring with hollow and empty eyes at the silent screen. "Hey, buddy," I said gently. "Are you Mickey?"

The boy glanced over at me and nodded.

"How are you doing?"

"Okay," he said in a tinsel voice, "except I'm a little hungry."

"Well, we'll get you some food right away, then. How's that sound?"

"Good. If you want."

"I do. I do want. Where's your mom, Mickey?"

Bettina, holding Tammy's hand, heard the question as she came into the room. "She's in her bedroom," Bettina said. "Maybe I should stay with the kids in here a minute, and you go see how she is?"

"On it," I said.

Mrs. Dade was in her bed, all right, and sleeping. But it wasn't the kind of sleep where you woke up.

The autopsy later revealed that she had died of an overdose of heroin, probably in the form of black tar, probably on the third or fourth day the kids had missed school. While we were waiting for the unnecessary ambulance, Tammy told us that her mother had lost her job at the Safeway a couple of weeks ago because of her drug problem, which was really a disease she couldn't help. She had told Tammy and Mickey that she knew she shouldn't be using drugs, that they were bad, and she was trying to stop, but it was really, really hard. The main thing, though, was that they must never, ever tell anybody because if the police ever found out, they'd come and either take Mom away or take them away from her.

Tammy took DARE at school, and she knew that this was true. Everybody agreed you shouldn't live with people who used drugs.

Which was why Tammy hadn't told anybody.

And this hadn't been the only time with Mom. Sometimes she would disappear into her bedroom for a couple of days. This was just longer than usual. Tammy didn't want to look in because sometimes her mom would get mad if she checked up on her. She didn't want her children to see her doing drugs. She was ashamed of it. In a day or two more, Tammy thought, her mom would probably come out of her bedroom, or she would go check when they were really out of food, and then they'd go back to school and Mom would go shopping and get them something to eat. Meanwhile, Tammy just fed herself and Mickey from what was left in the kitchen. She rationed it so it wouldn't run out. She needed to protect her brother, too, along with her mom.

I went and searched. They were down to three slices of mildewed white bread, some rice crackers, and about a tablespoon of peanut butter.

2 / (1996)

I had been on the job for five years and still didn't have my own office at Child Protective Services. I didn't really want or need one. Seventy-five to eighty percent of my work was, after all, in the field. The rest of it was writing reports of what I'd done. The supervisors got the offices, and as far as I was concerned, they could have them. Supervisors worried about closing cases and about numbers and about following established procedures. I cared about saving kids' lives. There tended to be a difference in approach.

After negotiating the gauntlet of homeless persons camped on the surrounding streets, I would arrive at the Otis Avenue building every morning somewhere around eight o'clock, check in for any possible true emergency calls, then most days pick up my daily allotment of "normal" cases. Every one of these was an emergency of some kind, although too often not designated as such by the bureaucracy.

To get an emergency declaration and hence the immediate attention of a caseworker or team of them, the home situation of the child had to be defined as life-threatening in the near term. Say, a woman holding her three-year-old by the heels out of a six-story window would be an emergency. Day-to-day problems were of a lesser nature and included chronic starvation or suspected physical abuse or a parent in some drug-induced or otherwise psychically impaired state. Or an uncle in a suspected carnal relationship with his eight-year-old niece.

The more or less routine call this morning was from Holly Park, a housing project near the southern border of the city. Due to its internal and conflicting gang affiliations, its grinding poverty and persistent air of hopelessness, and the astronomical percentage of its population that either used or dealt street drugs, it had the highest neighborhood homicide rate after Hunter's Point. And was undefeated for number one in most other crimes, violent and not.

I don't mind fog or rain, heat or cold, but I hate the wind, and today, a Thursday in early April, it was blowing hard. In an effort to save it from the vandalism that plagued Holly Park, I parked my already beat-up Lumina three blocks east of the project, then opened my door to a gust of Alaskan Express against which my parka was about as effective as chain mail. The day was bright and sunny, but the wind was relentless and bitter, bitter, bitter cold.

Hands tucked into the bottoms of my jacket pockets, I got to the address I'd memorized and, from across the street, stared at the tagged and scarred wasteland I was supposed to enter. I knew that fifty years ago the place had once been a showcase of sorts—the barracks-style apartment units freshly painted, with grassy areas and well-kept gardens, even trees. Residents got fined if they didn't mow their lawns, keep their individual porches and balconies clean and free of laundry or garbage. Now there wasn't one tree left, no hint of a garden, barely a blade of grass. From my vantage across the street, I picked up hundreds of glints of light in the packed tan earth surrounding the buildings—I'd been here many times before, knew that these were remains of countless discarded and broken bottles of beer, wine, liquor, anything alcoholic that came in glass. Pepsi and Coke weren't locked in combat in this arena.

Perhaps most disturbing of all, I saw no one. Of course, with the cold and the wind, people wouldn't be out to bask and frolic, but I kind of expected to see some soul passing between the pods of buildings, some woman hanging laundry, somebody doing something. But the place appeared completely deserted.

I wondered whether I should have waited a few more minutes at the office and hooked up with a partner for this call. One of the relatively new hires, maybe, who still had some fire in the gut. But finding someone in the office I could count on, with whom I could stand to spend much time, had become all but impossible.

Because the office had in the past couple of years become cancerous. This coincided with the appointment and arrival of Deputy Director Wilson Mayhew. From my line supervisors splitting hairs and playing power games, to so many of my fellow emergency response workers putting their experience to work dodging calls when they bothered to report in at all, most people in the department seemed to take their cultural cues from Mayhew. We were all county employees after all, covered by the union and essentially invulnerable to discipline. Without a motivational deputy director, caseworkers who cared about the work and about the kids tended to burn out after a few years. Now most of those who remained stayed on because they couldn't be touched—between accrued vacation and sick days and cheating on your time card in a hundred clever ways. Fully a third of the caseworker staff did nothing substantive ever. A couple never even came in to work, and it didn't seem to matter to Mayhew or the lower-ranking supes, who were then spared the hassle of having to confront them.

Bettina, still on the job, was having some substance issues herself in the wake of her divorce, and now I preferred to work alone.

Well, there was nothing for it but to go ahead. I was here now. And Keeshiana Jefferson needed help now. I had to go in and assess how bad it was. I took a step off the curb.

"Hey."

I turned, stepped back, double-taking at the absolutely impossible sight of another white guy in this neighborhood. Then, the features congealed into something vaguely then very familiar. "Dev?" I said. "Devin Juhle?" Juhle had been the shortstop to my second base on my high school team. Before college separated us, he'd probably been my best friend.

The other man broke an easy if slightly perplexed grin, then his own recognition kicked in. "Wyatt? What are you doing here?"

"Working," I said, more or less automatically reaching for my wallet, my identification. "I'm with CPS. Child Protective Services."

"I know what CPS is. I'm a cop."

"You're not."

"Am, too."

"You're not dressed like a cop."

"I'm an inspector. We don't wear a uniform. I'm with homicide."

I threw a quick look across the street. "You're saying I'm too late, then?"

"For what?"

"Keeshiana Jefferson."

"Never heard of her."

A rush of relief swept over me. At least Keeshiana wasn't the victim in the homicide Dev was investigating. I might be in time after all. "Well, hey," I said, "good to see you, but I got a gig in there."

Juhle put a hand on my arm. "You're not going in there alone?"

"That's my plan." Seeing Juhle's concern, I added, "Not to worry, Dev. I do this every day."

"Here?"

"Here, there, everywhere."

"And do what?"

"Talk to people mostly. Sometimes take a kid out."

Juhle cast a worried glance over to the projects, then back to me. "Are you packing?"

"A gun?" I chortled and spread the sides of my parka wide open. "Just cookies and chips in case somebody's hungry. I really gotta go."

"What's the exact address?" Juhle asked me. "I'm hanging here anyway with my partner, looking for witnesses. I'll stay close."

"No need," I said, "but I appreciate the offer. But really, catch you later. I gotta go check the place out now."

The wooden door to the barrack unit closed behind me, and the hallway went almost pitch-dark. Someone had painted out the long glass windows on either side of the door. I let my eyes adjust for a few seconds, then tried the light switch, which had come into view. It didn't work.

There was a stink in the hall, the familiar trifecta of mold, urine, animal. I also noted a whiff of pot and tobacco smoke, although the stronger smells predominated. The wind howled outside as it tore between the buildings, and hearing it, I thought to turn back and open the door again slightly to get some light. Just outside in a pile of rubble against the building, I spied a rock that would serve my purpose. I picked it up and propped the door with it, holding it open about five inches.

The Jeffersons lived in number 3, the back unit on the left side. I listened at the door and heard only the familiar drone of a television but couldn't really tell if it came from this apartment or one of the others. I knocked, got no response, knocked again. "Mrs. Jefferson."

Finally, a shuffle of feet, then a woman's voice from inside. "Who's that?"

I knew a few tricks myself. You say Child Protective Services to some people, the door never opens. But you say Human Resources, of which CPS is a part, they often think it's about their welfare payments, and it's open sesame. Mrs. Jefferson opened the door a crack, the chain still on. "What you want?"

"I'd like to talk to you a minute if I could."

"You doin' that."

"We got a call about Keeshiana. Is she all right?"

"Who called?"

"Your mother." Thank God, I thought. It should have been the girl's school, since she'd already missed two full weeks, but they hadn't gotten around to it by the time I called them to verify the absences. Luckily, the grandmother had come by the apartment yesterday and after leaving had called CPS. "She's worried about you both." I shifted to another foot, keeping the body language relaxed.

"Ain't nothin' to worry 'bout. I be taking care of my baby."

"I'm sure you are, Mrs. Jefferson, but when somebody's mom calls in and says they're worried, I'm supposed to come out and see if everything's okay." I pulled the parka closer around me. "If I could just come in and talk to you both for a minute, I could be on my way."

To my right, the door at the opposite end of the hallway suddenly opened all the way with a bang, and a posse of three men came inside amid a blizzard of profanity and posturing. All of them were layered up with jackets, all of them down with the perp walk. My testicles withdrew into my body as Mrs. Jefferson shut the door on me.

The back door stayed open. The leader of the gang, seeing me, stopped and looked around behind him, then down the hall behind me. "Yo, fuck."

I nodded. "'Sup," I said, dishing back some brilliant repartee. But I turned to face them, standing my ground.

"'Sup wi' this shit?" They'd come up close, surrounding me, all intimidation, the usual. The man's eyes looked a sickly yellow. He hadn't shaved in several days. Or, apparently, brushed his teeth ever.

I looked him in his yellow eyes. "It's no shit," I said. I held up my ID. "CPS, guys. Just checkin' on Keeshiana in here. See she's all right."

The front man took a beat, another look around. He swore again, cocked his head, and the posse moved past. The last man, eschewing his earlier mannerly approach, hawked and spit on the floor at my feet.

Tempted to tell them to have a nice day, I figured there wasn't any advantage in it and instead bit my tongue, then turned and knocked again on the door. "Me again," I said.

The door opened, no chain this time. "You some kind of fool or what?" she asked.

I followed her in, the door closed again and bolted behind. It was the kind of apartment I'd seen on dozens of similar occasions before. Kitchen, living room, two small bedrooms. Neither neat nor clean, with dirty clothes strewn on furniture, paper bags littering the floor, KFC and McDonald's containers stacked in piles on end tables and bookshelves that hadn't seen a book in half a century.

She'd pulled the blinds and covered most of the windows with drapes and what looked like sheets or pillowcases, so it was almost as dark as the hallway inside, but the corner of a sheet over the upper half of the kitchen window had fallen off and let in some daylight. "This is my baby, Keeshiana," Mrs. Jefferson said. The child was at the kitchen table. A sweet-looking diminutive six-year-old in a red T-shirt, her arms rested in front of her, hands clasped.

I didn't put out my hand, kept everything low-key, nodding only. "My name's Wyatt." I gave her my professional smile, and she nodded back warily. I turned to the mother. "Maybe we could all sit a minute?" And pulled out a chair. "So, Letitia," I began to the mother, "is that what they call you?"

"Lettie."

"Lettie, then."

But she cut me off, suddenly angry. "My momma got no call putting you on us. I ain't done nothing wrong, just protectin' me and my baby from evil."

"From evil?"

"Satan," she said.

"The devil?"

"Right."

"Is he after you in some special way?"

"He tole me. Said if she went out, he'd take her. He wants her bad."

"When did he tell you this?"

"Couple of weeks now. I seen him, you know."

"Where?"

She tossed her head. "Just out there."

"In the hallway?"

A nod. "And outside, too. That's why I got the windows covered. So he can't see in, know she's here."

I suddenly understood how the glass panes beside the hallway doors had come to be painted. I reached inside my parka, produced a bag of potato chips and a Snickers bar, and put them on the table without a word, sliding them down within Keeshiana's reach.

"It's okay, honey," her mother said, and the girl gingerly took the potato chips, pulled open the bag, and started eating them quickly, one by one.

I took advantage of the distraction to break the ice with her. "So, Keeshiana, you haven't been outside for a time?"

She looked a question at her mother, got a nod, came back to me. "No."

"You ever want to?"

She ate another chip, this time looking down at the table in front of her. "It's 'cause I'm bad, Momma says. That's why he wants me."

"I been prayin' every day," Lettie said. "Every night. She gettin' better."

I wasn't sure I understood, but I didn't like the sound of any of it. "How are you bad, Keeshiana? You don't seem bad to me."

"Momma says."

"No," Lettie said. "I don't say. But Satan, he callin' her."

"How does he do that? Lettie? Keeshiana?" I looked from one to the other. Finally settled on the mother. "Lettie. How long has it been since you've let her go outside?"

Her eyes went to her baby. She shook her head. "Since he got here."

"The devil? When was that?"

"I don't know exactly."

"A couple of weeks? A month?"

Lettie blinked against the onset of tears. "She go out and you can't fight him. He take her."

"He won't take her," I said. "I was just out there, and there was no sign of him."

At that moment, the wind gusted with a low shriek, and the kitchen window shook above us. "There's your sign," the mother said. "He laughin' at you, waitin' his chance."

"That was the wind, Lettie. Just the wind."

"No! He got you fooled."

"Momma," Keeshiana said. Now she was holding the Snickers bar. "Please."

Lettie again nodded.

Trying to escape the absurdity, I resorted to harsh reality. "Lettie," I said softly. "Mrs. Jefferson, listen to me. I need to know that you're going to let Keeshiana out of the apartment here so she can go back to school. Do you understand?"

"But I can't. I really can't. You can see that."

I didn't want to get into threats that I would take the child. If I didn't make progress, I'd have to get to that soon enough. Trying to remove the girl from her mother's custody would always be a last resort, and it was the last thing I wanted to do. "I tell you what," I said. "Why don't you and Keeshiana dress up warm and we go outside now for a minute all together? Lettie, we can each hold one of

Keeshiana's hands. We see anything that makes us uncomfortable, we come right back in here. Promise."

Lettie was frowning, shaking her head from side to side, but the young girl stopped her chewing and her eyes lit up. "You could just undo me a minute, Momma," she said.

Struck by the phrase, hairs raising on the back of my neck with premonition, I said, "What do you mean, 'undo,' Keeshiana?"

"You know." She wriggled in the chair. "So I can get up?"

Frustration crowded out any other expression on Lettie's face. "You fine," she said to her child, then spoke to me, her tone dispassionate, even reasonable. "She don't need to go gettin' up. She get up, she try an' go out."

My flat gaze went from Lettie to her daughter. "Keeshiana, I'd like to see you stand up, please."

Her eyes, panicked, flew to her mother.

Which was my signal. With an exaggerated slowness, I pushed back, stood up, and sidestepped to Keeshiana's end of the table. Pulling out her chair, I drew in a sharp breath. A clothesline wrapped perhaps a dozen times around her waist and legs held her in her place.

Devin Juhle, the homicide cop from my childhood, fell in next to me as I emerged from the darkened pod into the bright and windswept cut of packed earth and glass that led out to the sidewalks. I was carrying Keeshiana in my arms, a blanket wrapped around her legs, her own arms around my neck.

"What are you doing?" Juhle asked.

"Getting her out of here. Her mother had her tied up."

"She let you just take her?"

"I explained the situation, gave her the forms."

"Still. Anybody sees you or she come screaming out raising a stink, the people here . . ."

"The mom's gonna learn to live with it. I do this for a living, okay? There's a technique." I was walking quickly, breathing hard. "You got a car nearby?" I asked. "I'm three blocks away. Mistake."

"Yeah, but anybody comes out—"

"That's why I'm in half a jog here, Dev," I snapped, cutting him off. I indicated Keeshiana. "I'm worried about her."

"My car's just down here, around the corner," Juhle said, and led the way for us, double time.

3 / (2000)

Deputy Director Wilson Mayhew left a polite note in my cubicle asking if I could please come to his office at my earliest convenience. There was nothing ominous about the summons except that it was the first time I'd had any personal contact with Mayhew since we exchanged cordial hellos at the Christmas party two years before. At that time, finger right on the pulse of those he supervised, he had asked me what my connection was to the CPS. Since I'd only been with the department for eight years back then, and ever since Mayhew himself had come aboard five years before, I told him to keep it between us, but that I was really FBI, working undercover to ferret out the pimp who was running the illegal-alien child-prostitution ring out of the CPS. Surely he'd heard of it.

After that, at least he knew who I was.

So that October afternoon, I found myself standing in front of the DD's desk in his third-floor office on Otis Avenue. Though the furnishing and decor of the rest of the CPS offices could have been case studies in drab bureaucratic aesthetics, heavy on grays, greens, and metal surfaces, Mayhew's workplace, like the man himself, was done up in a semblance of style if not taste. The desk was an enormous redwood burl, polished and asymmetrical, without any apparent drawers, and a flat surface only large enough to hold a phone and a nearly empty in-and-out box. There was no sign of a computer or workstation of any kind. He had three Walter Keane paintings—large-eyed children on the verge of tears (get it?)—framed and hung to cover any free wall space. A teak credenza hugged the wall to my right, opposite the windows. It was covered by a large crocheted doily on which stood what appeared to be an actual silver Russian samovar. The bookshelves behind him held very few books and mostly featured silver-framed photographs of Mayhew with the past three mayors, the chief of police, Governor Gray Davis, Boz Scaggs, Danielle Steel, and a few other celebrities I couldn't identify. The top shelf was entirely devoted to Lladró ceramics. Touching.

Mayhew stood. His Armani couldn't disguise the extra forty pounds he carried. His round, faintly cherubic face glistened slightly over the double chin, as though perhaps he'd overscrubbed it. A high forehead wasn't improved or mitigated by his decision to comb what hair there was straight back. His own mother probably wouldn't have called him attractive, but he nevertheless exuded a confidence born of the exercise of power. The fat older white guy who'd made it, and if you didn't like how he looked, you could bite him.

He pushed his bulk up from in his chair and reached over the desk to shake my hand and thank me for coming so promptly. He was back in his seat by the time I answered.

"Sure. What's up? Is there a problem?"

"No, no. No problem at all. In fact, rather the opposite."

"Great." I waited.

"So how long have you been on the street now, working cases?"

"Eight years, sir."

He emitted a low whistle. "That's what I'd understood. Do you realize that you're the senior caseworker downstairs?"

"I hadn't really thought about it."

"And you've had nothing but glowing evaluations all that time."

I shrugged. "I care about the work, sir."

"Obviously. Obviously." Sitting back, he linked his hands over his stomach. "The point is that you've got a lot of firsthand street knowledge you could pass on to new caseworkers coming up into the department."

"I try to help when I can."

"Yes, well . . . but I was thinking we might want to formalize that relationship a bit." He came forward, his small eyes locking into mine, a smile of sorts appearing. "I'll put it right to you, Wyatt. Have you ever considered stepping up to supervisor?"

"I've never applied, no, sir."

"Why not?"

I gave it a moment's thought. "I guess I like being on the street."

"That's commendable. Where the action is, huh?"

"Something like that."

"Would you consider moving up?"

Again, I didn't answer right away. I must have appeared to be looking around the room at his pictures and trophies.

He blindly read it as envy. "With your stellar record to date," he said, "it's not out of the question you could be sitting here where I am in a matter of years."

Oh, be still, my heart.

Besides, this was a blatant lie. Mayhew himself had never worked the street. I didn't even know for sure that he had a master's in social work, which was a prerequisite for us street types. But casework was not one of the prerequisites for deputy director. Political connection was. Mayhew was the brother of a city supervisor, Chrissa Mayhew. I neither had nor wanted to have any part of that.

But we were being friendly, and I saw no reason to change the tone. "Well, it's flattering that you should consider me . . ."

He jumped in again before I could outright refuse. "It's quite a significant bump in salary, you know."

I shook my head. "It's not that."

"What is it, then?"

"What I said. I guess I'm just not much of an office person. I like going out on calls."

Sitting back, slumped in the chair again, Mayhew's face had closed down. "And you often go out alone."

It wasn't a question. Still, I said, "Yes, sir, I do."

"Why is that?"

Because most of my coworkers, whom you've hired, are unmotivated, you idiot. But I said, "Sometimes it's hard to coordinate schedules."

"And do you think that's particularly efficient?"

"Sometimes in the field, an inexperienced partner can be more a hindrance than a help."

"But how are they to gain that vital hands-on experience if veteran caseworkers won't go on calls with them?"

"Well . . . it's not a matter of 'won't.' Some of the people downstairs feel like they have to write up their reports, and that's their priority. And sometimes that keeps them at their desks." We were leaving the faux friendly arena quickly. "As to efficiency, you said I've had good performance reviews."

"On the calls themselves, yes. But we've got a ship to run here, and we need all the sailors to cooperate if we're going to keep it afloat."

The old salt in me failed to respond to the analogy. *So hire people who want to go out and do the work.* But I dredged up a hopeful smile. "I like to think I'm cooperating, sir."

For a long moment, Mayhew chewed on his thin lower lip. Sighing heavily with apparently deep regret, he said, "We've got several promising young people we'd like to bring on here, Wyatt, and frankly they could start at a much lower salary than you're drawing right now. Even if you moved up to supervisor, the impact on our budget would be positive if we could bring some of these people on."

So now it was a budget issue. Mayhew was pulling out all the stops as I began to see the bottom line. He'd promised a job—*my job*—to the son or daughter of one of his cronies.

"Who would I be replacing?" I asked. "As supervisor?"

"Darlene's been out on maternity leave for five months already," he said. "Two more than she applied for. I don't think she's coming back."

"Can I give it some thought?" I asked.

"Sure." The shiny face beamed. "Take a few days, Wyatt, as much time as you need."

I said no.

Two weeks after my refusal, Mayhew announced an administrative shakeup in the department whereby the three caseworkers with the most experience—that would be me, Bettina Keck, and a ten-year vet with chronically poor attendance named Lionel Whitmore—would evaluate both the seriousness and the credibility of abuse reports and assign caseworkers as appropriate. This was essentially the role that our level-one supervisors had filled before, and it was full-time in-office work, but no raise was involved this time.

Every actual case of child abuse was serious, of course, but not every call to report abuse was legitimate. When I'd first started working, I was surprised at the number of these complaints to CPS that turned out to be bogus—called in by fathers wanting to get their baby's mama in trouble or neighbors as payback for other neighbors making too much noise at night or an ex-wife wanting to hassle an ex-husband while he had the kids for a weekend. These and dozens of others like them were the all-too-common ugly, stupid, petty scams in which kids were used as pawns in the adults' games. Citing the facts that we were chronically understaffed, hammered by budget constraints, and overwhelmed by the sheer volume of legitimate complaints, Mayhew decided that his experienced caseworkers would be just the ticket to separate the wheat from the chaff among the complaints and thereby improve the efficiency of the CPS as a whole.

Mayhew's plan was as obvious as it was simple. From his point of view, I wasn't a team player, Bettina was a candidate for rehab, and Lionel was useless. If he could keep me off the street, I'd probably quit before too long. And without me holding down the fort on the false complaints, Bettina and Lionel would both screw up eventually if not sooner, clearing not just one but three caseworker spots. Mayhew could then make three of his wealthy friends happy and maybe get himself a new car—or at least another silver samovar or photo op with a famous person.

But truly outraged now, I would be damned if I was going to let myself be so easily ousted from a career I cared about. I figured I could outlast Mayhew. He needed good, solid caseworkers or he would begin to look bad from the outside. I figured it would be a waiting game, and I'd play it until the worm turned, then I would get assigned back to the street. And thereby win.

Wrong.

Late one Friday afternoon in February, alone at my cubicle—both Bettina and Lionel gone AWOL earlier in the day—with a stack of complaints that needed to be evaluated before the weekend in front of me, I fielded a mandated report from the emergency room at San Francisco General Hospital. A five-year-old Hispanic boy, Miguel Nunoz, had been admitted at a little before two o'clock that afternoon with a broken arm that struck hospital officials as unusual. I called the admitting station and talked to a Dr. Turner, who had discovered that this was the boy's third admission to three different hospitals—two broken bones and a dislocated shoulder—since his mother had taken up with a new boyfriend. Now they had casted the arm, and the mother was, even as we spoke, waiting to take Miguel home, but Turner thought somebody from CPS ought to get out there and talk to both the mom and her son and evaluate the situation before the doctor would feel comfortable releasing the boy back into his mother's custody.

I tended to agree.

Willa Cardoza and Jim Freed were just coming in for the swing shift. Inseparable, both were new hires within the past two years, which meant they were Mayhew's people. I'd never before had anything but professional interactions with either of them, and while not exactly gung ho, they showed up to work every day and seemed okay. At least, apparently, they went out on calls, filed decent reports, did the minimum. I also didn't know at the time—I was not a supervisor and so had no access to worker files—that neither of them had yet had to pull the trigger, i.e., forcibly remove a child from a parent's custody.

Nevertheless, they were the best, not to say only, choice at hand. My job was to evaluate the legitimacy of the complaint, and this one was no doubt as real as a heart attack. So I gave them the quick synopsis and told them they'd better hustle, the mom was sitting in the waiting room, anxious to take the boy home, and Dr. Turner wasn't going to be able to stall her forever.

By the time they left and I'd finished the last of my pile of evaluations, it was close to seven o'clock. Still concerned about the seriousness of the complaint, I swallowed my bile and went up to see if Mayhew was still in his office. His secretary had gone home, but he was there, drinking what looked like brandy in a snifter, talking to someone on the telephone. He made a fast excuse and hung up when he saw me in his doorway. It was my first audience with him since I'd turned down the promotion.

"Yes, Hunt, what is it?"

I'd been Hunt, not Wyatt, since the day. I briefed him on Miguel, told him whom I'd assigned, and said that I thought that this was a case he might want to keep an eye on over the weekend, to follow its disposition.

He thanked me for my responsibility in bringing this serious case to his attention and said that's just what he'd do.

Ms. Nunoz took Miguel home on Friday night. On that Sunday, he was again brought to the hospital, but this time with a concussion from which he did not recover. At the inquest, Dr. Turner testified that he had spoken to me and that I'd assured him that CPS would have someone out to the hospital within an hour, two at the most, but that no one from the department had arrived.

In both of their individual testimonies, Cardoza and Freed admitted that I had given them the case, but that I'd put no particular emphasis on it. Certainly, I had put nothing in writing (and in my haste to get them moving, this at least was true). They'd even gone on another call first—they had the address and case number to prove it—and had arrived at the hospital long after Ms. Nunoz had gone home with her son. Believing that Dr. Turner would never have released the boy if he'd believed there to be danger, they had gone to their next call and left a follow-up note on the Nunozes for Monday morning.

Wilson Mayhew, while I was sitting in front of him in the same small room at the disciplinary hearing, calmly and emphatically denied that I'd ever mentioned the case to him in any context whatsoever.

4 / (2001)

When all the administrative hearings and appeals ended, the bottom line was that I could stay with the CPS if I accepted a formal letter of reprimand they wanted to include in my personnel file. There was nothing else even remotely negative in that file, and I'd done nothing wrong in the Nunoz case. No power on earth was going to get me to take any part of the hit for Mayhew's betrayal and the incompetence and dishonesty of his protégés. I realized that the price for my refusal to accept the reprimand letter was my career at CPS.

So be it.

For ten years I've lived in a rent-controlled, barn-size warehouse south of Market, essentially in the shadow of the 101 Freeway. When I'd first moved in, it was empty space with a twenty-five-foot ceiling. I'd drywalled off and enclosed a little over a third of the three thousand square feet, and within that area, I'd put down industrial carpet and further subdivided it into three discrete units—a living room/kitchen, my bedroom, and the bathroom.

Five months after I quit, I was on my futon reading the final pages of *The Last Lion*, the great second volume of Manchester's biography of Winston Churchill. When I finished, I put the book down and sat for a while, contemplating the life of the man about whom I'd just been reading. Brilliant military leader, mesmerizing public speaker, superb watercolorist, Nobel Prize–winning author, prime minister of England and—oh, yeah—savior of the Western world. His personal trials between the two world wars, when he was discredited and vilified by enemies and friends alike, put my set-back with Mayhew and the CPS into some sort of perspective.

Which isn't to say I didn't have some issues with rage. Mostly I'd been working those issues off by windsurfing for a couple of hours nearly every day down at Coyote Point. I was also in two men's basketball leagues where elbows got thrown. I jogged the Embarcadero a lot. Plugged in my Strat and nearly blew the windows out of the warehouse. With Devin Juhle, several times a month, I'd stop by Jackson's Arms in South City and shoot a few hundred 9 mm rounds at what I imagined to be Wilson Mayhew's head. Amy Wu, a sympatico lawyer in town I'd met through CPS, was a good platonic drinking buddy with a light-handed knack for keeping in check my temper, always hair-trigger and worse since I'd quit work.

But as I say, I was working on it.

I got up and went to check the contents of my refrigerator. Standing barefoot in my kitchen area, the crud under my feet made me realize that I hadn't done a stem-to-stern clean of my rooms in a while, and without thinking too much about it, I grabbed a mop. When I'd finished with the floor, I emptied my hamper into the washing machine off my bedroom, added detergent, and set it for a heavy load. I wiped down the counters in the bathroom and kitchen, then scoured the corners for cobwebs and dust. Next, I ran the dishes that I'd been stacking rinsed in the dishwasher for the past week or so—mostly coffee mugs, a few utensils, and small plates.

Now I was undressed, ready for bed. My clothes spun, thumping in the dryer. The counters and floors were clean enough to eat off. The dishwasher was silent. My bedroom, like the living room, featured windows high in the wall facing Brannan Street, and because of the streetlights outside, my quarters were almost never entirely dark. With all of my own lights off, as they were now, the rooms and the warehouse in general retained about the brightness of moon glow.

The telephone rang and I picked it up. "French Laundry," I said.

"If this is really the French Laundry," a female voice said, "I'd like to make a reservation."

"I'm sorry. We don't do reservations."

"I thought if you called precisely two months to the day before you wanted to eat, exactly at nine A.M., you could get one."

"That's only if there's a free table and if the phone's not busy, which it always is."

"But not now."

"No, but it's not nine A.M. So I'm sorry."

"Is there any way I could get a reservation now?"

"Are the first three letters of your last name *m-r-l*?"

"Those aren't the first three letters of anybody's last name. Besides, my last name has only two letters."

"Then I'm sorry, we can't fit you in."

"You don't take people with two-letter last names?"

"Only very rarely." But we'd played that out as far as it would go. I asked Wu if she were looking for a partner to drink with tonight.

"Afraid not. I'm working."

"Still?" I looked at my watch. "At ten thirty?"

"Billable hours wait for no one, Wyatt. They're here, I jump on 'em." She paused for a beat. "You want to guess whose name just came across my desk?"

"Winston Churchill."

"Good guess but wrong. Wilson Mayhew. Ring a bell?"

"Vaguely."

"Have you heard anything about him recently?"

I wasn't entirely able to hide the jolt of excitement. "What do you know, Wu? Tell me it's bad news. He's not dead, is he? That would be too fair."

"No, he's not dead. But apparently he is hurt. Or at least he says he's hurt."

"What kind of hurt?"

"Terrible, fully debilitating, work-induced, stress-related back pain."

"Wow. Those are a lot of adjectives."

"Yes, they are."

"So what do they all mean? That somehow it's not physical?"

"No. The pain is real pain if, in fact, he feels it. But the exact physical diagnosis can be difficult."

"So how did you find out about Mayhew? Is he your client somehow?"

"No. But one of our biggest single clients is the California Medical Insurance agency, which handles workers' comp benefits for state workers. But we also have a section that specializes generally in exposing medical fraud."

"Okay."

"Okay. Well. Have you ever heard of Chief's Disease?"

"No. Does Mayhew have it?"

The question slowed her down. "Actually, that may not be a bad call. Do you know what it is?"

I had never heard of it and she filled me in. Evidently each one of the previous *six* directors of the California Highway Patrol had filed workers' comp claims for disability in the final months of their respective terms in office, and every one of them was now drawing over one hundred thousand dollars a year in disability payments on top of their regular pension from their retirements. One of the ex-chiefs, she went on, whose inability to continue working at the Highway Patrol had been caused by a diagnosis of stress-induced hypertension, had taken over as the director of security at the San Francisco International Airport, a post that paid over one hundred fifty thousand dollars per year. Between his full pension from the Highway Patrol, the disability, and the new job, this hardworking law-enforcement officer was making nearly four hundred thousand dollars, much of it tax-free, all from taxpayer funds.

"That's a good job," I said.

"It's a great job," she replied. "And we've been hired to see that he gets a chance to lose it or at least the disability-pay part of it."

"And how do you find that out?"

"Mostly legal stuff. We depose witnesses who work or worked with the guy, subpoena medical records, demand reexamination with our own doctors, check his medications, like that. But we also use private investigators to follow these people around, see for example if they forget to wear their neck brace when they go water-skiing and think nobody's looking. Or, in the case of our airport security director, if he still pursues the low-stress sport of bungee jumping with his son."

"You're kidding."

"We haven't caught him red-handed yet, but we've got hearsay witnesses. We'll find out one way or the other. But the point—the reason I called you—isn't Mr. Airport Security. It's Wilson Mayhew."

"You're reviewing his claim."

"No flies on you," she said. "We got the latest batch of paperwork from CalMed this afternoon, and I was doing my pro forma review of red-flagged claims, and I recognized Mayhew's name from our many fascinating talks."

"As well you should, Ames. So what happened? Wilson got flagged?"

"Yes, he did. But don't get your hopes up too far about that, Wyatt. It's automatic for all permanent, full-disability claims. Beyond that, it's any claim over a hundred grand a year. Then also Mayhew's claiming stress-related, nonspecific injury—back pain is the classic—where there's no immediate and apparent physical cause. He didn't fall down an elevator shaft and break his back, for example. He doesn't have a herniated disk or anything else we can see in the X-rays or pick up on the MRI. Evidently, he was helping one of his employees lift something at work, and he felt a bad tweak and went down. The next morning, he couldn't get out of bed, although apparently he's semi-ambulatory now." She took a breath. "So he gets flagged on all counts."

"He's lying."

"He may be. Although I have seen claims like his that turned out to be legitimate."

"I know the guy," I said, "and there's no way he helped somebody try to lift anything bigger than a paper clip."

She said, "You want to try to prove that?"

"What do you mean?"

"I mean, help us determine if his claim is legitimate."

"How would I do that?"

"Any way you could."

A hole opened in the conversation. Finally, I found a voice. "Haven't you got a bunch of private investigators you use for that kind of work?"

"Not a bunch, but some, yes."

"Then I don't get it. Why me?"

"Well, licensed, gun-toting PIs are expensive, at least if they're any good. Usually the firm does a preliminary investigation before we make the determination to bring in one of our PIs. We normally like to think there's some reason to suspect fraud before we send somebody out to make sure. Otherwise, we'd just be fishing on all our claims, and we'd have to go into the investigation business full-time, which we're not prepared to do. We're a law firm."

I sat with that for a moment. "That answers the general question of why, Amy. But not the 'Why me?' part."

"Well, frankly, don't be mad if I'm being presumptuous, but you've mentioned yourself that you were thinking about going back and looking for work. I thought you might be motivated about this, and besides, it might be good for you. Anyway, in the normal course of things, the firm would be spending a good deal of money over the next couple of weeks doing background on Mayhew's condition. We eventually might decide to put a tail on him, which will cost the firm more money, regardless of the outcome. But we may not, either. It depends on the preliminary findings."

"You want me to check."

She paused. "I've got to be clear that I'm not officially speaking for the firm, Wyatt. I'm not hiring you or even offering to hire you. I'm saying that in this case I'd be open to doing things a little bit backwards because it might save the firm considerable funds and man hours. If you told me you'd try to discover positive evidence of fraud in Mr. Mayhew's claim, I could be persuaded to put the preliminary legal steps on hold for a short while."

"And if I found something conclusive?"

"In that case, we could discuss some kind of reward contingency."

"I'll start tomorrow."

"Wow. Great. Just like that? You're sure?"

"I'm sure."

"You won't change your mind?"

"I won't."

"Okay, then." She paused. "You ought to try to be a little more decisive, you know. Nobody likes a waffler."

"I'm working on it. Meanwhile," I said, "tell me what I need to know."

I graduated from the University of San Francisco in 1989 and both because I craved life experience and because I didn't have any better ideas of what I was going to do for the rest of my life, I joined the army to see the world. Shortly thereafter, I got caught up in Desert Storm and sent to Iraq, which wasn't the part of the world I'd had in mind. As an English major with no job skills except the ability to write in complete sentences with verbs and nouns and other parts of speech in more or less the right order, I got assigned to the criminal investigation division to write up administrative and disciplinary reports.

Boring as the reports were, my experience with the CID was my first adult exposure to humanity's dark side. It's not something the army liked to advertise, but because of the tension, brutality, fatigue, emotion, crowding, and trauma to the human psyche, theaters of war are fertile breeding grounds for serious criminal behavior—predominantly rape and its variants but also murder and mayhem, theft, and general depravity. This is not breaking news, but it was to me. After a while, I got promoted and started to interview suspects, to go out on investigations. For the first time in my life, work was important and exciting—a rush, sometimes with an actual element of danger.

In my years with the CPS, many of the calls to the homes of abused children provided a similar buzz, and I came to realize that in some sense this feeling was my fix. In the five months since I'd been forced to quit, between my revenge fantasies and my anger issues, I'd given a lot of thought to the kind of professional path I eventually wanted to put myself on if I ever got myself out of the personal Dumpster. And one trait stood out. No matter what the eventual new career turned out to be, it wouldn't feature a whole lot of time in an office.

After Amy's call, I'd considered my options and finally pulled out my Canon 35 mm and my telephoto lens. I also owned a Sony video camera, which I dug out of the back of my bedroom closet. Miraculously, since I didn't even remember the last time I'd used either of them, both cameras seemed to have working batteries and film, and I put both of them and the ancillary junk into a backpack by the entrance to the alley in back off the kitchen. Then, turning off the brain, I went to bed.

When I opened my eyes to darkness for the fifth time, I finally gave up trying to sleep. Rain pelted the roof as I pulled on sweats and a windbreaker. By a little before six o'clock, the approaching dawn still not much in evidence, I was thoroughly soaked and making the turn at Cost Plus in Fisherman's Wharf, a mile and a half in eleven minutes. This was slower than I'd been at thirty, but I consoled myself with the news that it was undoubtedly faster than I'd be at forty-five.

Back home, I showered, changed, and decided to emulate Churchill while there was still time by opening a cold split of Veuve Clicquot champagne to have with my scrambled eggs. Coffee is my breakfast drink of choice as a rule, but what's the point of having a rule if you're not going to break it sometimes?

As the first order of business, I thought I'd wake him up for fun. Since I still had his home number from the CPS directory, I called him directly, heard his voice after the second ring, and hung up, smiling. I drove out to the address on Cherry Street that Amy had given me, a one-block dead end north of Lake that adjoined the south border of the Presidio. It was just past eight o'clock. Parking on the opposite side of the street and a few houses away, I noticed the black Mercedes with the vanity plates that read KIDSTUF, his cute little play on words about the work he did at CPS. So I was at the right place. I checked my cameras one last time, still uncertain about exactly what I was planning to do. Amy had described Mayhew as partially ambulatory, but she'd also told me that he was receiving a full-disability pension. So I more or less expected that ambulatory in his case meant he could get up out of his wheelchair to walk into the bathroom or something like that.

Fifteen minutes into my first stakeout, the rain picked up again, falling in vertical sheets that partially obscured my view of the front door to Mayhew's large, two-story house, which was up twelve steps from the street level. My Lumina's windows, nearly closed against the precipitation, began to fog up. It dawned on me that if my target stayed indoors, confined to his bed or not, it was going to be a slow couple of weeks.

Not my idea of a good time.

Two options presented themselves: Call again, or knock on his door?

At CPS, the direct approach tended to produce the best results. So I waited for a slight break in the downpour, then let myself out of the car and jogged across the street and up the steps. It was still by most civilized standards a bit early for an unannounced visit, but he'd been awake enough to answer the phone an hour before, hadn't he? Compared to my half-contemplated plot to have the man murdered only a few weeks before, this interruption seemed nearly benevolent.

I rang the doorbell, waited, rang again. After another moment, I heard footsteps, and then the door opened. His wife, presumably. A well-preserved fifty, in a green housecoat. At this hour, she did not exude graciousness. "Can I help you?" She was brusque, no-nonsense. "It's rather early to be knocking on doors, don't you think?"

"Yes, ma'am, I'm sorry, but I was hoping to talk to Mr. Mayhew."

"I'm afraid he's not available right now. He's not been well."

"I heard that, but this is very important. I won't take much of his time. I'm one of his former employees with CPS, Wyatt Hunt. I'm sure he'll want to see me."

Her mouth was a tight line. "I'm not so sure of that, but if you'll wait just a minute." She closed the door on me, and I did as she'd instructed. Waited.

More footsteps, heavier this time, and then I was looking at Mayhew. He was dressed for work, without the coat and tie. I doubted that his wife had rousted him from bed in those clothes, especially with the shoes on.

"Wilson." It was the first time I'd called him by his first name.

He hesitated, the unaccustomed informality throwing off his timing. "What are you doing here? What do you want?"

I conjured up a chill smile. "I want my job back, but it's too late for that now, isn't it?"

"That wasn't me, Mr. Hunt. You made that decision yourself."

"What decision was that, Wilson?" I kind of liked pushing the first name. It shifted the dynamic.

"Not to accept the reprimand letter. That was your decision."

"Yes, it was. And you know why I made it?"

"No, I don't. Doing so was foolish, though, your only chance to hold on to your career, and you threw it away."

"Close, but actually a little off. I couldn't accept the reprimand because I didn't do anything wrong. And you knew this and lied about it."

"You're delusional," he said. He stepped back and started to close the door.

Rage had begun to swell like a tide within me as soon as I'd laid eyes on him, and by now I was riding it. The power of my emotions took me somewhat by surprise. Acting without any thought, I jammed my foot up against the door and leaned into it. "You're telling me to my face that you don't remember me stopping by your office to brief you about Nunoz?"

He pushed against the door forcefully, to no avail, and gave up. "It was to your face last time, too, as I recall, at the hearing. It didn't bother me then, either, because it was the truth then, too." He smiled. "In case you're wearing a wire." The face went dark. "Now get your foot away from the door, Mr. Hunt, or I'll be forced to call the police." Then he added, "The last time we had a disagreement that went to a third party for adjudication, you got rather the short end of it, didn't you? Are you sure you want to go through something like that again?"

"No," I said, "you're right." I moved back, left the door free. "It's got to be handled differently this time."

Placid, his head cocked in a show of curiosity, he said, "That sounds rather like a threat."

"Does it?"

"Well, in case it was, let me just say I shall make a police report later this morning, and the next time our paths should happen to cross, I will apply for—and I assure you I will get—a restraining order issued against you."

"Thanks for the warning."

"If I were you, I'd take it to heart and move on with my life. We're not in the same league, Mr. Hunt. I thought you'd have realized that by now." Nodding, he said, "Have a nice day," before he closed the door.

I got Devin Juhle on his pager, and he called me back about a half hour later. The rain had been coming and going in fits and starts all morning, but now the random spot of blue had begun appearing through the cloud cover, which I chose to interpret as a sign of better things to come. At the big home down the street, not a creature was stirring. If I hadn't seen with my own eyes the evidence that Mayhew was suffering about as much back pain as I was, his apparent lack of activity might have discouraged me. Instead, encouraged by the certainty that his workers' comp claim was in fact bogus, I spent the time working the logistics of how best to expose him. I thought I had a decent idea.

By this time, Devin knew every nuance of my history with Mayhew. When I told him in general terms what I was doing, he perked right up, game for a little extracurricular activity on my behalf if there was even a small element of payback involved. I assured him that his involvement wouldn't take long, and my plan was so beautiful it might make him cry.

In another good omen for the home team, Devin and his partner Shane Manning weren't exactly swamped with critical homicide investigatory work at the moment. February tended to be a slow month for murder, and they were only working two cases. Beyond that, both of them were supposed to be witnesses in court that morning. Because of that they'd left the day open, but the trial had been continued for some reason, and now they faced a long afternoon with no scheduled witness interviews and no other work of burning importance. It was either come out and have some fun or sit around all day in homicide and catch up on writing reports.

Tough call.

I gave Juhle the phone number and cautioned him to make sure the call he made about Mayhew's flat tire came from a pay phone where it couldn't be traced back to anyone. "Wow, good idea, Wyatt," he said with his patented heavy irony. "I never would have thought of that." But in spite of the sarcasm, he and his partner were in. So I now had a makeshift staff of three, including myself, and two-thirds of it were trained police inspectors. I dubbed us all the Hunt Club. It didn't exactly make me light-headed with confidence, but the odds looked good.

What flat tire? you might ask.

The one I gave him as I hunched out of sight of the house behind his car, unscrewing the valve cap on the back right tire, then releasing the air in a satisfying hiss until the wheel had settled all the way down onto its rim. I admit that this could be seen as puerile, immature vandalism, very much beneath the mature adult I had become. But I took consolation knowing that it was, in fact, kid stuff, advertised by Mayhew himself, and I thought this gave the act a kind of elegant symmetry.

Nevertheless, my nerves were raw as I jogged back to my own car to wait. Juhle was going to make the call when he got near enough, and given all the variables with his schedule and with traffic, that might take an hour or more. Fortunately, he and Manning must have been chomping at the bit to hit the streets, and it wasn't more than twenty minutes before Dev called on my cell phone and told me he'd made the call. I should be ready.

Checking my video camera one last time, I got out of my car and went around to the passenger side, where Mayhew wouldn't see me even if he looked. I rested the camera on the car's hood to steady it and hunkered down as out of sight as I could make myself behind the vehicle. Of course, there was still a chance that Mayhew would simply call AAA or that the charming Mrs. Mayhew might come down to survey the damage and maybe even fix the tire herself. But I knew that Mayhew was already up and dressed and probably going stir-crazy in the house. He would also want to confront me if he got out fast enough and had the chance.

It might not happen. I realized that Mayhew might be cautious enough about the scam he was running that he'd keep the profile as at least a semi-invalid. But I also knew something about his arrogance and guessed that he believed that his connections and his social status would protect him from too much scrutiny. If there was any investigation going on about his workers' comp claim, he'd hear about it long before it got close enough to touch him, and he'd get back on his guard.

Besides, I had a slick backup idea involving my own suicide if this one didn't draw him out. But as it turned out, I wasn't going to need it today.

Sometimes luck does smile on the good.

As I zoomed in on videotape, Wilson came out onto his porch and, with his face set in a scowl, peered perfunctorily up and down the street. No doubt after getting Juhle's anonymous call, he thought it was me who'd flattened his tire in a fit of pique and then lit out. Certainly I wouldn't be so foolish as to wait around and take credit for the nuisance. Apparently satisfied, shaking his head in anger, he started down his front steps with a firm tread. He didn't put a hand to his sore back. He didn't reach for the metal banister that ran along the steps.

Down in the street, he circled the car. When he saw the flat, he swore violently—audible back even where I was filming—and turned a quick and, I thought, rather athletic full circle one more time, checking for a perpetrator. Swearing again, he stood still for a while, hands on his hips. I thought I might have captured enough on video already, with him walking easily down his twelve front steps, but more would be better.

I waited.

He did not disappoint. Opening the trunk, he leaned over (without bending his knees, I noticed) and rummaged a moment, then lifted out an apparently heavy bag of golf clubs, setting it down on the pavement. Another duck into the trunk produced the jack, and in under a minute, he had the thing in place, pumping with the tire iron, lifting the car.

I looked behind me at the corner and saw Juhle and Manning standing there, looking like a couple of guys taking a walk. We waved but stayed in place for another couple of minutes, watching as Mayhew undid the lug nuts. When he was just about finished, I stood up with the video camera and advanced, recording the whole way, getting to within about ten feet of him just as he pulled the tire from the wheel and stood up with it in his arms.

I kept the camera on him. I believe I may have been smiling. He half-turned, holding the tire, stepping toward the back of the car. Seeing me, he came to a shocked and abrupt stop.

"Yo, Wilson," I said. "How's the back?"

His eyes grew large and frightened as I lowered the camera and, pointing a finger gun at him, pulled the trigger. "Gotcha," I said.

That brought the bonus. Mayhew whirled halfway around, dropped the tire, and reached down for the tire iron that he'd used to lever up the jack. With an animal cry, he lunged at me as I danced away, capturing the Kodak moments as he continued to advance, swinging the iron as he came at me. If his back was hurting him, he didn't show much sign of it. But he was getting close now as I ducked and swirled away from another swing.

And then from behind me, Juhle's welcome voice: "Hold it right there! Police! Drop the weapon!"

The cavalry pulled up on foot and kept coming. Now nearly frothing at the mouth, Mayhew whirled on Juhle and Manning as they got him by the arms and tried to restrain him. He continued to resist them. The tire iron clanged to the street.

I caught it all on videotape. The steps, the golf clubs, pumping the jack, lifting the tire up, swinging at me with the tire iron, and—my personal favorite—the resisting of his arrest. This last guaranteed that the fraudulent back claim would now go all the way to the DA. Without resisting arrest, the DA might otherwise find himself tempted, coerced, or outright bought into forgetting about the fraud. With the assault on working homicide inspectors, he would then have to charge it all. Even Mayhew's connections would not be able to put a lid on the story once it came out that he had attacked two cops who just happened to be passing by and, witnessing an attack with a deadly weapon in progress, had charged in to restore order.

"Dismas Hardy," Amy said, "this is Wyatt Hunt."

We shook hands. Hardy was probably in his mid-fifties. He certainly looked good for the role of managing partner of one of the city's top law firms. He wore a gray suit with the thinnest of maroon pinstripes. Maroon silk tie, monogrammed silk shirt. High-end all the way, but he came across as one of the good guys. Plus, he'd had the good sense to hire Amy.

"Ms. Wu tells me you've made the firm some money this morning. We appreciate it."

"It was my pleasure. In fact, I can't remember when I've had more fun."

Amy spoke up. "As I mentioned to you when I first brought it up, Diz, Wyatt had a bit of history with Mr. Mayhew. I thought he'd be motivated."

"Still," Hardy said, "one day. That's impressive. Nobody does this stuff in one day." He nodded appreciatively. "I'm glad Amy thought of you."

"Me, too."

Hardy rested a haunch on the corner of his large cherry desk. "So now the question, Wyatt," he said, "is what can we do for you?"

I'd, of course, considered the payment issue, but it didn't rule my thoughts. Now I found myself saying, "Maybe this is one of those times when the work is its own reward."

Hardy grinned over at Amy. "This guy's too much," he said. Then, back to me, "Are you for real?"

I shrugged. "Sometimes it's not the money."

"In my experience, that's not as often as you'd think. Can I ask you a personal question? How long have you been out of a job?"

I shot a quick glance at Amy. She'd obviously had a somewhat substantive talk with Hardy before she'd invited me to look at Mayhew's case. "A few months, but I saved while I worked, and money's not a huge issue for me right now. I've kind of been trying to figure out what I wanted to do next."

"Well, if I'd just done what you did this morning, I'd be tempted to take it as some kind of sign. You ever think about becoming a private investigator?"

I laughed. "Not even once."

"Okay, but you deliver results like today, and within six months, you wouldn't be able to keep up with the work from this firm alone. I promise you."

Shaking my head, I still found the idea mostly amusing. "I don't have any idea how I'd even go about it."

"What's to know? You get a license, hang up a shingle, open your doors for business." He snapped his fingers. "Just like that."

This is now . . .

5 /

U.S. Federal Judge George Palmer met Staci Rosalier when she took his drink order one day at MoMo's, a San Francisco restaurant across the street from SBC Park, where the Giants play baseball. It was a warm September lunchtime, and Judge Palmer, known on sight to half the clientele and most of the regular staff, was sitting alone outside, awaiting the arrival of his appointment.

Staci was in her first week there at the waitress job. When she took the great man's order—Hendrick's gin on the rocks—they exchanged the usual lighthearted, mildly flirtatious banter. In spite of the age difference, it struck neither of them as incongruous. Staci was an experienced and sophisticated waitress, used to dealing with the well-heeled and successful.

And for a man at any age, Palmer's physique was admirable, his face captivating, his smile genuine. He was also personable, witty, confident, well dressed. He exuded the power of his position. The job God wants, so the saying goes, is U.S. federal judge.

As the crowd began to arrive, Staci fell into a rhythm with the work, and Palmer pretty much left her consciousness. She was after all serving half of the sixteen tables on one side of the outer patio, waiting on, among others, one superior court judge, the mayor's chief assistant, a gaggle of high-powered attorneys, a table of four of the 49ers, a city supervisor.

MoMo's was a happening place and had what they called a big yoo-hoo factor.

Over the next month or so, Judge Palmer came in nearly every workday, always choosing a table in Staci's section, arriving early enough, often enough that they got time to extend their repartee. His tips began at a generous twenty percent and grew to reflect the pleasure he took in her company. He learned that she was single, without a steady boyfriend, that she lived alone in a rented studio apartment just north of Market above Castro. She went to school part-time at SFCC and hoped to finish at junior college and go to Berkeley in the next couple of years, but the mission now was simply to make a living, which wasn't that easy on tips, in spite of the judge's largesse—not everyone was as generous as he was. She confided to him that she was thinking about taking another waitress job at another place on her days off here. But then she might have to quit school altogether and didn't want to do that. You didn't have a future if you didn't finish school.

She in turn found out, not only from him, that the judge had been married to Jeannette for nearly forty years. He lived in a big house in Pacific Heights on Clay Street. He had three grown children. He worked at the federal courthouse and worked on appeals to the Ninth Circuit. "Fun stuff," he told her. He also was an avid fly fisherman and something of a wine nut, as she'd already guessed from what he usually ordered to drink after his gin on the rocks for lunch.

After a while, they began to see each other outside of MoMo's, at quiet places down the coast where the judge would not be recognized. One day, he had come in much later than usual, close to one thirty, timing it so he was getting up to leave at around three, as she was finishing her shift. They walked together down the Embarcadero for a hundred yards or so, making easy conversation as they usually did at the restaurant. He asked her if she'd like to go over and walk by the water, where it was more private. He told her he had a present for her, which he so hoped she'd accept.

It was a solitaire one-carat diamond necklace on a platinum-and-gold braided chain.

6 /

Although he was now considered an official hero, Inspector Devin Juhle was coming off a very bad time. Six months ago, he and his partner Shane Manning were on their way to talk to a witness in one of their investigations at two in the afternoon, when they'd picked up an emergency call from dispatch—a report that somebody was shooting up a homeless encampment under the Cesar Chavez Street freeway overpass. As it happened, they were six blocks away and were the first cops on the scene.

Manning was driving, and no sooner than he had pulled their unmarked city-issue Plymouth into the no-man's-land beneath the overpass, a man stepped out from behind a concrete pillar about sixty feet away and leveled a shotgun at the car.

"Down! Down!" Juhle had screamed as Manning was jamming into park, slamming on the brakes. One hand was unsnapping his holster and the other already on the door's handle, and Juhle ducked and hurled his body against the door, swinging it open and getting below the dash just as he heard the blast of the scattergun and the simultaneous explosion of the windshield above him, which covered him with pebbles of safety glass. Another shotgun blast, and then Juhle was out of the car on the asphalt, rolling, trying to get behind a tire for shelter.

"Shane!" he yelled for his partner. "Shane!"

Nothing.

Peering under the car's chassis—he remembered all of it as one picture, though the images were in different directions, so it couldn't have been—he saw two bodies down on the ground by a cardboard structure and behind them a half dozen or so people crouched in the lee of one of the concrete buttresses that supported the overpass, penned in so they couldn't escape. At the same time, the man with the gun had retreated behind the pillar again. To the extent that Juhle was thinking at all and not just reacting, he thought the killer was reloading. But it was his only chance to get an angle and save himself and maybe these other people as well.

He bolted for the low stump of a tree that sat in the middle of the asphalt. It shouldn't have been there—Caltrans should have uprooted the thing before they poured, but they hadn't. Now there it was and he'd reach it if he could. Running low, then diving and rolling, he got to it in two or three seconds, enough time for the shooter, who had come out in the open again to fire his next round, which pocked into the stump in front of him and sprayed him with woodchips and pulp.

Juhle, on his stomach and with the side of his face and body pressed flat to the ground, knew that the stump didn't give him six inches of clearance and that the man was advancing now, sensing his advantage. He was still probably sixty or seventy feet away—and coming on fast. Once he got to forty feet or so, the shooter's height would give him the angle he needed. The next shotgun blast and Juhle would be history.

There wasn't any time for thought. Juhle rolled a full rotation, extended his gun gripped in both hands out in front of him, drew a bead, and squeezed off two shots. The man stumbled, crumbled, dropped like a bag of cement, and did not move.

Juhle called out for his partner again and again got no reply. Still in a daze, his adrenaline surging, he eventually got to his feet, his gun never leaving the downed man. In half steps, he warily crabwalked sideways toward him, with his gun extended across his body in a two-handed stance. When he got to his target, he saw that he had made the luckiest shot of his life. One bullet had hit the man between the eyes.

Which should have been the end of it. After all, Juhle had six witnesses to everything. Manning was dead, killed by the first blast. The car was a shot-up mess. It was clearly self-defense at the very least and heroism by any standard.

But not necessarily.

Not in San Francisco, where every police shooting is suspect. One of the homeless in the encampment, a highly intoxicated diagnosed schizophrenic, insisted that police had run up to the deceased and executed him for no reason. The fact that he claimed there had been five such officers and that he maintained that the man had not had a shotgun—in spite of Manning's death by shotgun blast—

didn't even slow down the right-minded public nuisances of the antipolice crowd.

Beyond that, Juhle's shot was so perfect that it led Byron Diehl, one of the city's supervisors, to opine that perhaps the killing had, in fact, been an overreaction by an overzealous and enraged cop. Perhaps it had, in point of fact, been an execution. Nobody could hit a moving man with a pistol between the eyes at fifty or sixty feet. That just wasn't a possible shot. The man with the gun might have already surrendered, laid his gun down, and Juhle—out of control because of the murder of his partner—had walked up and shot him point-blank.

The other witnesses? Please. Most of them wanted the shooter dead, anyway. Plus, they were naturally afraid of the police. If Juhle told them they'd better back up his story or else, they'd say anything he wanted. They were simply unreliable and their testimonies worthless. Except for the schizophrenic, of course, who was struggling with his substance abuse issues. The idiocy was so palpable that it may have been fun to watch but not to be part of.

So Juhle spent the next three months on administrative leave, under the shadow of a murder charge. He testified four times before different city and police commissions, not including a formal session defending his actions and confronting Diehl in the chamber of the board of supervisors. He was asked to demonstrate his prowess with a handgun on various police ranges in San Francisco, Alameda, and San Mateo counties, where they had pop-up targets that demanded speed as well as accuracy.

Finally, a couple of months ago, he'd been cleared of any wrongdoing. Returning to his place in homicide, though—Manning was of course gone forever—he found himself newly partnered with an obviously political hire, Gumqui Shiu, whose ten-year career didn't seem to have included much real police work. He'd been an instructor at the Academy, worked in the photo lab, and been assigned to various other details, where his progress had been rapid but unmarked by any real accomplishment. He clearly had juice somewhere, but nobody seemed to know where it came from.

This morning, Juhle was at his desk. Insult to injury, he still had his right arm in the sling from arthroscopic rotator cuff surgery—three little holes. His doctor had told him it was an in-and-out-in-the-same-day procedure, little more than an office visit. He'd be pitching Little League practice again in no time.

Not.

Like he ever wanted to do that again, anyway. Little League was pretty much the reason he'd thrown out the damn arm in the first place, letting his macho devils con him into a little *mano a mano* with Doug Malinoff—perfect baseball name—the manager of Devin's son Eric's team, the Hornets. Doug was a good guy, really, if maybe slightly more competitive than your typical major-leaguer during the playoffs, talking Assistant Coach Devin into playing a game of "burnout" for the enjoyment of the kids. Give them a taste of what it's like to *really* want to win.

Burnout's a simple game for simple adults and preadolescent boys: You throw a baseball as hard as you can starting from, say, sixty feet. You use regular gloves, no extra-padded catcher's mitts allowed, and you move a step closer after each round. First one to give up loses. Devin was no slouch as an athlete, having played baseball through college. He still had a pretty good gun of an arm. Nevertheless, he gave up, conceding defeat, after seven rounds, his opponent nearly knocking him down on his last throw from thirty-five feet. Malinoff had played shortstop in minor-league ball, made it to double-A. He could throw a baseball through a plywood fence.

Juhle caught the sixth toss not in the webbing but in the palm of the mitt. He never mentioned to a living soul and never would that on top of ruining his shoulder through his own stupidity on that cold and misty March day, he also allowed Malinoff's major-league fastball to break two bones in his *catching hand*.

Since then, Juhle had been having confidence issues. He found it hard to convince himself that he was among the most brilliant homicide inspectors on the planet when at the same time he considered himself a certified idiot for going at it with Malinoff.

It was Tuesday morning, May 31, nine fifteen. June, just a day away, is synonymous with fog in San Francisco, and today Juhle couldn't see the elevated freeway sixty yards to his left out the window. Awaiting the arrival of his partner, he was at his desk in the crowded, cramped, and yet wide-open room without interior walls that was the homicide detail on the fourth floor of San Francisco's Hall of Justice. He was sipping his third cup of coffee this morning, his right arm and still untreated opposite hand—damned if he was going to let anybody know—both throbbing in spite of six hundred milligrams of Motrin every four hours for the past ten days. He turned to the second page of the transcription of a witness's testimony in one of his cases that he was checking against the tape and suddenly took off his headphones, stood up, made his way past the shoulder-high, battered green-and-gray metal files that served as room dividers, and stopped at the door of his lieutenant, Marcel Lanier, who looked up from his own paperwork.

"What's up, Dev?"

"We gotta do something about the quality of people they hire, Marcel."

Lanier, only fifty-some and yet still a hundred years with the department, scratched around his mouth. "That's a song I've been singing for years. What kind of people this time?"

For an answer, Juhle handed him the printout he'd been reading. "You'll see it," he said.

Five seconds into his reading, Lanier barked out a one-note toneless laugh, then read aloud. " 'And what is your relationship with Ms. Dorset?' "

Juhle nodded. "That's it. You don't see a relationship like that every day."

"He was her power mower?"

"Must have been, since it's right there in black and white."

"Her power mower?"

"Yeah, except maybe instead of *power mower*, what he actually said was that he was her 'paramour.' " Juhle leaned against the doorpost. "And this is, like, mistake ten on one page, Marcel, not counting the big chunks that she has marked 'unintelligible' on the transcript, but that *I* can hear perfectly on the tape. Do they give an IQ test before we start paying these people? Of course, I've got to correct the transcript, anyway, but now it's going to take me two days instead of an hour. It'd be quicker to write the whole goddamn thing out in longhand."

Shiu floated up behind Juhle into the space left in the doorway. "What's going to take two days?"

Lanier ignored both the arrival and the question. His phone rang and he picked it up. "Homicide, Lanier." Frowning, suddenly all serious, he pulled over his yellow pad and started jotting. "Okay, got it. We're moving." Looking up at his two inspectors, he said into the phone, "Juhle and Shiu." When he hung up, there was no sign that he'd ever laughed or thought anything in the world had been funny ever. "Either of you already signed out on a car?"

The inspectors shared a glance. "No, sir. Paperwork day," Juhle said.

"Not anymore it isn't. Grab a ride in a black and white downstairs," he said, "and have 'em light it up out to Clay at"—he shot a quick look at his notes—"Lyon. Don't pass go, guys. I'll get word to the techs. I want a presence there yesterday. Somebody just killed a federal judge."

Jeannette Palmer had made the call to 911 at precisely a quarter to nine, her voice high-pitched and panicked, saying that her husband was dead, that somebody had shot him. Since Pacific Heights is a high-income neighborhood, emergency response tends to be prompt. In this case, a patrol car had been cruising within a couple of blocks down in Cow Hollow and was at the scene within two minutes. An ambulance arrived one minute later.

Jeannette was standing in the door—dressed, wringing her hands, crying—to meet the cops and guide them to the judge's office, a large room in the left-hand front of the house, with bay windows and thousands of books. This was where Jeannette had found her husband and a young woman she'd never seen before, both of them on the floor behind his desk, and where the responding officers then directed the med techs in the ambulance, who took one quick look and then left the bodies undisturbed. Both had been cold to the touch.

Juhle and Shiu, as ordered, got to the scene in fifteen minutes in a patrol car with lights and sirens clearing the traffic for them. Even so, a news van from Channel 4 had obviously picked up the dispatch and was already parked in the street out front, a harbinger of what was sure to be the full-scale media circus to follow. A knot of people—neighbors, probably—stood over by the van, chatting away with backstory. The good news was that there were already three other patrol cars at the premises, the officers out of the cars in uniform, securing the scene, denying access.

Juhle wasn't a native San Franciscan, but he'd moved up from the Peninsula for college at San Francisco State and had stayed. He had always loved Clay Street, especially this stretch of it. The gas lamp–style antique streetlights. The elegant gingerbread houses were set back a civilized distance from the sidewalk, usually with a low wall or discreet fence marking the property boundary. And then the landscaping, each house as though it were watching over its own small private park—no bigger than an average front lawn in suburbia—making a totally different statement about taste, urban life, civility.

Judge Palmer's place was in the mold. The house was a three-story Victorian, immaculately kept up. A low, tan stucco wall with a wrought-iron fence ran along the sidewalk. Then behind the wall, a circular driveway swept up to the steps of the porch. In the semi-circular garden carved out by the brick drive, a three-tiered stone fountain splashed down into a small lily pond surrounded by flowering shrubs, seemingly every one of which somehow contrived to be in bloom.

The two inspectors had gotten to the scene so quickly that the sergeant from the nearest station, who was supposed to superintend at these types of scenes, hadn't made it yet, but Officer Sanchez, a field-training officer, met them at the front door and told them they could find Mrs. Palmer, apparently in shock, with his rookie partner in the living room, off to their right. The office, with the bodies, was to the left. "Nobody's touched anything in there," he said, "and the wife says she didn't either, except the phone on the desk to call nine one one."

Juhle and Shiu, partnered in homicide now for two months, knew that within minutes they'd be joined by the assistant coroner and the crime scene investigation unit, who would quantify and memorialize, videotape, photograph, examine, fingerprint, and/or book into evidence everything in the room. Depending on how fast the word flew, they could expect a team of field agents from the FBI, since killing a federal judge could be a federal crime. Homeland Security might even want to explore whether there might be a terrorist angle to the judge's murder, and Juhle had to admit that this might not, in fact, be out of the question.

Meanwhile, this was Juhle's chance to get some impressions without interruption, and he wasn't about to pass up the opportunity.

The bodies lay, as advertised, on the floor, mostly hidden from the door behind the desk. The judge was dressed in pale brown slacks, a white dress shirt and darker brown pullover sweater. The chair, a big, comfortable-looking leather swivel, lay on its side next to the body. There was a small hole in the judge's right cheek and a congealed pool of black blood coming out from under the judge's head onto the clear plastic that protected his rug from the wheels of his chair. The room's lights were on overhead, as was a reading lamp on the desk, which looked pretty much undisturbed.

The woman was much younger than the judge—early twenties max. She wore stonewashed jeans, an undershirt of some kind, and a black sweater that left her midriff exposed. A diamond stud was visible in her navel. She lay flat on her back, her neck skewed a bit where her head had hit the wall behind her as she fell. There was no evident entry wound and no blood under her, although a thin thread of black came from her mouth and ended in a dark puddle on the floor beneath her. A large diamond glittered on a necklace chain out over the sweater.

"Well, it wasn't a robbery," Juhle said.

"No, and it happened fast," Shiu said. "She was standing next to him, the shooter whips it out, and it's bam bam over."

"Maybe." Juhle stood over to the side of the desk where he could see both bodies. But he wasn't looking at the bodies. He was looking at the bookshelves behind the desk. "But maybe bam bam bam. Three shots." Stepping over the woman, he leaned and pointed to a spot on a bookshelf at about the level of his waist, at what appeared to be a gap between two books. "There's a book pushed back in there. I'm guessing we got a slug." He looked some more. "Also good splatter all around it, pretty much the same height."

"Where do you see that?"

Juhle ignored the question. He wasn't here to give a class. "But only with one of them." He stepped back, scanned the bookcase over the woman's body. "Small caliber," he said. "No exit." He crossed over to his right, where a clutch purse was half-wedged into the cushion of a reading chair. He pulled on a pair of plastic gloves. "This ought to tell us who she is," he said.

But it didn't. It contained some cosmetics, a pack of Kleenex, eighty-five dollars and change in cash, a holder for a diaphragm, and a package of Trident chewing gum but no driver's license. No identification of any kind.

Shiu threw a look to the office door. "Where are those guys?"

Juhle shrugged. The crime scene team would get there when they did.

"I wonder if anybody heard anything."

Juhle wondered if his partner was making these inane comments to fill the dead air, like Dandy Don Meredith on a slow football night. Did Shiu construe this as helpful? The thought made his scalp itch. As for himself, he had no idea if anyone in the neighborhood had heard anything and didn't really wonder about it. He knew that canvassing the residents in the surrounding area was in his and his partner's immediate future. They would find out if anyone saw or heard anything, usual or not. They'd also double-check the 911 log to see about any possibly related calls. But he said, "Unless somebody was right out front, they wouldn't have heard anything. In fact, a bullet this small, I'm surprised there was enough firepower to knock him out of his chair."

"He could have been halfway up. After the first shot to her."

More inanity. Could have, should have, might have been—all of it a waste of breath until they actually had some evidence. Worse, preconceptions formed without evidence interfered with your ability clearly to see the evidence when you actually got it. A big part of the job was to work a case from the facts and not from imagination.

Juhle continued to look around, checking the floor, behind the drapes, just in case. Behind a leather wing chair, leaning over, he made the mistake of putting pressure on his hand as he pushed himself out of his crouch, and he swore as the pain from his broken bones shot up his arm.

"Is that still bothering you?"

"Continuous. I've been trying to figure out some game I can challenge Malinoff to where I can hurt him back. Except he's stronger and quicker than I am at everything. And that's when I'm not crippled and hurting. I'm going to have to cheat. Maybe hire someone to hurt him."

"You can't do that, Dev. You're a cop," Shiu said. "Kids look up to you."

"Oh, yeah, the role model thing. I forgot for a minute. But I wouldn't cheat, anyway, Shiu. It's against my religion."

"You don't have a religion."

"Yeah, I do. Just not a formal one like you do. And one of its main rules is don't cheat."

As far as Juhle knew, Shiu was probably the only Asian Mormon in the state of California. And now he couldn't pass up the opportunity for his continuing missionary work. "That's a main LDS rule, too, Dev. You're halfway to being one of us. With some training and prayer, you could—"

"Shiu." Juhle went to put up his hand, but the pain stopped him, and he grimaced again. "Haven't we done this? We're in the city of tolerance, right? Hell, we *celebrate* our diversity. I tolerate your religion. You tolerate me not having one."

"But I don't like it, Dev. Our jobs, you know, we could get killed any day without any warning. I don't want to see you die and cast into outer darkness."

"I know. And I appreciate it. I really do. And I halfway agree with—the die part. But meanwhile, all I'm trying to do is figure out what happened here and how I can hurt Malinoff as much as possible without getting arrested for it. That's all. Just those two things."

"I'll still be praying for you."

"I know you will, Shiu, I know you will." Juhle took a last look at the room. He was four years older than Shiu, and with his many more years in homicide, the acknowledged senior partner. When they'd seen all they needed to at any one given place, it fell to him to make the call, which he now did. "Well, while we await the arrival of our ace crime-team specialists, perhaps we should go see what the grieving wife can tell us."

The living room was done in soft tones of ivory and pink and lavender. The mirror-image footprint of the office where Judge Palmer and the current Jane Doe lay dead across the hall struck Juhle as singularly sterile—similar in its own way to those rooms in the projects where the furniture in the unused living rooms are sometimes covered with plastic so they will last forever. Even though Juhle was far from a connoisseur, he was struck by the display of wealth and good taste. The wide, gold-etched mahogany coffee table; the sideboard with its Venetian glass collection; the occasional table with its stunning and apparently fresh floral arrangement; both loveseats; the two matching crystal chandeliers; the eighteen-by-twenty-foot Oriental rug; the overstuffed couch—every article of furnishing was superb. And yet there seemed to be no life to this interior, no sense of play or even of excessive familiarity. As though it were a dollhouse that Mrs. Palmer had assembled not to live in but only to have, to rearrange, to impress others with.

In his career, Juhle had seen enough shock from victims' relatives that he knew he was looking at something very much like it now. The woman herself was large, though not fat. She sat at the very end of the overstuffed sofa with its pastel floral design, wearing a cream-colored tailored suit that ended at her knees and that now, with the sag of her strong shoulders, seemed to hang on her like a laundry sack. Mrs. Palmer's artfully honey-dyed hair showed signs that it had been carefully coiffed earlier, but every little while she would run a hand all the way through it, front to back, then pull at strands on the sides as though she were a distracted schoolgirl. Her face, probably a little more than conventionally attractive when she was made up, now was blotched and haggard, her eyes minimized behind the swollen lids.

Across from her in a loveseat, keeping silent watch, Sanchez's rookie Officer Garelia had stood when Juhle and Shiu came in and immediately crossed over to stand, silent and ramrod straight, at the door by which they'd entered. He didn't look to be more than twenty-three years old or so, and Juhle guessed it might be his first murder scene, perhaps the first time he'd seen a body or two up close.

But Juhle wasn't here to critique the furniture or observe the re-actions of rookie cops. Sparing his injured arm by using his foot, he moved the loveseat's ottoman closer to the couch and sat down. "Mrs. Palmer," he began, "I'm Sergeant Inspector Devin Juhle with homicide, and this is my partner Inspector Shiu. Are you up to talk-ing to us?"

She adjusted her posture, sitting back further into the sofa. Looking from Juhle to Shiu, her eyes took on a look of surprise, as though she hadn't noticed when they'd come in. "Yes, I think so." With an air of desperation, she let out a breath and asked, "Who is that woman in there with him?"

"We don't know, ma'am. We were hoping you might be able to tell us."

Mrs. Palmer's head moved from side to side as if she had little control over it. "I've never seen her before in my life. And now she's here, dead, in my house. What can that be about?"

"I don't know, ma'am."

"And what was she doing *here*? With my husband? This is our house. He wouldn't have brought her here." She looked from one of them to the other as though she sought their agreement. "He wouldn't have," she repeated.

Juhle and Shiu shared a glance. Shiu stepped into the silence. "You discovered the bodies this morning, ma'am?"

"Yes. When I got in." She drew another long breath, then pulled at a hanging strand of her hair. "I was at my sister's last night. Vanessa Waverly. That was my maiden name—she's divorced and went back to using it—Waverly."

Juhle noted the disjointed flow of her words. He had to remem-ber to keep the questions simple and see if she might settle down. "And where was that?"

"Novato." A Marin County town about a half hour's drive north of the city. "It's far enough, I usually stay over with her when I go up there."

"Do you do that often?"

"Every few weeks or so. She's my business partner—we run a spa and salon in Mill Valley. JVs."

"So it was a business meeting?"

"Yes, but I mean . . . she's my sister, too, mostly. We had dinner together. That's really all it usually is. We just talk."

"And you left here when?"

"Actually, early. Around four. I wanted to miss rush hour on the bridge."

"All right." Juhle tempered his voice. "And you were with your sister the whole night after that?"

"Yes."

"Can you tell me about when you got back here this morning?"

She sighed heavily, closing her eyes on the exhale. When she opened them, she took another weary breath. "I got in before eight but didn't want to wake him up if he'd managed to still be sleeping in. He's always had terrible insomnia, so I just left my overnight bag by the stairs and went into the kitchen to make myself some coffee. But then I thought I smelled something burning, so I went looking, and it was coming from his office. When I stopped at the door, I realized I couldn't see his chair, so I walked over . . ."

Juhle didn't have to close his eyes to reimagine the scene of carnage he'd just witnessed. Though it was, in fact, behind the desk, enough of the young woman's body showed around it that even a cursory glance from the door to the office would have revealed some part of it. Of course, he realized, Mrs. Palmer might not have even given the office that minimal glance. Although if she remembered noticing that she hadn't seen the chair . . .

She had closed her eyes again and now opened them. "I'm sorry," she said. "I do want to help you find who did this if I can."

"Do you have any idea who it might have been? Did your husband have any enemies?"

"Don't you think we have to know who that woman is first? Why is she here? Whatever it is, that's what this has to be about. Doesn't it?"

Juhle wasn't sure that was true. He could envision several scenarios off the top of his head that explained the girl's presence. But Jeannette Palmer was right. The overwhelming likelihood was that it wasn't about the judge by himself. Jane Doe was part of it.

"But all right. George's enemies." Her big shoulders heaved in a mirthless laugh. "This sounds awful for such a charming man, but it could have been anybody, really. You'd have to check his files. Every time he made a decision, he made an enemy, and he's been doing that for years and years. Then there's the CCPOA. . . ."

Juhle shot another quick look over to Shiu. The CCPOA, the California Correctional Peace Officers Association, was the prison guards' union, the most powerful and richest labor organization in the state. It was no secret that it wasn't doing much of a good job at policing itself. And suddenly Juhle, with a shock of recognition, put it together that the judge—who had been in the news looking into the possibility of putting the CCPOA into receivership, deposing its president, and freezing its assets—was George Palmer.

Jeannette Palmer didn't notice the silent exchange, and she was going on. "They're not nice people, and they were terrified that George was going to put them out of business."

"Did they threaten him?" Shiu asked. He had taken out the small notepad he used.

"Not that I know of. Not overtly, anyway. George would have told me."

Juhle waited for a moment, then asked if she knew what the judge had done on the previous night. She opened her eyes, brought him into focus. "He was home here when I left but said he was going out to dinner."

"Did he say with who or where?"

"No. It was casual. He just said he had to see some people about a horse, which was our code for cases he wasn't supposed to talk about. Even to me. Maybe his secretary would know. I'm sorry. But it wasn't the dinner. We know he came back from that, don't we? With her."

At the moment, Juhle didn't even know if he'd gone out at all, but he simply said. "Maybe not with her. Maybe she came later."

The thought seemed to give her a moment's reprieve. Perhaps grateful for that, she nodded. "Maybe she did," she said. "Maybe she came with the killer."

This, Juhle thought, was a pretty thing to think. But not very likely.

She ran a hand through her hair and sighed. "Oh, God," she whispered, "oh, God."

Juhle gave her a moment, then spoke her name, and she opened her eyes, but the faraway gaze she'd worn when they'd entered was back.

He tried again. "Mrs. Palmer?"

But she just looked at him and shook her head.

7 /

Snapping his fingers, Amy Wu's boss Dismas Hardy had told Wyatt Hunt that he could set himself up as a private investigator just like that. But it hadn't been exactly just like that. First Hunt needed to convince the Bureau of Security and Investigative Services of the California Department of Consumer Affairs that his time in the army as a member of the CID should count as the required education in police science, criminal law, or justice, and then that his years of work in the CPS gave him at least the equivalent of six thousand hours of investigative experience. Then there was his evaluation by the federal Department of Justice and the criminal-history background check. To say nothing of the two-hour written exam on laws and regulations. And finally the additional requirements for a firearms permit. All that took the better part of two months.

Then four years ago tonight, he had hung up the shingle.

Now he sat against the wall at a large round table in the power corner at Sam's, the classic restaurant and watering hole at Bush Street and Belden Alley. Fresh from a successful day locating a Piedmont dentist's nineteen-year-old daughter who'd dropped out of the USF dorms and moved in with her boyfriend in the Mission District, Hunt was the first one here for the anniversary party. Sitting alone at the table, he took a first sip of his Bombay Sapphire gibson and sighed with contentment.

He knew that in a few minutes he was going to be all but holding court with a high-energy, even slightly famous group of some of the city's most successful legal professionals. He wore a suit and tie. He could spout some of his high school Latin, his college French, and everyone would know what he'd just said—more, they wanted to know what he would say. They would be drinking fine wine and their waiter Stephano would call them all by their first names.

It almost seemed impossible. From where he'd been to here.

Hunt had been a foster kid in a succession of homes until he was eight when the then-childless Richard and Ann Hunt had miraculously decided to adopt him (and then proceeded to have four natural children of their own in short order).

When he opened his agency, there was never a question as to what he'd call it. In a practical sense, as a business name, The Hunt Club sounded substantial, as though a bunch of like-minded professionals hung out together and did good work. There might be fifty employees in an organization called The Hunt Club.

In fact, at first it was just him.

Next had come Tamara Dade. She and her brother Mickey were two of the very few kids Hunt had met in the course of his emergency work at CPS with whom he'd kept up. Tamara had looked Hunt up when she was about fourteen to thank him for saving her life back when she'd been Tammy and down to her last spoonful of peanut butter.

Beginning with that unexpected phone call, they'd stayed in touch with one another in a haphazard way. A few years ago, Hunt had attended her graduation from San Francisco State. After that, Tamara did some clerical work while she looked for a "real" job, but nothing exciting presented itself. Then Hunt opened his agency and found that business was good and he needed at least both an assistant and a part-time field guy. Now Tamara came in to the office every day, serving as receptionist, office manager, bookkeeper, secretary, and since she was going back to school in criminology and starting to log her investigatory hours, occasional partner. Though she was an efficiency machine in the office, she was even better getting her hands dirty in the field—totally fearless and a crackerjack interrogator in whom people naturally confided.

They weren't long in the business before Hunt had occasion to call on Devin Juhle for some classified DMV information he couldn't get through normal channels. Hunt got acquainted with some of the homicide guys' snitches, who tended to know where witnesses went to hide out. After that, Juhle and his partner Shane Manning had started to refer to themselves as Hunt Clubbers. Then one night when Hunt was over at Juhle's house for dinner—a regular occurrence—his wife, Connie, refused to put food in front of him until he made her a member as well.

After that, the whole thing took on a kind of insider's cachet.

One evening Amy Wu had stopped into Lou the Greek's with Wes Farrell, one of the partners in her firm, for a drink while Hunt, Juhle, and Manning, already a bit in their cups, were working on the club's bylaws, in this case, formally adopting Will Ferrell's *Saturday Night Live* bit, itself based on the original Fishbone lyric, as their official club cheer—"U-G-L-Y, you ain't got no alibi, you Ully, hey, hey, you Ul-ly."

Naturally, Amy and Wes lobbied for admission. Hunt and the guys played hard to get. After all, what was the point of having a club unless there were standards? What could Amy and Wes bring to the party? Wes didn't hesitate. He unbuttoned his dress shirt and showed off the T-shirt he wore under it, on which were written the words, EVERYTHING'S BETTER ON ANABOLIC STEROIDS.

"I wear a new one of these every day," Wes said. "I may have the world's most complete obnoxious T-shirt collection."

Nodding in silent admiration—Farrell passed the attitude test and was going to make the cut—Hunt and the cops turned to Amy.

She wiped away the tear that now somehow glistened on her cheek. "I have never, ever been in a club in my life," she whispered. "No one's ever let me join in. Oh, never mind, anyway." Obviously hurt, she turned, took a few halting steps away. Hunt, feeling awful, rolled his eyes and got up to undo some of the psychic damage if he could—after all, she was his friend, to say nothing of a significant source of his income. He gently put his hand on her shoulder. "Amy, we didn't mean . . ."

And she whirled around, beaming at him. "Are you kidding me?" she said. "You don't think people would kill to get me in their clubs?" She pulled him down and kissed his cheek. "Great liars are always in demand, Wyatt. You never know when you're going to need one."

Eventually, Amy hooked up with and was now engaged to Jason Brandt, another lawyer who worked mainly in the juvenile division but who made the club after he won a bet with Hunt that he could get the three of them into any Giants game any time they wanted without tickets or reservations. Or any other public concert, event, happening. Brandt didn't seem to understand why anybody ever paid or bought tickets to do anything. He told Hunt, who had come to believe it, that over the course of his senior-year summer—and granted, it had been before 9/11—he had toured the U.S. by commercial airliner, with stops in Chicago, Boston, New York, Miami, and Los Angeles, without buying one ticket.

Finally, Hunt hired another young stringer, Craig Chiurco, to help out with surveillance, and soon enough Chiurco and Tamara became an item. So now, since Shane Manning had been killed, there were eight of them—four, including Hunt, on the payroll— and another four irregulars who took the occasional break from their day jobs as lawyers and cops and even mothers to have a little fun on the edge of things, break up the routine.

This morning at the office, Hunt had given his employees each a five-hundred-dollar bonus. For the irregulars, the anniversary was a reasonably good excuse to have a dinner and a few laughs at Sam's.

Wes Farrell had grown out his hair again, though not as extreme as a few years before when it had gotten below his shoulders. Still, in a ponytail, the hair was a statement, like tonight's T-shirt he'd just shown everyone under his dress shirt that read, I WAS TOLD THERE WOULD BE NO MATH. He was explaining that he generally preferred nonverbal statements, such as his hair.

"So what's with the hair, anyway?" Wyatt Hunt asked him.

"You don't like it?" Farrell, hurt, put a hand to his heart. "I've been working on it for weeks."

"I know. I love the hair. I do. It's just not exactly the standard lawyer look."

"Tony Serra has it," Amy Wu said, referring to the defense leg- end they'd once made a movie about. "Long hair, I mean."

"Tony Serra's not your run-of-the-mill standard lawyer," Hunt said.

Farrell took umbrage. "Nor, might I point out, am I."

"No," his girlfriend said, "that you're not." Samantha Dun- can—no relation to the restaurant Sam's—put a hand over his and leaned over to answer Hunt. "And as for the statement, he's not cut- ting his hair until something makes sense. I tell him that's not going to happen until we've got a new administration in Washington." Sam was rather flamboyantly a Green Party person, which in San Francisco put her close to the mainstream, though not necessarily among this crowd of law enforcement types.

"Don't start, my love." Farrell covered her hand with his. "It doesn't have to be on the national front. A sign of anything making sense anywhere could propel me to a barber. But I see little evidence of it." Farrell looked around the table.

The dinner was going very well but hadn't exactly turned out to be the Hunt Club anniversary extravaganza that Hunt had originally billed it. Devin Juhle had pulled a huge case just this morning—a federal judge had been murdered—and he and Connie had had to blow it off. Hunt had reserved a table for nine, the empty chair for Shane Manning's memory and rather emphatically not for Juhle's new partner. When Amy had seen the crew from Trial TV—in for the current tabloid-fodder murder trial of Randy Donolan that was now in its sixth week at the Hall of Justice—which included her friend Andrea Parisi, she'd invited them to fill in the three open spots at the table. Now the party included Spencer Fairchild, the location producer; Parisi; and Richard Tombo, a black attorney, who along with Parisi worked as a talking-head expert on the trial.

"For example," Farrell said, pointing at Tombo, "if you, Rich, or Andrea, or both of you, actually do go large with Trial TV, that would make some sense."

"I'd make an appointment with your barber now, then," Tombo said. "Andrea's a lock for national anchor." He looked to his location man. "Isn't she, Spence?"

Fairchild tried not to wince. "As I believe I've mentioned, my friends, I just do local. This current Donolan circus ends in a couple of weeks, and I'm off to Colorado or Arkansas for the next hot trial. The big decisions are made in New York, not in the field."

But Brandt, always up to talk legal cases, got Fairchild off the hook. "You think Donolan's going two more weeks? I'm thinking after what he did on the stand today . . ."

Andrea Parisi finished applying her lipstick and looked at herself in the mirror in the women's room. She'd been trying not to think about yesterday and felt that she'd needed a couple of glasses of wine at lunch to keep her spirits up for the daily wrap-up broadcast. She and her producer and her male counterpart had had a little champagne in the limo on the way over here. In the past ninety minutes since they'd arrived, she'd had a vodka martini ("Belvedere, a little dirty, up") at the bar before they'd all sat down, then a glass of pinot grigio with her half-shell littlenecks, some Jordan cab (two glasses? three?) with the sweetbreads. She weighed 122 pounds and knew that she was probably legally drunk, although she felt fine.

She checked to make sure that the bathroom door was locked. Then, closing her eyes, she lifted her right foot slightly off the ground, touched the tip of her nose, and counted to five. Opening her eyes, she put her foot back down, and forced a bright smile at her reflection. "She sells seashells by the seashore," she whispered. She repeated it three times perfectly.

She would have bet that she'd be rock steady, and she was, but it never hurt to do a little inventory. Now she had verified for herself that she would easily be able to handle having some Amaretto or maybe, depending on her dinner partners, some Grand Marnier or a snifter of cognac with dessert. Then at least some of them would go around the corner to the cigar bar and have another round or two with their smokes, and she intended to be among them if that was the way the night went.

She took a last look, and something in her gaze held her for another moment. Oh, she supposed she was glamorous enough, to be sure. Her dark hair, a little below her shoulders, gleamed with red highlights—natural, thank you, since she was only thirty-one years old. A bridge of pale freckles rose off each smooth cheek and crossed a nose Modigliani might have painted. Perhaps in a technical sense her chin was too small, her lips too full, but for television, they were if anything a plus. Still, the mirror caught the trace of doubt, of what might be a flash of insecurity. At the corners of the startling green eyes, she saw a tiny web of worry lines form and then dissipate like an apparition. Leaning forward, she tried to see what was in those eyes that stared back at her. But there was no ready answer, and she couldn't stay in here any longer, not if she didn't want to call attention to herself as less than one of the guys, and she wouldn't do that. She would never let herself do that.

She pulled back, ran her tongue over her lips, over the bright red lipstick, and smiled at herself. A small sigh escaped, but she was unaware of it. "It's all good," she said aloud to her image. "Be cool. Don't push it." Now drawing a deeper breath, she steeled her shoulders, reached for the doorknob, and walked back out into the main dining room.

Hunt reached for his cabernet, brought the glass to his mouth, and a vision stopped him before he sipped. With the ongoing discussion into the fate of Randy Donolan playing in the background, he watched the sublime Andrea Parisi weave her graceful way back through the packed restaurant to their table. Because of his lucky seat against the front wall, she was going to be in his line of vision all the way.

The sound around him faded.

* * *

Dessert, and back with Trial TV. "Spence isn't leaving, anyway," Hunt said. "Not after the Palmer thing this morning hits. A federal judge gets shot, it goes national."

"But not right away," Farrell said. "Even if they find somebody and charge him, it won't get to trial for years."

"I'll bet a million dollars it's the prison guards' union," Brandt said. "He was going to shut 'em down; they took him out."

Farrell was shaking his locks. "Too obvious."

Wu agreed. "And the girl just happened to be there? I don't think so, Jason."

Tombo slugged back the rest of his wine. "Amy's right. We don't have to *cherchez la femme* here. She's already in it, the wife. She's going to be what it's about, guaranteed."

"Definitely the wife," Sam said. "She found out, confronted them, adios."

"Except I hear she wasn't home," Tombo said.

Sam shook an index finger. "You wait. It'll come out that she was."

"I'm with Sam," Fairchild said. "Either the wife did it, or she paid somebody."

"Any word on who the other victim is yet?" Wu asked.

Hunt realized that he probably had the latest news. "Devin says no. And even if he did know, he wouldn't tell me."

"Not even you, his close personal friend?" Brandt asked.

A nod. "I told him it didn't seem right and then cried a little, but it didn't work."

"Hunt breaks down," Wu said. "That I would like to see."

"Hey, now! That is so cruel." Hunt put a hand to his heart. "I cry. I feel things. I cry at Hallmark commercials, weddings. Sometimes I cry just for fun. Crying is the new laughing."

"I'll try it sometime," Wu said. "So how old was she? The girl?"

"Devin did know that," Hunt said. "Low twenties." Pause. "Palmer was sixty-three."

"Okay," Fairchild said, "now we're talking. That trial opens, every camera in America comes back to San Francisco. Especially if it's the wife."

"It's going to be the wife," Sam said again. "It's always the wife, except when it's the husband." She patted Farrell's hand next to hers. "That's the main reason Wes and I aren't married, in fact. So we don't kill each other."

Wu looked down at her engagement ring, then over to her fiancé. "I still want to get married," she said. "I promise not to kill you."

Brandt planted a peck on her cheek. "Me, too."

Tombo said, "You ought to put that in your vows."

Everybody had a laugh, and in the middle of it, Hunt glanced at Andrea Parisi, who seemed to be somewhere else until she caught him looking and put on a smile that was no less appealing for being so obviously forced.

Sam and Wes went home after dinner, while the rest of the party decamped to the Occidental Cigar Club, a short walk around the corner from Sam's, on Pine. The Occidental had a sign on its front door, THIS IS NOT A HEALTH CLUB, for those oblivious to the clouds of cigar smoke who might otherwise have wandered in to work out, wearing their Lycra and sweatbands.

The Occidental's owners had figured a way to beat the city's stringent antismoking ordinances. No purveyor of alcohol, quoth the city fathers, could permit smoking in an enclosed premises since second-hand smoke was unhealthy for the people who worked inside. The exception was where the owner of a small bar was the only employee of that bar. So at the Occidental, all the employees had a share of the business.

Hunt, sitting with Jason and Amy in the front window—they all had to work the next day—had backed way off on the alcohol during dinner and drank decaf coffee. Wu smoked a small Sancho Panza, and Hunt and Brandt smoked Monte Cristos.

Hunt's eyes kept returning to the bar. He saw that Fairchild, Tombo, and Parisi were now working on fresh rounds that came in snifters. Serious drinks. "They're going to be hurting tomorrow," he said.

Wu glanced over. "Andrea's been slamming 'em back all night, Wyatt, as if you didn't notice. She's going to be *dying*, but look at her now . . ."

"You don't have to tell Wyatt to look at her," Brandt said. "He's got that part down."

Hunt deadpanned him. "I'm facing them, Jason. Should I avert my eyes? Besides, there are far worse things to look at."

"Whoa, screaming endorsement," Wu said. "I'll tell Andrea you said that."

Hunt sipped his coffee. "I don't see my opinion impacting her worldview."

"Don't kid yourself," Brandt said. "She speaks very highly of you from time to time."

Hunt said, "I'm sure." Then trying to sound casual, "What does she say?"

Brandt blew some smoke. "She likes when you happen to meet up on your morning runs. Says it's often the high point of her day, just the two of you, puffing along the Embarcadero."

Hunt had been doing business with Parisi as the representative of her firm—Piersall-Morton—for nearly a year. He thought she was attractive enough, but the relationship was strictly professional. Then they had inadvertently met up during their respective jogs one morning a couple of months ago. Six A.M. in dense fog, Parisi telling him she didn't realize he was as much an idiot as she was. He'd run with her until she turned off at Bay, neither of them saying much.

Since then, it hadn't been inadvertence. Now most mornings, Hunt left his place at the same time and ran the same route, and without ever discussing it, they'd met up more than a dozen times. He never considered that she might have been timing it herself.

"What does she like about it?" Hunt asked.

"You don't hassle her," Wu said.

"That's true enough. I don't think I've said a hundred words to her."

"That's what she likes," Brandt said. Obviously, he and Wu had talked about this. "You treat her like a normal person."

"She *is* a normal person," Hunt said, his eyes flicking over to the bar again, "in sweats with her hair up." He lifted his chin, indicating the media trio. "But that person over there, that's not a normal person. That's a star."

"Well," Brandt said, "she's that, too. Although I don't think she's as happy with that or committed to being that person."

"She doing a great imitation, then," Hunt said.

"She's trying to figure it out." Wu exhaled smoke. "I mean, can't you see the attraction? New York. Fame and glamour. On TV every day. Huge bucks. You know what she's been making all this time she's been doing Donolan?"

"I guessed minimal," Hunt said. "I thought mostly it was advertising for her firm."

Brandt shook his head. "Nope."

"She started at five grand a week," Wu said, "and got great ratings. Now it's twenty."

Hunt nearly choked on his drink. "Twenty thousand dollars a week? For three sound bites a day if she's lucky?"

Brandt said, "She goes to New York, it's five hundred K a year—and goes up fast."

"Which," Wu added, "beats seventy hours a week with Piersall."

"It beats anything I've ever heard of," Hunt said. He took in the scene at the bar. "No wonder she's hustling it."

"Well." Wu, almost wistful, turned her head to look. "But as you say, she's a normal person at heart." Over at the bar, as they watched, Parisi clinked glasses with Fairchild, and her wonderful contralto laugh carried across the room. Wu sipped her espresso. "I'm just afraid she's fighting herself."

Hunt leaned in closer to Wu. "What do you mean?"

"She wouldn't have to tank herself up so much if it came easy. I mean the big personality, the star stuff. You don't need to drink that much if you're happy, Wyatt. Believe me, I know whereof I speak."

Hunt had his eyes on Andrea. "Maybe she's just partying."

"Maybe," Wu admitted, "but when I was partying like that not so long ago, I wasn't happy. I was hiding."

"And I found you," Brandt said.

She lifted his hand and kissed it. "And thank God you did."

"You guys should get a room," Hunt said.

Brandt's hand moved over Wu's back. "Maybe we should," he said.

Again Parisi's laugh carried over to them. At the bar, they seemed to have ordered yet another round and clinked their glasses again.

A half hour later, Wu and Brandt were gone. His cigar finished, Hunt got up to leave at the same time they did, but after stopping by the bathroom on his way out, he caught another glimpse of Parisi at the bar. Without conscious thought, he boosted himself up onto an empty stool against the wall in the back corner, where he was all but invisible.

Tombo was gone, too. It was just Fairchild and Parisi, heads close to one another. From the suddenly drawn and empty look on Parisi's face, Hunt found it hard to imagine her laughing about anything. She turned her face away from Fairchild, and the bar's dim amber light reflected off the line of her cheek, and Hunt realized with a start that he was looking at the track of a tear and that she was crying.

Fairchild was leaning over, in toward her, when in a flash, she straightened and turned back to him. Her hand moved in a blur. At the same instant, Hunt heard the bitterly angry "Fuck you!" that brought the bar to a sudden silence along with the report of the slap against Fairchild's cheek. Again, "Just fuck you, Spencer!"

And then she was off her stool and moving unsteadily around the end of the bar to the front door. In the tense silence, Hunt heard a throaty sob escape as she pushed the front door open roughly enough to slam it against the side of the building. Outside, she stood for a half second, looking both ways, and then turned to her right and began to run.

Hunt was on his feet before the door closed, out onto the sidewalk and after her. She had less than a hundred feet on him. The sound she was making echoed between the downtown buildings. She seemed almost to be wailing—a continuous if staccato moaning punctuated by her footfalls. Hunt called her name and broke into a run after her.

Before the next corner, the street fell off more sharply and Parisi's voice rose in a startled yelp as she pitched forward, went down, and rolled to a whimpering stop into the gutter on Montgomery Street. In seconds, Hunt was next to her, trying to turn her over, see if she was all right.

But hearing a man's voice, her eyes clouded with tears and she lashed out at him wildly, screaming, "No! No! No! Leave me alone."

He didn't let her go but held her as she struggled against him. "Andrea, it's okay. It's okay. It's Wyatt."

Parisi, struggling against him, saying, "No, no, no, no."

"It's Wyatt, Andrea. Let's get you up."

"Can't." Closing her eyes, "Going to be sick."

Her body began to spasm. Hunt turned her head and held her as she lost her last couple of drinks and most of her meal.

"Okay," he said, "it's okay. Just let it go. You'll be all right."

When she seemed to have finished, he pulled off his tie and cleaned her face with it, leaving it in the gutter. Getting her to her feet, he backed her away from the curb. Her purse had flown away from her on her fall and was now in the middle of the street. He set her down against the nearest building while he went to get it. When he came back, her eyes were closed, her breathing ragged. Going into a squat, he touched her cheek.

"Andrea, can you hear me?"

She barely moved.

"Do you think we can get you home?"

No response.

He opened her purse, found a wallet, opened it up for her address. She lived someplace on Larkin Street, which ran way the hell up to the north end of the city. Hunt looked at his watch—nearly midnight. For all of its congestion during the workday, this time of night Montgomery was deserted. No cars had passed the whole time he'd been here.

Now he saw a cab on its way toward them. He got to the side of the road, put his hand out. The cab pulled up and stopped, and Hunt went to the driver's window. "My girlfriend's had too much to drink," he said, pointing over to Parisi. "If you can just give me a minute."

The cabbie was a middle-aged black man in a Giants cap and jacket. "You need some help?" he asked.

In a minute, they had her in the backseat, passed out.

"You want to take her to emergency?"

Hunt almost said yes, then decided that it might cause her more trouble. She was breathing. She'd had way too much to drink, but she wasn't going to die. And the emergency room meant complications with her job and her TV work. He didn't want to cause her any further problems. He just wanted to get her through this.

"I don't think so. Just home." He gave his address.

The cabbie turned the corner and stepped on the gas.

8 /

The morning interviews with Jeannette Palmer and the briefing sessions with both the FBI and Homeland Security blew Juhle and Shiu through lunchtime. After hitching a ride back downtown with Assistant Coroner Janey Parks, they picked up their normal car and headed back out to Clay Street to start talking to neighbors and look over anything else CSI turned up.

Which was not much.

A slug in the book that Juhle had noticed verified the murder weapon caliber as .22. Mostly based on the accuracy of the shots and gunshot residue on the desk, the forensics folks had determined that the shooter was probably standing very close to if not at the very front of the desk. Although further tests would seek to amplify the initial data, which was sketchy at best, this in turn led Shiu to surmise—based on the blood splatter and trajectory angle through the book—that the shooter was either a short man or a woman.

Juhle flinched. He knew that there were too many variables in the relative positions of the gun and the targets to draw conclusions. How could one possibly distinguish, for example, a tall man who shot from the hip from a short man holding the gun at shoulder height? He couldn't stop himself. "So, a man or a woman. Imagine that. As opposed to, say, a chimpanzee, which was my first choice."

The neighborhood was a bust as well, with one perhaps important exception. Shari Levin, who lived directly across the street from the Palmers and who had gone out to her bridge party at about seven thirty, had noticed what she thought was Mrs. Palmer's car parked out in the street. She noticed because she wondered why she hadn't parked as usual in her own circular driveway. At least it was the same basic type of car—"one of those sports convertibles you see everywhere nowadays."

She knew Mrs. Palmer drove the same BMW Z4 that was parked in the driveway now, and she thought it had been that car, although it had been near dusk and the car was dark, too. Juhle and Shiu filed the information, knowing full well that if it hadn't been Mrs. Palmer's, the car in question might well turn out to be an Audi, a Porsche, or a Mercedes. Even a Honda. In more rigorous questioning, all Ms. Levin had finally given them was that she'd barely glanced and hardly noticed, but there had definitely been a car on the street, parked up flush to the driveway, and she thought at the time that it had been Mrs. Palmer's. Whose else would it have been?

So they hadn't exactly broken the case wide open in the first few hours. Not that they expected to, but public forbearance over slow progress would be short-lived. Chief Batiste made that crystal clear in his afternoon press conference when he said that the murder of a federal judge struck at the very heart of our free society and that the apprehension of the guilty party for this atrocity would be the top priority of his police department until the case was solved. The "my police department" was ominous. He would take the credit for success and the blame for failure. He promised results—and fast.

Juhle hated when they did that. Batiste had no idea what they had, what they were working with; he hadn't the vaguest notion of the complexity of the crime. In fact, no one did yet. But Batiste was promising quick results. Stupid and counterproductive, and now all on the heads of Juhle and Shiu.

Thanks, chief. And you wonder why morale's in the toilet?

At the press conference, amping it up another notch, Batiste also announced that he and Mayor West had assigned an Event Number to the case, meaning that they were freeing up nearly unlimited funds from the city's general fund, outside of the police budget, for the investigation.

No mistake about it: If Juhle and Shiu hadn't felt the pressure from the beginning, and they had, they were in a cooker now. And they still hadn't even identified the female victim. All the usual inquiries failed. No criminal history, no military record, no applications where she'd submitted fingerprints to any agency. Fingerprints sent to DMV came back negative.

She didn't even have a driver's license?

Now, Shiu driving and closing in on one in the morning, the two inspectors parked in the cops' lot behind the Hall of Justice. Groggy and silent, they walked up the dimly lit outdoor corridor that led them to the morgue, just across the way from the jail.

It was a clear night, cold and quiet.

Shiu rang the coroner's night bell—Juhle hadn't taken any pain medication since the morning, and his hand was throbbing. After a moment the silhouette of Janey Parks appeared back in the darkened recesses of the outer office. She was the efficient yet generally friendly bureaucrat with whom they'd hitched a ride downtown twelve hours before.

When she opened the door, leading them back through the desks the way she'd come, she started right in: "The witness is Mary Mahoney. She's a waitress at MoMo's. Twenty-seven. Came down by herself. No question on the ID. Positive."

This last wasn't much of a surprise, since the young woman's face hadn't been touched by the bullet, a mystery which Ms. Parks had solved earlier in the day at Palmer's house by opening the victim's mouth with her rubber-gloved hands and looking inside with her flashlight, thereby discovering the entry wound at the back of her throat. The girl had had her mouth open when the shot was fired. All the teeth were intact. The slug didn't have enough punch to penetrate the skull, so there was no exit wound, either. "But, man, it did some damage inside," Janey was saying. "Ricocheted up and kicked around in there like a pinball. The brain was scrambled eggs."

"Hey, great. Good detail. Thanks, Janey." This was the kind of image that tended to stick with Juhle and wake him up with the sweats. But he shook it off—it would come back to haunt him, anyway, get him on the ricochet, as it were.

They got to the office of John Strout, the medical examiner who was now in his mid-seventies and had long since ceased caring about the formal appearance of professionalism. The place was a museum of the bizarre, the outright macabre, and the dangerous. Three hand grenades, reputedly live, served as paperweights on his desk. By the entrance to the morgue's cold room, a skeleton with a pipe in its teeth and a silken rope around its neck relaxed on an authentic antique Spanish garrote. On the bookshelf counter, Strout kept his collection of knives, brass knuckles, sharp and deadly ninja paraphernalia. Several rifles and shotguns leaned against the walls. In an immense terrarium in the center of the office—and completely illegally as a technical matter—he kept his favorite murder weapons from actual cases he'd worked, many complete with bloodstains: an ice pick, a beaker full of empty syringes, a baseball bat, various pokers and blunt objects, a couple more knives of particularly creative design.

Even if you hadn't just come from having identified a deceased acquaintance, the place could be unnerving. And on top of all this, Parks had kept the lights dim, which maximized the terror factor.

Juhle flicked the switch and the room lit up. It helped.

And here was Mary Mahoney, sitting with her arms crossed tight over her chest, her eyes reddened from recent tears. Juhle moved a wooden chair over beside her and sat down. Parks, he noticed, had gone to sit in Strout's chair.

On his own footstool, Shiu broke the ice. "I want to thank you for coming in tonight. It's not something everyone would have done."

"I didn't know what else I should do," Ms. Mahoney said.

"Well, you did the right thing," Shiu said. "Every minute we save early on in the investigation increases the odds that we'll find who did this."

"I kind of thought that." Ms. Mahoney had short, spiky black hair, wide-set liquid brown eyes—her best feature—lips that had been collagened, a nose she hadn't been born with. The effect wasn't negative.

"So how did you come to think it might have been . . . your friend?" Shiu asked.

"Staci. Staci Rosalier." In her small voice, she continued, "Well, when I came in about four, everybody at the restaurant was talking about the judge, about what happened. He ate there, you know, just about every day. Nobody could believe it. And then, I don't know when exactly, but after the rush started, I heard something about a woman being with him. A young woman. Not his wife." She looked from Shiu to Juhle, who nodded, encouraging her to go on. "And so—we were jamming all night—but it got me worried. So when I got a minute—by now it's, like, ten thirty?—I went and asked one of the managers if she could check and see if Staci was in today. She worked lunch, which I did, too, when I first met her. Which is how we became friends, you know?"

"So," Juhle said, "you asked the manager if Staci had come in?"

"Right. But she hadn't even called in. And Staci never missed. She was like the rock at lunch." Mahoney closed her eyes, drew a deep breath. "So, anyway, when I found that out, now I'm really worried."

Shiu stepped in. "So what's the connection between Staci and Judge Palmer? That you were so concerned about?"

But suddenly Mahoney was shaking her head from side to side. Tears appeared in her eyes. "I just can't believe that's all that's left of her in there. I mean, she was the sweetest person. Who would do that to her?"

"That's what we're trying to find out," Shiu said.

Mahoney went silent. Shiu gave her a handkerchief, and she dabbed at her eyes. "I might be the only one who knew about it, but Staci and the judge had a thing."

"You mean an affair?" Juhle asked.

"Well, not exactly. Maybe more than that. He put her up, you know. Paid her rent."

Juhle saying, "Do you know how long this had been going on, Mary?"

"Him and her? I don't know exactly, but at least since last fall. Although the new place, she just moved in there only a couple of months or so ago."

The two inspectors exchanged a glance. Juhle came forward. "The new place?"

"Just across from the store. MoMo's. In those lofts, the new ones."

Juhle knew them. Prices on the one-room studios started at around four hundred thousand dollars and topped out at well over a million for the penthouses. If Judge Palmer had put Staci Rosalier in one of these places, he'd made a serious commitment to her.

"Have you ever been up to her place?" Shiu asked.

"A couple of times, although she was pretty private about it. She couldn't let anybody find out about them, which you can understand."

"But she let you," Shiu said.

"We were real friends. Plus, it was so cool, she just had to show *somebody*." The tears spilled over. "I just . . ." she began, then lowered her head and fell silent.

Juhle gave her a moment. Then gently, "You're talking the new condos on Second, right directly across from MoMo's?"

She looked up at him and nodded. "Why did this have to happen?" she asked.

Juhle had no answer.

The building supervisor, Jim Franks, wasn't thrilled to get woken up at 1:50 A.M. It took the sallow, potbellied, middle-aged man nearly ten minutes to get to the door, another very long minute to find the one key on his twelve-key ring that would open it. Juhle and Shiu stood outside all the while in the now fully gathered cold—impatient, unspeaking, unamused.

Franks had thrown himself into a wrinkled pair of brown slacks and a stained Corona beer T-shirt. When he opened the door, he backed away a few steps. "This couldn't wait till the morning?"

Juhle held his warrant up for Franks to see, dredged a tolerant expression from somewhere. "Mr. Franks," he said in a conversational tone, "you have my word we'd rather be doing this in the morning, too. But a woman who lived in this building was shot dead the night before last and we don't feel like we've earned any rest until we've got some kind of jump on who might have killed her, which we don't have yet. We thought we might find something in her apartment that might help us. Can you understand that?"

The little speech hit its mark. Suddenly Franks was less hostile. "You said Staci Rosalier? She dead?"

Juhle nodded. "She just got identified an hour ago by a friend of hers who told us she lived here. That's why we're bothering you."

"You want to see her apartment?" But then a thought struck him. "Don't you need to have some kind of warrant for that?"

Juhle sighed and produced it again.

"Okay," Franks finally said. They walked down a dark hallway on the first floor to the office of the building, where Franks went to a file cabinet, unlocked it on the third try, and pulled a key off a hook. "There you go," he said, handing it over to Juhle, "now if that's all . . ."

Shiu, unable to fake equanimity, hung back by the door, his arms crossed over his chest. Juhle looked at his partner, came back to Franks. "Just one or two questions."

Sighing extravagantly, Franks lowered a haunch onto the corner of his desk. He brought a hand up to his eyes and rubbed them. "Okay, what?"

"Would you notice when she had visitors?"

"No, I don't think I ever did. She could have anybody come anytime they wanted."

"But you didn't notice anyone special?"

"People are coming and going all the time. I don't pay much attention." Franks checked the wall clock. "You said only a couple of questions . . ."

"Yes, I did." Juhle's humor actually seemed to be improving—in spite of the hour, in spite of his broken bones. "Here's another one:

Do you remember if anyone came to see her in the past few days? Anyone unusual?"

"I'm sorry," Franks said, "I just never pay attention to that. We've got almost a thousand tenants, and all of them have friends and families, most of 'em unusual one way or another. People are coming and going all the time." He straightened up off the desk. "Now if you don't need me anymore, I'm going back to bed. You can drop the key in the box when you're done."

"Thank you, sir," Juhle said, "we appreciate your cooperation."

Franks shrugged. "No problem."

In the elevator, Juhle shot a glance at Shiu. "Personable guy."

"If that was no problem," Shiu said, "I'd like to see him when he thinks he's got one."

Juhle shrugged. "He's tired."

"Who isn't?"

"Offer it up to the poor souls in purgatory."

"What's that?"

"Purgatory? Kind of like a waiting room outside of heaven, although I vaguely remember hearing it doesn't exist anymore. Wouldn't that be a bitch? What happened to all the souls waiting around in there when they decided it wasn't there?"

"Is that a real question? Let's make this quick."

Staci Rosalier had lived on the fourth floor, three steps across from the elevator, where the judge would face little danger of being recognized when he came to visit.

They opened the door and turned on the light. The condominium was high-end and modern in style and adornments but smaller than Juhle had imagined it would be. Twenty-five feet deep, maybe fifteen wide.

Four stools fronted a bar that ran along to their left. Behind it was a kitchen area with a sink and two-burner stove. The bar ended at a door to a small, shower-only bathroom. Directly across were full-length closet doors and built-in bookshelves filled with paperbacks. The far wall was all window, drapes open both sides, the ballyard across the way. He guessed that the couch was a sofa bed. There was a coffee table on an artsy-fartsy throw rug and a comfortable-looking brown leather chair under a reading lamp in the corner.

"The good life," Shiu said.

"You don't like it?"

"It's a hotel room. Nobody lives here."

"No, look," he said. "Daffodils on the bar there. Books in the shelves." Juhle was pulling on his surgical gloves. On the small table next to the sofa, he turned on a three-way reading light and picked up two framed photographs, one—badly out of focus—of a smiling young boy, and the other of Judge Palmer. "Personal photos. She lived here, all right, Shiu. She just didn't have much room."

Shiu was already behind the bar, poking around in the cabinets, the drawers, the refrigerator. He was reaching into a closet when Juhle grabbed his arm. "Gloves," he said.

Juhle opened another closet filled with clothes and a dozen or more pairs of shoes. Staci had color-coded the hangers. He turned. "Here's the wallet." On a built-in chest of drawers. Moving out into the room, he sat on the sofa and began emptying the wallet's contents onto the coffee table in front of him. More cash—four fifties and four ones. Credit cards. Library card. Social Security. Costco. A smaller version of the same fuzzy snapshot of the boy. One of the judge—much more casual than the formal office shot she'd framed and taken in this room, Juhle realized—in the reading chair, grinning.

Juhle made an unconscious noise and the sound stopped Shiu. "What?"

"That's weird."

"What?"

Juhle shrugged, held up a business card. "Andrea Parisi." At Shiu's blank look, he thought fast and said, "The TV expert on the Donolan trial?"

"Ah." Shiu placed the name, but neither it nor the card had any significance to him. "What is weird about her? She hangs out with the judge, she's going to know some lawyers. Plus," he added, "you know as well as me, MoMo's is famous lawyer land."

"Yeah, you're right." Juhle didn't see any need to tell his partner that his friend Wyatt Hunt was sometimes her jogging buddy. And that he had been regaling him with Andrea Parisi fantasies for the past six weeks or so. Instead, he placed the business card back with the other contents of the wallet. "But it's funny that this is the only card she kept."

Shiu didn't think so. "Maybe, like every other waitress in the world, she wanted to get into television."

"That's not here. That's in L.A."

"It's everywhere," Shiu said. "It's a universal truth. Anyway, I bet we find a stack of other business cards in some drawer here. Either that, or Staci got that card and hadn't thrown it away yet.

Besides, you and I know this doesn't have anything to do with Andrea Parisi."

"We could pretend. Spend a little time with her cute little self." Juhle cracked a grin, got no response from his partner, tried again. "Spend a little time with her cute—"

"I heard you."

"That was a stab at humor."

"Adultery's not something you joke about."

"You are *so* wrong, Shiu. Adultery's no lower than number three on the list of all-time joke topics. In fact, there's this Irishman, Paddy, who hasn't been to church in something like twenty years, and this one day—"

"Dev." Shiu held a palm up. "It's something *I* don't want to joke about, okay?"

"So along with religion and ethnic and gay and women, now you don't do adultery. Christ, what's left?"

"Why does there have to be anything?" Shiu sat down on one of the stools. "Devin," he said, "it's the middle of the night. We're investigating a double homicide that's all about adultery, okay? We know we're going to arrest Jeannette Palmer in the next week, maybe sooner than that. Her life will be ruined, already is ruined. This young woman is dead. So is a federal judge. None of this is funny. And Connie wouldn't find it funny that you want to get cozy with Andrea Parisi."

"Yeah, you're right, I'm sorry, my bad." Juhle hung his head. "Getting cozy with Parisi, that would be wrong," he said with deep sincerity. Then he suddenly brightened. "But, hey, maybe I could invite Connie? If you wanted in, we could make it a foursome."

In his bed Juhle pulled the covers up over his sling with some care. Next to him, Connie stirred. "What time is it?"

"Unreasonable. Near three, I think. You awake?"

"No." Then: "How'd it go?"

"I think we solved the case. Surprise, it's the wife. But I've got to get a new partner."

"You always say that. What'd he do now?"

"Nothing. He's perfect. I hate him. I even invited him to get into a love thing with you and me and Andrea Parisi, the TV fox with the Donolan trial. Turned me down flat."

"I didn't know you knew her."

"I don't, but I could definitely meet her around this case."

"Is she involved in it?"

"I can't see how. But the victim had her business card, and I'm sure I could finagle an introduction."

"Maybe it's me. Maybe Shiu doesn't find me attractive."

"Impossible."

"It *would* be weird," she agreed. "Are you tired?"

"I could probably stay awake another few minutes in a crisis."

"You know how long it's been? Since the operation."

"Is that the last time? Nine days?"

"Actually, it was the day before that, if you're counting, which makes it ten. That qualifies as a crisis," she said, and rolled on top of him.

9 /

Out in the warehouse, practicing silent scales on his unplugged Strat, Hunt heard a muffled scream, Parisi coming back to consciousness. He stepped into the doorway where she could see him.

She was sitting up on his bed, the covers thrown off, in the clothes she'd been wearing last night. "Oh, my God! Wyatt? What am I . . . ?" Her hands came up to her face, and she moaned again.

Hunt unslung his guitar and laid it on the rug. By the sink, filling a glass, he grabbed a bottle of aspirin and crossed over to her. Handing her the glass, he shook out some pills.

"Thank you." She took them all at once, knocked back the water. "What time is it?"

"A little after eight."

Her eyes widened, but the effort was too much. She lowered the glass into her lap. "It can't be that. I've got to . . ." Swinging her feet to the floor, she tried to stand but didn't make it. Putting the glass on the floor, she fell back onto the bed.

Hunt picked up the glass, went and filled it again, and came back to her. "Drink more water. You need to get hydrated."

She raised her head. "I don't think . . ."

He wasn't hearing it. "Water. Water will save your life."

She pulled her body up and drank.

"All of it," Hunt said. "You'll be glad you did."

She forced the rest of it down, tried to straighten up again. "I've got to get back home. I've got . . ."

"You want to give it a minute."

"I can't. I've got . . . what day is it?"

"Wednesday."

"How did I get here?"

"I didn't know where else to take you. You passed out."

She picked at the memory. "We were . . . Spencer, that bastard." Parts of it coming back. "All along, he knew . . . he couldn't do anything about . . ."

"New York?"

She lay back into the pillow, threw an arm over her eyes. "I've got to call work."

"I can do that for you."

"No." But she didn't move. Lying on the bed, breathing through her mouth.

Hunt got the phone. He had worked for her firm enough that he knew the number by heart. He also knew her secretary, Carla Shapiro, but didn't want to talk to her because she would ask him questions. So he talked to the receptionist. He was Andrea's doctor, and she had a bad case of food poisoning. She was resting and on fluids now and wouldn't be in till tomorrow.

Andrea tried to object. "Wait," she said. "That's too . . ."

"Maybe this afternoon," Hunt said into the phone, "but I'm recommending against it."

When he hung up, she collapsed back down. "I've really got to get home."

"You've got to get up, you've got to call work, you've got to go home. What you've got to do, Andrea, is give the alcohol time to dissipate. Get more water inside you. You're okay here. Lay back down, close your eyes, cover up. I'll unplug the phone. You go back to sleep."

"Maybe I should."

"No 'maybe' about it."

"But I need to use the bathroom."

"Can you get up?"

"I don't know." She sat up, tried to stand, went back down. "Maybe not."

Hunt leaned over her. "Put your arms around my neck."

"You don't want to . . . I stink," she said. "My clothes—"

"Shut up. Arms."

She obeyed him. He got her upright, walked her inside the bathroom, then stepped outside it, and closed the door behind him. After the flush, he heard the water running.

"Wyatt." The voice feeble.

He opened the door. She was sitting down on the seat cover, tears in her eyes. Again he got in front of her, went to one knee. "Arms," he said.

After a minute, she moved, and he walked her back and helped her down again to the bed. "You can take off your clothes if you want. You'll be more comfortable. I won't look."

"Okay," she said. But instead of making any movement to do that, she lay on her side and pulled the blankets over her. Hunt took the pillow and tucked it in under her head.

Before he straightened up, she was asleep.

When she woke up next time, she took four more aspirin with two more glasses of water that Hunt made her drink. In the bathroom, she used the new toothbrush Hunt had given her. Now she turned off the water and stepped out of the shower. With the clean white towel Hunt had supplied, she wiped the bathroom mirror in a couple of circular strokes. Her clothes lay where she'd put them in a pile on top of the hamper, under her purse, which she now brought over to the sink. The purse still contained her hairbrush and compact. She wasn't going out without using them.

When she was satisfied, she wrapped the towel up under her arms, then around her, barely preserving a technical modesty.

Wyatt Hunt wasn't in any of the rooms she'd seen, so barefoot and towel-wrapped, she walked out through the bedroom and opened the door. She got a surprise. Hunt was on her right, facing away from her, by an old, cracked leather couch and in front of a six-foot television screen that was turned off. Surrounded by several amplifiers and four guitars on their stands, he was holding a fifth and quietly playing scales on it.

Parisi's gaze went up to the ceiling, way above her. She took a silent step out into the huge open space that looked pretty much like what it was, a converted warehouse. Over to her left, a silver MINI Cooper squatted in one corner. The far wall facing her contained a desk with a computer and file cabinets. On the right-hand corner was some kind of backstop, with a few bats stuck in the fencing. Then, coming around, a set of weights. Finally, the pièce de résistance, one half of a hardwood basketball court, backboard and all, with a Golden State Warriors' logo in the key.

"Wyatt."

He turned. His eyes immediately went to her legs, then nearly as fast came back up. "Hey," he said. "Better?"

She couldn't go that far. "At least there's some hope I might live." She gestured around. "This is very cool."

Unslinging the guitar, Hunt put it back on its stand. Took the moment as an excuse not to stare at her. He cast his eyes around his space. "Yeah. I like it. You want the grand tour? You notice my professional basketball court, bought used from the Warriors for a mere four grand?"

"No. Where is that?" Joking with him. Now looking down at herself. "You wouldn't have something I could wear, do you? I couldn't bring myself to put my old clothes back on."

Hunt decided not to say that she looked pretty damn good to him just like she was. "I'm sure I can find something," he said.

Now she was wearing one of his black pullovers over a T-shirt and a pair of his jeans with a length of rope to gather the waist. They were drinking coffee at the table in Hunt's kitchen. "So how do I thank you?" she asked.

"No need. You were in trouble. I'm supposed to leave you passed out in the street?"

"Some people might have."

"No human beings."

"Well . . . thank you." She sipped at her coffee. "It keeps coming back to me. I hate a public scene."

"I've seen worse," Hunt said.

"Did I hit him?"

"Yes, you did. A slap, really."

"That's inexcusable."

Hunt shrugged. "He'd been lying to you."

"Still. That's no excuse. Once the hitting starts, excuses get lame pretty quick."

"I have noticed that."

Something about the way he said it stopped her, the cup halfway to her mouth. "That sounds like personal experience?"

"Maybe a bit."

"If you don't want to talk about it . . ."

"No, it's all right. I spent time in a few foster homes when I was a kid, that's all. I found that once the old corporal punishment barrier got broken . . . as you say, any excuse became a good one."

She put her cup down. "You were a foster kid?"

He nodded. "For a while. Till I was eight. I was lucky. I got adopted."

"At eight?"

"I know, it's unusual." He made a face. "I must have been cuter then."

"Well," she said, "maybe in a different way. But you know, then, too, about getting hit."

"Too? Who hit you?"

She drew in a deep breath and let it out. "My mother's second husband. Richie. He was a big believer in discipline, and I was his favorite."

"Why was that?"

"You're sure you want to know this?"

"I asked."

She sighed. "I think because I tried to fight him off. Note the key word, 'tried.' Luckily, he was only around for a year."

"What happened?"

"Mom found out. About me. She got him to come at her, and she killed him. They called it self-defense."

"Sounds like it was."

A small smile began, faded. "Close enough, I guess." Twirling her cup on the table now. "I apologize for all the melodrama."

"It's all right. I can take it."

"Anyway, it's why I'm so disgusted if I hit Spencer, even if he's a shit. I thought I'd trained myself never to do that."

"You think maybe you got drunk and saw a little of Richie in Spencer?"

"I don't want to think that. I don't want to see Richie in anybody."

"But he's always around?"

"The memory. Somewhere, yes. And I know what you're going to say next."

"If you do, you're a step ahead of me."

"I doubt that."

"Okay, so what was I going to say?"

"That you know why I crave this public adulation, the anchor thing."

"Do you? Crave it, I mean?"

"I must. Deep down, I don't think I feel too worthy of any one person's affection. I'm damaged goods. So maybe enough love from the masses makes up for the lack of it from any one person. How's that for a theory?"

"Painful." Hunt started to move a hand across the table to cover hers, the comfort of a sympathetic touch. He didn't let it get there.

She went on. "I can't think of how else . . . why else . . . anyway, I'm sorry."

"Yeah," Hunt said. "Love. That's a bad thing for a person to want." He finished his coffee, put his cup down. "No more apologies, okay? How's the head?"

"The head pounds. The head is going for a new record."

"Well, as long as you get something positive out of it."

A feeble smile, then the structure of her face seemed to break somewhat. Tears threatened again. "What's really funny is that Spencer was really just the last straw. You know why I got involved with him in the first place?"

"You wanted to be a star."

"Okay, that. But mostly to get out of San Francisco. To New York or anywhere else. And to do it as a celebrity. That would just show . . ." She twirled her coffee cup.

"Show what?"

"Not what. Who." She drew a breath and spoke under it. "Another guy. We broke up six months ago, just when Donolan was starting. I was too serious, he said. He didn't want serious. Besides, he had a new girlfriend. Two years we're together, and he didn't want serious. We were adults, colleagues. The professional side would just be the same."

"And it was?"

"That's the killer. It was." She met Hunt's eyes. "Then Spencer showed up. And the new gig. And suddenly that all became a way to get out."

"To get away from this other guy?"

She nodded. "I couldn't stand to keep seeing him, but we had to meet all the time. Work. Prison guard stuff, CCPOA. Piersall's bread and butter, as you know."

But Hunt hadn't realized that. "I thought they were just another client."

"Not exactly. In fact, they're number one for us. Six or eight million in billings."

"Every year? Are they in the market for their own private investigator?"

"I don't think you'd like working for them."

"For any whole number percentage of eight mil I'd try. I'd try really hard." Hunt came back to the nut of it. "So you had to keep seeing this guy professionally? You couldn't just bail on him?"

"You don't bail on that kind of business and stay employed. Not at Piersall."

"So New York was the answer?"

"Well, it was *an* answer." She spun her cup, forced a weak smile. "I think it's time I called a cab."

"You don't need a cab. I'll take you home."

"No. You've already done too much. I'll just get a cab."

"We're not arguing about it," Hunt said. "Grab your clothes. It's time I got out in the world today, anyway. I can drop you."

10 /

Juhle didn't get into the homicide detail until a little after ten. He assumed that since he'd been out working the Palmer—now the Palmer/Rosalier—case until the wee hours of the morning, Lieutenant Lanier would be inclined to cut him some slack on his regular hours. This turned out not to be the case for a couple of reasons.

First, his partner was at his desk before eight o'clock, shaved and polished and writing up a report on Mary Mahoney's identification of Staci Rosalier, including the fact that the young female victim had been Palmer's kept woman. CSI was searching the condominium again more thoroughly this morning and hoped to have a lot more to give homicide, plus next of kin information, before the end of the day.

The other reason that Lanier wasn't in a forgiving mood was that the two special agents of the FBI who were also on the case had arranged with him to convene an informal task force meeting at nine thirty in his office with Juhle and Shiu and the other two investigators with the Department of Homeland Security.

So everyone wouldn't step on each other's toes.

By the time Juhle arrived, it was clear that Shiu had sold their case pretty well. He had shared his information about the relationship between Rosalier and the judge, as well as the testimony of the neighbor, Ms. Levin, about Mrs. Palmer's car being out in front of the house at the time of the shooting while she was supposedly in Novato. In spite of all the potential jurisdictional issues confronting them, Shiu convinced every one of the other five professional investigators in Lanier's office that the most likely scenario for the double homicide was that the wife had discovered her husband's infidelity and somehow had known that he and the girl would be in her home while she was supposed to be away. Either that or she'd lured them there under some pretext.

All that remained, Shiu had told them, was to break Mrs. Palmer's alibi with her sister and, if they were lucky, find the murder weapon, although she had probably disposed of it somewhere along the road or in the Bay on her drive back to her sister's house in Novato. The bottom line was that it appeared to be a crime of passion, personal and local, and hence under the jurisdiction of the San Francisco Police Department.

One of whose two inspectors had failed to appear for the meeting.

"It was a pure miracle you were there," Juhle was saying. "What were you doing in at work already, anyway?"

Shiu was driving through the tunnel behind Sausalito on the way to Mill Valley. "I didn't want to have them spin it the wrong way, Dev. Besides, you know, I try to be in when the shift starts. And the meeting didn't begin until nine thirty, which should have allowed anybody plenty of time to get in."

"*I didn't even know about the goddamned meeting.* And don't tell me not to take the Lord's goddamn name in vain, which you were just going to do. Because the actual fact is that I *do* have to swear because I am goddamned pissed off. You know how that is?"

"I feel anger myself, sure. Everybody feels anger." Shiu glanced sideways again. "For the record, I thought Lanier was a little harsh myself."

"A *little* harsh!" Juhle did a good Lanier imitation: "*Did it ever occur to me that the murder of a federal judge was more important than my beauty rest? Would it be reasonable to expect that I'd be giving priority to this case because if not, he's sure these federal employees would be happy to help us out.* Who does he think got the ID on Rosalier and the connection to the judge in less than twenty-four, huh? It sure as hell wasn't the goddamned FBI."

Shiu took an exit ramp off the freeway. "He was embarrassed, that was all."

"There wasn't anything to be embarrassed about. We got a judge with a million cases pending, any one of which could have brought assassins out of the woodwork, kept us following false leads halfway to Tombouctou and back, and still we got this thing all but tied up in under a day. It's unprecedented. Hell, it's close to divine intervention. We ought to be given citations, and instead he's busting my chops. It isn't right."

"Maybe he wants it completely tied up. He's under a lot of pressure himself. If he calls the FBI off, and he's wrong . . ."

"He's not wrong. We're not wrong."

"I didn't say we were. I said 'if.' "

"Don't entertain negative thoughts," Juhle said. "We're the good guys and we're right."

JV's Salon in Mill Valley was much bigger than Juhle had envisioned. Taking up several suites in an upscale mall, it provided full-service personal care for its female clients. In the glass-enclosed, antiseptic reception area, Juhle and Shiu waited for Vanessa Waverly to come out and give them some of her time. They'd made an appointment, so in theory Waverly should have been expecting them, but she hadn't responded to the receptionist's call, and now the pretty young redhead looked for her boss somewhere inside the labyrinth behind her.

Shiu walked around the room, checking out the services. "What's exfoliation?" he asked.

"Hair, I think. Removal of. Although it might be skin. I'm not sure."

"Removal of skin?"

"Just the outside."

"It must be skin, because they have waxing listed separately. Waxing's got to be removal of hair, don't you think?"

Juhle cast him a look of pure exhaustion. "Do we have to talk about this?"

"Listen to everything they do here—manicure, hair color and styling, spa, massage, facials, tanning, makeovers, exfoliation, waxing. Have you ever done any one of those things?"

"Sure. I get a haircut every month or two, bite my nails off when they bother me."

"So that would be no."

"Shiu." Juhle held up a hand. "Beauty in women, it's like sausage, okay. You don't want to know too much about how it's made. You ask me, a place like this, it's God's way of telling some women they've got too much free time, too much money, and maybe, just maybe, they're a little too self-absorbed."

"Well," said a female voice behind him, "there's an enlightened observation." She wore a welcoming smile—her teeth had been done, too, Juhle thought—and extended her hand to him. His sling kept his right arm close to his body, but he put out his left hand quickly and got his already-broken bones crushed again for his trouble.

Vanessa Waverly was an athletically built, chestnut-haired Venus of a certain age in a black bathing suit with a multicolored wrap tied around her hips. Juhle thought she made a terrific walking advertisement for cosmetic surgery. At a glance, it appeared that everything doable on her had been done. "I'm sorry I wasn't out here to meet you," she said. "We had a problem with one of the dryers, and then Jeannette just called again."

Shiu proffered his ID and badge, which Waverly studied with some care before saying that maybe they'd be more comfortable in her office. Without waiting for a response, she turned and led the way down a carpeted hallway on whose walls were framed beauty magazine covers interspersed with tasteful enlarged color glossies of beautiful unclothed females of every age, from babies to, apparently, grandmothers. Waverly's office, with tinted windows and a view of an oak-studded hillside, reiterated the same themes but in a slightly more austere fashion. Four bronzed sculptures of idealized naked women rose from pedestals in the corners. A sheet of glass atop a large reclining nude in black marble served as the coffee table, which was surrounded by white leather couches and chairs. A glass tube desk held a telephone and computer terminal, but no paper, blotter, or clutter of any kind, and no in-box. It was a power desk, plain and simple, although Waverly did not cross over behind it.

Instead, she turned back to the inspectors. "Can I offer you some coffee, tea, bottled water? No. Do you mind if I just get some for myself? Meanwhile, please, sit down wherever you'd like." Again, without waiting for any response, she turned and went to a refrigerator which was all but hidden in the shelving behind her desk.

When she came back with her Evian, she took the couch. The inspectors had each taken one of the chairs. "This is a terrible day," she said without preamble. "What can I do for you gentlemen?"

Juhle cleared his throat. "First, about what I was saying in there . . ."

"Please, inspector, I've heard it all before, believe me. I've developed a very thick skin. You've come here to talk about George and Jeannette." It wasn't a question.

"Yes, ma'am," Juhle replied. He took out his pocket tape recorder. "I don't know if you're aware, but in any homicide investigation, we usually tape-record our interviews. It's standard procedure. Is that okay with you?"

"Yes, of course. Why would I object?"

Juhle shrugged. "Some people do. I like to ask." He smiled, turned on the machine, gave his introduction—case and badge number, date, place, name of witness. Then, "You said you'd just talked to your sister when we got here?"

She nodded. "Yes. She's staying at my house for a time. Until she . . . well, until it feels all right to go back to her home. Which may be never."

Juhle took the lead in the questioning. "What did she want? The call just now?"

Vanessa Waverly, perhaps struck by the abruptness of the question, canted her head to the side. "She wanted to know if you'd arrived yet. She didn't understand why you wanted to talk to me. Frankly, I'm not too clear on it, either, to tell you the truth."

"So she knew we were coming?" Juhle asked.

"Yes. I told her after you called me. It seemed a natural thing to do. Why? Was that a problem?"

"No, ma'am, just a question."

"How's she holding up?" Shiu asked.

Waverly let out a quick breath. "She's devastated, of course. What else could she be under the circumstances? And I don't mean just George's death, which was bad enough, but the other victim, the young woman. Have you discovered who she was yet?"

Shiu nodded. This would be public information by the evening news, and there was nothing to be gained from trying to withhold it. "Her name was Staci Rosalier. Have you ever heard of her?"

"No."

"She was a waitress at MoMo's, where Judge Palmer often had lunch. There were pictures of him in her condo."

The woman hung her head. "Damn it, George!" she said. "Damn you."

"You had no idea?" Juhle asked.

"I had no idea. I honestly thought George and Jeannette were the one couple I'd ever known . . ." Shaking her head from side to side, she swore again. "You try to keep a little faith in the human race, you know? But it tends to let you down."

Shiu said, "So you had no indication that your sister knew anything about this, either?"

"None. She didn't know. She may not know yet. Not for sure, anyway. Although, of course, she suspects it. But why would they have been there in their house? Especially if she had a condo nearby. Was he just trying to insult Jeannette by bringing his little chippie home?" She shook her head again. "I mean, that would just be so out of character. I *know* George didn't hate Jeannette, and that's what it would take for him to do something that cruel. Even if he was having this . . . relationship. Okay, he's a man and men do that. But he respected her. He just wouldn't have brought another woman home. He wouldn't have insulted Jeannette like that."

"We don't know why he did bring her there yet, ma'am," Shiu said, "or even if he brought her at all. It's entirely possible she came over on her own. Somebody could have dropped her off. Maybe she had another boyfriend, and that's their killer. Maybe she took a cab. Maybe she wanted a showdown with your sister or with the judge. We just don't know."

Somewhat to Juhle's surprise, Shiu was doing a decent job, talking to this woman, keeping her interested, informed, motivated to respond back to them. It was almost more of a surprise that he had such an apparently keen understanding of the various scenarios that could have resulted in the double murder. Maybe he'd actually thought about it in some detail. Would wonders never cease?

And beyond that, Shiu wasn't giving away the store at random, either, as often seemed to be his habit. For example, there was no reason to tell Vanessa Waverly, as they'd discovered from the medical examiner's office that morning, that Staci Rosalier's diaphragm had been inside her and that she'd recently had sex, probably with the judge, maybe even in the bed upstairs, although there'd be no corroboration of that until the DNA results from the diaphragm and the sheets came in later.

After a little silence, Juhle spoke. "Your sister told us she was with you that whole night." Juhle and Shiu had carefully avoided any intimation in their earlier interview with Jeannette that she was a suspect—and in fact the prime suspect—in the slayings. Perhaps there would be a crack in the respective stories. "I wonder if you'd mind going over those hours again with us."

"What on earth for?" Her reaction of shock and even disbelief as it dawned on her that her sister might be under suspicion was in some way gratifying. Whatever other subjects the two sisters had talked about in the time since the murders, Juhle was suddenly certain that Jeannette's alibi hadn't been one of them.

It left a clear field, and he stepped into it. "Jeannette told us she left the city at around four to avoid the traffic. Do you remember what time you met up with her?"

"This is ridiculous," Waverly said, angry eyes flashing. "Jeannette did not kill George. She didn't know he was seeing this girl." She flung her hair, ran her hand through it. "But all right. It was . . . I got home at my usual time, which is around seven."

"And you met her there? At your home?" Juhle asked.

"Yes."

"So she was there when you got home?" Shiu wanted to lock it down.

"No." She threw them both a challenging look. "I work all day. Usually I don't keep much food at home, and when Jeannette comes, she often goes shopping so we can cook something together."

Juhle kept up the press. "Is that what she did the other night?"

"Yes."

Shiu: "And what time did she come home, then? From shopping?"

"I don't know for sure."

Juhle: "But she wasn't there when you arrived?"

"I've already said that."

Shiu: "You'd been working. Did you pour yourself a drink when you got home? Or take a shower? Read your mail? Do you remember?"

Still obviously frustrated by this line of questioning, Waverly nevertheless sat back on the couch and gave it some thought. Finally, she opened her water and took a long drink. "I pulled into the driveway, got my mail, went inside, and made myself some iced coffee from the morning leftovers. Jeannette called me from her cell."

Juhle met his partner's eye for an instant. "What did she want?"

"She didn't know if I had any wine chilled, and she'd forgotten to pick it up at the grocery. She called and asked me to check, which I did, and we didn't have any, so she said she'd swing by Adriano's and pick up a bottle. Adriano's is just up one-oh-one, the next exit."

"So ten minutes?" Juhle clarified.

"Maybe that, yes."

Shiu said, "And ten back. So she got to your home when?"

This brought a rise. "Well, if she left the city at around four as she said, then I'm sure she got there at about four forty-five. One of the neighbors might have seen her. You could ask them."

"We will do that." Juhle adopted a gentle tone. "Of course, we'll do that."

"Then, as I've just been explaining to you, she went out to do some shopping."

Juhle kept on. "But you didn't actually meet her and see her at your house until closer to eight, maybe eight thirty. Would that be about right? Was it dark out, do you recall?"

Waverly leaned back into the couch and closed her eyes. At last she said, "It was just dark. I remember because when she pulled up, I opened the door to say hi and saw that she'd forgotten to turn off her car lights."

On up to Novato, Shiu said, "So she forgot to check if they had wine, then forgot to buy it, then forgot to turn off her car lights . . ."

"Must have had something else on her mind."

It was a clear afternoon with high clouds. Juhle looked over at the bay and almost dared let himself think they were going to have some nice weather. But he said, "That woman—her sister—she's a force of nature."

"You shouldn't covet thy neighbor's wife," Shiu said.

"I got one for you," he said. "How about 'You shouldn't say *shouldn't*'? Besides, she's not married. Therefore, she's not anybody's neighbor's wife."

"You're married, though."

"Gee, thanks, Shiu, that had momentarily slipped my mind. I wasn't coveting her, whatever the hell that is. I was just commenting that she was a force of nature. This is our exit."

"I know."

Adriano's was a small boutique liquor store in yet another Marin County mall with an unreasonable percentage of luxury cars in its parking lot. Shiu parked directly in front of the door, and the two inspectors walked into the empty shop. Classical music was playing in the background, and a bell sounded as they crossed the threshold. A well-dressed, short, white-haired man with a neat mustache came out of the back.

After introductions, it appeared that for once things might be simple. Mr. Adriano told them that he worked the outer store alone. Noon to nine, six days a week. It wasn't difficult at all, and he'd been here twenty-seven years. No one got into the cash register except him.

Of course, he knew Mrs. Palmer on sight. She had been in here many, many times with Vanessa Waverly. "Her sister, right?"

But he'd rather talk about Vanessa. Just between them—had they met her? *Mamma mia!* "I would gladly give up my left nut for one night, you know what I'm saying? Although I'm afraid I would have to get in a very long line. But what is it you want to know about her sister. Mrs. Palmer? Jeanne, is it?"

"Jeannette," Shiu said.

"Ah, that's right. Jeannette. I must remember." His habitual smile faded. He put a finger to his forehead at the flash of memory. "It just came to me. You gentlemen. The judge. Her husband, right?"

"I'm afraid so, sir. Do you remember the last time she was in here? Mrs. Palmer," Juhle asked.

Adriano scratched his cheek for a moment. "Not recently, I don't think. A month ago, maybe."

"Not two days ago?" Shiu asked.

"Oh, no. Definitely not."

"You're sure? Late dinner time? Say eight or so."

He stared off into the distance. "No. She may have stopped in and bought nothing if I wasn't out here and then maybe left. I might have missed that. I always try to hear the chime and come out if I'm working the back of the store. Like just now with you gentlemen. But she didn't buy anything where I had to use the register. That I would have remembered. And eight o'clock, not a busy time. Of course," the impish smile returned, "if she ducked under the chime and stole a bottle . . ."

"No," Juhle said. "She wouldn't have done that."

"I'm sorry, then," Adriano said. "I haven't seen her."

11 /

"Home sweet home," Parisi said. "If you want to come in and wait ten minutes, I can give you your clothes back."

"I can pick them up later. Or you can drop them by my place."

"Except we're both here now."

"Okay, sold."

Parisi lived in a stand-alone one-story house adjacent to a grassy park almost all the way north on Larkin, as it turned out, a block up from Ghirardelli Square. The house was a Spanish-style stucco beauty with a tiny front lawn strip, a covered stoop leading to the front door. There was a parking spot between Parisi's driveway and the one next door that wouldn't have held anything much bigger than a shoebox, but that's why Hunt had bought the Cooper.

"You've got a whole house?" he asked as they got out of the car. "How do you own a house in San Francisco nowadays?"

She shrugged. "Says the man who lives in a warehouse."

"Yes, but I rent. More than that, I rent-control rent."

"You'll see," she said. "It's a small house. A friend of my mom's retired and gave me a deal." She fished in her purse, and the small garage door started up. "Don't ask me why, but I never use the front door."

"I wonder why you don't use the front door?" Hunt mused.

She laughed and said, "Don't ask." Then, "Come on, follow me," taking his hand.

They walked into the garage past the black Miata convertible parked there. At what turned out to be the door to the kitchen, she pressed another button on the wall to bring down the garage door again.

Hunt was close up behind her, close enough to smell her perfume. She was still holding his hand in the darkness, then released it to open the door. "Wait just a second," she said. "Checking something. Good. You can come in now."

It was a small kitchen, modern and functional, that looked like it got a reasonable amount of use. She'd hung several pots and pans on a metal canopy against the wall next to the refrigerator, and a block full of what looked like good knives sat next to a canister of cooking utensils—wooden forks and spoons, spatulas, and brushes—on the counter by the stove. "What did you check for?" Hunt asked.

"To see if I did the dishes. I wasn't sure. I didn't want you to think I was a slob."

"I wasn't going to think that. But if there are dishes to do, that must mean you eat here."

"Of course, I eat here. What do you think?"

"I thought you probably ate out every night. Finished your show and then went to some fine restaurant. The high life. Like last night."

She shrugged. "Sometimes. But no. Most nights I'm here, alone, late, working. Ask Amy. She's got the same schedule. But you should know for the record that I'm not a bad cook. In fact, I may be a great cook. You can't be Italian and not be a good cook. It's illegal."

"What's your specialty?"

"Well, of course, my tomato sauce is incredible. And eggplant parmesan. What I was going to . . . no."

"What?" Hunt asked.

"Nothing."

"Not fair. You can't start and then stop."

"You're right. That would be wrong." She laid a light hand on his arm, then took it away. "I was going to say that as soon as you left, I was going to make my patented peasant spaghetti carbonara, which is really one of the best hangover remedies in the world, and then I was thinking I would see if you wanted to stay and have a bowl with me. But I've already taken up too much of your time."

"I know," Hunt said. "It's been awful."

"Don't you have to go to work?"

"As it happens, yesterday I closed a case that I thought would take at least two days but only took one. So lucky for you, as it turns out, I'd cleared my schedule for today, anyway."

"Lucky for me." Parisi glanced at the wall clock. "Well, despite my doctor's orders, I've got to go in later. I've got an appointment at three. But that still gives us plenty of time. If you want."

"To stay?"

"For lunch."

"You're going to have to twist my arm." Hunt held out his hand. And it worked, she took it again. "That's enough," he said before she'd even pretended to start.

While the bacon cooked and the water boiled, she showed him around. The rest of the house lived up to its billing—small. But like the kitchen—modern, efficient, warm. Parisi kept the house more neat than surgically clean. No clothes lying around, no dishes in the sink. Hunt did stand mesmerized for a minute, surprised by the contents of a locked glass case in the dining room; she had a collection of handguns—pistols and revolvers; a couple of tiny, derringer-style weapons; old-fashioned gunbelts with leather holsters; what looked like snuff boxes.

"You like guns?" he asked.

"Not so much nowadays."

"This looks like a pretty good collection."

"I know. When I was younger I went through a Wild West phase. But I never touch these anymore."

"But they work? They shoot?"

"Oh, yeah. All of them shoot. No point in having a gun that doesn't shoot, is there? But don't worry, they're all registered."

"I wasn't worried."

"I should probably just get rid of them, but . . ."

Hunt threw a look at her. "Richie?"

Nodding, she sighed and said, "Maybe a little. Come on." She took his hand and led him to the adjacent living room. "After your place, it seems a little cramped, doesn't it?"

"Cozy is more like it. Does the fireplace work?"

"Perfectly. It's the best part of the house."

"Although it might be a little dark."

She squeezed his hand and went to open the plantation shutters over the double-wide living room window. The light brought out a sense of life that had seemed missing before. The blond hardwood floors shone. The framed prints were bright with cheerful color, yellows and reds and greens. Turning, she said, "I don't really open the blinds too often, and I should, shouldn't I? It makes a difference, doesn't it?"

"It's beautiful," Hunt said. "I mean it. You were really getting ready to leave this place?"

She looked around. "I've kind of stopped seeing it, Wyatt." A sad smile. Then, abruptly, "The bacon!"

While the water boiled in the kitchen, she made a comment about how warm it was and took off Hunt's pullover, draping it over a chair. "Do not, I repeat, do not forget this," she said. She was braless under the T-shirt, which was sleeveless and tucked tight into his jeans. He sat at the table and watched her move from the utensil drawer to the table, the table to the stove, the refrigerator to the table. Putting out a bottle of Pellegrino and two glasses. Placing the cooked bacon on paper towels to drain. Some large pinches of salt went into the water pot. She put place mats down on the table, set out red-and-white checkered napkins. One fork and one large tablespoon each. A wedge of Parmesan and a metal grater, then a pepper grinder in the center of the table.

He watched her stir the spaghetti, a fetching frown of concentration on her face, her elbow up and the T-shirt shimmying with the movement. She pulled a strand from the water. "You know this?" and tossed it up against the wall, where it stuck. "That's the test, you know. It's al dente when it sticks to the wall." She turned the flame up under the bacon fat.

He watched her take the large pot of boiling water and pasta and pour some of the water into a huge glass bowl, then dump the remainder of the pot into the colander in the sink. He watched her lift the bowl filled with heated water and pour it off over the spaghetti in the colander. And then—so quickly he couldn't believe it wasn't burning her hands—she poured the drained spaghetti back into the heated bowl.

All of it was fluid, with no wasted motion. But fast. She crunched the bacon over the spaghetti. He sat entranced, and as she turned back to the stove, she stopped for just a second, grabbing the bacon pan, to smile at him. "Twenty more seconds," she said. "You're going to love it."

Next he watched her crack two raw eggs over the spaghetti in the large bowl, then pour all the hot bacon grease over it. Now finally using pot holders, she picked up the bowl and brought it over to the table where Hunt had his front row seat. She held a wooden fork in one hand, a wooden spoon in the other, and she began to toss the eggs and bacon and fat into the pasta until it was well mixed. Grabbing up the wedge of Parmesan, she grated furiously, again with that frown of deep concentration, until the cheese covered the spaghetti like a fresh dusting of snow.

He watched her now turn the pepper mill a dozen times over the dish. She brushed a rogue hair away from her forehead. She had the wooden fork and spoon in her hands again now and tossed the pasta one last time before lifting a perfect serving and placing it in the center of Hunt's plain white bowl. Then she did the same with her own and sat down across from him. "More Parmesan and pepper is okay. You can't have too much," she said. "How is it?"

Hunt was nearly swooning from the smells coming off the dish as well as from the simple and stunning beauty of the ballet he'd just witnessed. Twirling a few strands onto his fork with the spoon up under it to catch the strays, he brought the bite to his mouth. "It's the best thing I've ever eaten," he said.

They were in the middle of eating. "Okay, now what about you?" Parisi asked.

"Not much," Hunt said. "What don't you know?"

"Well, I know you weren't a cop before you became a private eye, and that's pretty unusual. You worked with kids, right?"

"Correct. CPS. But actually I was a cop first."

"How can that be, if Amy doesn't know about it?"

"I know. It can be our secret. I guess I don't talk about it too much. It wasn't in the city."

"You're going to make me guess, aren't you?"

He laughed, feeling good. "No. Here's the exciting story. I was CID during the first Gulf War. But when they sent me back stateside, I had another year or so on my hitch, and I got involved dealing with abusive home situations with service families. By the time I got out and came up here to the city, I'd had enough of the army and the police, both. But the kid thing . . . I don't know. That seemed to matter." He smiled at her. "And we've only got time for a few more questions."

"All right. Where did you grow up?"

"I'm a Peninsula guy. San Mateo."

"Really? I had you as a city boy all the way. I mean, how you know your way around. I've been here six years now, and take me outside of downtown or west of Van Ness, and I'm lost. I just figured somebody who knew the place like you do must have been born here."

"Nope. Moved here at twenty-five."

"Same as me."

"Except with me," Hunt said, "it wasn't six years ago. It was fifteen."

She furrowed her brow. "That math doesn't work."

Bowing, acknowledging the compliment. "You're too kind, but, yes, it does."

"All right, I'll believe you. But one more question?"

"One."

"How'd you get to be buddies with a homicide cop?"

"Actually," Hunt said, "it was pretty cool the way we reconnected. Dev and I used to be best friends. We played high school baseball. Then college, you know, and the army for me. Anyway, I hadn't seen him in something like ten years, then . . ." He gave her a truncated version of his reunion with Juhle—the Holly Park projects, Keeshiana tied up to her kitchen chair.

When he finished, Parisi was sitting forward, turned to him, one foot on the floor and the other tucked under her. "But that's an incredible story, Wyatt," she said. "Is that the kind of thing you did all the time?"

"No. Sometimes. Not all the time. Thank God. Anyway, after that," Hunt said, "Dev and I just kind of picked up where we'd left off in high school, except, of course, for the small details like him being married and the three kids."

"And what about you?"

"What about me?"

"Have you ever been married?"

"No."

"Kids?"

"Never married, no kids." He didn't want to lie to Andrea and this, technically, was the truth. Never married, no kids. Engaged, yeah, and only six weeks from a wedding. Sophie had been twenty-six years old, two months pregnant, in otherwise perfect health, when the aneurysm had struck her down.

He must have struck the right carefree tone. Andrea kept on. "Do you wish you had? I mean, all your years of working with children . . ."

He lifted his shoulders, came out with the response he'd perfected long ago: "I guess I've seen too much of the way a lot of families turn out."

"But not all."

"No, not all. That's true."

Parisi's expression had turned inward.

"What?" Hunt asked.

"I was just thinking about all I've been doing for all this time, with Spencer and . . . other guys before him and the relentless pursuit of this career and . . ." She let out a long breath. "Suddenly it all seems a little empty."

"All that food you put inside you, you can't be empty now."

He sensed that she understood what he was trying to do, which was to let her give all of her demons a little rest for a while. Her last twenty-four hours had been painful, humiliating, trying enough. She shouldn't beat herself up anymore. Not today.

She met his gaze, then stood up and walked over to stand in front of him. She put her hands behind his head and pulled it against her belly, holding him there. After a minute, she released him, and he stood up, cupped her face in his hands and brought his lips down to hers.

She pulled away enough to say, "I've got to take these clothes off to give them back to you, anyway."

Hunt would have stayed in her bed all afternoon, maybe all week, but she told him that she really needed to go and put in a few hours of work. But she would like to see him again that night. "Someplace nice for dinner, your choice, my treat?"

"What could beat what we just had?"

"Nothing," she said. "Although some people eat more than once a day, you know."

"I'll consider it," Hunt said. "But at the risk of bringing up a touchy subject, what about the Donolan gig?"

She shook her head. "The courtroom's dark today. I'll find out where that stands tomorrow, and probably go on until the damn trial is over."

"Okay, then." Hunt was holding the clothes of his that she'd worn. He stood at the open and rarely used front door. "If you're still up for it when you're through with your work. But if you would rather just go back to sleep, I get it."

"You're such a good guy," she said. "I mean it." Again, he read gratitude in her eyes. "How about we leave it open," she asked, "and I'll call you one way or the other. Say, by seven?"

"That sounds fair. One way or the other."

She nodded. "I'll call."

12 /

Predictable in retrospect, unforeseen at the time, the result of the interrogation at JV's Salon was that as soon as Juhle and Shiu left, Vanessa had called her sister and told her that whether or not she realized it, she was a suspect in the murder of her husband. The inspectors had made that abundantly clear.

By the time they left Adriano's, Shiu—showing by now nearly constant signs that the pressure to identify a suspect was affecting his judgment—was actually arguing that he was more than halfway to thinking they should go and have a discussion with one of the assistant district attorneys. Right now. They should lay out what they had on Jeannette and start talking about the logistics of charging her with murder—whether to arrest her before she could flee or do something equally precipitous such as kill herself or whether they should wait and bring their evidence to the grand jury for a formal indictment.

Juhle wasn't against either of those alternatives per se. In fact, he more than halfway believed what he'd been raving about to Shiu on the drive up—that they'd all but solved the case in a day. But regardless of the pressure to press charges against Jeannette, they simply didn't yet have the guns.

True, they had a window of the wife's time that they couldn't account for and during which she could conceivably have committed the murders for which she had a strong and even compelling motive—assuming she'd known about Staci Rosalier in the first place. But the fact that she probably hadn't gone to Adriano's to buy wine didn't come close to telling them anything about what she did do during those critical four hours. Besides, they hadn't even put the screws to Jeannette herself yet. It would be bad luck if they presented her as their suspect to the DA or to Lieutenant Lanier or worst of all to Chief Batiste, only to have her show up with a witness or two who'd seen her at her sister's house or talked to her at the grocery store.

Or anything.

After convincing Shiu that they had to talk to her again—and soon—Juhle called her on his cell phone to see if she'd be able to give them an hour or perhaps more of her time. This was when he learned that Vanessa had called her. Jeannette would, of course, be happy to see them whenever they'd like, but the meeting would have to take place at the San Francisco office of her attorney Everett Washburn. She gave him the address on Union Street, said she'd meet them there in forty-five minutes, say 4:30 P.M.

But their drive back down to the city was significantly extended when a deer decided to take a break from his rural environment on the Marin Headlands and seek a bit of impromptu urban culture, perhaps some nightlife, down in San Francisco. To do this, of course, he had to cross the Golden Gate Bridge. The three-mile crossing, ultimately successful with the help of a California Highway Patrol six-car escort, tied up traffic in both directions on the bridge for nearly four hours.

Everett Washburn was pushing seventy and affected a homespun style—baggy brown dress pants, red suspenders, an over-wide rep tie under a wrinkled rack sports coat. A walrus mustache and a florid, frankly beefy complexion gave him a vaguely Captain Kangaroo-ish appearance, although Juhle thought that the blue eyes under the mane of snow-white hair were about as warm and inviting as glacier ice. If Mr. Green Jeans pulled one of his dumb stunts on this guy, he'd take a bite out of his ass. Then again, Juhle realized, the lawyer had his game face on as he pulled open his front door, six or eight feet below street level under the Café de Paris. Ostentatiously, he consulted his watch.

"Eight-oh-six," Washburn said by way of introduction. "I really should bill the city, rather than my client, for the time I have been kept waiting after you scheduled our appointment for which I had to drive all the way from Redwood City."

From the way he said it, Redwood City might have been a hundred miles or more from where they stood, when in fact, it was more like thirty, most of it freeway and none of it, today, deer-ridden. "If Mrs. Palmer wasn't such a valued personal friend as well as my client, and if it had not been her wish to cooperate in every way that she could in your investigation, I never would have remained until this ungodly hour. I had a heart attack two years ago, and my doctor has recommended against me working outside of business hours. But she wants her husband's killer caught. That above all. I assume you have some identification. May I see it, please."

Juhle had, in fact, offered to cancel the appointment when it became apparent that they weren't going to make their time, but Washburn had blustered about his drive, the fact that he'd already come into the city just for this one interview. He was a very busy man and didn't know when he could guarantee a return trip. If they wanted to talk to his client, they were ready to cooperate fully today, whenever they could. Afterward, he would try to be flexible, but it might be a while, and of course, he wouldn't allow his client to talk to the police again without his presence. In short, he'd played them.

And now was doing it again.

Tempted to call the whole thing off and dare the old bully to let his client come before the grand jury on her own if she wouldn't talk to them, Juhle bit his tongue. It wouldn't help. He and Shiu had to move somewhere on this investigation, and until they could eliminate or implicate Mrs. Palmer, they'd be treading water.

Washburn had them and he knew it.

He practiced law from the basement of an old Victorian building and now without another word led them down a dark and narrow hallway with suites off the left side only. At the end, the hall opened into a wider but still small receptionist's station. Behind this was Washburn's office, a comparatively spacious octagonal room with windows on six sides and books in every other inch of wall space. There was no desk, no sign that business was conducted here. To all appearances, they were in a living room—lots of living greenery, Oriental rugs, low tables, and a couple of seating areas. Outside, through the windows, dusk had nearly settled, but the room was well lit with shaded lamps.

Jeannette Palmer, on a loveseat, did not stand as they entered. Dressed in black, she looked brittle and exhausted. Washburn took a straight-backed wooden chair and indicated the couch on the other side of the coffee table for the inspectors. Juhle took out his tape recorder and placed it on the table between them all, getting a nod from Washburn as permission. He recited his standard introduction, then met his suspect's furious and fragile gaze.

"Mrs. Palmer, how are you holding up?" Juhle began.

Obviously, she'd been coached to say nothing without her attorney's approval. Now she looked sideways at Washburn, a mute question.

Which he answered. "Frankly, inspector," he said, "she'd be better if she didn't have to deal with the absurdity of evidently being considered a suspect. And it is an absurdity."

"Are you going to let her talk?" Shiu asked.

"Of course. I told you she wants to do everything she can do to help you with your investigation. Isn't that right, Jeannette?"

"Completely."

"All right," Juhle said. "Then maybe we can make this easy on all of us."

"It's already been far too difficult," Washburn said. "Too unnecessarily difficult."

Again, Juhle resisted the temptation to get tough with this lawyer. There was no point in getting into a pissing contest with him, which seemed to be what he was trying to provoke. Instead, Juhle again looked Mrs. Palmer in the face. "Yesterday," he began, "at your home, we asked you about what you did on Monday afternoon, and you told us you had driven up to spend the night with your sister, leaving about four o'clock to avoid the traffic. Is that about right?"

"Yes."

Juhle lowered his voice. "Mrs. Palmer. It would be very helpful to our investigation," he said, "if you could tell us specifically everything you can remember about the time between leaving your home and arriving at your sister's house."

Again Mrs. Palmer looked at her attorney, and this time he nodded and let her respond. "All right. As I've already told you, I left at four. I don't remember any traffic problems or really exactly what time I got to Vanessa's, but I'd be surprised if it was five yet."

"Where did you park there?" Shiu asked. And Juhle, who just wanted to keep her talking, shot him a warning glance.

But she answered him. "Just in the driveway. But I don't know if anybody saw me. I didn't talk to anyone."

Shiu couldn't seem to let her alone. "How about phone calls?"

She shook her head. "There really wasn't anyone I needed to call. I'd already called Vanessa, so she'd know I'd be there, and George was . . ." The mention of her husband's name took an immediate and, to Juhle, somewhat shocking toll, from which she recovered only after a small but unmistakable struggle with herself. "He was going out to dinner, as I said." Looking from Shiu back to

Juhle, she sighed again, and went on. "Anyway, I'm afraid I didn't do much. The driving had made me sleepy, so I must have just dozed off for a while, but eventually, I picked up Vanessa's copy of *Sunset*, and they had this recipe for stuffed chicken breasts that looked delicious, and I decided to surprise Vanessa and make it for dinner, so I went shopping."

"Let's go back just a second," Juhle said. "You said you'd already called your sister?"

"Yes."

"Was this from home?"

"No. The car. I usually called her when I got about to JV's. Just to say we were still on."

Juhle looked over at Shiu, wondering if his partner had picked up the import of this admission. If Mrs. Palmer had used her cell phone on the freeway passing through Mill Valley between four and five o'clock, they could pinpoint her location within a mile or two by finding the cell site that had picked up and relayed the call. If she were really in Mill Valley, it was much more unlikely that she had returned back home to San Francisco to shoot her husband and his mistress. If on the other hand, the call had come from the city—or, better, from near her home—they were in business.

But he couldn't give her up that easily. The motive was too good, the symmetry too perfect. They had too much invested. They still had the groceries, the wine, the difficulties with that story. It was still possible.

"Okay, let's go back to your grocery shopping," he asked. "Where did you do that?"

"Just the Safeway there in Novato. I don't know the exact address, but it's back a freeway exit from Vanessa's."

Shiu spoke up. "What time was this, would you say?"

"I don't know exactly. Six? No. I think I napped until six. Closer to seven, I'd say."

Shiu kept at it. "Did you have any discussion with anyone there?" he asked. "Anybody who might remember you?"

Evidently, Washburn had endured his own silence long enough. "Inspectors, excuse me," he said. "Might I suggest you ask my client if she used a Safeway card to make her purchase?" Again, it was clear they'd had this discussion. He looked expectantly at Mrs. Palmer.

"Yes," she said, "I did."

"So there'll be a record of that?" Juhle said.

"With her name on it, and the exact time, as a matter of fact."
Washburn sat back, rested an ankle on his opposite knee.

Shiu, his frustration now at full simmer, said, "What about
Adriano's?"

Mrs. Palmer turned to him. "What about it?"

"You called your sister and told her you'd forgotten to get any
wine, and you were going to go by Adriano's to pick some up."

For a moment, Mrs. Palmer's weary brow clouded again. She
sank back into the cushions of the loveseat, then brought her hand
up to her temples and squeezed them. "Adriano's," she said.

Shiu prompted her. "The liquor store."

"Jeannette." Washburn leaned over and touched the arm of the
loveseat.

"No. It's all right, Everett," she said. Coming forward, she almost managed a smile. "It's hard to remember what you didn't do,"
she said. Then, to Shiu, "I didn't go to Adriano's. I went back to
Safeway. I remembered that I'd forgotten to get some cash when I
paid for the other groceries, and they have an ATM at the cash reg-
isters, so I just went back there instead."

This time Juhle was up to speed. "And used your card again?"

"Well, my Safeway card, and then I paid with my ATM."

13 /

Hunt reached Juhle on his cell phone just as the inspectors were leaving their interview with Everett Washburn and Jeannette Palmer. He'd tried him at home first, and Connie had told him that he wasn't there and, no, he probably hadn't had dinner, either. She'd talked to him while he was stuck in traffic on the bridge, and he was going to be working late. By the time he got done, she'd be putting the kids down—not Juhle's favorite time. If Hunt wanted to meet up with him someplace, Connie thought Juhle would probably welcome his company.

Having finally given up on getting his "either way" phone call from Andrea Parisi, Hunt told Juhle that he'd gotten stood up and that the evening yawned open before him. If Shiu would drop him at the Tong Palace on Clement, they might salvage some remnant of this otherwise shitty night.

Now, as the ancient waitress at the dim sum place had done every five minutes or so since they'd sat down, she came by with another tray of delicacies. Hunt and Juhle pointed at what they wanted—sign language was the lingua franca here—and soon their table had plates of shrimp wrapped in transparent won tons, fried oysters, little steamed bundles of dough stuffed with seafood or meat or vegetables, a plate of siu mei, rice noodles with spicy pork. This was their third round, and their enthusiasm for the food hadn't dimmed much. Juhle held his hands apart to indicate a large bottle and said an actual word, "Asahi," while Hunt lifted the teapot and pantomimed for a refill.

"So Jeannette didn't do it?" Hunt said.

Juhle, on five hours of sleep, sagged at their corner table. He tipped up his tea and made a face. "Not if she called her sister from

Mill Valley at four thirty and was paying at the Safeway at both seven thirty and quarter to eight. She didn't drive all the way into Marin, then remember, Oh, yeah, I was supposed to shoot George and his girlfriend tonight, so she turned around and went home, did the deed, then turned around again and went back to Novato."

"That does seem unlikely."

"At least. Besides, her neighbor on Clay Street who saw the car parked by her driveway? That was at seven thirty, when she was pretty definitely at the Safeway. You know Everett Washburn, the lawyer? No? Well, he somehow got the manager up there to go back and find her receipts and fax them down to him at his office. We're going to go back and check ourselves, but I'm not optimistic. She was there."

"So who's that leave?"

"As suspects? Approximately the whole world."

"Not me." Hunt held up his right hand. "Monday night, I was down in Palo Alto with my dad. He'd vouch for me."

"All right, except you. And probably Connie, who was feeding me dinner at the time, so I guess she's out, too. Everybody else, though."

Popping an oyster, Juhle chewed and thought for a moment. "The problem is, I can't understand Staci Rosalier being there if it wasn't personal. I mean, it *had* to be about her."

Hunt shrugged. "Maybe she was just there."

"But why?"

"I don't know. She wanted to do it in the wife's bed. *He* wanted to do *her* in the wife's bed. Any combination thereof. Whatever, he knew his wife was going to be gone, he's trying to get away with that much more for the thrill of it. Maybe it was just bad timing."

"And somebody else showed up while they just happened to be there? In other words, a coincidence." Juhle shook his head. "I don't believe in them. Not at murder scenes."

"Maybe this is the exception."

"It isn't. Somebody else was there because they knew Palmer and the girl were there. Count on it. Or, thinking out loud now, Palmer might have been seeing somebody else, too. He invited her over to his house, but the dead girl—Staci—found out about the new one and came by to confront them both." Juhle savored a bite of pork bun. "So Staci brings the gun with her, shoots Palmer . . ."

"Out around the front of the desk?"

"Sure. Why not? There's a struggle. The gun goes off—the extra round in the book. In the scuffle, the other woman grabs the gun away from Staci and shoots her, then sees what she's done and takes the gun and splits."

Hunt waited for Juhle to take his beer from the waitress and pour it into the chilled glass. "So what actual evidence do you have?"

Juhle drank half the glass. "Damn little. Shiu thinks the shooter might have been short, as in not tall, so as you can see, we've really narrowed things down there. I personally favor the midget-standing-on-a-box theory. Nobody in the neighborhood heard or saw anything, except for a sports car that might have been a BMW Z4 or some look-alike. But there's no connection between that car and anything else inside the house or out. It wasn't a robbery or burglary gone bad, and a burglar's not going to park his car in the driveway." After a long, futile day of investigation, Juhle clearly had wrung about all the amusement he could out of this case.

Hunt picked up a shrimp. "I heard a rumor the judge was thinking about messing with the prison guards' union."

"Where'd you hear that?"

"A source who, alas, must remain unnamed. But the gist of it . . ." Hunt gave him a succinct rundown of what he'd learned that day about the CCPOA and Palmer's interaction with it. Of course, Juhle knew about Palmer's well-publicized battle with the union, but the inside details of the allegations surprised even the veteran cop.

When Hunt finished, Juhle was sitting back again, beer and food forgotten. "The wife, Jeannette, she mentioned them, too, the union," Juhle said. "Of course, this was back yesterday when we thought it was her, so it didn't make much of an impact. Now, though, you've got me wondering. If Palmer was really going to bust them, it's someplace to look. Who told you about this?"

"A lawyer friend of mine. Her firm, Piersall-Morton, represents the union."

"Great. You can save me a phone call. You got a connection there?"

Hunt said, "Of course. Connections are my life. But she's busy, Dev. You're a cop. You call the office, they'll direct you."

Juhle had to take it. "All right, all right," he said. "Piersall. Why is that name familiar?"

"It's a huge law firm?"

"No, that's not . . . wait." Juhle went to snap his injured fingers and winced against the pain. "Ah. The brain comes alive and it all comes back. I've been meaning to ask you. Andrea Parisi?"

Hunt's frown was pronounced. "What about her?"

Juhle came forward and leaned into the table. "What about her is that as I believe I've mentioned, there are no coincidences, and we found her business card at Staci Rosalier's place last night."

"At *the victim's* place?"

"In her wallet. So if she's in this somehow, Parisi, I mean, I need to know about it."

"How would she be in it?"

"I don't have any idea, but maybe you do."

"Nope."

"But you've been going out jogging with her."

"Occasionally, Dev. Only occasionally. And so what?"

"So did she ever mention Staci."

"No. Never."

"But Staci had her card."

"Wow. That really narrows it down all right."

"All right. How about the judge?"

"Yes. She mentioned the judge."

"In what context?"

"In the context that Andrea and I were talking today, and Palmer got himself killed two days ago. The topic's come up with just about everybody I've seen in the past couple of days, Dev. Now including you. What exactly are you thinking?"

"Just that if Parisi's with Piersall, that puts her around the guards' union, right? It's a lead. It's something." He snapped his fingers again. "She's your connection there. At Piersall."

Hunt forced a smile. "No comment. Except to say that it's a matter of public record that I bill out some reasonable hours to Piersall. So what? I think I've already told you I didn't kill Palmer. I'm pretty sure Andrea didn't, either. Although you could always ask her."

"I'm not saying she did. But I'd like to know why Staci had her card."

"Coincidence?"

"I hate that."

Hunt shrugged. "It happens. Maybe she saw her at MoMo's and is trying to break into TV."

Juhle shook his head. "That's what Shiu said, too, so it can't be right."

"Okay, so how about the next time I talk to Andrea, I ask her about how Staci might have got the card? If she even remembers at all."

Their waitress arrived with another raft of selections, but after forty-five minutes of continuous eating, both men were done. Juhle asked for the check and came back to Hunt. "So one last question: Who stood you up?"

Hunt decided to tap-dance. "I haven't yet decided if, technically, it was exactly a stand-up. She just decided not to have dinner. She got pretty wrecked last night, and I think she still was hurting. Physically, I mean."

"You're making excuses for her? Do you have any idea how pathetic that makes you? Are you in love?"

"Marginally, maybe a little more."

"Connie will be so relieved. But not if you're in love with somebody who gets wrecked one night and stands you up the next. As qualifications go, those kind of suck."

"She's had a tough week."

"Maybe we should start a Tough Week Club. Now who are we talking about?"

Hunt sat back, drained his teacup, shook his head, put on a smile. "You know me better than that, Dev. I don't kiss and tell."

"But you didn't kiss her. You couldn't have if she stood you up."

"As I said, that point is technically unresolved. I may have kissed her before tonight, in which case I still wouldn't tell."

"You moved on her last night when she was wrecked?"

"That would have been ungentlemanly, so we can rule it out."

"You're not going to tell me, are you?"

"See. That's what makes you so good at your job. The trained inspector sees things other people would clean miss."

Hunt drove by Andrea's house on the way home. It wasn't on the way, and he didn't really plan for it. He pulled up across from where he'd parked that afternoon. The house was completely dark. It was still early, a little short of ten o'clock.

He wanted to see her again. It was as simple as that.

Hunt pulled into her driveway, turned off his ignition and lights, and got out of his car. Her garage door had small windows at eye level and Hunt looked in. Her car was gone. Nevertheless, he walked over to the stoop and peered through the glass panes in the top of her door into pure darkness.

Back in his car, he sat behind the wheel with the motor off for the better part of another half hour, until the cold had eaten through him. If she came home and found him sitting there, what was going to be his pathetic excuse? He'd come across as clinging, needy, lovesick, maybe even a potential stalker.

He turned on the ignition. He'd catch up to her tomorrow. Backing out of her driveway, he drove half a block down to Bay Street and turned south, heading for home.

Alone in the front of his warehouse, Hunt shot hoops.

Basketball wouldn't ever hold the place in his heart forever reserved for baseball, but besides shortstop, he'd played point guard on his high school team and still got in at least twenty-two games a year with a city league team that played through the fall and early winter, although ironically he wasn't much of a fan of the pro sport. He and Juhle called the NBA the TMA—the Tattooed Millionaires Association—and he also wasn't really fond of the music they played at the games.

But shooting hoops—shooting hoops was the best therapy in the world.

And tonight he needed some, self-administered. So he'd start right at the edge of his half-court hardwood, take a shot, move up a few steps, but still outside the three-point range, take another, get to the top of the key, then the free-throw line. Whenever he missed, he, of course, charged the basket for a layup, then ran it out for another round until he tired. He stood six foot two, and when he'd been a teenager, he'd considered his ability to stuff one of the great athletic achievements of his life, but somewhere in his twenties, that skill had left him. He still tried every time he suited up in his sweats, though—the springs might come back for one fleeting day, and he didn't want to miss them.

Finally, though, the industrial clock over the backboard said it was 11:42. He was dripping and about done in. He liked to go out with three in a row, and he'd made his first two and now stood at the free-throw line, bouncing the ball at his feet a couple of times. Then another two times. Then once. Held the ball for maybe thirty seconds. His breathing slowed.

Dropping the basketball, he stopped the bounce with his foot, pushed it back under him, and sat down on it.

Without taking that last shot, he walked off the court and turned out the lights on the playground side of his place, flipped on the overheads on the living side, went in and showered. When he finished, he went into his bedroom, opened his dresser, pulled out another pair of gray sweats and put them on, then opened another drawer and reached under the T-shirts where he kept the picture.

He hadn't taken it out in a couple of years. He didn't even remember the last time.

It was the only one he had kept of Sophie. The night he'd burned all the rest of them, he'd taken this one out of the frame, but something about it had stopped him. He hadn't been able to make himself erase all signs that she'd ever existed. He couldn't do it.

It wasn't a glamour shot, which was maybe what he liked about it the most—although God knew she'd had the capacity for glamour when the mood struck her—but it captured her. The laugh, the skin, the *magic* of her. It might have been the night she got pregnant, or, as her glow revealed, she may have already known. But in this shot, she was in her medical scrubs, just off her rounds at the Med Center, on a Saturday evening at the Shamrock Bar where they'd met.

She'd given him a new telephoto lens for his birthday, and Hunt had been shooting extreme close-ups of birds in Golden Gate Park all day. When she'd come in and sat down at the bar, he'd been in the bathroom—timing was his specialty—camera and new honking lens around his neck. When he'd come out, she hadn't seen him. She was talking to the bartender there, laughing at something he was saying. And Hunt had raised his camera, brought her up close enough to touch, and caught her in that moment. When he saw what he'd captured, he'd blown it up to eight by ten and framed it and put it next to their bed, along with her favorite shot of him— on a windboard flying over the bay.

Now he moved the glossy over under the light and laid it flat on the dresser. His face softened by degrees until he put his hands down on either side of the picture and leaned on them.

He'd considered sharing his life with someone back when he was with her. But since then, that feeling had left him. There had been a few women since—nice enough, attractive enough—set-ups by Connie, that type of thing, but if the kind of involvement he'd had with Sophie was going to empty his soul out so thoroughly, his own preservation demanded that he avoid it. He just wasn't going to open that door again. It wasn't worth the pain.

He didn't even know Parisi. Not really. And what he did know wasn't all good by a long shot. But she'd gotten inside him.

"How dumb is this?" he said aloud to the picture.

But, of course, Sophie couldn't answer.

14 /

The following morning—Thursday, June 2—Hunt was moved by two considerations to walk the fifteen-odd blocks from his home to his detective agency's two-room office over the Half Moon Café on Grant Avenue in Chinatown.

First, an unexpected break in the fog had created a glorious morning.

The other was that the waiting period was over today—he'd circled the date on his calendar—and he could stop and pick up his new gun, a 380 ACP Sig Sauer P232, which gave him about an inch less barrel and an inch less height than the weapon he'd been carrying for the last couple of years, the Sig P229.

He'd fallen in love with the new weapon the last time he'd been to the range with Devin Juhle, who'd been trying one out and ultimately decided against it. For Devin, it was too small, and he didn't feel he could be as accurate with it. But Hunt had found the opposite to be true. Lighter and easier to handle, the gun performed better for Hunt than anything he'd ever shot. Plus, though the actual spec difference in size wasn't that great, it felt far less bulky in his back-of-the-belt holster.

Armed with his new toy, knocked out by the beauty of the day, Hunt surprised himself by stopping in and buying a bag of freshly made, still-hot *char siu bao*—sticky dough buns filled with pork in a sweet sauce. The Chinese food last night with Juhle had been so good that he was unable to resist the craving for more this morning. Back out on the street, Hunt's sense of well-being got so much the better of him that he emptied his pockets and put all his coins in the hat of a homeless guy who was sleeping in one of the doorways.

In his office, Tamara was out from behind her desk watering the plants. She wore a red miniskirt, red low-heeled shoes, and a demure white blouse that nevertheless stopped in time to display a couple of inches of taut flat stomach and a faux-diamond navel stud. "If you ever get a job in a real office," Hunt said, "you know they probably won't let you show off your tummy."

She flashed him a tolerant smile. "That's why I won't work in a place like that. Craig likes my tummy."

"It's a fine tummy," Hunt said, "but old guys like me—not saying me personally, but guys like me—might find it distracting in a business environment."

"Well, that's their problem. Not saying you personally, but people like you. We're never going to have this be like a real office, are we? With dress codes and everything?"

"It's unlikely," Hunt said. "Except maybe if Craig pierces anything I can see."

"Does his tongue count?"

Hunt held up a hand. "Tam. Please. Not before breakfast. He hasn't done his tongue, has he?"

"No, but we were talking about maybe the two of us . . . You wouldn't really fire us, would you?"

"No. Never, I hope. But I also would find it a little hard to have a casual little chat like we're having right now because I would be creeped out."

She smiled at him. "Maybe I shouldn't tell you, then, about Craig's . . ."

Hunt stopped her. "Better left unsaid," he said. "But speaking of the boy?"

"He's process serving. Six subpoenas."

"Six in one day? Don't tell me somebody's actually getting to trial."

She nodded. "Believe it or not. One of Aaron Rand's clients. Craig's on his cell if you need him." She pointed to the white bag in his hand. "Tell me those are fresh *bao*."

"I'll play your silly game," he said. "These are fresh *bao*, but sadly I only bought a dozen."

She gave him a look, held out a be-ringed hand punctuated with red nail polish. "A dozen feeds a hungry family of four. Give."

"Besides, they're just out of the oven. Way too hot to eat."

"I'll blow on them."

Hunt sighed theatrically. "It doesn't seem right." He opened the bag, handed her one of the buns. He turned and let himself into his office, closing the frosted glass door behind him. Taking off his coat, hanging it on the rack by his door, he reached around and took out his new gun, just to look at it again. But holding it now, he suddenly realized that he needed to run downtown and get his CCW—carry a concealed weapon—permit updated to cover it. Technically, he shouldn't be walking around with the thing in its holster on him until he'd done all the paperwork. He reminded himself to remember to take care of it at lunchtime, then put the gun back where it belonged and went around to his desk.

The office was good-sized, square, utilitarian. When he'd first seen it, it had essentially been a large windowless closet—a major factor in its affordable rent. His first improvement was to knock out a three-foot-square section of the wall and put glass between Tamara's office and his own to let in some natural light.

Next Hunt installed wall-to-wall carpet throughout. He had a standard-issue IKEA blond desk with a computer and phone and a matching swivel chair and a double stack of light tan metal filing cabinets. From his home, he'd brought down two acoustic guitars—one steel and one gut—and hung them for easy access on the wall to his left. On his right was a Corian counter with a sink and hot plate and printer and fax machine on top and a small refrigerator with drawers for surveillance supplies—night goggles, binoculars, pilot bags when pit stops to pee weren't an option—and photo equipment underneath. He thought that the bunch of framed old black-and-white baseball photographs that he'd gotten cheap at the ballpark didn't look too bad above the counter.

He'd resisted the urge to call Andrea when he'd gotten up. He knew that he could have pretended that he was just checking up on her, making sure she was feeling okay, that her hangover had abated, but he didn't need Juhle to tell him how lame that would be. He'd get in touch later in the day, casually. No mention of the phone call she had promised yesterday.

Now that he'd made it all the way into work without having yielded to the temptation to call her, he resolved that he'd put it off until later and simply ask her out. She'd either say yes or no. He didn't really believe it, but he knew it was possible that their moment yesterday could after all have been her exhaustion and vulnerability, and he didn't want to play to those cards. If anything real had been there yesterday, it would still be there today—or even tomorrow.

He forced her out of his mind.

After his day off yesterday, his workload had backed up and was fairly heavy. At noon, he was scheduled to assist in some predeposition statements from some witnesses in a fraud case at one of his clients' offices, which might take up a good portion of the afternoon. He had three surveillances of one kind or another that were in more or less active status. A doctor had also hired him to find out some history about his very rich mother's new and much younger boyfriend. And when things got slow, he could always fall back on locating witnesses—there were always a few that needed to be found.

But he had some computer work to get out of the way first. He was taking an online class on information technology and computer forensics, pumping up his skills set to compete with the big PI firms should his specialization as a legal investigator become a liability. When he finished today's lesson, he was planning to search the Net as part of a background check on one of the job applicants with an executive headhunting firm that he'd snagged as a client.

Engrossed in the intricacies of computer forensics, he never heard the telephone ring outside on Tamara's desk. He had told her that he was doing his lesson online and didn't want to be disturbed for an hour. So he jumped when the phone went off at his elbow.

"That was a short hour," he said.

"I'm sorry, but it's Amy Wu. I thought you'd want to talk to her. She sounds upset."

If it was Wu, he would talk to her. He punched at the phone. "Amy, what's up?"

Her voice unusually serious, Wu said, "Maybe nothing. Maybe I'm just paranoid. I was wondering if you've talked to Andrea recently."

"Not since yesterday afternoon."

"Okay, maybe that's good news. What time was that?"

"Two. Two thirty. Why would it be bad news?"

Wu paused. "I've been calling all around. Nobody's seen her. Well, nobody I've talked to at least. I've called Spencer, too, and he hasn't heard from her since Tuesday night. He told me to try you."

Hunt knew well enough the reason that her Trial TV producer hadn't heard from her. He also assumed that Fairchild must have seen him rush out after Parisi at the Occidental.

But Wu was going on. "Last night I paged her and also left a message at her home, asking her to call me no matter what time she got in, and she never did."

"Call? Or get in?"

"I don't know for sure. Both."

"What was so urgent?"

Wu hesitated. "Did you hear they identified the woman who was killed with Judge Palmer?"

"I did. Staci something, right? Waitress at MoMo's. I didn't know her."

"We did. Andrea and Jason and I. We all knew who she was at least."

"So that's why you wanted to get to Andrea? To tell her about Staci?"

"Originally. You know, to talk about it a little. But then when she didn't call back . . ."

"Did you try her at work? She was going in there when I left her."

Another pause. "When you left her? You're saying you didn't just talk to her yesterday afternoon, you were *with* her?"

"She passed out, and I took her back to my place." He gave her the short version. "Anyway, after she got herself together, I took her home. She was talking about going in to work."

"But she didn't go to work. Not yesterday. And she's not there now and hasn't called this morning."

Hunt, frowning, checked his watch. True, it wasn't yet ten o'clock. And okay, Parisi could have gotten in sometime after he left her driveway last night and be out having an early meeting with a client. She could be doing a morning workout. She could be out jogging. She could have simply decided to sleep in and not answer her telephone. She might even have stood him up to go out with another guy and wasn't back home yet. But Wu, not really given to histrionics, was upset. Hunt felt a seed of real concern in the bottom of his gut. "Was her secretary worried?" he asked.

"Not particularly. She said that sometimes she comes in later."

"That's probably what it is."

"Maybe. But you know Andrea, Wyatt. You page her, she calls back. Her cell phone's surgically implanted in her ear."

"Maybe she's turned it off."

"That would take us to the outer fringes of reality."

Hunt believed Wu, but so what? Given the events of Parisi's last couple of days, he considered it plausible that she might have turned off her cell phone and simply checked out for a few hours. She'd given him every sign that she wanted to think about things. But again, Wu was their mutual friend, and her worry was genuine and somewhat contagious. "Who else have you tried?" he asked her. "Does she have family nearby? Maybe she's staying with them."

"I know her mom teaches at Cal and lives in Berkeley, I think, but I don't have her number, and I'm not sure if I want to get her worried, too."

"I could find her and call and make it sound innocuous. I promise."

"Do you think it would be dumb to check anywhere official?"

"Like what?"

"I don't know. The police? Hospitals?"

"Not yet, I don't think. How long has it been? Am I the last one who talked to her?"

"So far."

"And what's that? Eighteen, twenty hours ago?" Though those numbers startled him in some way, Hunt kept up the optimistic front. "She's a big girl, Amy. She could be anywhere. She could just be hiding out."

"From what?"

"Fame. I don't know. Figuring out what she's going to do with Spencer. Or her law career. It really could be anything."

"You really think so?"

"I really don't know. But why don't I find her mother's number, and after that, if she's not there, I'll call around, the official places. Meanwhile, you wait and see if she calls you back. And when she does, you call me, right?"

"Okay."

"Okay, then. Later."

They hung up and within fifteen minutes, Hunt was talking to Deanne, one of Andrea's sisters in Berkeley, keeping his questions generic and low-key. Identifying himself as a private investigator, he said he was doing a background check on the résumé for someone who had given her sister as a reference at this number. Deanne certainly didn't sound as though she'd experienced any trauma recently in her life. She laughed and said her sister hadn't lived there for years, so whomever Hunt was checking up on wasn't very current. Deanne hadn't seen Andrea in a month or so, but she was fairly sure that her mother had talked to her last weekend. Hunt thanked her for her time and hung up.

So Andrea wasn't at her mother's house. Feet up on his desk, Hunt thought for another minute or so, then picked up the phone again and punched in some numbers he knew by heart.

15 /

"Juhle, homicide."

"Hunt, Chinatown."

"Wrong."

"How could I be wrong? I haven't said anything yet."

"Why do I have to explain everything, Wyatt? If I say, 'Juhle, homicide,' you don't say, 'Hunt, Chinatown.' You say something like 'Hunt, investigations.' It's the work, not where you do it. Try again later." And he hung up.

Hunt sometimes thought that the only thing worse than dealing with someone who had a personality was dealing with somebody who didn't. He punched up Devin's number again, got his deadpan, "Juhle, homicide," and this time said, "Hunt, investigations."

"Wyatt," Juhle boomed, "how've you been all this time?"

"I've been good, Devin, but I'm investigating right now even as we speak. I need you to find out something for me."

"That would be *me* investigating, not you. And I believe I've mentioned I do homicide. Are you calling about a homicide?"

"I hope not."

"Then I'm not your man. Shiu and I, we're out the door in about two minutes on a murder case, which is what we do. And it's all we do. So good luck."

"Don't hang up!" Hunt was surprised to note the sharper edge in his voice. In spite of his assurances to Amy Wu that everything probably was fine with Andrea Parisi, Hunt was aware that the knot in his stomach where the last pork *bao* had settled had not gone away. "You remember last night we talked a little about Andrea Parisi . . ."

Juhle's voice fell half an octave. "Yeah."

"I just got a call from Amy Wu."

"What about?"

"About Andrea not returning her calls since yesterday and not showing up at work this morning."

"Hey, I almost didn't come in myself. It happens. My arm was killing me. I had to drop a Vicodin."

"Not the same thing, really." Hunt tried to keep the impatience and worry out of his voice. "I wondered if you could make a few calls around and see if a thirty-something Jane Doe has turned up somewhere."

"She wouldn't be a Jane Doe if it's Parisi. Somebody would recognize her."

"That would depend on how she looks, wouldn't it? Say if she was beat up . . ."

"You're serious, aren't you?"

"Yep."

"Why can't you make those calls and look for her?"

"I'm tied up with clients for the next several hours. You could do it quicker through one of those magical networks you cops employ, where you can find out about anything. Besides, you answered your own phone, which indicates that you're in your office either doing paperwork or screwing around until something more important comes up. And this is it."

Juhle looked down at the first stack of Judge Palmer's bank records on his desk in front of him. "How long has she been gone?"

"Since before dinner last night."

"And you want me to check where?"

"Everywhere you'd look if you were looking for somebody. The morgue would be my last choice, but hospitals. Maybe she got herself drunk and arrested last night and isn't checking her messages."

"You want missing persons," Juhle said.

"They won't start looking until somebody's gone three days, Dev. You know this, and that's too long."

"Not really, since it gives the missing person time to show back up if they've had a change of heart and decided to come back to their spouse or boyfriend or mother and father."

"This isn't any of those."

"You checked her house, her work, her . . . ?"

"Yes to all the above. Some of us—Wu, Tamara, me—we're going to be calling around, but you know you can cover more ground a lot easier."

Juhle hesitated for a couple of seconds. He said, "Now you mention it, I kind of wanted to talk to her myself about what you mentioned last night."

"What was that?"

"Palmer, basically. The prison guards. Lanier thinks there might be something there after all."

"So you're admitting you owe me?"

Juhle sighed into the line. "All right. I'll see what I can find out," he said.

Tamara opened the door before Hunt put the receiver down. "Do you really think she's in trouble?"

"You've been listening in on my calls."

"Just the last two, and only to save you the time it would take to brief me. Are you really worried?"

"Let's say I'd feel better if we heard from her."

"What are you going to do next?"

He consulted his watch. "I *was* going to be finishing this class on the Net and then getting some business done, but I'm due at McClelland's, and that's going to take most of the afternoon."

"Do you want me to call anybody else in the meanwhile?"

Hunt was up, gathering papers, snatching up his briefcase. "Try Andrea's office again and make friends with her secretary, try to avoid getting her all worked up. Find out the last clients she saw, what they talked about, where she was last night . . ."

"Whoa!" Tamara raised a palm, stopping him. "I'm trying to avoid getting her all worked up, right? I'll just talk to her and see what she gives me."

"Okay, you're right. Otherwise, stay near the phones in case Devin calls back. You can page me. Or if you hear from her, of course."

Marcel Lanier closed the door to his office in the homicide detail. He went behind his desk and sat, leaving his two inspectors to wonder if he wanted them to remain standing or to sit. Shiu had come in before Juhle and apparently didn't intend to move. He now blocked access to the two chairs in the small area facing Lanier's desk. So they stood, unnaturally close together, by the door.

"If it's not the wife, you understand," the lieutenant began in a low and brooding tone, "we're going to be having jurisdictional issues again." He meant the FBI and Homeland Security. "What do you suggest we do about that?"

Juhle, with a little sleep under his belt and a Vicodin easing his hand and shoulder pain this morning, cracked an easy grin. "The Feds? How about we don't tell 'em? Yesterday, they backed out of it, thinking it was local. Maybe it still is; there's just a few complications. So today we just leave it. If they don't ask, we don't tell."

Lanier's mouth turned upward briefly in a parody of a smile. "That's a fine idea, Devin, except for the press conference that I'm supposed to be giving in about two hours."

Juhle shrugged. "The investigation is continuing. Tell 'em we're making progress. Which we are. Reporters love progress."

"We all do. But what would that progress be in this case?"

"Eliminating suspects. We don't have to tell them Jeannette's out because, in fact, maybe she's not. We're just pretty sure she wasn't the shooter."

Lanier didn't like that. "Pretty sure?"

Shiu stood at attention. "My money, she's still in it."

Lanier turned his head. "What about you, Dev?"

Not exactly exuding enthusiasm, Juhle lowered his chin an inch, which served as a nod. "Barring something pretty weird, it's probably true she couldn't have been there for the shooting, sir. She was up in Marin."

Shiu spoke up in a hurry. "But that doesn't mean she couldn't have planned it and hired someone."

"That's where you're going with this?"

"I think it's still our best shot, sir. One thing's sure—if Mrs. Palmer knew about the Rosalier girl, she's got the best motive. We'll be trying to find out if she did and if so, how."

"So she's still the focus?" Lanier asked. "Just on the off chance somebody with the feebs comes and asks."

"We're not ready to abandon the motive, Marcel," Juhle said. "Oh, and I did mention she got herself lawyered up, didn't I? Everett Washburn."

Although retaining an attorney was universally viewed by the cops as nearly tantamount to an admission of guilt, in this case the news didn't rock Lanier much. "You'd expect that, wouldn't you? Judge's wife. She knows the game. But Washburn, shit."

"Yes, sir," Juhle said. "High-powered. Good news is maybe it takes a couple of years before it gets to trial and he'll die before then."

Lanier shook his head. "I wouldn't get my hopes up. Prosecutors have been saying that for the past ten years. The old fart's going to live forever. He's too smart to die."

But clearly Mrs. Palmer's choice of legal representation wasn't his main concern. He leaned back in his chair, cast his gaze up to the ceiling for a minute. When he came back down to his inspectors, his face was set. "I want you to understand, Shiu, that I agree with you that she's got a good motive. Hell, the classic motive, no question. So I'm just being devil's advocate here a minute."

Juhle was starting to like this. In the old days, when he was paired with Shane Manning, the two of them would toss case theories back and forth all day long, dig into them for nuances, contradictions, contexts. Lanier might be the boss, but he'd come up through the ranks and had been an inspector himself for fifteen years. This was what cops did, how they talked, the way they thought. Juhle wondered for the hundredth time what he'd done to deserve his current partner, who just didn't have a cop's imagination. Standing here by the desk, rooted to the floor, for example.

"Excuse me, before you start," Juhle said, "my esteemed colleague here actually likes standing at attention all day, but I'd really like to sit down." Amazingly, his partner moved, crossing behind the desk to the far chair while Juhle took the near one. "Okay," Juhle said when he'd taken the load off, "advocate."

Lanier wasted no time, held up a finger. "First, professional hit is your call, am I right?"

"Right," Shiu said. "Best case."

"Okay, a couple of questions. Like, how do you explain the slug in the book? The shooter's three, four feet max, from his targets, who at the very least aren't moving much. Palmer's in his chair. How does he clean miss? And okay, of course, gun's go off by themselves, but just to think about. Next, what's this nonsense about how they can tell that the shooter is probably short? Like kid-size, small-woman-size."

Juhle snapped his fingers. "That rent-a-midget place," he said.

Shiu painted on a frustrated look that Lanier ignored and went on. "The other question is where does a woman like Jeannette Palmer find a professional killer first, who's going to trust her, and second, who she's going to know how to talk to once she finds him, if she can get that far? How does she even ask? What, she's doing research for a book or something?"

Shiu spoke up. "Are you suggesting we drop it?"

"No. But I do think it's a reach."

"Why is that?" Shiu asked.

Lanier gave it another moment, considering. "Okay, the stuff I've just mentioned, for starters. Not insignificant, especially setting up the deal in the first place. Next, no scuff marks on any of the slugs, which means no silencer. Another small point, I grant you, but if I'm shooting somebody—make that two people—during daylight hours in a street-facing room in a house in a quiet, high-end residential neighborhood, even if I'm using a .22 pistol, I'm trying to keep the noise down, you know. Simple precaution."

Lanier paused, picked at a spot on his right ear. A silence built in the small room, but the lieutenant obviously had more to say, and evidently even Shiu saw the wisdom in letting him get to it uninterrupted.

"You know what's the real thing, though?" he asked. "I'm picturing the moment, okay. Palmer's in his big leather chair, the girl is next to him, the shooter's across the desk." He shook his head. "I just don't see it."

"Why not?" Shiu asked.

"May I?" Juhle asked.

Lanier nodded.

"It's too far away," Juhle said. "The judge let him in—we've got no sign of forced entry. Okay, say, he showed the gun at the door, backed everybody in. No way do they get to the office with the judge sitting in his chair. No, the second he's inside, the shooter pops him in the head right now—you're right, Marcel—with a silenced gun, then goes for the girl. They are not all somehow chatting in the office."

"I have no trouble with any of that." Shiu had sat back, crossed his legs, spoke to Juhle, while including Lanier. But a tone of defensiveness crept in. His back was straight and stiff against the wooden chair. "But maybe the person didn't appear to be a threat. Maybe the judge knew him. Or her. And the victims thought they were going to be able to talk things out."

The guy even *sits* at attention, Juhle was thinking. He said, "It's not a deal breaker, but there is one more thing." He turned to Lanier. "He shoots the girl again, am I right, Marcel?"

"I think so," Lanier said. He lowered his voice, shifted to face Shiu a bit more. "She went down after the shot, but there's no visible wound. What do you do if she's your contract? He's already missed at least once. She might have fainted, or even ducked. A pro doesn't leave her there without making sure. He comes around the desk and puts another one in her brain. And probably another one for the judge as well."

"At that range, he would know they were dead if he hit them in the head." Shiu sat with all of their objections for a long moment. Finally, he said, "I still think that somehow it has to involve Mrs. Palmer."

"And I agree that it's a strong assumption," Juhle said. In fact, he'd seen enough homicides to know that the taking of lives almost always involved a great deal of sloppiness. Retaliatory gang hits would as a matter of course take out four bystanders and leave the intended victim untouched. A woman would plan to kill her cheating boyfriend, wouldn't put enough rat poison in the peas—or he'd taste it halfway through—and they'd wind up in a knife fight that left them both dead. Strung-out, part-time hit men had been known to hit the wrong guy. Oops.

But beyond the randomness that often accompanied violent death, depending on who you asked, Juhle knew that the going rate to take someone's life in San Francisco ranged from down around one thousand dollars to somewhere in the neighborhood of fifty thousand dollars. Obviously, if you hired from the low end of that spectrum, your junkie street person looking for dope money to get right might make any number of technical errors in planning and execution. Of course, Juhle figured that if Mrs. Palmer had hired out the job, she had drawn from the upscale side, but maybe not.

He just wanted Shiu to have a little perspective. On the other hand, he and Shiu lived most of each day together, and there wasn't any point in alienating him or helping to make him look bad. "There is one way it might have worked, though," he said.

"What's that?" Lanier asked.

"You been following this thing in the papers between Palmer and the prison guards?"

In one of his well-tailored Nordstrom suits, Hunt was in a room full of very serious adults, talking about financial details of a million-dollar partnership that had gone awry because one of the principals had played loose with the books. It was important stuff to everybody else there—Hunt knew that the associates at McClelland, all younger than he was, made a minimum of one hundred fifty dollars per hour and that they lived and breathed these details.

Now he was there, at a mere eighty dollars per hour, to ensure that his witness, a sixty-year-old gentleman named Neil Haines, was going to say substantially the same things in his deposition testimony as he'd told Hunt in their discussions about four months before, discussions that Hunt only vaguely remembered, but which fortunately he'd recorded. He'd also taken copious notes.

Looking out over the sun-drenched city from the thirty-fifth-floor conference room windows inside McClelland, Tisch & Douglas, Hunt passed the rest of the morning in a haze of detail and tedium. When the depo team broke for lunch, he checked with Tamara. Andrea was still AWOL. Apparently she'd called in at work yesterday on her way to see a client at her home.

"Who was the client?"

"Carol Manion. And, yes, if you were wondering, that's *the* Manions."

Hunt whistled. Unless she'd known the Manions personally beforehand, Andrea Parisi had obviously bartered some of her notoriety into hard billings if she was scoring this level of client. Ward and Carol were a well-known couple who had made their initial money in the grocery business but since had branched out into wineries and restaurants and sports teams. They owned a good portion of the 49ers. They had also been regulars on the society page, but Hunt seemed to recall that recently their son had died in a boating accident or something, and since then their public appearances had tailed off. "So did you talk to her, Mrs. Manion?"

"No, are you kidding? How do I get to her?"

"Andrea's secretary?"

"Wyatt, come on. No way is Carla Shapiro giving out Manion's private number."

"Did you ask?"

"Did I ask? Am I slightly insulted by that question?" Hunt could almost see Tamara pout over the line. "She pretended she didn't have it. I'm *sure*."

"So we don't know if Andrea ever got there?"

"Right. I did call their corporate offices—the Manions's—and asked, too, but evidently it was something more personal. At the main office, they didn't know about any connection between Carol and Andrea."

"Okay. What about Dev? Any word from him?"

She told him that Juhle had called to report that no local hospitals had unidentified accident victims, the morgue had no recent Jane Doe, the jail hadn't acquired an attractive, young female-attorney inmate overnight. All this, as far as it went, was good news— Parisi wasn't verified as hurt or dead—although it was nowhere nearly as good as a sighting would have been.

"Have you heard any more from Amy?"

"No word."

"I'll call her." But as soon as they hung up, the young McClelland turk who was directing their efforts in the depositions knocked on the glass conference room window and motioned to Hunt, indicating that they were going to start. Time was money, and the lunch break here at McClelland was thirty minutes. But whatever it was, they needed him in there, and the call to Wu would have to wait.

16 /

Spencer Fairchild had been the line producer on more than twenty-five trials nationwide for Trial TV, and in his opinion, the trial of Randy Donolan for the double murder of his wife, Chrissa, and her lover, Josh Eberly, was the absolutely best one he'd ever been involved with.

It had it all.

Randy Donolan was thirty-one to Chrissa's twenty-six to Josh's seventeen. Both of the adults were attractive, though neither matched Eberly for sheer heartbreaking sex appeal. Chrissa had been substitute-teaching PE and history at Lincoln High School when she met Josh, and they'd begun their affair within a couple of weeks. Right up until the day of his arrest over a year and a half ago, Randy had run a small but enthusiastic fundamentalist Christian ministry (and Web site startup business) out of his house in the Sunset District.

Although Josh and Chrissa's bodies had not been found to date, samples of blood types matching both of theirs, as well as DNA-matched hairs from each of them, had turned up in the truck bed of the vehicle that Randy used for his pastoral and Web-master duties. That truck turned out to be owned by a parishioner named Gerry Coombs. When the police discovered the blood and hair in Gerry's truck, Mr. Coombs found an altogether different religion and became the chief state witness against Randy, with whom he'd been having a homosexual affair.

Among the dozens of allegations of one type or another that came out before and during the trial were the proposals that Gerry, Randy, and Chrissa had been involved for some time as a three-some; that Josh had decided to cut Randy out and leave Gerry and

Chrissa; that Chrissa loved Josh and wanted to marry him; that Gerry had actually done the killings at Randy's request; and just about all other possible variations on the theme. Which in the San Francisco environment were nearly endless.

From the get-go, the case had been a gold mine for Trial TV.

And now, as if the case didn't already have enough complications, the extremely coolheaded, logical, and knowledgeable babe, Andrea Parisi, who'd been explaining the meaning and nuance of every defense strategy and move since Day One had apparently disappeared.

Wu's early morning call to Spencer Fairchild had alerted him to this fact before he'd left his apartment. Andrea had been upset the other night, of course—he really didn't blame her—but it never occurred to him, even if she weren't going back to New York, that she would do anything to jeopardize the position she'd created for herself here in San Fran. After all, she was definitely on the inside track for any future trials here. She had kicked ass on camera. And the money they were paying her, even given that in her everyday life she was a highly paid lawyer, was not chump change. To say nothing of the notoriety and branding, both for her and her firm.

Even if her one first shot at the Apple hadn't worked out, Fairchild didn't doubt that she would realize that she was still young. A little more seasoning, a different break here or there, and she would be ready. And even if she wasn't, what she had here was not just good—television is a career-making medium, and she was already a star. She'd get over the affront to her *amour propre*. It was part of the business.

So his initial feeling after he talked to Wu was that Andrea was probably off pouting and would be back in plenty of time, at least for the afternoon court session and definitely for when she was really needed at the wrap-up. This was the segment after the court adjourned for the day, usually no earlier than four o'clock, when she and Tombo would not only review the day's major events but put them in context from the defense and prosecution sides, respectively. Great television, especially when they'd get into it with one another, as they sometimes did.

But he didn't like to lose tabs on the "talent," and just to be safe, he'd done a little calling around—to Andrea's completely private, off-limits-to-anyone-else, emergency-only Trial TV–issued cell number, then to Richard Tombo's home. Knowing that Wyatt Hunt had run out after her the other night, he had called The Hunt Club and talked briefly with Tamara, who was trying to locate Andrea herself.

At Piersall, he talked to Carla, whom he knew and who, he felt sure, admired the hell out of him, and she really, truly hadn't heard from her boss. She was worried.

Now Fairchild was sitting across from Richard Tombo about to order what passed for lunch at Lou the Greek's, a semi-subterranean, dark, and marginally hygienic bar/restaurant across the street from the steps of the Hall of Justice. Today, Judge Villars had dismissed the Donolan morning session at eleven thirty, and so there were still a couple of booths available under the small and grimy alley windows along one side. In spite of Lou's drawbacks, which to Fairchild were legion—the food, the atmosphere, the lighting, the food, the smell, the food, and particularly the daily special, which was the only menu item—it was a popular place within the legal and law-enforcement communities and had been for more than twenty-five years. It was SRO from noon until about one thirty, two and three deep at the bar.

Tombo was either an old thirties or a young forties. Wide-shouldered, substantial without being fat in the waist, a little above average height. His skin was very dark, his head buzzed, his dark suits always impeccable. Hints of gray accented his well-trimmed goatee. A wide, somewhat flattened nose bisected an almost exactly symmetrical face, and this gave him a definable and pleasant look—perfectly normal and yet somewhat unusual at the same time. His deep chocolate eyes, potentially so soulful, often winked out between laugh lines. In his own way, Tombo was as attractive as Parisi, and this, of course, was a large part of the reason Fairchild had chosen them.

Fairchild was finally getting around to telling Tombo about Parisi's reaction two nights ago. "That's what this disappearing act is about, I'm sure. But let me ask you, Rich, did I ever pretend that I had that kind of pull? Haven't I always told both of you to just enjoy this ride while it's here because there's no telling when it's going to come again?"

Tombo picked up a green pod of edamame from a bowl of them on the table, popped it open, and emptied the beans that were inside into his palm. "Evidently she didn't get that message somehow."

"I never lied to her."

"I'm not saying you did." He picked one bean and put it in his mouth. "She might have gotten a different impression is all I'm saying. With you both being so tight and all."

"No tighter professionally, I mean, than you and I have been. It's been a team all the way, the three of us."

The laugh lines showed. "Yeah, well, I wasn't just talking about the professional thing."

"Okay, fair enough. But the first time I got a vibe that she was really thinking New York was on the plate was Tuesday night. That is no bullshit. That's the first time. I mean, that she was counting on it as the next step, that it was actually going to happen. As soon as she said that . . . well, I had to set her straight. And that's when it started to get a little heavy. What are those things, anyway?"

Tombo, opening another shell, looked down. "Edamame. Soybeans. Great stuff." He looked around the crowded room. "Lou's stepping it up, going gourmet."

Fairchild said, "You notice the special coming in? Tempura dolmas? What is that?"

"As you say, it's the special. Sui generis." Tombo paused, translated roughly. "It's own thing."

"Maybe that, but we've got a ways to go to get to gourmet."

Tombo shrugged. "Depends on your definition. In the Sudan, this stuff would cause food riots." He threw some soybeans into his mouth. "So where is she, you think?"

"Laying low. Sending a message. Trying to get to me."

Tombo clucked sympathetically. "Thinking it's personal."

Fairchild cocked his head, wondering if Tombo was mocking him. "Exactly," he said. "She'll be back by the wrap-up, I'm sure."

"Let's hope."

"Well, if not, you'll carry it fine." The waitress came by with a tray of water glasses, put two on their table, took their unnecessary order for the record—the dolmas special. When she'd gone, Fairchild picked up his glass. "Tell me honestly, Rich, what did you think you were doing after this trial?"

Tombo shrugged. "Going back to billable work. God, that sounds horrible now that I think about it." The eyes lit up again. "Hey, maybe we can pull a few strings and get George Palmer's killer into trial in ten days or so. Wouldn't that be great?"

"Terrific. But wouldn't they have to catch him first?"

"If it's a him. Speaking of which, check this out." Tombo's gaze had gone to the crowd by the door, where two figures who were familiar to him had broken through. "Juhle and Shiu," he said. "And it looks like they're coming our way."

*   *   *

Tombo had been an assistant district attorney for nine years before going into private practice. He knew both Juhle and Shiu and had followed their assignment in the Palmer case. When they got to the table—he'd called it; they were coming right to him and Fairchild— he made the introductions. He and Fairchild made room for the inspectors by sliding over on their benches, and now the seating in the booth was a little tight. And Shiu started right in. "We were just on our way over to Andrea Parisi's firm, and Devin thought you guys would be down here, so we could hit you first. In fact, we were kind of hoping that Parisi would be with you."

"No," Fairchild said. "It's just us guys so far. As you can see."

"Have you talked to her today?" Shiu asked.

"Not yet. She's not due till the afternoon gavel, and sometimes she's got other work and misses that." Fairchild shrugged as though this were no issue at all. "I expect her around for the wrap-up, though, you want to stop by then."

"What's up, guys?" Tombo asked.

"Well, since we're here, anyway, for starters," Shiu said, "we wonder if either of you could tell us a little about the extent of her involvement with the prison guards' union?"

"You mean, beyond them being her client?" Fairchild asked.

"Piersall's client, you mean," Shiu said.

The producer shrugged. "Okay, sure, but she worked on their stuff all the time."

"Maybe I'm missing something," Tombo said. "You guys are on Palmer's murder, right? What's Andrea got to do with that? Or the prison guards, for that matter?"

Juhle stepped in. His partner had said too much already. "We don't know," he said. "All we've got are some dots we thought Parisi could connect."

"About Palmer?" Tombo asked, followed by Fairchild's, "Like what?"

Juhle didn't like to give information out to television people. He offered both men a bland smile and asked his own question instead. "Has she ever mentioned a young woman named Staci Rosalier to either of you?"

Tombo shook his head. Fairchild frowned.

"Ring a bell?" Juhle picked up something in Fairchild's expression.

"No. Not from Andrea. The name's familiar, though."

"She was the other victim," Shiu said. "The other woman with Palmer."

"That's it," Fairchild said. "That's where I heard it. What's her connection to Andrea?"

Juhle reached for an edamame. "That's what we want to know."

Tombo and Fairchild shared a blank look.

Shiu said, "Okay, let's go back to the prison guards for a minute." He turned to Fairchild. "You said she worked with them all the time. So she must have been aware of Palmer's, um, problems with them."

"Sure," Fairchild said. "But who isn't? Some article's in the paper every couple of weeks, right? Inmates killed by their guards by mistake up at Folsom. Mexican Mafia's making a fortune running drugs out of Pelican Bay. They're staging gladiator fights to the death with the prisoners at Corcoran. Half the prison doctors have rap sheets of their own, don't have current licenses, give the wrong prescriptions. And every time, Palmer's threatening that this time he's shutting the union down. The guards are out of control. If the union can't discipline itself, he'll put it under federal jurisdiction. Well, guess who he communicates all this to the union through?"

"Wait a minute." Tombo came forward, no sign of laughter in his eyes now. "You think the CCPOA had something to do with Palmer's death?"

"We don't know," Shiu said. "We do know the union has muscle and isn't afraid to use it. We also know that people who run against the candidates it supports, especially in the rural counties, have had bad things happen to them, to their campaign headquarters, like that."

Juhle had listened to enough of Shiu's irresponsible chatter. Next he was going to tell them that they were looking into the possibility that Jeannette had paid somebody, maybe one of Palmer's union enemies, to kill him. This was where they'd been in Lanier's office early in the day. But since then, having come that far, Shiu might tell them that they'd realized that they didn't need Jeannette as the prime mover at all. It might have been some union henchman all on his own. Pretty soon, if Shiu kept it up, they'd hear all of their theories on television. "Anyway, what we'd like to see Parisi about," he said, "is maybe some context on this, that's all."

"But you've got her with the other victim somehow," Tombo said. "Isn't that right?"

Juhle evaded. "Again, context." He was getting out of the booth, his body language bringing Shiu up and out along with him. "When you do see her," he said in his most amiable tone, "would you mind

THE HUNT CLUB / 135

telling her we'd like to talk to her? If we don't before, ask her to wait around, and we'll catch her on the wrap-up."

"This incredible story she was going to break." Fairchild didn't appear to be having any trouble with the dolmas. He was finishing his fourth. "That was why New York was really going to want her. She was going to be this amazing investigative reporter. Anyway, that's what started it."

"You told her it didn't matter."

"I had to." Fairchild shrugged. "It didn't matter. It doesn't."

"She tell you what it was?" Tombo asked. "The story."

"Some. But I got a better sense of it right now, talking to these guys."

"What?"

Fairchild leaned in over the table, lowered his voice. "It's one thing you get some union thugs to mess with people, right? But how about if you actually spring inmates for a night or two to do crimes? That's what she was looking at."

Tombo had already pushed his plate away, mostly uneaten. He was filling up on water. "To do what?"

"Whatever needs to be done. Trash a campaign headquarters. Intimidate some assemblyman leaning the wrong way on prisons appropriations. I don't know, maybe assassinate somebody. And meanwhile, they've got the perfect alibi if anybody ever comes and looks—they were locked up."

Tombo raised his eyes, shook his head. "No."

" 'No,' what?"

"No everything. It couldn't happen."

"Why not?"

"Because, Spencer, here's what happens you let a convict out. He keeps going. He doesn't go do the job you've kindly asked him to do. He probably leaves the state. At the very least, he doesn't come back to his friendly local prison, having just killed somebody for you, or trashed a campaign headquarters, to peacefully serve out the remainder of his term."

Fairchild chewed for a moment, considering. "He does if, say, his brother's in the slammer with him and might have a fatal accident if you didn't come back."

"Oh, yeah. The ever-popular two-brothers-in-the-same-prison trick."

"Might not be a literal brother. Might be another relationship.

Or," getting into it now, Fairchild said, "or how about you get conjugal rights every night, plus dope, plus liquor, cigarettes, any combination of the above? They bring it all in for you."

"Who does?"

"The guards."

"The guards who are guarding you?"

"Yeah, those guys."

"And where's the warden all this time?"

"He's in on it. He's just taking care of the union's business. It's grateful. He gets a bonus under the table every week. Not surprisingly, it's not a credit business."

Tombo was frankly smiling now, enjoying the idiocy. "How about they get him a Harley to drive around the yard with, too? I agree to go out and kill somebody, I'd demand a Harley."

"Maybe not the Harley," Fairchild said. "Too visible. Piss off the other inmates."

"Like conjugal rights wouldn't?"

"They might at that."

"This doesn't happen, my man. I can't believe Andrea was really looking into this."

"I think she was. She might be still. And I mean this minute."

"Even after you told her it wouldn't get her to New York?"

"Maybe it was the Palmer case. If she thought that it could have happened with him. I mean an assassin out of one of the prisons. She could break the case, get famous on her own, make the move to New York without my help."

Suddenly serious, Tombo went silent and twirled his empty water glass on the table.

"You think that hard, I can actually hear the cogs turning," Fairchild said.

"They don't spring inmates," Tombo said in a nearly breathless whisper. "They use parolees."

"What are you talking about?"

"Spencer, what have we been talking about? Union muscle. Andrea was onto something, but it wasn't the inmates. It's the parolees. They get their parole violated and sent back to the joint if they don't do what they're told. Then whatever they do, maybe up to murder, they're alibied by their parole officers."

"That's a stretch, Rich. I can't believe you'd get many cops who'd have any part of that."

"No. I don't think many cops would, either. But parole officers aren't cops."

"Sure they are."

"No, they're not."

"What are they, then?"

"Technically. They're prison guards. CCPOA."

Devin Juhle's opinion was that Gary Piersall had too much hair for a guy in his fifties, all of it a perfect shade of gray, and not a one out of place. At least six foot four, he probably didn't weigh two hundred pounds, and his perfectly tailored light gray suit was shot through with almost but not quite invisible threads of neon blue. A strong aquiline nose under a wide forehead gave him a patrician cast that was only accentuated by piercing milky blue eyes.

They were in his office, seventeen floors above San Francisco. The firm had four floors in the building on Montgomery Street, and Piersall's lair was about a third of the way to the top, in the northeast corner, which afforded views of the bay, Alcatraz, the Golden Gate. Piersall had greeted Juhle and Shiu at the door and had offered them the wing chairs that faced his desk while he had gone around to put the ornate piece of cherry furniture between them.

"I'm afraid I still don't understand why you've come to see me," he was saying. "What connection do you have between George Palmer's murder and the CCPOA?"

Juhle, unruffled, sat back comfortably in the oversize chair, one leg crossed over the other. "Well, sir, it wasn't much of a secret that the judge was threatening to freeze the union's funds and put it into receivership."

Piersall assayed a thin smile. "The key word there, inspector, is *threatening*. You have to understand that this was a game he liked to play, although frankly he had cried this version of wolf enough that the entire exercise had become much more tedious than worrisome."

Shiu, in contrast to Juhle, sat in the front six inches of his chair, his feet planted flat on the carpet. "So you're saying that he didn't have enemies with the union?"

"No. I'm sure he had several. He was biased and unsympathetic to the guards and loved the limelight. He bought all the bullshit the cons were selling and was a loud, sanctimonious son of a bitch on top of that. So, yeah, he had an enemy or two, Jim Pine maybe being the most visible of them."

Pine was the president of the union and, because of the vast sums of money he controlled, one of the state's most powerful political figures. He had personally spearheaded the drive for California's Three Strikes law, which vastly increased the state-prison population and in turn created the need for more guards and, hence, more union dues. Pine was also the driving force behind the Victims' Awareness Coalition, which constantly lobbied for harsher criminal penalties to keep inmates in prison for longer periods of time. Every get-tough-on-crime prosecutor and legislator in the state of California had benefited from the lobbying efforts and political contributions of Pine and the CCPOA.

"But I must tell you, inspectors," Piersall went on, "that Mr. Pine doesn't have to resort to strong-arm tactics, which is, I gather, what you're implying here. George Palmer wasn't going to take him down, and even George Palmer knew it. He just wanted to keep the pressure on with the union's efforts at self-discipline, which—I'll be honest—sometimes historically have come up a little short. But the whole interaction with George and Jim was all very much in the spirit of checks and balances between judicial and executive functions, and that's all it was."

Juhle toyed with his own idea of a smile. "That's good to hear and all to the good, except that we've just come from Judge Palmer's office before we came here. We talked both to his secretary and to his clerk, who had already drafted the preliminary order to put the union into receivership. It's hard to believe you knew nothing about that."

Piersall all but rolled his eyes. "He's gone that far several times before. It's just another stage in the threat." With a sudden show of impatience, he rubbed his hands together, put his palms flat on the expanse of desk. "But let me ask you this, gentlemen: Doesn't the presence of the young woman, the other victim, provide a more compelling theory here for George's death than some obscure and frankly tortured reading of union shenanigans? I'm assuming you've established an intimate relationship between her and the judge? And in that case, I'd expect that you'd be looking a little, shall I say, closer to home."

Juhle instinctively mistrusted anyone who overused the word *frankly*, his experience having taught him that it was a nearly infallible indicator of mendacity. "Mrs. Palmer has a very solid alibi. And you're right. That leaves us pretty much at square one. So, frankly," he purposely repeated, "we came here to ask for your help and cooperation. We're exploring not only alternatives to Mrs. Palmer as the suspect, but ways that someone in her social position could have identified and maybe even contacted someone from the, shall we say, enforcement side of something like the CCPOA."

This brought what appeared to be an expression of geniune shock, then a sympathetic smile. "If that's where you are," Piersall said, "then you gentlemen really are nowhere. You're saying that you are reduced to thinking that Mrs. Palmer might have contacted someone in the union to help her kill her husband?"

Shiu nodded. "Let's say we'd want to rule that out, yes."

"And leaving out," Piersall said, "that the CCPOA doesn't have an enforcement side."

"No?" Juhle came forward. "So those little problems last year with folks running against your candidates in, what was it? Seven counties? What were they? Acts of God?"

Piersall shrugged. "I don't know. A lot of that is rumor, and I've heard the theory that some of them might have been the candidates themselves, trying to create the illusion that the union was behind the incidents. But if you don't like that, I'd suggest the random spark, maybe even simple carelessness, I don't know. Local vandals, kids' pranks. And might I point out, frankly, that if memory serves, no one from the union was ever arrested in connection with any of that mischief."

"The coincidence factor doesn't speak to you, does it?"

"The coincidence . . . ?"

"Seven different political races, and only your opponents hit?"

"Hit? Somebody gets a flat tire, and it's a conspiracy? As a matter of fact, some pro-union candidates were harassed, too, although these weren't as well publicized. So, no, the coincidence doesn't compel me much. And to extrapolate from that and think that Mrs. Palmer somehow . . ." He stopped, shook his head. "I'm sorry, but it's just ludicrous."

Juhle said, "To tell you the truth, sir, it would be ludicrous except for one thing."

"And that is?"

"Andrea Parisi."

Piersall's ice-blue eyes squinted down. "What about Andrea?"

"Well, as I understand it, she was your representative with the judge."

"One of many actually and less so since she's been involved with her TV work on Donolan. Half of our associates work regularly on union billings. But, yes, she had a comfortable relationship with Judge Palmer. The court respected her, and she him." Cocking his head to one side, he continued, "But I'm afraid I'm still not getting your drift."

"Staci Rosalier, the other victim, she had Parisi's card in her wallet," Shiu said. The junior inspector seemed incapable of talking to anyone without giving up every shred of information that their investigation had uncovered. "That makes her the only person we have who has a demonstrated connection to both victims. And the intersection with Palmer is the CCPOA."

"Slim pickin's," Piersall said.

"Yes," Shiu agreed, "but now that she's apparently missing, there's . . ."

Juhle, at the end of his patience, uncrossed his legs, held a hand out toward his partner, hoping to stem the flow.

Piersall reacted as though he'd been jabbed. "What do you mean, apparently missing? She's not . . . excuse me a minute, would you?" He picked up his phone. "Carla? Gary Piersall," he said. "I'd like to speak with Andrea, please. I see, since when? All right, thank you. Have her call me as soon as she gets in, would you? Thanks." He hung up, the confident face suddenly slack.

Juhle had gotten to his feet. He wanted to get Shiu out of the room before he could do any more damage. He managed to place his business card on Piersall's desk. "We're really not trying to waste your time, sir. If you hear from her, we'd appreciate it if you had her give us a call. ASAP."

Three floors down in the same building, Juhle, Shiu, and Carla Shapiro were in an employee lounge that was larger than the entire homicide detail—six tables with four chairs each, vending machines for coffee, tea, sodas, candy, snacks. The smells of popcorn and stale coffee hung in the air. Andrea's secretary was thin, bespectacled, frizzy-haired, earnest, and sick with worry now about her boss, she told them. Just sick.

She was talking, all nerves, as they took seats at one of the tables. "She called at about quarter to three and said she was feeling a little better and wanted to come in and catch up on some of her work, but first, she was going to go out and visit a client at her home, then probably be in after I went home, no doubt till pretty late. I didn't have to wait around—she'd leave stuff on my desk for the morning."

"But she didn't?" Shiu asked.

"No. She never came in. At least she never signed in down-stairs. After hours, we have sign-in here in the building, you know." Then, as though it had just occurred to her, "She'd missed most of yesterday, too, you know? And she never misses work. I mean, never."

"So what was she doing yesterday?" Juhle asked. "That made her miss."

"Food poisoning, they said."

"Who was that?"

"Her doctor, I think. He called and talked to reception, not to me."

Shiu had his small notepad out and glanced down at it, then looked up. "But then she was apparently better by about quarter to three?"

"Yes, I think so."

"You talked to her personally," Shiu asked, "and she was going first to meet a client at her house. Did she do that a lot? Meet clients at their homes?"

"I think so, yes. Sometimes. It depended."

Suddenly Juhle broke in. "Do you know the name Staci Ros-alier? Was she one of Andrea's clients?"

Carla shook her head. "No. That name isn't familiar. I'm sorry."

"Nothing to be sorry about, ma'am," Shiu said. "Did Andrea tell you who she was going to see?"

"Yes. Carol Manion. You know the Manions? Except she never got there."

"How do you know that?" Shiu asked. "Did you call her?"

In Carla's nervous state, the question appeared to startle her. "Who?"

"Mrs. Manion."

A haunted expression of guilt settled in Carla's dark eyes. "Well, no. I mean, there was no reason to last night before I left, and then . . . because she called here instead. I mean, the office. Later last night. There was a message on Andrea's line when I got in this morning."

"From Mrs. Manion?"

Head sunk into her shoulders, she nodded. "Wondering if An-drea had forgotten or gotten the wrong day or something. Which of course Andrea would never do."

"No." Juhle made circles with his index finger on the table. "So she never made it to the Manions? If she was going there at all."

"I think she was. That's where she told me she was going. Then coming back here."

"And that," Juhle asked, "is the last you've heard from her?"

She reached under her glasses and brushed away a tear. "As far as I know," she said, "that's the last anyone's heard from her."

17 /

Wes Farrell's work environment didn't bear much resemblance to the other law offices Hunt visited throughout the city. It took up nearly the entire third floor of a stately renovated building in the heart of downtown. A casual visitor who came up via the elevator in the underground parking lot—thereby avoiding the formal reception area and bustling legal offices on the floors below—might reach the conclusion that this was the private residence of an eccentric and spectacularly slovenly person.

Farrell's mostly unused desk sat over in the corner under one of the windows, which left the rest of the space free to resemble a living room, with an overstuffed couch and matching easy chairs, a couple of floor lamps, a Salvation Army coffee table. A Nerf basketball net graced the wall by the door. Farrell had willy-nilly pinned up some old and unframed advertising prints from the Fillmore era and one poster of Cheryl Tiegs walking out of some water somewhere wearing a see-through bathing suit and a killer smile. The counter and cabinets on the left-hand wall might have been a college student's kitchen, with the sink and coffee machine and mugs out, and binders of stuff, legal pads, and books scattered about everywhere.

But nobody was enjoying the place at the moment. Farrell, slouched on the couch, his feet up on the table, summed it up for all of them. "I'm getting a bad feeling here."

Wu slumped in one of the easy chairs, hands folded in her lap. Hunt, who'd charged out of McClelland's a few blocks away after his depos finished up, was standing by the television perched on a low wall unit under the street windows. He reached over and switched the thing off. They'd just finished watching today's

Donolan wrap-up on Trial TV, featuring only Richard Tombo, no mention at all of Andrea Parisi. "Amy and I, we're ahead of you on that one, Wes," he said. He turned to Amy. "You talked to Spencer recently?"

"Forty-five minutes ago," she said. "She hasn't called. He's thinking it's serious."

"He's right," Hunt said. "So, as far as we know, nobody's talked to her since she left to go to the Manions?"

"Do we know she even did that?" Farrell asked.

Hunt nodded. "She took her car. We know that. It was in her garage when I dropped her off at her house, and it wasn't there last night."

"So where's the car?" Wu asked.

"*No lo se.*" Hunt blew out in frustration. "And apparently she never made it out to her meeting. Manion called her office and asked where she was—if she'd forgotten the appointment."

"So she just gets in her car and disappears?" Farrell asked.

"So far," Hunt said, "that's what we've got. It's not good." He walked over to the seating area, straddled the armrest on the other easy chair. "And while we're at it, here's the other thing I've been wondering about most of the day. She'd just found out she wasn't going to get the anchor gig in New York, right? She was badly hungover. She even thought that slapping Spencer might cost her the regular gig on Trial TV, with ramifications if it got out at Piersall as well."

"You're saying she might have killed herself?" Wu asked.

Hunt didn't want to think that but knew that it wasn't impossible. People were complicated, endlessly unknowable. What he had interpreted as a hopeful beginning, she could have seen as another possibly tawdry episode in a life that might have been filled with similar connections. He said, "I've got Tamara calling emergency rooms all around the state because it's the only thing I can think of. But you know her better than I do, Amy. What do you think?"

"Do I think she might have killed herself? I want to say no, but . . ."

Hunt's cell phone rang and, holding up a finger to Wu, he got it and moved over to the window for better reception. "Yeah, we just saw it, too," he said. Then, "I know. Uh-huh. Sutter Street, Wes Farrell's place upstairs. Yeah, we're all here now. What about? Okay, just a sec." He turned back to face the room, spoke to Farrell and Wu in a suddenly husky voice. "Devin wants to come up and say hi to all of us. It's about this. We all gonna be here for ten more minutes?" He got nods all around and went back to the phone. "Okay, Dev, we're here. Sure, it's your call."

When he closed the phone, he remained standing by the window, facing out. His shoulders rose, fell, rose again.

"Wyatt," Wu said with some concern. "What is it?"

Finally, he turned around. "It's just that Devin and Shiu are homicide, and they want to come up here and talk about Andrea." He let out a long breath. "Homicide means somebody's dead."

The next few minutes passed in an agonized semi-silence. At one point, Wu said, "If they had anything definite, it would have been on the news. Especially what we just watched. They can't have anything."

"Unless the police didn't tell them or asked them to sit on it. But let's hope," Farrell said.

Hunt called Tamara again, found out that Andrea hadn't been admitted to any of the emergency rooms she'd called so far, although she still had another ten or fifteen to call in the nine-county Bay Area alone, to say nothing of the state at large. It was going to be a while.

The conference phone buzzed and Farrell picked it up and said, "Good. Send him up."

The first sight of Juhle's face was reassuring. He looked done in after a long day of work, but it didn't look like he was here to deliver the kind of bad news they'd all been fearing—his eyes, in fact, appeared lit up with a kind of expectation. But the sense of relief hadn't gotten any chance to take hold before Wu asked if they'd heard anything about Andrea.

"Just tell us she's not dead," Farrell added.

Juhle shook his head. "Not that I know of. You got any reason to think she's dead?"

"You do homicides, Dev," Hunt said. "You wanted to talk to us."

"I did. I do. And it's a homicide, all right, but not hers." He looked into the three concerned faces in front of him. "I just came from talking to Rich Tombo down outside the Hall after his gig. He'd called and left a message that he felt there was something he needed to tell me. Any of you guys hear the rumor that Andrea Parisi had been romantically involved with Judge Palmer?"

Hunt felt the blood drain out of his face. Because immediately the rumor rang true. How had it not occurred to him? Palmer, of course—the "other guy" Andrea had been seeing for two years before Fairchild, who didn't want a serious relationship, who had dumped her, who worked with the CCPOA. And now, who had been murdered.

Wes Farrell harrumphed. "It's hearsay, Dev."

"Well, yes, it is." Juhle wasn't here to fight anybody. "But we're not in trial, and this is the kind of hearsay that makes us feel like it would be a good idea to question the object of it if at all possible."

"Which, right now, it isn't," Hunt said.

"So it seems," Juhle said.

"Wait a minute," Amy said. "You're saying you want to ask Andrea about George Palmer's death?"

"Right."

"As a suspect? That's ridiculous."

Juhle shrugged.

Farrell was unconvinced. "It's just a rumor."

"Granted," Juhle said. "But we know about when Palmer started up with Staci Rosalier. The other victim. About six months ago. Right about when Donolan began. Which, according to Tombo, is when the judge broke it off with Andrea."

Shiu amplified. "Tombo's opinion was that she wasn't over him."

"Yeah, but Dev," Hunt said, "they broke up six months ago. And then she kills them both last Monday?"

"I'm sorry," Farrell said. "There's just no way."

"No? Were you with her, Wes, on Monday night?"

"No, but . . ."

Juhle looked from Wu to Hunt. "Either of you? Okay, then. Here's what we know. She did the broadcast with her TV people at four thirty and another one at five, after which her limo dropped her at her firm at five thirty or so. She worked for an hour and a half and signed out of the building at seven-oh-eight."

"And then what?" Farrell asked.

A shrug. "Then we don't know. It's why I wanted to talk to all of you. Tombo told me you guys all were out with her the next night, Wyatt's little anniversary soiree, which I now so wish I'd attended. Maybe she mentioned something about what she'd done the night before to one of you."

"This is insane," Wu said. "I know she saw the judge every week or two with the union stuff they did. In fact, she'd just . . ." Suddenly, Wu stopped.

Juhle didn't miss the slip. "I'm listening, Amy."

Wu looked for help from Hunt to Farrell, but neither could offer anything. "Well, she had seen him having lunch that Monday."

"And how," Shiu asked, "do you know she did that, ma'am?"

"She told me at Sam's. She couldn't believe it about him having been shot. She'd just seen him at MoMo's the day before."

Juhle's eyebrows went up. "MoMo's is where Staci Rosalier waited lunch tables."

"Wait up, Dev," Hunt put in. "So your theory is that six months after Andrea and Palmer broke up, she sees him and his new girlfriend at MoMo's and out of the blue succumbs to this mad fit of jealousy and decides she has to kill them both that night? At his house? Doesn't that seem a little out there?"

"Absolutely. I don't pretend to have the answers, just questions. The primary one being where is she? But add that to her apparent motive . . ." He shrugged. "I don't know how out there it is anymore."

Hunt was out on Sutter Street alone with Juhle, who'd hung back while Shiu went to get the car. "So you want to know what she was doing Monday night?"

"Yeah. First, though, same as you, I'd just like to find her." His face set hard, he went on. "And it's funny, we heard from Tombo that your very own self left your cigar place hot on her tail Tuesday night. You catch her?"

"She was drunk, Dev," Hunt said. "I took her back to my place to dry out. Then brought her back home around noon."

"That would be yesterday, the last anybody's seen her." Juhle paused. "You fuck her?"

The question, completely unexpected, left Hunt tongue-tied just long enough.

So that Juhle said, "Shit. You did."

"I never said that."

Juhle had no patience for it. "Yeah, you did. Give me a break. And now you're also the last one we know to have seen her."

"And now I'm a suspect, too?"

"It's not as funny as you seem to think. I'm not kidding. It's going to occur to Shiu, too, I guarantee you."

"And then what? He's going to arrest me?"

"Don't push it, Wyatt. Don't give him an excuse. He might." After a second, Juhle said, "So Parisi's the one who stood you up last night." It wasn't a question. He had figured it out, and now took a step forward into Hunt's personal space. He lowered his voice to a whisper laced with anger. "Maybe you remember last night when you told me she didn't do much work herself involving the prison guards' union? Except for meeting with my murder victim every week or so? Did you know she was sleeping with him, too?"

"I didn't know that. I never suspected that."

"Good for you. But the rest of it, you just didn't think it *mattered*?"

Hunt's guts roiled and he felt the flush rise in his face. He'd asked for this. "I know it matters, Dev. What can I say? I should have told you. I fucked up. I'm sorry."

"Damn straight you fucked up."

"Right. I know. She was hurting. She was a mess. I guess I was trying to protect her."

"From me?"

"From everything. But you, too. Right."

"You know what? That really pisses me off. If she's innocent, she doesn't need protection from me or anybody else. You get that?"

"Yeah, but if any of this gets out, it won't matter if she killed those two or not. If she's been having an affair with the judge on her biggest case, she's toast."

"Not my problem. Not yours, either. I need to find her."

"So do I."

"If you do, I need to see her."

"Dev, I won't hide her from you."

"No? Let's hope not. But while we're on this, what else haven't you told me?"

Hunt said nothing.

"No hurry, Wyatt. I've got all day."

"You'll find this out, anyway, when you get to looking in her house," Hunt said at last. "She's got a gun collection in her dining room."

"Swell. Terrific. Fucking peachy."

"She . . ." He stopped. There was no point in arguing with Juhle about this or trying to explain it away. It was what it was.

"Anything else," Juhle asked, "that you know about her that might matter?"

After another minute, Hunt said, "Nothing." Then: "No. Wait." He considered whether it was, in fact, something and at last he spoke. "I don't think she stood me up."

Juhle moved away a half step, squinted with still-angry eyes. "I'm so happy for you. What the hell does that mean?"

"She's the one who brought up the idea of us going to dinner. She said she'd call me one way or the other. She doesn't do that if she's planning to light out of town. She would have called. So whatever's up with her, it wasn't her choice. It happened to her."

"So she's a victim? Like every single convict in every jail in the world."

"I'm not saying she sees herself as a victim, Dev. I'm saying she might be one. That's my truest call."

The cop backed up another step. "Your truest one? Okay, I'll take it into consideration." Shiu pulled the car up to the curb and gave a polite little honk. Juhle turned, got to the door and opened it, then turned back. "But I'll tell you what, Wyatt. Your truest call meant a hell of a lot more to me yesterday than it does today."

The dressing-down left Hunt literally shaking. Or maybe it was the information—still just a rumor, he reminded himself, although he intuitively believed it—about Andrea and Palmer. He stood out on the sidewalk in front of the Freeman building staring after Shiu and Juhle's car until long after it had turned a corner and disappeared.

When he came back to himself, he returned to the main doors of Freeman, Farrell, Hardy & Roake, rang the after-hours bell, and waited for the click that unlocked the door. In a minute, he was up the stairs, knocking on Farrell's door, letting himself in. Wu was sitting on the couch, talking on the telephone. Farrell had undone his tie and taken off his dress shirt, leaving him in today's T-shirt, which read, SEEN ONE SHOPPING CENTER, SEEN A MALL. Farrell was standing behind the easy chairs and had just shot a Nerf ball toward the basket. Neither attorney was facing the television set, which was back on, albeit silent. On the screen was a picture of Andrea Parisi. Hunt ran over and hit the sound.

"... not been seen since midafternoon yesterday. Further cause for concern among authorities is the fact that Ms. Parisi's legal work brought her into regular contact with Judge George Palmer, who was shot to death at his home last Monday evening. Anyone having any knowledge of Ms. Parisi or her whereabouts is urged to call the police or this station at . . ."

Hunt muted the sound. Wu still held the phone but now was standing, staring at the screen. Farrell, too, had turned, and his face had clouded over. "Well, now it's official at least," he said. "Maybe Missing Persons will move on it after all."

"Don't count on it," Hunt said. "The TV saying somebody's missing doesn't necessarily mean that they're missing."

"But she is missing," Wu insisted. "I know something's happened. We all know that. She'd never go this long without telling somebody."

Hunt pointed at the phone in her hand. "Who are you talking to?"

"Oh." With an I'm-stupid expression, she spoke back into the phone. "Jason. Did you hear that?"

Farrell sat on the arm of the easy chair, his jaw tight. "Devin doesn't really consider her a suspect in Palmer, does he, Wyatt?"

Hunt lowered himself down onto the wall unit next to the television. "I'd say close to as good as the wife."

"What do you think?"

"You really want to know? You don't want to know."

"You think she's dead, don't you?" Wu had hung up and now sat, her hands nervous little birds in her lap. "I'm afraid of that, too."

Farrell's expression showed he wasn't far from that thought himself, but he said, "What about kidnapped?"

Hunt shook his head. "Why? And no ransom demand. It makes no sense."

"Neither does her disappearing," Farrell said, "unless she just split up the coast or somewhere to get her head straight. Between this thing with Palmer and her fight with Spencer, I could see her just laying low for a few days."

But Wu was shaking her head. "She would have told Carla, at least. And probably Gary Piersall."

"Maybe she did, Amy," Hunt said.

"No, not Carla, anyway. I talked to her enough times today. Nobody's that good an actress."

Farrell said, "Maybe she just wasn't thinking straight and forgot to tell anybody."

Wu shook her head. "That's just not her."

Hunt said, "She was fine when I left her. She wasn't freaking out. She was going in to work. Besides, if she's taking a mental health day or two, the story breaking on TV is going to bring her back in. If that or some ransom demand doesn't happen in the next few hours, and I don't think they will . . ." He let the sentence hang unfinished.

"So what do we do?" Wu asked. "Just sit and wait?"

"I don't know what else we can do," Farrell said. "She turns up or she doesn't."

"Well, maybe not." Hunt lifted himself up from the credenza, the nebulous idea of why he'd felt he needed to come back up here beginning to form into something more cohesive. "If she's dead, nothing we do makes any difference. But if she's not . . . if she's hurt or trapped or crashed and skidded off the road someplace or anything besides dead, there's still a chance we can do something."

"All right, maybe," Farrell said, "if we could get the police . . ."

But Hunt was shaking his head. "Think about it, Wes. We've already got the police. Juhle wants her. He'll pull out all those stops." He took in both of them. "I'm talking about us."

"Us? You mean you and me and Amy?"

Hunt nodded. "And Jason. And my troops, Tamara and Craig and Mickey."

Wes cracked a thin smile. "And do what?"

But Wu said, "I'm in. Whatever it takes."

"Here's what I see," Hunt said. "Wes, hear me out. We've got three options. One, Andrea's already dead. Two, for some reason she went away on her own. On that, she'll either come home on her own, too, or she plans to stay away indefinitely, in which case she's left the country and we'll never see her again."

"I don't think that's it," Wu said.

Hunt nodded. "I don't, either. But she also might have had a bona fide accident going where she was going, and then the cops will probably find her or her car. So forget one and two. Those are just out of our control."

"Okay," Farrell said. "What's three?"

"Three, somebody took her." Hunt held up his hands, forestalling the response he saw in both of their faces. "I'm not saying that's what happened, but it's the only thing we can look at, and possibly effect, rather than just sit and wait. If somebody took her, they did it for a reason—something she did, someone she knew, something she was involved in. That's what's left."

"So what do we do?" Farrell asked.

"How about if you go talk to Fairchild and Tombo. Between the two of them, they're going to know more than any of us but may not know what they know."

"What do you want me to do?" Wu asked.

"You and Jason, maybe you could get with Carla Shapiro. Find out who Andrea hung with at work, what her caseload was, her personal life outside of Trial TV. Meanwhile, I'll put Tamara and my stringers on the phones and try to pick up any other lead I can."

"Where?" Wu asked.

"I don't know exactly. I'll start digging. Maybe, as you say, Wes, talk to Devin some more."

"He's a good guy, Wyatt, but he's a cop on a big case. He's not going to be inclined to share." Farrell came forward, elbows on his knees, hands clasped in front of him. "Don't get me wrong. I'm on the team here. But this is a helluva long shot, the whole idea."

"I realize that," Hunt said. "But what's the alternative?"

18 /

Hunt got lucky with Mickey Dade.

Besides the occasional work he did for Hunt, Tamara's twenty-three-year-old younger brother also drove a cab in the evenings while he sporadically attended chef's school during the day at the California Culinary Academy when he could afford classes. Hunt thought the interest in food might have had something to do with Mickey getting down to his last spoonful of peanut butter when he'd been ten, but they'd never discussed it.

Tonight, though, Mickey was circling Union Square, not four blocks from Farrell's office, when Hunt got him on his cell phone. Picking him up out front, Mickey left the meter off and started to drive. Hunt, sitting in the passenger seat next to him, wasted no time. "How's it look for work over the next day or two, Mick?"

"Clear enough. I could probably find a few hours. What do you want?"

"I don't know yet. You hear about Andrea Parisi?"

"Who?"

"I guess not, then. She's on TV about the Donolan trial almost every day."

"I don't watch TV. Waste of time."

"I know. It's one of the things I've always liked about you most."

"Except for the *Iron Chef*. I love that show."

"Mick."

"Yeah."

"Andrea Parisi."

"Okay."

"She's missing. We're going to try to find her."

"Who's we?"

"You, me, Tamara, Craig, some of my pals from the legal world."

"Where'd she go?"

"Was that a smart or dumb question?"

Mickey took a beat. "Dumb. I get it. If she's missing, though, don't the cops automatically look for her?"

Hunt explained about Missing Persons, as well as where they stood with Parisi in a general way, while Mickey managed to run three reds and hit fifty miles per hour between every other stoplight on the way down to Brannan. He got Hunt home in a little under ten minutes, but before he sped out in a hail of gravel for a dispatch fare at Lulu's, he promised Hunt he'd keep his cell phone on and await instructions.

"You got your camera on you, right?" Hunt asked him. "Just in case."

Mickey patted the small leather case on the car seat next to him. "Always, dude, always."

Back home, Hunt changed out of his business suit into jeans, hiking boots, an old flannel Pendleton. By the time he'd changed, his computer was up, and he sat at his desk where he Googled the names Ward and Carol Manion. Andrea Parisi had not made it to her final appointment with Carol Manion, true, but if the two women had talked after Hunt had left Parisi, that made Mrs. Manion perhaps the last contact Andrea had had before she disappeared. She might have said something, left some hint.

He spent nearly a half hour scanning through a selection of the hits—there were over seventy thousand of them, so anything greater than a cursory look was impossible, even after he winnowed his searches down to the narrowest parameters he could. The Manion name hadn't quite made it into the very pinnacle of the San Francisco pantheon inhabited by the Swigs and Gettys and Ellisons, but they seemed to be well on their way to getting there. Hunt already knew about their statewide—rumored soon to be nationwide—chain of discount specialty grocery stores. Likewise, in just the last couple of years, they had acquired huge brand recognition for their fledgling Manion Cellars label by producing some extremely cheap, remarkably high-value Napa cabernets and merlots. Hunt himself had a couple of bottles of their stuff in with the rest of his minimalist collection on the floor next to his refrigerator. The family had been among the biggest bidders at the Napa Valley Wine Auction for the past several years, last spring paying more than one hundred thousand dollars for a jeroboam-size bottle of '96 Screaming Eagle from the birth year of their younger son, Todd. In sports, aside from their involvement with the 49ers and NFL football, they owned a minor-league baseball team in Solano County and were big-time sponsors of the U.S. Winter Olympic Ski Team. The tragedy Hunt had vaguely remembered concerned their older son, Cameron, who'd died in a waterskiing accident just last summer. The twenty-four-year-old golden boy was a competitive racer who'd been training in Lake Berryessa for the Emerald Bay Classic at Lake Tahoe when he'd hit a submerged log at seventy miles per hour.

Hunt did quite a bit of this kind of computer work and knew exactly what he was looking for, and suddenly there it was. The Manions' private residence was the site of the Kidney Foundation dinner in 2000, and the society write-up of the event included the information that the home on Seaview Drive in the Seacliff neighborhood "commanded a stunning panoramic view from the Golden Gate to the Farallones."

Hunt punched in Mickey Dade's cell number again, and this time gave him his marching orders: Would he try to get out to Seacliff before it got dark, ask around if he had to, and get the exact address of the Manions' home? With that, Hunt would be able to find their personal telephone number, where he could then reach Mrs. Manion and maybe get a few words with her.

Finally, in his kitchen, suddenly ravenous, realizing that he hadn't eaten since the morning's *bao*, Hunt cut a three-inch chunk of dry salami off the roll that hung from a peg inside his refrigerator. It would have to do.

He had to move.

Hunt didn't go to the Little Shamrock much anymore. Directly across the street from Golden Gate Park on Lincoln and Ninth Avenue, the bar used to be the local hangout for him and Sophie, but he didn't live in the neighborhood anymore, and it really wasn't much of a destination place in its own right. Even if it had been, Hunt wouldn't normally have chosen to frequent it. He'd put away and buried that part of his life.

Still, tonight, no one had been home at Juhle's when he'd gone by. He cursed himself for not calling first, but he hadn't wanted to endure more scorn and perhaps rejection on the phone. If he simply showed up with another apology to his friend, though, he might get in the door. And from there make some kind of pitch for information. He wasn't, in fact, sure of exactly what he was going to say.

But the Shamrock was on this side of town, and now something else—the recent though mostly oft-repressed memories of his life back then, the photograph of Sophie at the bar—was drawing him back to revisit the old haunt.

On a Thursday night at seven thirty, Hunt expected that the place would be crowded wall-to-wall with people, which wouldn't have been saying much since on its best night the watering hole's maximum occupancy probably peaked at a hundred souls. Sophie and Hunt sometimes used to get in here when there were only a couple of customers before the cocktail hour, and it had always struck them as almost impossibly small for the flourishing concern which it obviously was—the establishment had first opened its doors in 1893 and had been in continous operation ever since.

The old wooden bar ran halfway to the back of the place. Directly in front of the bar, the place was only about eight feet wide. Three tiny tables with four chairs each provided some seating. The facing wall was further cluttered by antique bicycles and other turn-of-the-nineteenth-century memorabilia, including a grandfather clock that had stopped for the last time during the 1906 earthquake. In the back by the dartboards and jukebox, the room widened out a bit, but a couple of seating areas with sagging couches and over-stuffed chairs took up a lot more room than tiny cocktail tables would have and gave the spot a homey feel.

Now out the wide front window the sun cast its last long shadows on Lincoln. A couple in matching black leather sat on stools at the far end of the bar, nursing pints of stout. A lone dart thrower pegged in the back. Cyndi Lauper's "Time After Time" played quietly over the speakers. The television was dark, and no bartender trod the boards behind the bar.

Hunt took one of the stools nearest the door, wondering if he should just leave, unsure why he'd stopped by here in the first place. For most of a minute, he sat waiting and had just about made up his mind to go when the dart player ducked under the far end of the bar—"With you in a sec."

Parking his darts in the gutter, the bartender started toward him, and Hunt said, "Mr. Hardy?"

The man stopped, cocked his head. "Doctor Hunt," he said, then lowered his voice. "You can drop the Mr. Hardy when I'm here behind the bar. It's Diz. And what brings you all the way out to the frontier on this fine night?"

"I've got a better one," Hunt said. "What's a top-dog lawyer doing tending bar at a place like this?"

Dismas Hardy—Amy Wu's boss and Wes Farrell's partner—flashed a craggy grin. "I own some of this place," he said. "A quarter of it, to be precise."

"And you bartend part-time?"

"Very part-time. As in almost never. My brother-in-law's usually back here, but he's . . . well, he's doing a bit of rehab, and he asked me to fill in for a few days. I didn't realize you came in here."

"I don't, really. Not in a few years."

"Well"—Hardy threw a napkin down onto the bar—"you seem to be here now. So what're you drinking?"

"I'll have a beer. Tap. Bass."

"Coming up." Hardy walked to the spigots, drew two brews, then walked back, carrying both of them. He placed one on the napkin in front of Hunt and took a sip from the other, putting it down in the gutter. "So. You working tonight?"

"Not for money." Then. "You hear about Andrea Parisi?"

Hardy nodded. "Amy and Wes were telling me earlier. She still missing?"

"Yep."

"You're looking for her?"

"Starting, yeah. I was just with Wes and Amy at your offices, in fact."

"Doing what?"

"Putting them to work on it."

"I thought it went the other way. The law firms hire the investigators."

"Usually that's true." He hesitated, wondering if he was shooting himself in the foot. He and Hardy had always gotten along, but in Hunt's experience, the average managing partner usually wasn't overjoyed to hear about billable hours that didn't get billed to some client or another. "But we're all pretty worried." He ran through his quick analysis of Parisi's chances. "We figure we might have a day, maybe two."

"How long has she been gone?"

Hunt checked his watch. "Thirty hours, give or take. It doesn't look good, but at least her body hasn't turned up anywhere. On the slim chance . . ."

"Where are the cops on it?" Hardy asked.

"Missing Persons won't do anything for at least another day or two. But do you know Devin Juhle?"

"Sure. Homicide."

"Right. And, most of the time, a pal of mine." Hunt delivered it straight. "He considers her a suspect in the Palmer murders."

Hardy narrowed his eyes. "We're talking the same Andrea Parisi? Trial TV?"

"Right. So now Juhle wants her as badly as we do, maybe worse. I'm hoping to leverage him to do what Missing Persons won't."

"A homicide cop? And what do you want from him?"

"What he knows."

Hardy seemed to find that amusing. "And he's just going to tell you? How are you planning to make him do that?"

This was, of course, Hunt's problem. Especially after Juhle's last words to him. "We go back a ways," he said.

Hardy appeared to get a kick out of this. "Because you're friends, you're just going to ask him?"

"That was the original plan, but I knew a couple of things, and I didn't tell him right away. So now he thinks I was holding out on him."

"Sounds like you were."

"Well, there you go. Anyway, it's a problem."

"Well, the bad news," Hardy said, "is that he wouldn't tell you anything if you just asked, anyway. It's the same gene that predisposes these guys to homicide. He probably wouldn't tell his wife, either. The good news is it happens that I've had a little experience with exactly this sort of problem." He paused. "Abe Glitsky's one of my best friends." Glitsky was San Francisco's Deputy Chief of Inspectors. For a dozen or more years before that, he'd been the chief cop in the homicide detail.

"That's impossible," Hunt said. "You're a defense attorney."

"It is impossible," Hardy agreed genially enough. "If you knew Glitsky like I do—and count your lucky stars you don't—you'd know how impossible. But I'd be lying if I told you he hasn't been a help to me more than once."

"On the defense side?"

"Sometimes kicking and screaming, I might add. But, yeah."

"How did that happen?"

Hardy lifted his beer out of the gutter, took a sip. "When you can't just ask," he said, "you trade."

Hunt couldn't decide if what he liked the most about his Cooper was the turbocharged power; the cool, high-tech, vaguely Art Deco dashboard; or the fact that it could fit into parking places only a little bigger than the size of a toaster. He pulled up right in front of the familiar small house on Twelfth Avenue between Ortega and Noriega and parked between its driveway and the house next door, in maybe eight or nine feet of curb space. Though it was dark out now, he knew that the garages on either side and all the way up and down the block sported signs that read: DON'T EVEN THINK OF PARKING HERE! And in his own personal experience, he knew the home owners meant it. A couple of times, he'd hung half a foot over the outer lip of somebody's driveway and come out to find himself towed—one hundred and twenty-five bucks plus the ticket, thanks.

Juhle's home looked like all the other houses on the block—two-story stucco with four steps up to the front stoop, the built-in one-car garage taking up a third of the footprint. In the daylight, the house's fresh, bright green trim distinguished it somewhat from its neighbors, and at this time every spring, the flower boxes in the windowsills bloomed with daffodils, impatiens, and angel's hair. But by now it was a few minutes after nine, none of these amenities were visible, and it was just another shivering house squatting out in the fogbelt of the Sunset.

After the clear and cloudless day, the fog was in and now obscured most of the rest of the street. But he could see lights on inside at Juhle's. They'd gotten home.

As he mounted the front stoop, Hunt found himself fighting his nerves. Constant action since he'd finished his deposition work at McClelland's in the late afternoon had insulated him somewhat from his growing visceral worry—by now nearly a physical sickness—about what had happened to Parisi. With every minute, the odds that she was alive grew longer. And yet he couldn't accept her possible death, if only because he wanted to believe that life wouldn't do this to him again—give him hope, even a deluded perhaps foolish hope, only to steal it away.

All he knew was that he needed to find her. To find out, if nothing else, where it all could go with her. And without Juhle's help and even active cooperation, he didn't think it was going to happen.

He pushed the doorbell, heard the chimes within, and waited in the fog.

Connie met him at the door with a kiss on the cheek. "You've got guts, Wyatt, I'll give you that."

But then she led him back to the rest of the family. Juhle, his arm in his sling and his other hand in a bucket of ice, looked through him. The kids—Eric, Brendan, and Alexa—all jumped up from the kitchen table, where they were eating their pizza. Uncle Wyatt was a favorite. He often arrived laden with coins, candy, other treats for them, and tonight was no exception. For some reason, their parents tolerated these gifts from Hunt but from no one else, and it set a tone of acceptance. That, plus the fact that their father usually seemed looser when Hunt was around. Juhle would play games with them that he otherwise didn't have all that much time for—Foosball and Ping-Pong out in the garage, football or baseball catch out in the street, hoops on the driveway. Occasionally, the two men would play guitar together or listen to new CDs. Wyatt was cool.

Tonight after they'd pilfered his pockets for Necco wafers, the kids went back to their places. Hunt moved around behind them and pulled a quarter, one at a time, out of each child's ear. Eric was still in his Hornets uniform. "How'd you guys do tonight?" he asked him.

"We killed 'em, nine to two," the older boy replied. "Dad was coach. He let me pitch."

"How'd he get to be coach? He looks like he's hurting right now."

"He's okay," Alexa said. At seven years old, she was the queen of fatherly protection. "Nothing like Coach Doug."

"Are we talking about Mr. Malinoff?"

"Yep," Brendan said.

"What happened to him?"

Finally, Juhle relaxed the frown he'd been cultivating. "Pickle," he said.

"Malinoff played pickle?"

"In spikes," Eric said. "On the grass."

"You know pickle, right, Uncle Wyatt?"

"Sure, Brendan. In fact, I invented it. Run back and forth between bases, slide under the tag, right?"

Alexa caught him with a suspicious glare, turned to her father. "Did Uncle Wyatt really invent pickle?"

"If he says so," Juhle said, then added with some edge, "I know he wouldn't lie."

Hunt turned to Connie. "So what happened to Malinoff?"

"He challenged the kids. Said he'd give five bucks to anybody who could beat him."

"Daddy told him not to," Alexa said, "but Coach just called him a wimp. I heard him."

"He was kidding, honey," Connie said. "Just teasing. He knows your father's not a wimp. It was kind of an adult joke about how he hurt his arm, that's all."

"It wasn't funny." Alexa was in full pout. "I didn't like it."

"God didn't like it, either," Juhle said, "which is why he punished him."

"What did God do?" Hunt asked.

Connie was having trouble keeping a straight face. "He broke Coach's leg," she said.

"Ow!"

"That's what Doug said, too."

"Not exactly, Dad," Eric said.

"No, I know. And I bet Uncle Wyatt can imagine what he really said, too. But we don't use that kind of language, do we? It's bad sportsmanship. Right?"

To a chorus of "Rights," Juhle stood up, took the dish towel Connie held out for him, and wrapped it around his catching hand. "Okay, you guys, finish your pizza, and I hear there's still homework to be done. And no Neccos tonight, either. Con?"

"No Neccos," she repeated, " 'til tomorrow after school."

"Where are you and Uncle Wyatt going, Dad?" Brendan asked.

"Out to the living room," Juhle said, "for some private adult conversation."

"Dev, listen," Hunt was saying. "When you told me about it last night, maybe you don't remember, but you were all over the wife. Parisi wasn't any part of it, and even if I had thought about it and mentioned it to you, you would have said no way, that she was ancient history. If there was anything between Parisi and Palmer, they broke up six months ago. She is not jealous of Staci Rosalier all of a sudden now. The wife had the better immediate motive. Why else get 'em both to her house? Plus, you must admit, this isn't exactly something we've dealt with every day, you and me, withholding information. I didn't know it was information. Next time, I tell you everything before I think it. Promise. You'll be telling me to shut up before I've opened my mouth."

Juhle still didn't like it. His face hadn't softened except for the instant after the door to the kitchen had closed behind his family when he'd been referring to Malinoff and said, "It was a beautiful moment, I tell you. You should have seen it. The ambulance and everything." But after that, the fun was over.

Now he reclined—head back, feet up, eyes closed—in his big,

brown leather lounger. His features looked drawn with fatigue, pain, and irritation. Connie's footfalls came from the back of the house, and in a moment, she appeared with a glass of water and some pills. She looked at her husband first, then over to Hunt, who was sitting forward on one of the other chairs, elbows on his knees, jaw set, eyes bright, tightly wound.

"Excuse me," she said, "time for medication." She dropped the pills into Juhle's hand, waited while he threw them into his mouth, then handed him the water. Then she turned to Hunt. "These usually make him sleepy," she said, and walked out.

When the two men were alone again, Hunt said, "I'd hate to have her mad at me."

Juhle opened his eyes. "Don't fuck with your friends, their wives won't be mad at you."

"How many times you want me to apologize?" No answer. "Dev, I need your help."

"What? Finding Parisi? You're dreaming, Wyatt."

Suddenly remembering Hardy's advice, Hunt said, "Listen to me. I can help you, too."

Juhle let out a short, aborted chuckle. "Sure you can. And you're motivated, right? You find Parisi, you'll give her to me. No, if you find her, you'll hide her from me. Or she'll hide herself, keep herself hid is more like it."

"That won't happen. I'm giving you my word it won't happen. If she's findable, I can help you," he repeated.

With a sigh, Juhle brought his lounger back to a sitting position. He still looked weary, but there was a hint of interest. "Why are you going to do that, Wyatt? And first, I've got to believe that you *will* do that."

"I just gave you my word, Dev."

Finally, Juhle nodded. "All right. That leaves how."

Hunt let out a breath. "You know what I do for a living about half the time in my job: I find people. And right now I've got people talking to everybody she knew, everybody we can find, personally, firm, family, you name it. If she's dead, she's dead, and she'll probably turn up someday. But last I saw her, I guarantee you she wasn't going into hiding on this murder rap. Somebody picked her up, and I'm just praying right now that they didn't kill her right away. That's where I'm coming from. Have you heard anything about a ransom note? Did you track any credit card use yet? Any sign that she's on the run?"

"All that's classified."

"Okay, so do we have a deal, or what? I'm telling you, I'll give you everything I get, the minute I get it. But I need to know what you've got about Parisi, every little thing. If I'm missing something. Someplace I could be looking."

"And what would that be?"

"If I knew, I'd know, wouldn't I? But give me that and I could take Parisi off your plate entirely and leave you free for everybody else. Mrs. Palmer, whoever. But that's the other thing I can give you that you don't have and I really believe you need."

"What's that?"

"A partner."

Juhle narrowed his eyes, his mouth tight. "I've got a partner."

"Right. I've met him. He helping you much?"

"He's a cop."

"Yes, he is."

"I don't go behind his back."

"Of course not. Go in front of him. See if he notices. Meanwhile, you and me, we do what you and Shane used to do—try to figure this stuff out."

Juhle looked down at his swollen hand, closed it and opened it again a couple of times. Finally, he gave it up with a sigh. "No. No note. No credit cards. No cell phone. No nothing. And why do you think," he asked, "we haven't gotten any kind of line on Staci Rosalier's family?"

"So I've got Wes talking to Fairchild and Tombo about what she might have been doing Monday night, which could eliminate her from your equation all by itself. Meanwhile, Amy Wu's with Carla—" Hunt said.

"Parisi's secretary Carla? We talked to her today," Juhle said.

"She give you anything?"

"Pretty much the same timetable you've already got. Not much else."

"Okay, but speaking of the timetable, I've got Mickey Dade going to find out where the Manions live so I can get to Carol, the wife."

"You don't have to bother," Juhle said. "Shiu and I already talked to her today. She lives out in Seacliff. Incredible spread. We waltzed in like we own the place."

"How'd you do that?"

"It doesn't get talked about much out in the world, but all her security guards are off-duty San Francisco homicide inspectors."

"Even Shiu?"

"Only the best for the Manions, Wyatt. I'm probably the only cop in the detail she doesn't call by his first name. Shiu called on her security number, and we got the red carpet."

"See." They'd been talking the case for ten minutes or so and by now the friction had bled out of the room. Hunt was all the way back in his chair, legs crossed. "This is why we need to communicate on this. So what did Mrs. Manion know?"

"Basically nothing. She never saw her. Parisi never showed. That's a dead end."

"She tell you what they were supposed to be talking about?"

Juhle stared up at the ceiling, dredging it back. "She's a bigwig on some committee—the Friends of the Public Library? Something like that—Shiu's got it in his book, I'm sure. Anyway, they've got a fund-raiser later on in the summer, and they wanted Parisi to be, like, the local celebrity master of ceremonies, so she wanted to feel her out on it. I guess they liked her work on TV, the new face and all."

Hunt let out a breath, finally shook his head. "So she leaves her house, gets in her car, and vanishes?"

"Right. That's what we've got."

"You get her phone records?"

"Working on them, Wyatt. She just became a live suspect today. We should have something by tomorrow, Monday the latest."

This wasn't nearly soon enough for Hunt, but he had no say on it. "And you've talked to Palmer's office, too?"

By now, Juhle's pills and weariness were slowing him down. He took a couple of seconds to respond. "Yep. He was probably thinking about moving on the union, although Gary Piersall says it was a bluff."

"So where would Andrea play there?"

"I've been trying to work that connection all day. It's a dry well."

"How about if she thought she knew or had discovered who'd put the hit on Palmer? She goes to . . . what's his name, the union chief?"

"Jim Pine."

"Right. She goes to Pine—or not to Pine directly. Maybe even to one of her colleagues at Piersall, maybe talks about her suspicions. She's going to blow the whistle, and somebody decides they've got to stop her—"

Juhle interrupted. "You're stretching it pretty thin here, Wyatt. Although let me ask you one. The union connection with Jeannette Palmer?"

"Which is what?"

"Invisible at the moment, except in Shiu's mind. I'm asking your opinion about it: She finds out her husband is having this affair and decides to have him killed? She's heard all these stories about muscle in the union, and she knows where they live, maybe how she can get to them."

Hunt shook his head. "No offense to your partner, Dev, but no."

"Just 'no'?"

A nod. "Think about it. She even gets to step one, she's blackmail bait forever. The union wants to knock off the judge for whatever reason in the world, they'll just do it. They wouldn't need the wife to ask them. They wouldn't believe her if she did. It's just stupid."

"My partner doesn't think it's stupid. He thinks that's what probably happened. I've been trying to get behind it, but it's been giving me this monster headache." Juhle pulled his hand down across his face, pressed at his forehead.

"I think you're right about one thing, Dev. I think Andrea's connected somehow. But she's the third victim, not the suspect."

"Well," Juhle forced himself up and out of his lounger, "that's your theory. But either way, let's find her."

19 /

Farrell reached Fairchild on his cell phone and met him at Terrific Tennis, the large indoor facility at the edge of the Moscone Center. He was finishing up a set with someone who looked like a pro to Farrell's untrained eye—dressed like one, played like one. Farrell stood behind the Plexiglas in the hallway that ran along the back of the courts, caught the producer's eye, and five minutes later, the set—or the lesson—was over. Dripping in his whites with a towel draped over his shoulders, Fairchild stopped at the desk for a bottled water, then sat across from Wes at a wafer-size, waist-high table.

"You see that guy? Andy Bresson?" he began without preamble. "Forget the governor. He's the terminator. Six-oh, six-oh. Or should I say, oh-six, oh-six?"

"What's the difference?" Farrell asked.

"Depends on who's serving."

"But you were both serving."

"Yeah, it changes. I gather you don't play." Fairchild mopped his brow, took a long drink. "So," he said, "Andrea. Still missing, I presume?"

Farrell eyed him carefully. Fairchild wasn't even bothering to feign interest. "You don't seem too worried about her, I must say."

"That's because I'm not worried about her. A little pissed off perhaps, since she blew off the show tonight. But worried? No."

"Why not?"

"Because she's doing this to me. You hear we had some words the other night?"

"I heard it was a little more than that."

Fairchild shook his head. "She slapped me, that's all. She was drunk and chose to believe I'd been using her when it turned out I couldn't do much to help her score the New York gig. Now she's making the point that she can screw around with me and my job, too."

"That's what this is?"

"My call, anyway. Plus, she's getting some press, all this attention. It might even go national, she stays underground long enough. So she won't need me anymore. Na na na. Spoiled and idiotic, that's what she is."

"So you haven't seen her since she slapped you?"

"No."

"Talk to her?"

"She's not going to talk to me. I think she went crying to Wyatt Hunt."

"Well, he took her home, if that's what you mean. Now he's trying to find her. He's worried. We're all worried, tell the truth."

Fairchild went to put his sweaty hand on Farrell's arm, then stopped himself. "Wes, save yourself the grief. My guess is she's already called her mother, maybe her firm, to let 'em both know she's all right. Meanwhile, look at all the attention." He dried his hand, shook his head into his towel. "Trust me, she's just taking a few days."

"So you and her weren't out together Monday night?"

"Monday. Just a sec. What's today?"

"Thursday."

"So we had the fight on Tuesday, that's right. So Monday. No. We had a date, but she went in to work for a while and then called me from there and canceled."

"She say why?"

He shrugged. "I don't know. Something must've come up."

Farrell knew Richard Tombo from back when he'd been a newly minted assistant DA. They'd faced each other in court probably a dozen times. Since the younger man had gone out on his own, they'd run into each other regularly around the Hall of Justice, at Lou the Greek's. They seemed to inhabit the same basic restaurant and legal universe. Tombo worked out of a quaint, brass-railed, beautifully restored carriage house in the shadow of the Transamerica Pyramid. He was in his office, tie undone, suit jacket on a valet beside the desk. His legal pad was full of scribblings. Three empty

coffee mugs held down his desk blotter. A folder filled with plead-
ings was open in front of him.

"What do you mean, 'Why am I still here?' " Tombo said in his
modulated, professional announcer tone. "Wesley, my man, this is
when I work for my money."

"I thought they paid you princely sums to stand in front of the
camera down at the Hall."

"Princely enough. But that ends in a week, maybe two. Meanwhile," he gestured to the work before him, "I abandon my clients
and lo, I have no steady income. So no, I'm not even semiretired. I'm
still billing sixty, seventy."

Farrell remembered those days in his own life when he'd been
just starting out with one of the big corporate firms. He'd been
thrilled that they'd pay him the big bucks if he worked all the time.
And by *all the time*, they meant every single waking minute of every
day, including weekends and holidays. Billing twenty-two hundred
hours a year meant twelve-hour days, minimum. Now, looking at
the relatively young and still vibrant, energetic, charismatic Tombo,
he wondered how long he could keep it up. How long he'd want to.
How long his family could take it. "If this is billable time I'm on,"
he said, "I don't want to keep you."

"Not to worry," Tombo said. "If it's Andrea, whatever I can
do . . ." He picked up one of the mugs, saw that it was empty, put
it back down, and sighed. "So there's still no word."

Farrell shook his head. "I've got to tell you, Rich, it's somewhat
refreshing to hear your concern. I just got through with Fairchild,
and he thinks it's all about him."

Tombo waved that off. "That's just Spencer. He's in television.
He thinks everything is all about him."

"So you don't think that?"

"No. Not at all. She's not going to miss a scheduled shoot, Wes.
It's not in her bones."

"That's what I'd always thought, too. All of us—Wyatt Hunt,
Amy, me. Hunt's trying to find a way to get some police cooperation, although last we heard from them, they thought she might be
on the run."

"From what?"

"Them. The cops." A pause. "They apparently think she might
have killed the judge and his girlfriend."

"No, really?"

"Really. So it would kind of help if you, for example, could remember anything about Monday night, since you were with her un-

til five or so for the wrap-up, right? Just tell me you guys all went out to dinner and burned down the town."

Tombo thought a minute, reached for his mug again, this time grabbed it, and stood up. "No," he said, pouring another cup over at a sideboard, "that was Tuesday, wasn't it? You and me and all of us at Sam's? Her fight with Spencer?"

"Right. But I'm talking Monday."

Tombo cricked his back, a lion stretching, then settled more comfortably against the counter. "Okay." He closed his eyes, brought the coffee to his mouth with a loud slurp. "No," he said at last. "Dinner with a client. I remember because Spencer originally had had other plans for the two of them."

"That's what he told me. Do you remember who the client was?"

"I never knew, so it's not a matter of remembering. But I don't think she mentioned it. And, Wes? I don't think I have to familiarize you with the old dinner with a client trick, do I?"

"You got that sense Monday?"

"I can't say it was as strong as a sense. She just dropped the excuse early enough, it could have been preemptive, that's all. The New York thing was coming to a head. Maybe she saw the writing on the wall and didn't want to face it yet with Spencer."

Farrell said, "You know anybody who might have wanted to hurt her? Anybody she was afraid of?"

"Andrea? Afraid. No. And I can't imagine anybody wanting to hurt her."

But his brow clouded briefly, and Farrell saw it. "What?"

Tombo hesitated again, then drew a deep breath. "Just something Spencer mentioned this morning, that maybe she'd stumbled on some great story, some big scoop."

"About what?"

"Dirty operations—I guess wet ops, even—being run out of the prisons. Except that, as I told Spencer, for about a zillion excellent reasons, that can't happen."

"But Andrea thought it could? Or it was actually happening?"

"All I can say, Wes, is she never mentioned it to me."

Wu was with Jason Brandt and a distraught Carla Shapiro at the secretary's apartment on Grove at Masonic when she got Farrell's call from Tombo's office about Andrea's possible Monday night meeting with a client. They sat around a kitchen table on the fourth floor of the older apartment building. The floor was black-and-white checkered linoleum, the counters white tile. The sweating window over the sink looked into an open shaft and then across fifteen or twenty feet of open space to the kitchen of another mirror-image apartment. Getting the dishes cleaned and out of the sink didn't appear to be a priority either for Carla or her roommate, who was out for the night.

Wu closed her cell phone. "That was somebody else we're working with, Carla. He says Andrea might have had a client meeting Monday night, too. Does that ring a bell at all?"

The poor young woman was drained with anxiety and lack of sleep. She'd changed from her prim and preppy work clothes into some oversize, formless gray sweats, which diminished her underweight frame even further. Her reddened eyes seemed to plead that she'd taken all of the questioning she could handle, but she steeled herself for another effort. "God, Monday," she said. "I don't even remember Monday anymore."

Because Andrea would often call her after normal business hours, Carla had gotten into the habit of keeping her desk calendar up to date on her Palm Pilot. They'd already gone over Andrea's appointments for the past couple of weeks, but now she dutifully punched in Monday again, scrolled to the evening, sighed. "I don't have anything for it in here."

"Maybe we can talk about Tuesday, then." Brandt spoke in an understanding, even sympathetic tone. "Let's start with the last time you saw Andrea, how's that? And that was Tuesday, right?"

"Right. It was, let's see, about ten thirty or eleven. We'd all just heard the news about Judge Palmer, and I went into her office to see if she was all right." Carla looked to each of them. "She wasn't. She was just sitting there in a daze."

"Crying?" Wu asked.

"No. Like she was in shock. She said she'd just seen him the day before."

"There you go," Brandt said. "Monday."

Carla nodded. "Okay. Okay, now I'm remembering. She was at lunch with the judge that Monday."

"Was that their semiregular monthly status conference?" Wu asked.

"Yes. They usually had it on Mondays."

Brandt kept it on point. "Do you remember her coming back after lunch?"

Carla closed her eyes for a moment, trying to bring it back. When she spoke, it was with a kind of relief. "All right. She did come back. She had a meeting in his office with Mr. Piersall, which was the norm after she saw the judge. It went on for a while, longer than usual."

"Do you know why?" Wu asked.

"I think so. Evidently there was a problem at Pelican Bay—you know, the prison—last week that got the judge really upset. But she barely mentioned that to me, other than saying she had to talk to Mr. Piersall about it a little. So by the time she's done with that it's now almost three fifteen, and the Trial TV limo comes to get her at three thirty." Suddenly she gave a little start, looked off into the middle distance. "Oh."

Wu came forward. "What?"

"This is probably nothing, but I just remembered, Betsy Sobo."

"Who is?" Brandt asked.

"Another associate. Upstairs."

Wu asked, "What about her?"

"She called twice while Andrea was with Mr. Piersall. Andrea had asked her if she'd come down and talk to her about something. So she'd blocked out a half hour and was a little upset when Andrea wasn't back from Mr. Piersall."

Brandt asked, "Do you know what Andrea wanted to talk about with her?"

Wu asked, "Were they friends or something like that?"

Carla shook her head. "No to both. You know, we have a hundred attorneys. It's not like everybody knows everyone else. I don't think I've ever seen her. She's not in the union group and works on another floor. I didn't know Andrea even knew her, but I guess she did."

Wu pressed. "And she'd made an appointment to see her?"

Brandt amplified. "This was after she'd come back from seeing the judge?"

"I'm not sure of that. It might have been anytime, really. But it was for that afternoon."

"But they didn't get together that day?" Brandt asked.

"No. I know they didn't. Andrea ran out of time."

"So maybe they connected that night." Wu's color was up. If Andrea had met this Sobo person for any length of time on Monday night, she would no longer be a suspect in Palmer's murder. "Can you get in touch with her?" she asked.

"Now?" Carla glanced up at the wall clock: 9:40. "I'm sure I can somehow."

Carla obviously had tracked down associates before. She called the firm's night number, got the directory, connected to Sobo, who, of course, as a young associate was on permanent call, never off the clock.

Wu punched in her pager number, and they all waited in a kind of suspension for about three minutes. And then Wu's cell phone rang.

"This is Betsy Sobo," the voice said. "Can I help you?"

"Betsy, hi. This is Amy Wu. You don't know me, and I'm sorry to bother you at this hour, but I'm an attorney with Freeman Farrell and I'm over here now at Carla Shapiro's apartment. Andrea Parisi's secretary?"

If Sobo had been angry at Parisi on Monday, there was no sign of it now in her voice. "Oh, God. Have they found her?"

"No. Not yet. That's what I'm working on. You had an appointment with Andrea on Monday afternoon, is that right?"

"Yes. I said I'd give her a half hour, but she . . . she got busy and couldn't make it."

"So here's my question. Did you reschedule or anything? For Monday night by any chance?"

"No."

In the cold, humid kitchen, Wu's shoulders fell. "So you didn't see her Monday night?"

"No. What would I have seen her about?"

"That's the other thing I wanted to ask. Why she wanted to meet with you."

"I didn't know that, either, specifically. She just asked me if I could spare some time while she picked my brain, and I said sure, she being such a star and all."

"Did she say what she wanted to pick your brain about?"

"Again, not specifically. She was rushing out to a meeting with Mr. Piersall."

"So she called you after her appearance before Judge Palmer?"

"I don't know about that." Suddenly, it hit her. "Wait a minute. You mean *the* Judge Palmer? Who got shot? You're saying Andrea was with him on Monday?"

"Yes."

"Oh, my God." The voice took on a desperate edge. "You're saying she's probably dead, too, then, isn't she?"

"We don't know. We hope not. We're trying to find her." Wu

hesitated. "I'm assuming she hasn't gotten in touch with you since Monday, either, is that right?"

"Yes. I mean yes, that's right. No, I haven't heard from her."

"And you have no idea what she wanted to talk to you about?"

"Well, some idea, of course. I figured it must have been something about some kind of family benefits with the union. That's what she worked on."

"But Carla tells us you weren't on the union team?"

"Right, I know. We're the poor stepchildren of the firm. But still, I guess I'm kind of the house whiz kid on family law."

"Family law?"

"You know—divorce, annulments, adoption, custody, restraining orders—where those good times just keep on comin'."

20 /

Checking his calls driving back from Juhle's, Hunt got the message from his answering machine at work. "Wyatt Hunt, this is Gary Piersall. I'd like to talk to you as soon as you can get back to me. No matter what time. It's about Andrea Parisi, and it could be very important." He left three telephone numbers.

He got him on the first one. Piersall was still at the office and told him to come on down as soon as he could get there. He should just park in one of the partners' spaces under the building. They were marked.

Hunt checked his watch. It was closing in on ten thirty. "Do you want to tell me about it on the phone?" he asked.

"Are you on a cell?" Piersall asked.

"Yeah. In my car."

A pause. "No. I don't think so."

Hunt rang off, intrigued. Piersall was a smooth and experienced attorney, used to going up against some big boys. If he was suddenly paranoid, that in itself was instructive. But if Hunt was going to be meeting with Piersall now and maybe learning something he'd have to move on, there was a very good chance he wasn't going to be able to stick with his original plan. Which had been to talk to Mary Mahoney, the witness who'd identified Staci Rosalier, during her nighttime shift at MoMo's. A minute later, he was back on the phone, talking to Tamara, turning her and Craig loose on it.

His sense of urgency was increasing with each passing hour. If Andrea were already dead, time would not matter. Maybe this was his way of putting off that ultimate acceptance, but whatever this need to move was, he was not remotely inclined to fight it. He would find out as much as he could as quickly as he could, from whatever source he could tap. It was the only thing—if, in fact, there were any hope left at all—that could possibly, possibly make any difference. More, it was the only thing he could do.

The garage elevator in Piersall's building automatically stopped on the ground floor, and Hunt got out there and jogged to the guard's station in the vast, glass-enclosed lobby. Piersall had already called down and told them to expect him, and as he signed in, the guard called up and announced that he'd arrived. Jogging back to another of the four banks of elevators—floors 11–22—Hunt almost allowed himself to feel a glimmer of hope. Clearly, Piersall had something.

The elevator opened onto a reception area that was designed to impress. The fog hadn't made it this far inland, and the city glittered all around and below out the floor-to-ceiling glass. A massive, shining waist-high bar of finished redwood, probably thirty feet long, gleamed even in the dim pinpoint after-hours lights. Several trees grew from their enormous urns and threw subtle shade patterns across the redwood, over the cushy wall-to-wall carpet.

Keyed up as he was, Hunt almost jumped as Piersall slid off the plain desktop where he'd been sitting in the semidarkness.

"Thanks for coming down on so little notice. I appreciate it. And let me make this clear: You are working for this firm on some CCPOA matters, and what I am telling you now, I tell you as my investigator, so it's all covered by the attorney-client privilege."

The man exuded tension. Hunt had never before seen him without his tailored suit precisely arranged. Now he wore neither coat nor tie, and he'd unbuttoned the shirt at his throat, both sleeves at the wrists, and rolled them up. "You want to sit down?" Piersall walked back over to one of the waiting couches and plopped his long, lean frame down into it. Without waiting for Hunt to settle, he began to talk. "I don't know exactly how to put this in a favorable light, but by now you've done enough work for us, you know how it is sometimes." He inhaled, then blew out a stream of air. "I had to lie to the police this afternoon."

"What about? Andrea?"

"Not directly, no." He hesitated. "About our main client, which as you know is the prison guards' union. I told the inspectors looking into Judge Palmer's murder that they didn't have an enforcement arm. Which, of course, they do."

"The cops suspect that anyway, sir. Your telling them one way or another isn't going to change anything."

"No, but you see the position I'm in. I represent these people. I

can't very well sic the cops on them. That's what they pay us all—
and very handsomely as you know—to keep from happening. Look
around us here, all of this comes from CCPOA money, all of it."

Silence. Hunt didn't need to look and verify what he already
knew. He said, "You think they've done something to Andrea."

Another lengthy silence. Piersall exhaled. "Have you ever heard
of Porter Anderton?"

"No."

Piersall clucked in frustration. "Doesn't seem anybody has.
Porter Anderton was the DA in Kings County up for reelection last
year. But he'd made the mistake of investigating some allegations of
prisoner abuse by some guards at Corcoran, then moving forward
with the cases. Twenty-six guys."

"Twenty-six guys? All prison guards. What'd they do?"

A weak smile. "You mean what did they *allegedly* do, remember.
These are our boys. We defend them. These particular guys evidently had a tough day out with their work crew, so when the crew
were getting off the bus back at the yard, they needed to let off a little steam and choked and punched and beat up their prisoners, who
by the way were still apparently shackled."

"Cute story," Hunt commented.

"Yeah."

"Just out of curiosity," Hunt said, "how many cases like that do
you get every year?"

"This firm? Against all prison employees? About a thousand."

Hunt whistled. "That's every year?"

"Ballpark. Of course, most of those don't get beyond the investigation stage. For obvious reasons," Piersall added, "like cons as
witnesses deciding they couldn't exactly remember what they'd seen
after all."

"So what about this Anderton?"

"Ah, well, Porter went all gung ho on these guys, the guards. He
decided they had a huge problem with the whole correctional system at Corcoran, which was in his jurisdiction, and he was the one
who was going to stop it. He got in touch with George Palmer, too."

"And something bad happened to Porter." Not a question.

Piersall nodded. "Huge coincidence, isn't it? He had a hunting
accident. Shooter never found. Just one of those things."

"Imagine that. And what about his prosecutions?"

"Well, we're their attorneys. We did our job. The cases fell
apart."

"Yeah, but a bus full of victims? Didn't any of the other guards see this happen, too?"

Piersall shrugged. "The other guards, no. You ask any prison guard if he's ever seen one of his colleagues cross the line into brutality, you get a categorical denial every time. It never happens. And in their defense, I must say that if your job is making some three-hundred-pound gorilla get in his cell when he doesn't want to, you might have to get a little creative from time to time. But the inmates? They all eventually decided it was really in their best interests to just let the matter slide."

"All of them?"

For a response, all Piersall could manage was a thin, tight smile.

"So you're thinking," Hunt said, "that Palmer, and maybe Andrea . . . ?"

"I don't know. I don't know. I almost can't bear to think about it, to tell you the truth." Piersall's head hung as though by a single thread in his neck. "I've worked with and built a career around these people for the past fifteen years. My family has gone on vacations with Jim Pine's family. I don't want to believe he'd order what I can't help but think he might have."

"But why now?"

"That's just it. Just now is why it's suddenly feasible. I don't know if you've been following it, but the prison system's had a bad few weeks. They just indicted eight guards at Avenal for blood sport. . . ."

"What's that?"

"Human cockfights. Gladiator contests to the death."

While Hunt tried to fit this degree of organized brutality into his worldview, Piersall continued, "On top of that, we had four inmate deaths at Folsom. . . ."

"In one week? How did that happen?"

Again, the tight smile. "One bad fall. One complication from—I'm not joking—a pulled tooth. And two pneumonias that didn't get diagnosed in time, which isn't much of a surprise considering the head physician up there doesn't have a license to practice in hospitals anymore. But, hey," he added with a bitter laugh, "at least no shootings, so it wasn't the guards."

"Does that happen a lot? I thought that was mostly the movies, guards shooting prisoners?"

"Depends on where you happen to be locked up. Here in California, happens about once every two months. Rest of the country, maybe once a year, and that's usually only if you're actually about to kill somebody else. In any case, the situation is bad enough that Palmer's already appointed both an investigator and a special master to get a plan going, how to deal with the constitutional issues of prosecuting these things. You want more?"

"I think I'm getting the picture."

"Well, but you need the last piece, which just came to a head over this last weekend. Palmer had ordered an audit. . . ."

"So he's all over this, isn't he?"

"Oh, yeah. He's the man—or was—no doubt about it. Anyway, a while ago, he got wind of money being laundered through the prisons, so he ordered an audit on the prisoners' books at Pelican Bay."

"I don't know what they are, prisoners' books."

"Inmate trust accounts. All prisoners get one so their friends or family can get them money inside to buy stuff—food, bathroom supplies. That stuff's legit at the commissary. Under the table, of course, you've got cigarettes, dope, booze, women, boys, whatever they can score."

"This is in the prisons?"

"Right."

"Pelican Bay? Toughest lockup in the country?"

"That's the one."

"With the guards there?"

"Yeah. Probably cutting half the deals, taking a percentage on all of them."

Hunt had to break the tension. "You're not making this up?"

It brought back the tight smile. "So what did the audit disclose? Half the guys in the SHU—the Security Housing Unit—meanest place on campus, trust me, half of the books on these guys, had over twenty thousand dollars in them. Two of them had over forty thou."

"Thousand?"

"Thousand."

"That'll buy a lot of Snickers," Hunt said. "How'd they get that kind of money?"

"You'll love this. It's Eme."

"It's getting so I need a scorecard. Who is Emma?"

"No, no. EME. Mexican Mafia. Bad, bad, bad dudes, the worst. Their guys are all over the state but mostly down south—I'm talking dealers on street corners—they're paying protection to the EME heavyweights in the joint. So it's just another extortion racket, but it seems to bring in big money, which then goes back out to buy

THE HUNT CLUB / 179

more drugs or support the con's family. I don't know, maybe they send their kids to college with it. But the point is it's large, and by the time it goes out, it's clean. Laundered through the prison."

"Jesus."

"Yeah, well, you put all this together. The audit was the last straw, and Palmer finally ran out of patience. He had his office drafting up an emergency order to federalize the entire state prison system, which meant taking the union out of the equation. He had some jurisdiction issues, but it's not impossible he would have had the damn thing signed by now."

"Except he got killed."

"Right. Except that." Laying it all out seemed to have calmed Piersall's nerves to some degree, but now the reality of his situation settled on him heavily again. He came forward on the couch, feet flat on the floor, elbows resting on his knees, his shoulders sagging under the load. "I've been sitting in my office since early today." He was whispering, perhaps afraid of being heard even up here. "Ever since I heard that Andrea was missing. I just don't know what I'm going to do, except I know I can't go to the police." He looked up across the space between them. "I'll be honest with you. I'm scared shitless."

To Hunt, this seemed like a justified response. He'd be scared, too. Perhaps he should be now, though he wasn't. All the prison stuff felt far removed from him. Although if Andrea was involved in it, he knew that this wasn't the case. He was in up to his neck. "I'm assuming," he said, "that Pine knew about the judge's order."

Piersall nodded. "We called him from my office, as soon as Andrea told me about it. This was early Monday afternoon. So now look at this." From his shirt pocket, he took a small newspaper clipping. "Yesterday's *Chronicle*."

Hunt took it. He had to stand up and move under one of the lights to read it.

INMATE LAST SEEN GOING FOR A SMOKE

A 35-year-old ex-convict who recently had violated his parole escaped yesterday from San Quentin, where he was awaiting transport to Vacaville State Prison, when he left his cell in midafternoon, apparently with permission to go smoke a cigarette.

Although a tracking canine unit was dispatched to the scene, the dogs were apparently unable to pick up any scent of Arthur Mowery, and in response, the Department of Corrections has expanded its search to outlying counties.

Mowery was originally arrested in July of 1998 for burglary and possession of a firearm by a felon and, since that time, has been paroled twice. Both times he was re-arrested for violating his parole.

Hunt looked up. "Yesterday's *Chronicle*. That makes the escape Monday afternoon."

Piersall lifted, then dropped his head. "Yes, I noticed that."

Coming back to his own seat, Hunt said, "So what do you want me to do? You think this guy Mowery is . . . ?"

Piersall held up a restraining hand. "I don't know," he said. "That's my mantra for this whole situation. I don't know anything about him, except what you've just read. But I do know that most of the work you've done for us, you got through Andrea. Her secretary told me that your office had called several times asking about her." He drew a deep breath, finally made eye contact. "Look, Wyatt, I can't be any traceable part of anything that results in problems for the union. I want you to understand that perfectly. But someone needs to know about all this if it's hurt Andrea. Someone needs to look into it. You seemed the logical choice."

"Okay, I'll buy that. But how do you read this?" Hunt asked.

"I don't think . . . I know that Jim Pine put Mowery on the payroll for a couple of months several years ago, after he got paroled the first time."

"On the payroll doing what?"

Clearly, this confession was weighing heavily on Piersall. He wiped the shine off his forehead. "Security. He went up the second time because he got a little too enthusiastic. That's when I heard his name the first time. I couldn't believe Pine had hired him on the books, and we had a discussion about it. It couldn't happen again. You hear what I'm saying?"

"I think so."

"But he got paroled again."

"During the campaign season," Hunt said, "when there were all the problems."

"Correct. And he's been out ever since, until last Saturday when he got violated back in again—I checked when I saw that article. For the record, I think the escape was legitimate."

"So what happened, you think?"

"I think his controller gave him the job to kill Palmer, and he decided the job was too hot for him. I mean, killing a federal judge isn't vandalism to a campaign headquarters. Mowery said no, and they violated him back in for disobeying."

"And what about the breakout?"

"He either got the message that they were serious, and he was going down for hard time, so he changed his mind, or he broke out on his own."

"So this kind of activity is really going on? This is what Andrea had been looking into?"

"Maybe. She mentioned the possibility to me on Monday. She didn't know about Mowery, though. Not by name, anyway."

"Did you mention her suspicion to Pine?"

Miserable, Piersall pulled at the sides of his face. "Maybe enough for him to get the idea."

Craig Chiurco and Tamara Dade came across exactly like what they were, a couple of young lovers. They had known each other—both working with Hunt—for almost two years but were still in their first six months as sweethearts. This was the first time Wyatt had assigned them to the same job, and it had the feel of a date about it, especially here at MoMo's, which neither of them felt they could afford to frequent in their regular lives. But they were here now, on the job, long after the dinner crowd had gone home.

Which didn't mean the place was empty and dragging by any means—to the contrary, the meeting and greeting seemed to be at a high pitch.

This meant that Mary Mahoney wasn't going to be able to get with them for a while. After she'd talked to Hunt and gotten his instructions, Tamara had called to make sure that Mary was working tonight. And then they'd gotten themselves a bit turned out and cruised downtown.

Now, by the front door so they wouldn't miss Mary if she forgot that she'd promised to see them, Tamara sipped a cosmo, and Chiurco a gin and tonic. It was a good night for celebrity sightings—they spotted Robin Williams and Sean Penn in separate parties at the back. The mayor, Kathy West, was holding court at a large table by the front windows. They were just trying to identify who was sharing the table with her when a well-formed black man walked by them on the way to the men's room. Chiurco pointed and said to her, "Jerry Rice."

"That isn't Jerry."

"Number eight-oh in the flesh. Bet?"

She held out a hand, palm up, and paused. "Five bucks," she said.

He raised his hand and slapped it down on her own gently. "Five it is." They turned to their drinks, each harboring smiles as Mary Mahoney emerged from the crowd in the bar and came over to them. "I don't know if it was going to free up here for a couple more hours, so I asked Martin—my manager—if I could take a break since it was about Staci. He was cool, but it can't be too long, okay?" There wasn't another free stool to be had, so Chiurco got up and offered her his, asking her at the same time if he'd just seen Jerry Rice walk by.

"Oh, yeah, that's him. He's in here all the time."

Chiurco flashed his girlfriend a smug little grin, and the waitress said, "I still can't believe we traded him, you know. That was so dumb."

"I don't know," Chiurco said. "I've got to believe it's better than the Giants trading *for* all these guys who are at the end of their careers, instead of trading them away."

"Yeah, but Jerry. It's like if they would have traded away Montana."

"I never would have traded either one," Tamara said. "And now I'd let Jerry play until he didn't want to anymore, then make him a coach and keep him around forever."

"Then rename the park after him." Chiurco, having fun, going with the moment, letting the ice break naturally.

"I like it." Mahoney nodded. "Rice Park? Rice Field?"

"How about *The* Rice Field?" Tamara asked. "The Rice Field."

"Perfect," Mahoney said. "We'll tell him when he comes back."

"Except he's not a Niner anymore," Chiurco said.

Mahoney made a sad face. "Oh, yeah. That." With hardly a pause, she switched gears. "So you guys said you're with a private investigator, not the police?"

"Right," Tamara said. "The Hunt Club." She had a card with her name on it and presented it to her. "Right now we're hunting for Andrea Parisi."

Mahoney wore her expressions on her sleeve; now she looked a question. "The trial person? I saw that on TV, but I didn't really . . . she's really missing?"

"Why wouldn't you believe it?" Chiurco put in.

A shrug. "No real reason. I mean, she just missed one show,

right? And they only had it on one channel. I thought it was probably some ratings thing."

"No," Tamara said. "She's really missing. Since yesterday afternoon."

"And she's got something to do with Staci?"

Tamara kept it low-key. "We don't know. That's what we're trying to find out."

"Evidently," Chiurco said, "Staci had one of Andrea's business cards in her wallet."

"That's it? That's the connection?" Reaching down into her apron, she pulled out a thick deck of business cards and placed it on the table. "That's tonight," she said. "That's every night." She took Tamara's card and placed it on the top of the stack. "Now you're in it." She turned to Chiurco. "You got one, you can buy in, too. I hope that's not all you have."

Tamara, cool and elegant, took a sip of her drink. "Not exactly."

Chiurco leaned in, elbows on the high table. "So we're trying to figure out if there was some connection between all three of them. If Staci knew Andrea, for example."

"She never said anything about that to me." Mahoney felt on firm ground here. "And she would have. Definitely, I think. She was a big Trial TV fan."

"So you two were close?" Chiurco asked.

Just like that, the liquid eyes threatened to overflow and she dabbed underneath them.

They waited.

Mahoney sighed, sighed again, then shrugged. "I was nice to her when she first came on here, and maybe that hadn't been so normal for her in her life before. That's the impression I got anyway."

"So you didn't know her before she started working here?" Tamara asked.

"No."

"Do you know if she grew up here in the city?"

"I don't think so. Just the last couple of years. Before that, I don't know."

"Because," Tamara continued, "no one has turned up from her family. The police haven't been able to get any kind of background on her yet."

The waitress frowned. "Nothing?"

"Not a thing."

"That's just so wrong." She brightened for a second. "But wait.

I know she has . . . had, I mean, a younger brother. She had his picture in her room."

"Did you ever meet him?"

"No."

"How about his name?" Tamara was carrying on the interrogation while Chiurco stood, arms crossed, letting her go with it.

"I don't know what it is," Mahoney said. "She just called him her brother." She looked over at the bar; she'd been on break about long enough and this brother stuff wasn't going to help Staci or find Andrea. "We never really talked about him. I just saw the picture and asked who he was and she said, 'Oh, that's my brother.' We didn't really go into it. He was just her brother."

"This couldn't have been her first waitress job," Chiurco said, taking a different slant, trying to get Mary back into it.

"No. She worked, I think, at a Thai place out on Ocean. She was going to school at City College and lived out on that side of town before she got the place here."

"What's here?" Tamara asked.

Mahoney pointed behind them out the window. "Right there. Those condos just across the street. The judge got it for her."

"We're almost done, Mary," Chiurco said. "Can you try to remember? Did Staci ever mention Andrea Parisi to you at all, in any context?"

Her collagen-enhanced lips tightened with a few seconds of concentration. "I'm sorry, but I don't really remember anything like that."

"Okay, last one," Tamara said. "Is there anything you remember about Staci that you think might help us? Any reason somebody might have wanted to kill her?"

"I just can't believe anybody wanted to kill her. I think it must have been all about the judge, and she just happened to be there."

"But to your knowledge," Chiurco added, "had she ever gone there before, to his house?"

"No. I'm pretty sure of that, actually. She would have mentioned it."

Tamara seemed to be asking it as much of herself as of Mahoney. "So why then?"

"I don't know." Mahoney offered a broken smile. "Why any of it, you know?"

21 /

Hunt and Piersall rode down to the main lobby together in silence, then took the walk around to the basement elevator, got in, and Hunt pressed the button marked "4," where he thought he remembered parking. Still without a word, Piersall reached around him and hit "5."

When the door opened, Hunt stepped out and quickly looked both ways. The only car on that level was a black Miata. He didn't see his own distinctive car and stepped back inside the elevator. At "5," they both got out. At this time of night, theirs were the only two cars on that level. Piersall had put on his suit coat again and carried a large briefcase. He beeped open the trunk of his Lexus, dropped the briefcase inside, and went around to his driver's door. There, he paused, seemed to consider saying something, but instead merely gave Hunt a minimal nod, opened the door, and got in.

Hunt sat in his own front seat, trying to make some decision about what to do next. Next to him, he was vaguely aware of Piersall's car backing out of its spot, then driving off.

While all of Piersall's information about the CCPOA might be relevant to Judge Palmer's murder, Hunt couldn't quite get into focus how it could help him find Andrea. Taking the newspaper clipping from his shirt pocket, he reread it for the fourth or fifth time, wondering what it meant.

If anything.

If, as Piersall seemed to believe, this escaped convict Mowery had anything to do with Palmer's murder, *and* further if Mowery had come to set his sights on Andrea, then Hunt had little doubt that she would, in fact, be dead by now.

But that was a lot of *ifs*.

None of them contemplated the reality that Hunt had chosen to believe and act on—that somehow she was still alive. Though as each hour passed, that position became more difficult to sustain. He knew that he would have to call Juhle first thing in the morning and convey Piersall's information, but none of that seemed capable of helping him in his primary objective. Which even now he was beginning to recognize as more of an irrational hope than a realistic possibility.

But until she was found, while she might still be alive, he couldn't abandon the pursuit.

Alone on this parking level, down in the bowels of the building, Hunt suddenly understood with a jolt something that had been nagging at him. Hitting the ignition and throwing the car into reverse, he peeled out with a screech of rubber, got to the end of his row, and turned up, following the exit sign.

Stopping at the entrance to level four, he drove down to the elevator bank and pulled into the space next to the Miata he'd briefly glimpsed on the elevator ride down when the doors had opened and he'd stepped out for a moment to look for his own car.

Getting out of his Cooper, he went to the Miata driver's window and peered in. There was nothing to identify the owner—no purse, no article of clothing, no junk. Just black leather seats. He went around to the back and checked the license plate, trying to remember if he'd even glanced at Andrea's plates when the car had been in her garage. But for the life of him, he couldn't dredge up anything he recognized.

But his adrenaline was up, and though it was irrational, he *knew*. This was her car.

The scenario flickered in his mind, frames in a silent movie. She'd come to the office on Wednesday after all, not driven directly to the Manions. Her assailant therefore had very possibly not killed her on sight—certainly not by gunshot, anyway, not in the middle of an afternoon in what would have at that time been a crowded parking structure. But had taken her somewhere, where conceivably she might still be alive.

Hunt had to take the elevator back up to the lobby again and get outside before he could get reception on his cell phone. Standing on the dark and empty sidewalk, he listened to the rings on the other end of the line. "Come on, come on, come on. Pick up. Connie! I know, I'm sorry, but it's important. I need to talk to Dev."

* * *

Juhle wasn't the happiest Hunt had ever heard him with the idea of running the license plate at this ungodly hour to find out whom the car belonged to, but by the time he called Hunt back, having gotten somebody on the night shift at Central Station to do the two-minute computer check, he sounded wide awake. It was Andrea's car all right.

While he waited for the first black-and-white to arrive, Hunt used the time to check in with his troops.

Farrell, smart man, was off the clock, his phones either turned off or unplugged, and Hunt left a message, calling a meeting for the morning on Sutter Street at eight o'clock sharp.

Amy and Jason were still awake and watching television, having drawn blanks from Carla Shapiro. Amy mentioned the tenuous, tantalizing near meeting with Betsy Sobo, perhaps on family-law/union-benefits issues, that Parisi had scheduled and then bailed on for Monday afternoon. Brandt and Wu also reported that by now all the local television channels had picked up the story of Andrea's disappearance and were giving it a lot of prominence—they were watching *News 4 Late Edition* now, and the story was heading up the hour. Amy had also called Parisi's mother, who had already been contacted by several media types. She was now distraught and had no idea where her daughter was or what could have happened to her.

Tamara and Chiurco didn't have much to offer, either, on any possible connection between Staci Rosalier and Andrea Parisi. Hunt only now remembered that he hadn't yet caught up with Mickey Dade, who didn't seem to be answering his cell phone either.

Hunt left a message, asking Mickey to check out Thai restaurants on Ocean Avenue that might have once had a waitress named Staci Rosalier. He knew that if this trail grew hot at all, Juhle would find a way to get some manpower on that aspect of it, and Mickey's work would be largely redundant.

But Hunt couldn't think of any other assignment for the cabbie before the first patrol car finally arrived. It really hadn't been that long since he'd woken up Juhle—maybe twenty minutes. He met the police vehicle at the garage entrance and led the way down. The uniformed officers had him move his own car while they laid out the yellow tape around the Miata. Treating the car as a potential crime scene, which perhaps it was.

Juhle pulled up—no Shiu, no comment—eight or ten minutes later. A CSI unit was on the way to do a once-over before they towed Andrea's convertible downtown. If there was anything on or in the car, Juhle was confident that they'd find it. At this time of the morning, they didn't need crowd control, so Juhle dismissed the uniformed officers. When they'd driven off, he boosted himself onto the hood of the family car he'd driven down and said, "So what do you make of this?"

Hunt ran down his scenario.

"You're saying somebody snatched her out of here?"

"That's my guess. They've got video cameras coming out of the elevators in the lobby, so we can find out for sure as soon as we can get to them. But there's no way she ever made it up to her offices. Someone would have seen her."

"How about if she just parked, then walked back up through the garage here and out onto the street? Then away."

"Remotely possible, I suppose," Hunt said. "But why would she do that?"

"Maybe after she left her house, she heard something or talked to somebody and decided she had to disappear."

"So she wants to disappear and immediately dumps her best way to get out of town? Plus, she doesn't hit the ATM and she hasn't used any of her credit cards." Hunt shook his head. "There's only two ways to go, Dev. Either somebody picked her up or she was snatched."

"Not saying I don't agree with you, but we keep coming back to why. If somebody wanted to kill her, they'd have killed her. If it was a kidnap, where's the ransom demand? You're saying somebody just took her because they wanted to look at her or something? The most logical thing, admit it, is that she's on the run or killed herself. And if you've got a better reason for her to do that than because she killed Palmer and Staci, I'd like to hear what it is."

Hunt hesitated, but he'd brought Juhle along with him this far already. He had to tell him about Piersall and the CCPOA. Screw the attorney-client privilege. But before he could really begin, he got interrupted by the arrival of the crime-scene unit. When the techs went to work, Hunt started again, and by the time he'd finished, they'd dusted the outside of the car for fingerprints and now were setting up to tow it to the PD garage to do a thorough search of the interior, luminol it for blood, and check it for gunshot residue.

Juhle was pacing, all the prison guards' union facts making an impression. "You're telling me that Palmer was already drafting this order to federalize the whole prison system on Monday? I talked to his secretary, and she never mentioned anything about it."

"Did you ask her?"

"I asked her if she knew of anybody who might have had a reason to kill the judge."

"Maybe she didn't think of the order in those terms. Maybe she thought it was another piece of paper like the thousand others she'd typed up before. Slow grind of the court."

"So how did you find out about it?"

"What's more important than that is whether it's true. And I'm sure you'll check it out, but this will save you some time: It is."

"And Jim Pine got wind of it and sent somebody, some parolee, to make sure the order didn't get signed? That's the theory?"

Hunt nodded.

"What about the girl? Staci. That was just bad luck, her being there at precisely that time? I have some troubles with that."

"Me, too. But I can also think of ten ways to explain it."

"But all of them, I bet, some variation on the theme of luck or coincidence." Dissatisfied, Juhle pushed absently at the source of the pain in his shoulder. "But let's leave that for a minute and go back to Parisi. When the judge got killed, say, she had a feeling Pine must have been behind it. So what? You're saying she went to Pine and asked him about it? Only if she was an idiot, which she wasn't."

"How about if she mentions it to Piersall, just to float the idea, and he lets enough of it slip to tip off Pine?"

"We did this earlier," Juhle said, "when I said you were reaching. You still are."

"I don't think it's any kind of a reach to see a connection between the union and Parisi, Dev. She worked for it. The judge was all over it. The timing is perfect. It all fits."

"Staci Rosalier doesn't fit."

"Again, bad luck. Or—and I know you hate this—coincidence."

"No. I've got a better one. How about this?" Juhle held up a finger. "One, Rosalier had Parisi's card." Juhle pointed at the Miata, held up a second finger. "Two, a car that looked a lot like this one right here was in the street in front of the judge's house when he got shot. Three, regardless of what you may think, there wasn't anything professional about the job on the judge and Staci. We've got one missed shot and no coups to the head. Not a pro. Four, by your own admission, Parisi might be a jealous woman with at least some propensity to violence—the slap?—and a gun collection. Further, she has just maybe that day come to believe, contrary to what she's been thinking for the past six months, that she isn't going to be able to move three thousand miles away from the man she still loves and who she's forced to see all the time because of business. Finally, and again, just that day, Monday, she goes to lunch and sees the judge and puts it together that the sweet young thing who's waiting on him is the girl he's fucking instead of her! You think that doesn't get her just a little upset?" Back to pacing now, Juhle had gotten himself wound up. "Hell, Wyatt, the more I think about it, the more I like her for these killings. And then she blows Dodge."

Hunt, leaning against Juhle's car, was silent. It was an impressive litany, he had to admit. All of Piersall's theories and concerns about the union and all of the apparent linearity of the crises that had forced the judge to begin drafting his order lacked the immediacy and passion of Juhle's argument. The only reason Hunt couldn't bring himself to accept it was because he didn't want to or couldn't bear to, he wasn't sure which.

"And you know what I would have done after that?" Juhle stopped in front of him. "I would have tried to tough it out, to go on with my work, my normal life. But the very first night, I get so drunk I pass out. And the next day, I'm so distracted and lost that I leave for an appointment and wind up in my parking lot at work, never having thought about where I was going or what I was doing. And I realize it's hopeless. I'm not going to pull it off. I'm going to get caught, arrested, and tried, and then spend most if not all of the rest of my life in prison—and that's something I know more about than almost anybody who hasn't been inside because I work for the people who guard them."

"You're thinking she killed herself."

A brisk nod. "I'm thinking she walked out of here on her own two feet, got herself out to the Golden Gate Bridge by the time it was dark, and then walked halfway across. That or something very much like it is really what I think happened here, Wyatt, and my heart goes out to you if it did. Now, am I going to check the security cameras here in this building in the morning? Will I have a talk with Mr. Pine and follow up with Jeannette Palmer and maybe even take an interest in how Mr. Mowery managed to get himself out of a high-security prison environment and what he might have done or be doing right now in his hours of precious freedom? You bet I am. All of the above.

"But until I find even a little tiny bit of actual evidence that connects anyone in the union or anywhere else to these murders, I'm going to stick with what makes the most sense, leaving coincidence and luck out of it. And that is Andrea Parisi. And I hope like hell I'll find some evidence that proves either theory. I don't care which. I just want proof." Finally, Juhle tried a smile. "Meanwhile, though,

I think I'll get back home and try to squeeze a little sleep into this night while there's still time. And you might want to try the same thing."

"I'll give it some thought," Hunt said.

They said their good nights and got into their cars and headed through the lot and up the ramps. At the top, Hunt flashed his brights and honked, then got out of his Cooper and ran up to to Juhle's window. "Let me ask you one last thing."

"Sure. Why not? You're going to, anyway."

"I know you've got a warrant in to check Parisi's phone records, and you'll get a look at them soon enough. But I also know you've got somebody in security with SBC and Cingular and every cell phone company in the world who you could call right now. I've seen you do it. What I want shouldn't take five minutes."

"You're shitting me." Juhle's shoulders heaved in a soundless laugh. He looked at his watch. "One fifteen in the morning?" But, in fact, it wasn't a completely unreasonable request, and he sighed in resignation, set his parking brake, pulled out his phone. "What do you want to know?"

Hunt had both Andrea's cell and home telephone numbers, and he wanted to check traffic to or from each phone from noon on Wednesday. That's all. As it turned out, Juhle did this kind of thing often enough that he knew the number he needed to call by heart. When he got connected, he explained that the paperwork—the warrant to look at the phone records—had been signed by the judge and was on its way but that they were hot in a murder case. It was life and death, and they needed some information right now.

It took a bit longer than the five minutes Hunt had predicted. Andrea Parisi hadn't made or received any calls on her cell phone after noon on Wednesday. She had received one call on her cell phone that day at 2:48 P.M. It had been placed from a pay phone in the lobby of the Saint Francis Hotel, about six blocks from where they were right now, and it had lasted forty-two seconds.

When he rang off, Juhle didn't seem too impressed with the new information. "It could've been anybody, Wyatt. Hell, forty-two seconds, it could have been a wrong number."

Hunt mostly agreed with him. It could have been anybody. But Hunt did not think it was from just anybody. Hunt was going to choose to believe that it was from the person who had ultimately met Andrea in the firm's parking garage, after telling her that they'd meet in her office. More than that, of far greater significance in

Hunt's mind, the call's existence went a long way toward debunking Juhle's vision of what may have been Andrea's final hours.

She had not been so distracted and confused that without any thought she'd more or less automatically driven to work, then realized how hopeless her existence had become. No, she had taken a quick business call that had changed her immediate plans. It was a small enough thing, but it meant that Juhle was not right in all respects.

Logic or no, Juhle might not be right at all. And this in turn meant, logic or no, that Hunt might not be wrong.

22 /

After the Army, then CPS, then as a private investigator, Hunt had come to the conclusion that there was a joke about everything. No matter how grotesque, depressing, horrifying, just plain awful, stupid, venal, or tasteless any given situation was, if there was anything that could remotely be construed to have a shred of humor in it—hell, bring it on! Somebody's gonna laugh. Dead babies, mistreated animals, AIDS and all variants on every STD, medical mishaps, sexual dysfunctions, murders and suicides, infidelities, accidental mayhem, severed limbs—you're killing me here.

And sure enough, Wes Farrell dredged up this morning's gem about that old comedic standby, the U.S. federal judge. They were all just checking in, sitting around his upstairs office before the business day had officially begun downstairs, and Farrell asked conversationally if anybody knew the difference between a federal judge and the Ku Klux Klan. To a roomful of blank, groggy stares, he finally said, "Nobody? Okay. The KKK wears white robes and scares the shit out of black people."

There were five other people in the room—Hunt, Tamara, Chiurco, Amy Wu, Jason Brandt—and nobody reacted with so much as a smile. It wasn't much of a happy moment, what with Andrea still missing and now, according to Hunt, with Juhle still considering her the most likely suspect in the murders of Palmer and Rosalier. And a probable suicide at that.

But that didn't stop Brandt from chiming in with his own contribution. "So this psychiatrist shows up at the Pearly Gates, all pissed off because he was young and in perfect health and he shouldn't have died so soon. It wasn't right. Saint Peter says he's sorry, but no real reason, they had to take him a little earlier than they'd originally planned. So the shrink is all, 'You mean you ended my wonderful life on earth early for no reason? Why would you do that? Just because you could?' And Saint Peter looks both ways, leans over and whispers, 'It's God. He thinks he's a federal judge.' "

Hunt was wide awake in spite of only five hours of sleep. He gave the moment its due, which wasn't much, then threw a glance around the room at his partners and said, "Maybe we could talk about what we all did last night and see if it gets us anywhere."

But as they started to revisit their individual interviews, it became clear that the earlier desultory banter was covering up a more profound shift in the general mood. Now it was Friday morning, and Andrea had been gone since Wednesday afternoon—one and a half days ago. Forty-two hours. They'd all read the *Chronicle* story this morning, front page. Now the whole world was looking for Andrea, the photogenic television personality.

And now the three lawyers had their daily billable work looming ahead of them. Tamara and Chiurco were still obviously ready to take instructions and run with them—whatever Hunt wanted—but Mary Mahoney hadn't gotten them one step closer to Andrea Parisi. And finally, Tamara was the one who said it out loud: "I'm starting to believe she must be dead, Wyatt."

There were somber nods all around.

"It may not matter at this stage," Brandt suggested, "but maybe the best thing for us would be to try to contact Missing Persons again. Tell them everything we know and see where they can take it."

"They're not going to find her if Juhle can't," Hunt said. "He's got her as his main suspect in these killings. He's got people working on it, believe me."

Farrell, who'd been sitting forward on the couch, his head down, now lifted it. "This phone call to her cell phone," he said. "That's the last time we know of anybody talking to her?"

Hunt said it was.

"So you know for a fact—you found this out last night?—that she hasn't used her cell phone since then?"

"Right."

Farrell let out a heavy breath. "Well, it seems to me, then, whether she's on the run or whether she's dead, either one, there's no trail left to follow. None of us found out anything that goes anywhere, did we?"

Again, a silent, bleak consensus.

Which Hunt still wasn't ready to accept. "Okay, I'm discouraged myself. But let's talk for a minute about Juhle's idea, that Andrea is either on the run or has killed herself. Anybody here besides me see the tragic flaw in that argument?"

Wu spoke up. "It assumes that Andrea's a double murderer."

Hunt turned to her, his face all but lit up. "There it is," he said. "Now I know that you, Wes, and Tamara, and Craig, didn't know her very well. But Amy and Jason did, and I was getting close, and there is just no way I can accept that she killed anybody."

"Me neither," Brandt said. "Amy and I have both known her since law school, and I agree with you. I can't imagine it."

"All right," Hunt said. "If we believe that, we can eliminate the fact that she left the parking garage of her own accord. In fact, what happened is she met somebody, probably whoever called her from the Saint Francis, who either talked her into coming away with them or outright snatched her."

"Somebody she knew," Wu added.

"Probably. Okay," Hunt said. "So that's where we are. And I still believe that's ahead of the police."

"Yeah, but Wyatt?" Brandt seemed to have taken some signal from the group, making him its spokesman. Now he cleared his throat. "However it happened, she's been gone two nights now. I'm trying to imagine some scenario where this went down, even exactly as we described it, where she isn't already dead. And I hate to say this, but I can't find one."

Hunt took in his assembled team, looked around the room from one set of eyes to the next. Wu had tears in hers. Tamara and Craig were holding hands. He saw no sign of any more hope and realized that all of these smart people had reached the same all but inescapable conclusion.

Hunt, Tamara, and Craig said their good-byes to Wu, Brandt, and Farrell at the Freeman Building. Mostly in silence, they walked the few blocks back to The Hunt Club offices and climbed the stairs. Once they were inside, Tamara went around to her desk and sat down, while Hunt crossed to the front window and stared down onto Grant Avenue, and Chiurco went over to start the coffee.

Putting the phone on speaker, Tamara pushed a button, and they heard that they had seven messages.

"Seven? A new record," Chiurco said. "Great timing, huh?"

Scowling, Wyatt turned away from the window and came to hover, arms crossed, over the phone.

Beep. Yesterday, 6:18 P.M. "Wyatt, Bill Frazier." This was the doctor who wanted background on his mother's new boyfriend. "Just calling to check on progress. You'd mentioned that you might have something by tomorrow, and things are heating up pretty quick with the two lovebirds. I don't want Mom to do something dumb, like elope before I get a chance to stop her. Sorry to push, but if you've got anything, I'd like to hear it sooner than later. Thanks."

Beep. Yesterday, 7:04 P.M. "Hey, Wyatt, you there? Pick up if you can. Where are you, man? You got your cell turned off? This is Peter Buckner." The lead attorney in the depositions Hunt had attended at the McClelland offices on Wednesday. "All right. We got a problem with Jeremy Harter. He didn't show for his depo this afternoon, and he's not answering. . . ."

Hunt reached down and punched the button to kill the sound. He turned to Chiurco. "Did you get all your subpoenas served yesterday?"

"Four of 'em."

"Man." Hunt shook his head. "When's the court date?"

"Tuesday." Which meant Craig shouldn't really take any time for other business such as Andrea.

Swearing, Hunt pushed the button again, heard the end of Peter Buckner's message, then a chirpy voice of someone identifying herself as Melanie was telling him that he'd been preapproved for a platinum . . .

Tamara hit the skip button. "I've never been glad to get one of those before," she said.

Beep. 9:19 P.M. "Mr. Hunt. My name is Ephraim Goldman and I'm a senior associate at Mannheim Shelby, referred to you by Geoff Chilcott at . . ."

Hunt skipped over the rest of that one. "Later," he said.

They all listened to the next three, Tamara taking notes. Every message was new or continuing business, and none of them had anything to do with Andrea Parisi. Hunt sat himself down on the chair by the door and tried to get his mind to focus. He had a business to run here, he knew, but those demands suddenly didn't seem remotely compelling. He was starting to realize that the business was growing so fast that soon he'd have to bring on some more stringers, of which luckily there was a plethora—off-duty cops and even some of the other PIs were always ready to make some extra spending money. But he didn't have the time right now even to interview, much less hire.

"Do you know where Mickey is today?" he asked Tamara.

"I think he was cabbing. He's off his phone, though. I tried this morning."

"I know. I tried him last night. You think there's any way we could get him to leave it on so we can reach him?"

Tamara smiled. "I doubt it."

"Well, if he checks in, tell him to call me. You know what," Hunt said. "It's true. Good help *is* hard to find."

"Fortunately," Chiurco said, "you've got us."

Hunt nodded. "That is fortunate. There's just not enough of you two to go around."

"So what do you want us to do?" Tamara asked.

With a game plan that was anything but strategic, Hunt found himself approaching the Piersall building he'd left only about eight hours before. All he knew was that, business be damned, his personal priority was Andrea Parisi. He'd told Tamara and Craig that somehow they'd have to handle what they could among all these callers and somehow put off the others. Be self-starters. Manufacture brilliant excuses. Figure it out. That's why he paid them the big bucks. If they lost a client in the process, so be it. He'd take responsibility. And they should also be ready to drop everything in ten seconds if he needed them on Andrea.

His employees might truly believe she was already dead—and, in fact, he saw that they clearly felt sorry for his inability to accept that truth—but he was not going to presume that she was gone until he was forced to. It was going to take a lot more than everyone else believing it.

In contrast to last night, Montgomery this morning was clogged. The usual deliveries and normal heavy street traffic crept along around several police cars and the vans representing all of the local and a couple of the national television stations. A crowd of onlookers ebbed and flowed around the broadcasters and their crews.

Hunt was only somewhat surprised—it wasn't yet nine o'clock—to recognize Spencer Fairchild and Richard Tombo hovering by the Trial TV van, sipping from Styrofoam mugs, and he picked his way through the crowd over to where they stood. When Tombo saw him, he motioned him inside the perimeter of their cameras, lights, and wires.

"What's all this about?" Hunt asked. "Is there anything new on Andrea?"

"She hasn't turned up if that's what you mean," Tombo said.

"But suddenly she seems to be in the middle of everything. You heard they found her car in the garage here?"

"That wasn't any 'they,' Rich. That was me."

"No joke?"

"I've got no jokes left in me. I found the car last night."

Spencer Fairchild, next to them both, didn't miss a beat. "You want to be on television, Wyatt?"

Hunt might not have any jokes in him, but he still had half a laugh left, and he used it now. "Like I want a root canal. But what's so important about the car that it's drawn all you flies? Did the crime-scene people come up with something?"

"Not that we've heard," Fairchild said. "As to all the cameras, it's another development in Donolan. We get a different shot than down at the Hall of Justice. Breaks up the monotony."

Hunt swiveled his head, took in all the activity. "Help me out here, Spencer. What's Donolan got to do with Andrea at this point?"

Fairchild clearly wondered if Hunt was putting him on. "Andrea *is* Donolan. The beautiful commentator goes missing in the middle of the trial? You couldn't have scripted it any better. And now suddenly because she's gone, Judge Palmer is Donolan, too. As we speak, Wyatt, this is turning into the hottest story in the country. I've got to hand it to Andrea. Even if she didn't plan all of this . . ."

"What are you talking about?" Hunt was surprised to hear the anger in his voice. "She didn't . . . nobody planned anything here."

Fairchild's condescension fairly dripped. "I know that's your story. Farrell told me the same thing last night. But I find it interesting to learn that you were both the last person to see Andrea on Wednesday and then the very same person to find her car. What made you think, out of the whole city to choose from, to look here? I wonder if it could have been because you drove down behind her, then drove her away to wherever she's hiding out now."

Suddenly Tombo stepped in. "Hey, Spence, easy . . ."

But the producer didn't back off. "Hey, yourself, Rich. It wouldn't be the first time Andrea's hooked up with some guy to boost the old career another notch. First me, now maybe Wyatt here . . . they're fooling everybody, the two of them, thinking this is just a hell of a lot of fun." He turned. "What do you say about that, Hunt? True? False? Any comment at all?"

"Yeah," Hunt said, "here's a comment. You're pathetic." Every impulse in his body wanted to take a swing at Fairchild and deck him, but he forced himself to turn away.

Fairchild walked several steps after him. "When you see her, tell her she's played this out too far already. There's no getting back from where she's gone! She'll never work in television again!"

Nearly blind with anger, Hunt willed himself through the lobby doors and across to the elevators. The elevator doors would open in a couple of seconds on the fourteenth floor, and he still had very little conscious idea of exactly what had brought him up here. It was more than the need to escape from Fairchild's insane accusations—he'd been on his way over here before he'd ever seen the video cams outside. He'd been wrestling with the logic of what he thought he knew about Andrea and what he could accept, what he felt. For if she were dead, as they all now feared, Hunt still in some obscure way felt a degree of responsibility.

Not for her death itself, of course, but for the last hours of her life, when he'd voluntarily taken on the role of her protector. And lover. With a stab of guilt, for the first time, he realized that he perhaps unknowingly had, in fact, taken advantage of her fragile state, her vulnerability. He hadn't seen it like that at the time. But he didn't want to fool himself—that might have been the true dynamic after all. The thought curdled his stomach.

And then, after he'd left her, someone had abducted her and done her grievous harm.

He did not believe, as Juhle did, that she had killed Palmer and Rosalier and then taken her own life.

He did not believe, as Fairchild did, that she'd plotted her own disappearance as some sort of publicity/celebrity-making stunt.

Hunt believed that he knew what had happened with a certainty that was startling. And that certitude—in its first flowering now after everyone's hope but his for Andrea's life had flown away—was rearranging his interior landscape back into something that he thought he had long abandoned and that he now recognized as both terrifying and familiar.

The anger that had nearly literally blinded him downstairs wasn't occasioned by the ravings of a prancing jackass like Spencer Fairchild. But those irrational stupidities had shattered somewhere within him the last resistance to the deep and abiding rage that he'd come to believe in the past four or five years he'd finally tamed.

A rage that had ruled his days from his sense of abandonment through his succession of foster homes until he'd finally moved in with the Hunts. A rage that had fueled his CID work in Iraq, then delivered him to his work rescuing children, finally blossoming into a general rage at the world he'd been left in when Sophie and their unborn baby had been taken from him. A wide-ranging rage at bureaucracy, at venality, at the incompetence and outright villainy of men like Wilson Mayhew. A rage, finally, that had almost undone him with its power and intensity. Day to day, night to night, unyielding and terrible rage. For the world seemed to promise so much. And that promise so often was a lie.

And then, after he'd established his business and worked as a private investigator for a while, the rage had gradually started to subside. His work was a job now, not a vocation. Wyatt Hunt read, he did his sports, he played his music, he satisfied his clients. He would not feed his rage any longer with his overwhelming desire to excel, to make right, to care, to love. The inevitable failures—and he'd come to believe that at least partial failure was always foreordained—had taken too great a toll on him. He didn't choose to live at that level anymore, and he'd been content. Marginalized, perhaps, never too deeply involved. But content.

And now suddenly, a toggle switch thrown, that inner contentment was over. And this was why he had felt so disoriented at Farrell's, so distracted on the walk over here, so unable to connect with what should have been sorrow at the idea of Andrea's death. He was not really sad, not unfocused, not lost. With a kind of terrible joy, he realized that what he felt now was pure—the rage for justice that had nearly consumed him before but that had also given his life ballast, moments of real connection and meaning.

If someone had killed Andrea Parisi, had rent the fabric of his world so thoroughly, he was going to bring whoever it was to justice. Nothing else mattered. He would take whatever help he could get, but if he had to do it all alone, then he would.

The elevator door opened, and he strode out to the first desk to his left, where a young woman stopped her typing to look up at him. "Can I help you?" she asked.

"Yes," he said. "I need to talk to Carla Shapiro."

Juhle said, "No. No evidence."

He was in Lanier's office, sitting awkwardly forward because of his sling. Shiu stood one step inside the closed door, at rigid attention. It was a small room with a big desk in it. There were three windows, two in the wall behind Juhle and one in the wall behind Shiu. None of them opened to the morning's sunshine in the real world. None of them opened at all, in fact. Just beyond Shiu's window, about a million miles away, Juhle could see four of his fellow homicide inspectors shooting the breeze and laughing about something. When Juhle brought his gaze back inside, Lanier wasn't laughing. "No evidence at all?"

Juhle looked over at Shiu—no help. "Maybe if we can get Mrs. Levin—the Palmers' neighbor—down to see Parisi's car, she might give us a positive make."

Lanier grunted, leaned back in his chair, and pushed himself away from the desk until he got to his back wall, where he stopped. "Maybe she might, huh?"

Juhle shrugged. "What we've got, Marcel, are connections. Six or seven of them, which taken together are pretty damn compelling if you ask me and Shiu, and you did."

"We don't have any other suspects, sir," Shiu said.

"Here's a tip, my son," Lanier said. "That's probably the kind of thing you don't want to mention out loud to somebody who does your performance reviews." He turned to Juhle. "But Parisi?"

Juhle shrugged again. "I didn't just make it up, Marcel. I think she did it, tried to bluff it out, made it a day or two until guilt or remorse or whatever the hell else you feel made her kill herself."

"I don't feel anything," Lanier said.

"I know, me neither. Feelings, I mean. I don't feel any feelings. I do feel my shoulder."

"He won't take ibuprofen," Shiu said.

"I did for the first ten days. Not only didn't it work, it hurt my stomach."

"I'll tell you what hurts my stomach," Lanier said. "My stomach hurts when I start thinking about going out in front of our ravenous media representatives with the announcement that the case on Federal Judge George Palmer—did I say *federal* judge?—only the fourth *federal judge* to be killed in the entire history of the United States—"

"Is that true?" Shiu asked. "Only the fourth one? Wow."

Lanier risked a quick, conspiratorial I-know-why-you-hate-this-guy glance at Juhle. "Right. So I tell the jackals we've solved this case, locked it up tight in only three days. The murderer's Andrea Parisi. But you'll just have to take our word for it because we don't have any evidence. What do you think, Dev? You think they'll go for it?"

Juhle sulked. Lanier was right, and Juhle was dead beat after the last couple of sleepless nights. "What do you want us to do, Marcel?

I could drive out to Andrea's house, find some hair in the sink or something, drop it off over at the judge's . . ."

"We can't do . . ." Shiu began.

Wincing, Juhle held up a hand. "Kidding, Shiu. Back off."

"But all kidding aside," Lanier said, "we've already got some issues—well, especially you, Dev, are not going to get any slack here. Whatever you get has got to be rock solid."

Juhle's eyes turned dark. "What the fuck does that mean?" He shot an I-dare-you look at his partner.

Lanier pushed off from the back wall and wheeled his chair forward, up to the desk, and put his arms on his blotter. "That means that there are some people in positions of authority who were not completely convinced by your exoneration on the OI." The officer-involved shooting that had cost Juhle three months of administration leave but had finally resulted in his merit citation.

"Well, how can I put this? Fuck them."

Shiu straightened up more, tightened down his jaw. Even Lanier seemed to wince. Profanity was tolerated in the field, but Deputy Chief of Inspectors Abe Glitsky frowned on it in the various units under his command.

Immune to this sensitivity, Juhle didn't slow down. "I mean it, Marcel. Who are they? No, I know who they are. Maybe I should . . ."

"Maybe not, Dev. Maybe nothing, okay? We both know who they are, and they're wrong, and you're up for cop of the year, okay? You want my opinion, I hope you get it. And you might as long as you don't say 'fuck' too often around Glitsky. But my point is that these couple of supervisors have the ear of the mayor and the chief. And not only is this the biggest case in the world, but we've finessed the FBI to keep the hell away from it because it's not political. So it's all yours, both of you guys, and welcome to it. But don't come to me without any evidence, please. If Parisi did it, show me something that'll prove it. Or at least find something that eliminates everybody else?"

"You want us to prove a negative?" Juhle asked. "That can get tricky."

"Don't get smart, Dev. You know what I want. I want more. If it's on Parisi, fine. But we don't even have next of kin on one of the victims if I'm not mistaken. To the critical soul, this might bespeak a lack of vigor in the investigation. Am I making myself clear?" His eyes went to Shiu. "You really don't have any other suspects?"

"I don't know who they'd be at this point, sir."

"You don't. Not with all these union hassles? Nobody the judge had ever ruled against? Maybe the girlfriend had another boyfriend? Don't I remember the wife has a sister? What was she doing Monday night? I don't know squat about this case, and I can think of half a dozen questions you haven't even asked yet."

"I *have* asked them, Marcel," Juhle said. "I've asked every goddamn question you just gave us, and the other half dozen you didn't mention on top of those. And for the record, we went down to the judge's chambers first thing and spent a fascinating few hours talking to his staff, and found out that he's got lots of cases with people who are mad at him. Not just the CCPOA. And believe me, they're all rattling around in my brain every single second. And sure, I might be wrong, but it's good police work to follow the clearest trail." He paused to grab a breath.

Shiu stepped into the breach. "And that, with respect, sir," he said, "looks like Parisi."

Lanier held up a hand. "I've heard. I get your message. But traditionally we like those little links in what we call the chain of evidence that maybe—"

Juhle had heard enough. He was already on his feet, interrupting. "You want us to shake some more trees, Marcel, sure, we'll do it. But there's no more evidence in those directions than there is with Parisi. It's going to look like what we're really doing is covering our ass."

Lanier blew his frustration out at them. "There are worse ideas," he said. He gestured toward his closed office door. "Keep me up on developments. My door's always open."

23 /

Betsy Sobo's oversize tortoiseshell glasses didn't fool Hunt. With the dorky specs, the tousled dirty-blonde hair, only the barest touch of makeup around the eyes, and no lipstick, the young associate in the family-law division of Piersall obviously tried to pass herself off in her professional life as plain, even bookish. Today, she was even dressed in the Catholic school uniform of a plaid skirt and white blouse, black leggings, no-nonsense black shoes. It was a nice try, but Hunt thought she could be in sackcloth and ashes and draw admiring stares.

She'd stood up to meet him and shake his hand, then had gone back behind her desk. Hunt sat across from her on a folding chair, which was about all that fit in her office after she'd squeezed in her bookcase and files. She had six feet of window behind her, a nice view over downtown to the east. Hunt asked her permission to record their conversation, and she said yes.

"I talked to someone last night about this," she was saying. "A woman. Another attorney."

"Amy Wu?"

"I think that was it. I don't think I helped her much. I told her I didn't know what Andrea wanted to talk to me about."

"But she called you herself to set up this appointment? I just talked to her secretary, and she said it wasn't her."

"Yes. She called me herself."

"To ask if you could give her a half hour or so of your time?"

"Right. But that's about all. I said sure."

Hunt leaned forward. "According to Carla, she called you just after she'd seen Judge Palmer for lunch, isn't that right? So my thought is that maybe she dropped a hint of something we haven't heard about yet."

"I don't know what that would be. And wouldn't she have mentioned whatever that was to Gary—Mr. Piersall—at their meeting?"

"She might have," Hunt said, "but I don't think she did. I think what she wanted to talk to you about was different. I talked to Mr. Piersall last night, and apparently the big topic between him and Andrea was this order the judge was threatening to sign. He and Andrea didn't talk at all about union benefits."

"But I'm not even sure that's what she wanted to talk to me about. I just assumed."

"Is there anything specific she might have said that made you assume that?"

"I don't know what it could have been." Taking a breath, Sobo put her elbow on the desk and rested her forehead on the fingers of her left hand. She closed her eyes for a moment, then opened them. "Okay. She said that Mike Eubanks—he's the partner for our unit— he told her to call me. And if Mike told her, it would have been benefits."

"There you go," Hunt said.

"Then she said, 'This person I met at lunch.' And then she stopped and said she only had a minute but there were some pretty big players involved and she didn't want to start anything unless she was solid on the law."

Hunt didn't move for a long moment. "And that would have been family law, right? She said somebody she met at lunch. Those words?"

"I think so. Yes. Pretty close."

"As in met for the first time? Rather than just met for lunch."

"Maybe. I'd say so, yes."

"So not the judge." Not a question, either. "Let me ask you this: With all the union work this firm does, have you ever worked on benefits issues before?"

"Me, personally? Not usually. I'm mostly into the custody battles and restraining orders, stuff like that. There's just a ton of divorces with these poor guards' families. You wouldn't believe."

"So what did you think this was? That Andrea wanted?"

Sobo considered for a minute. "Maybe some kind of divorce coverage into the members' package, attorneys fees or counseling, so it doesn't come out of pocket for these guys and their families. We make the case that it's the stress of the work that's a proximate cause of the marital breakups." She shrugged. "We've prevailed on this kind of thing a few other times—the stress in the job *is* a killer. I mean almost literally."

"I'm sure it is," Hunt said. "So the pretty big players Andrea was talking about?"

"I figured some insurance companies. But it may have been one of the heavy politicians, the governor, even, if we were bringing the issue to the legislature."

"So it made sense to you? Andrea wanting to see you?"

"Sure. It's the kind of thing we would do. Definitely."

Judge Oscar Thomasino was the warrant magistrate on duty today, and he was a much easier sell than Marcel Lanier had been. It took Juhle about forty-five seconds to explain to His Honor what he and Shiu would be looking for at Parisi's home and why a search was necessary, and the judge signed off before Shiu had finished filling out the affidavit.

Twenty minutes later, they were inside her house, standing over the handgun collection. The cabinet wasn't locked, and Juhle started picking up the pieces one by one, smelling them, then placing them on the table next to them. All the guns were in working condition, firing pins intact; most appeared to have been cleaned relatively recently, although in their enclosed cabinet, they might have simply been protected from dust over a period of months or even years. But they still smelled of oil. There were nine of them in all. Seven Old West–style revolvers. When Juhle looked down the barrels of both derringers, however, he could tell that they hadn't been cleaned since they'd last been fired. And they were .22 caliber. He had Shiu bag the tiny guns to bring to the police lab for ballistics comparisons on the slugs retrieved from Palmer's study.

Pretty sure that he'd found his evidence, Juhle let some cockiness show. "Are we glad we came here, Shiu, or what? I'm tempted to run those puppies down to the lab right now and be back in Marcel's office by noon with the results."

"They might not be a match."

"Well, we'll find out. But I've got to tell you, I feel lucky."

Juhle closed the cabinet back up, made his way slowly back through the kitchen, then across the living room and into the hallway that led to the bedrooms and a bathroom, which Juhle entered, turning on the light.

"What are we looking for in here?"

Over by the hamper, Juhle said. "You know those videotapes

you didn't want to watch the other day? Monday's Trial TV?" He rummaged around for a second and then pulled out an instantly recognizable purple blouse. "Look familiar? I don't think she changed after they shot the show. First, she went back to work, right. Then I think she drove right out to the judge's and shot him still wearing this blouse. So let's bag this sucker for GSR and blood. And I'm betting we find the suit she wore still in her closet. And if we're lucky, the shoes."

Jim Pine worked in West Sacramento.

He liked being nearby the capital so that he could schmooze the lobbyists and legislators and direct the workings of the political action committees that did his bidding. Controlling a yearly income of over twenty million dollars in annual dues, he was the largest contributor to California's political scene—bigger even than numbers two and three, the California Teachers Association and Philip Morris, respectively. Every election cycle, the CCPOA was the major backer of between twenty and forty state lawmakers, and dozens of local office candidates, not to mention the governor, lieutenant governor, secretary of state, and state attorney general, regardless of party. Pine had also teamed the political clout of the prison guards' union with three of California's powerful Indian gaming tribes and formed the Native Americans & Peace Officers Independent Expenditure Committee, another superpowerful PAC, whose offices, too, were in West Sacramento.

Over the years, under Pine's direction and leadership, the CCPOA and its supporters had lobbied for tougher and tougher laws, with more and bigger prisons to house the criminals that broke these laws. In the process, the California Department of Corrections, the CDC, grew from thirteen to thirty-one prisons, with a total population of one hundred sixty thousand inmates, and to have a yearly operating budget of nearly five billion dollars. And while the twenty-five thousand prison guards now earned a yearly salary of fifty-four thousand dollars, it was far from uncommon for an individual guard to actually make more than one hundred thousand dollars or more with overtime and sick-leave benefits.

Now Pine was not in West Sacramento, though, but in the office of the managing partner of his attorneys, at Piersall in San Francisco. After the slaying of Judge Palmer on Monday, he had deemed it necessary to be close to the investigation, should anyone in authority need to contact or question him. He knew that sometimes there had been apparent animosities between the judge and the union, and Pine was here to keep the story straight. He'd given over a dozen interviews in the past couple of days to various handpicked members of the media, always with the same message: George Palmer and Jim Pine had been adversaries from time to time in their professional lives, but personally they got along. They attended the same fund-raisers and functions and supported many of the same political candidates. And now, today, Pine would be at Palmer's funeral, in conspicuous mourning.

Mostly to be sure the bastard was really dead.

Gary Piersall wore black, too. He hadn't finally gotten more than four hours of turbulent sleep last night and now sat on the leather couch across from his client, on his third demitasse of espresso.

They would be leaving together for Saint Mary's Cathedral in a few minutes. Pine was sixty-three years old and looked ten years younger, as always, in his business suit. Carrying about 220 pounds on his six-foot frame, he was a robust forty pounds overweight, with a marine cut and the rosy cheeks of either a choirboy or a heavy drinker.

But for all of his cheerful, upbeat public persona, Pine was not happy. He'd been nearly assaulted by reporters downstairs when he'd gotten to the building—everyone gathered in the street and even in the lobby for this new angle on Andrea Parisi. And the rumors had begun again—that her disappearance had to do with the Palmer homicide and somehow, mysteriously, with the union.

Where did they come from? Pine wanted to know. How could he stop them? "I mean, what do they think, Gary? I'm putting hits out on people? First George and then Andrea? Christ! I liked that old son of a bitch. And I loved Andrea, I really did." He leveled his gaze across the room. "You look like shit, Gary. Are you feeling all right?"

"I'm fine, Jim. Just a little done in with all of this."

"Well, don't let them see it down there, let me tell you. You want to go throw some water in your face, you go ahead. You show any weakness, they'll eat you."

"Don't worry about me."

"But I do." He kept his flat gaze on his attorney. "And I'm worried about Andrea. Do you have any idea what could have happened to her?"

"None."

"You sure? You have any thoughts? Opinions?"

Piersall forced himself into a rigid calm. What was Pine doing here? Feeling out what he knew? Testing his loyalty? "I think she may have killed herself, Jim. She wanted to ride this Trial TV thing to New York, and when that fell apart—"

"So you also don't think there's a thread running through us?"

"Us?"

"Me, you, the union."

"No," Piersall said. "How could there be? What kind of thread?"

Pine sat back, the picture of relaxation, although his eyes were pricks of almost feline intensity. "I have people on the street who hear things, Gary."

And at that moment, Piersall resolved to have the outer lobby swept for recording devices, as he regularly did with his own office. If Pine had heard what he'd confided to Hunt last night . . .

"Then this morning they had it on the Net, the Trial TV site. Where do they get this shit? But anyway, the point is by tonight it's everywhere. You know what I'm talking about?"

Piersall cleared his throat, tried to get down a swallow of his coffee. "I've tried to steer clear of all that, Jim. It's just these irresponsible journalists one-upping each other. It breaks on the Net, you know its unattributable bullshit."

"Yeah, but then the legit stations pick it up. What I'm saying is we've got to treat this story as beneath contempt."

"And the story is . . . ?"

"That Andrea knew something, and we had to shut her up. That's hysteria talking, and we don't want to feed it. We shouldn't discuss it on any level."

"I have no intention to, Jim. It is beneath contempt."

"She ever talk to you about anything like that?"

"No. Not even remotely. She was a company girl all the way, Jim."

"And you're a company man?"

Piersall put down his coffee cup, mustered his calmest tone. "I have been a company man for fifteen years, Jim. It's a little painful to me to think you'd have to ask."

Pine studied him for a long moment. "Okay. Just so we're on the same page."

Carla had called Gary Piersall as soon as Hunt had shown up unannounced at her desk. She liked Wyatt, and the boss had told her to cooperate with him in every way she could. Beyond that, she knew that he was on Andrea's side, and that was also the firm's side. They were considering her a victim of abduction, and Piersall had given Hunt the okay to look wherever he needed. Wherever.

And, just back from his talk with Betsy Sobo, he'd hesitated, trying to decide on his next move, before he told her he'd like to look through Parisi's office. There might be something in her files, her notes, on her tapes or answering machine, almost anywhere, that might provide a clue to what had happened to her.

But to allow Hunt access to the intimacies of Andrea's office— Carla felt this was beyond the pale. She called Mr. Piersall again to get his specific permission but was told that he was in his office now with Mr. Pine and absolutely could not be disturbed. So she'd stalled, first having trouble locating the key, then taking a trip to the bathroom, until finally Piersall was still unavailable, bunkered down with Pine, and there was no alternative.

"Dev. Wyatt."

"Talk to me. Where are you?"

"Piersall's again. In Parisi's office."

"Are you shitting me? I'm on my way over there right now, stuck in traffic with Shiu. Why is it, you think, I'm the cop in the case and you're already inside?"

"Maybe the personal-charm thing?"

"Can't be that. Don't touch anything."

"Too late. And you've got to see this."

"I thought you didn't consider Parisi a suspect?"

"I don't. She's not."

"That's funny, because we just pretty much sewed that up with what we found in her house just now."

"Good for you, but I wouldn't go public with it until you see what I'm looking at."

"In a contaminated scene."

"What does that mean?"

"It means you're in it. So whatever you've got, it's no good as evidence. Who's to say you didn't put it there?"

"Me. And even if I did, you're still going to want to see it."

Hunt had been in the room—really not much larger than a cubicle— for nearly fifteen minutes, the door closed behind him, and here in front of Carla's desk now was a man identifying himself as Devin

Juhle, homicide inspector, accompanied by the firm's security officer and asking for Wyatt Hunt.

Carla Shapiro thought her heart might stop. This was not supposed to happen. She'd made the final decision on her own to allow Wyatt into Andrea's personal space, and now the police had come to find her out. She struggled a second for a breath, then managed to string together the words. "Our investigator's in Ms. Parisi's office."

The inspector's face didn't do much to ease her sense of dread. "I know that," he said. "Where's the office?"

Carla was already standing, though she didn't remember getting up. She walked over the few steps, grabbed the knob, and pushed the door open. The inspector was right behind her.

Behind Andrea's desk, in her chair, Hunt closed the lower left-hand drawer next to him and looked up. "Where's Shiu?"

"On his way to the lab. We're going to settle this thing once and for all. What do I need to see?"

Hunt had the manila folder ready and handed it over. The inspector put it down on the desk and opened it. Inside was a half-inch stack of newspaper clippings of various sizes as well as several printouts of what looked like Web pages. Carla risked another step into the room so she could see the headlines. The one on top read: "DA Killed in Hunting Accident."

As the inspector turned to the following pages, Hunt was saying, "You'll notice the folder has no title on the tab. It was under her regular hanging folders in the back of the desk file here. The first one's Porter Anderton, who was the DA prosecuting some prison guards at Avenal. Then there's all seven of the stories about vandalism to candidates' headquarters up and down the state. Sixteen stories all told. Four deaths of people—Anderton's hunting accident, a couple of hit and runs, one suicide. Every one of the victims had dealings with one prison or another. One prosecutor, two whistle-blowers, one physician." Hunt reached across and tapped the printouts. "If you're still not believing in coincidence, then she was on to something."

"She was building a case."

Hunt nodded. His eyes were so cold that a chill seemed to come off him. "Maybe more than a case, Dev. Maybe a story. And she'd already built it. And she told it to the wrong person."

24 /

Mickey Dade finally checked in and got through to Hunt while he was still at Piersall, and was double-parked outside ready to play chauffeur when he and Juhle came out of the building. Hunt gave him Staci Rosalier's address and told him to hit it. Most of the way over to her condo, Juhle was on his cell phone with Shiu, who was still at the lab. They were backed up and the various tests might keep him there for most of the afternoon. No, they hadn't even done the ballistics. That would be the first test, they promised. Yes, Shiu would call immediately the second he had the results.

Juhle's response was clipped. "Shiu, listen to me. We need those results *now*! Exert some goddamn authority, would you? We're homicide, for Christ's sake. Top of the food chain. Kick some ass. Threaten to get 'em fired. Whatever it takes." He snapped the phone shut. "Idiot."

Mickey Dade and Juhle had never met each other before, and now the young cab driver threw a worried glance first at his boss and then into the backseat, where Juhle sat smoldering. Next to Mickey in the passenger seat, Hunt turned halfway around and said, "You're scaring my driver."

"That's another thing," Juhle said. "How is it you have an on-call, off-the-meter cab to drive us around wherever you want to go, while I'm a goddamn inspector of homicide and I'm reduced to hitching rides?"

"It's got to have something to do with karma," Hunt said.

Now they had gotten the key again from the marginally cooperative Mr. Franks and were on their way up in the elevator. This stop was necessary, Juhle was explaining, because Lanier's criticism that they hadn't even identified next of kin on one of the victims wasn't completely off the mark. They should have moved on that already if only for credibility's sake. So he needed to come here and grab the larger, framed, but still very fuzzy photo of the young boy and then get one of the papers to run it with a DO YOU RECOGNIZE THIS PERSON? tag. They'd blown up the other photograph that had been in Staci's wallet and brought it back to the station, and it had been useless. The kid must be some relation to Staci, didn't Hunt think?

Hunt knew. "He's her brother."

"How do you know that?"

"Mary Mahoney. The waitress at MoMo's . . . ?"

"I know who she is, Wyatt. I'm the one who gave her to you."

Hunt wasn't going to fight. He didn't blame Juhle for his frustration. In the last hour, Juhle had gone from what he considered a probable closing out of this case to an entirely new and increasingly plausible theory of it. Particularly if the ballistics on the derringers didn't match and he found himself back at square one. And it didn't help that the new theory was one that Hunt had pressed him to consider from early on, and Juhle had flat out rejected.

Hunt decided to be conciliatory. "That's right, Mary was your ID on Staci, wasn't she? Anyway, she told Tamara he was her brother."

"Did she get a name?"

"No, I don't think so."

"Of course not. That would be too easy."

"Right."

They got to the fourth floor, crossed the hallway to suite A, and Juhle opened the door. The drapes were still open as Juhle and Shiu had left them the other night, and the room was fairly bright. Juhle walked straight across to the table next to the sofa bed and picked up the framed photo of the boy and, in sort of a slow-motion double take, stared at it for a long moment, his frown growing more pronounced.

"What?" Hunt asked, crossing over.

"This is her brother?"

"According to Mahoney."

"How old do you make him?"

Hunt looked. "From that picture? Good luck. You're the one with kids. Six?"

"That's about right, I'd guess. And she was twenty-two?"

"So?"

"So fourteen years. That's a good stretch between babies, don't you think?"

Hunt shrugged. "Happens all the time. Plus, that picture might be six, ten, fifteen years old. They could be as close in age as Mickey and Tamara."

Juhle's face went a little slack. He rolled his hurt shoulder, let out a heavy breath, and suddenly, surprisingly, turned and sat down on the sofa bed. "I'm losing it, Wyatt, I swear to God," he said. "You know that? I'm losing it."

"What are you talking about?"

Juhle hung his head, shook it as though it weighed a ton. "This goddamn shooting. The scumbag I shot last year."

"What about it? You didn't have a choice, Dev. Plus, you saved a bunch of lives."

"Yeah, but suddenly I'm the tall poppy."

"What's that mean?"

"You know, a field of poppies, one of them sticks up too high, that's the one you chop off. Ever since the . . . the incident, everything I do gets second-guessed. Lanier just brought it up again this morning, more or less saying that if it wasn't me on this Palmer case, it'd go a lot easier on him. On everybody. So what do I do? I know I'm under the magnifying glass, right? So that's what I'm thinking about. How things get *perceived*—if you can believe that bullshit."

"Don't worry about that. Just do your job."

"Easy for you to say. I tried to convince Lanier this morning that I'd actually considered other suspects, and I have, but I couldn't get a one of them to gel, except Parisi. I don't seem to be able to get my brain working the way it used to."

"You followed a lead till it gave out, Dev. That's what you do."

"No. It's more than that. Like this picture just now." Juhle put on a voice. "Oh, really? It might not have been taken in the recent past. It might, in fact, be ten fucking years old." He looked up at Hunt, shook his head again, continued in his regular voice. "Jesus Christ! Where's my brain?"

"Your brain's fine, Dev."

"That's nice to hear, but you're not inside my head with me, Wyatt. Now I'm second-guessing *myself*. This job's about half instinct, you know, and I'm getting pretty damn close to zero confidence in mine. And that, of course, makes me act that much more certain of everything, even when I'm not or shouldn't be. It's eating me up."

Hunt walked over and stood by the window for a second, then came back and sat down next to his friend. "If it's any help," he said, "I personally think you're still the same horse's ass you've always been. And the only way you're going to convince other people that you're a good cop is to be one over time. Don't get pushed into having to defend something that might be wrong. The investigation is continuing. You don't know yet and you don't say until you do. Then your mind isn't cluttered with all this confidence crap. You just do what you do."

"He was coming at me, Wyatt. He'd already killed Shane and opened up once on me. I had no choice at all."

"I believe you. So does every cop in the city. Including Lanier."

"I'm still waking up a couple of times a week. See the double barrels coming down. Connie's even trying to talk me into going to see a shrink."

"It might not kill you."

"Maybe I should."

"Couldn't hurt."

After a small silence, Juhle checked his watch, said, "Funeral," and stood up.

They were driving up Second Street, this time Juhle in the front passenger seat, heading eventually for Fifth and Mission, the *Chronicle*'s offices. Hunt spoke from the backseat. "Hey, Mick, are you all right?"

"Great. Why?"

"Because I've driven with you approximately four hundred times, and you've never once before driven close to the speed limit."

"I never exceed the speed limit," he said. "I don't know what you're talking about."

"Inspector Juhle here doesn't do traffic," Hunt said. "He just does homicide."

But Mickey Dade knew that Hunt was capable of a lie like this one—trying to get him to slam it up to sixty—and Juhle would write him up a ticket while Hunt got a chuckle out of it. So he turned to Juhle, sitting next to him. "Is that true? You don't write tickets? I thought all cops kind of did everything."

"Are you kidding?" Juhle asked. "Traffic division does traffic. I do murders. You want to know the truth, I get pulled over myself for speeding or running a red or some damn thing about every month or two."

"They tag you?"

"No. Of course not. They see the badge, and they either back off or I shoot 'em. But in theory, I'm not on lights and sirens, I'm at the limit or I get tagged. Just like you or any other citizen would."

"Awesome," Mickey said. "That's really true?"

"Scout's honor."

"Cool." And Mickey punched it up to forty-five before the next intersection.

When Mickey pulled the cab up in front of the *Chronicle* Building, Juhle opened his door. "You don't mind waiting?"

"No sweat."

Juhle disappeared into the building, and Mickey looked back over his shoulder. "So how'd you like the pictures? That's an awesome house. Manion's."

"Oh, yeah, sorry. I should have called you off that. I'll pay you for the time, but as it turned out, Juhle had already gone out and talked to her. Then I got busy and never got the time to call you."

"No big deal. I shot the house anyway, though, and JPEG'd it off to you, home and work. You should check it out."

"I will."

"Someday, I'm a famous chef, I'm going to have a house like that."

"I hope you do, Mick. I hope you do."

"Goddamn it! God *damn* it!" Standing on the Geary Street edge of the wide expanse of concrete in front of Saint Mary's Cathedral, Juhle snapped closed his cell phone.

"Shiu again?" Hunt asked mildly.

"You know how long it takes to run a ballistics test, soup to nuts? On a bad day, maybe one hour. You know how long Shiu's been waiting for them to start?" Juhle consulted his watch. "It's already been two and a half hours."

"And you're thinking you should have gone down with him, exerted some authority, as you say, but it's probably just as well you didn't. Since Andrea never shot either of those guns at the judge or anybody else, those tests aren't going to turn out like you want, anyway, and then you'd be really mad. Besides, if you'd have gone down there, you wouldn't have come to Andrea's office, and then where would you be? Still thinking she's your suspect. Now, you're here, with an actual chance to see if not talk to somebody who might have had something to do with the case you're trying to solve."

The last couple of days, Hunt was almost getting to where he was starting to expect television crews wherever he happened to go. Certainly, all three local channels and a couple of the cable stations were again represented here, although it looked as though Trial TV had for some inexplicable reason decided that they didn't need to carry Palmer's funeral live and direct.

A fitful sun broke through onto the throng of arriving mourners. Juhle at first hung back on the periphery of the property, getting the lay of the land, but then he nudged Hunt, who buttoned his suit coat against the steady breeze, and the two of them began to stroll down the row of Minicams.

Hunt pegged the crowd at already between two and three hundred. He recognized quite a number of the city's elite and powerful milling about, possibly waiting to be interviewed themselves—life as one big photo op. They stopped and listened for a minute as the mayor, Kathy West, extolled Judge Palmer's virtues to the blonde from Channel 4. Chief of Police Frank Batiste led a phalanx of his top brass, decked in their dress blues, up into the cathedral's mouth. A woman Juhle knew as another federal judge shared an anecdote with the hunk from Channel 7.

Many, many civilians, of course, kept arriving in a steady stream as well. Juhle pointed out the judge's wife, Jeannette, and her sister Vanessa, who was flamboyant even in black. Palmer's secretary and his clerk.

An elderly couple caught Juhle's attention for a moment. He knew them. It was right there . . . then he snapped his fingers and said, "Carol Manion, and I'm thinking spouse."

Hunt spotted Dismas Hardy—in black pinstripes looking nothing like his bartender persona—walking with a very pretty red-headed woman and his two partners, Wes Farrell and Gina Roake. Farrell gave him a somber nod.

Hunt saw Gary Piersall by one of the vans up ahead, standing with his hands in his pockets, the walking dead. After giving Juhle a quiet heads-up, when they got up to him, Hunt touched the attorney's arm lightly. "Mr. Piersall. Good morning."

"Mr. Hunt. Inspector . . . Juhle, right?" Piersall extended his hand. The men shook. "It's a sad day," Piersall said. "Are you making much progress?"

"Not enough." Juhle gestured with his head to the interview going on in front of them. "Who's that?" he asked.

"Jim Pine," Piersall said. "A client of mine. He and the judge were acquainted."

Hunt threw Piersall a sideways glance to see if he were joking. But no, this was the drill for today. Hunt realized that Piersall wasn't going to be debriefing him on their discoveries in Andrea's office. "He runs the prison guards' union, doesn't he?" Hunt asked, telling Juhle.

Piersall's eyes flicked between them. "Yes, he does."

"What's he talking about?" Juhle asked.

"Apparently, some irresponsible parties have been trying to establish a connection between the judge's death and some recent actions he'd been contemplating with respect to union matters. Mr. Pine is debunking that speculation as ridiculous, which, of course, it is."

"Really?" Juhle said. "That's your position? Because I must tell you, I've heard a little bit about it myself, and it doesn't sound so far-fetched to me. Especially with the Andrea Parisi situation."

"Well, inspector, if that's the direction your investigation is leading you, it's a small wonder you've not made much progress. Now if you'll excuse me, it looks as though Mr. Pine is about done, and we've got to be getting inside." Piersall leveled a last glare at Hunt and stepped around him to get next to his client.

"Let him go," Hunt whispered, moving Juhle along. "It's an act for Pine's benefit. He's got to be the good attorney in public. He told me last night that he was scared to death."

"Of Pine?"

"Keep walking. Yes, of Pine."

The light going on in his head, Juhle stopped in his tracks. "You saw him last night. That's how you found Parisi's car. You were there on something else."

"I was there on what I found this morning, Dev. I just didn't know it then 'cause I hadn't found it yet."

"Well, I've got to have a few words with Mr. Pine."

"And he's going to talk to you?"

"I'm a cop, Wyatt. It's not like he gets to choose."

"He'll be lawyered up. He's already lawyered up. It'll just waste your time. You know it as well as I do."

"You got a better idea?"

"You know," Hunt said, "I think I do."

* * *

They decided to check out the inmate who'd escaped from prison.

On the plus side, San Quentin occupies a large waterfront site with harbor views. Juhle was telling Hunt that he thought a developer could make a fortune here with a small city of condo complexes and an upscale mall, a marina with bay-front dining. The main buildings currently on the property—enormous, industrial-looking concrete structures in a square around an inner yard—would have to go, of course, and they'd have to think up some way to purge the bad karmic load that had accumulated from the decades that the facility had spent housing, feeding, guarding, and executing its inmates. But once they got that done: "They give it a fancy name. The yuppies would be lined up for a mile to bid on the suckers. Hey, 'Q by the C'—get it? Just the letters?"

"I get it. You missed your calling, Dev. I'm serious." Hunt driving, they had left the main road a mile before and joined a surprising albeit short line of vehicles that were now pulled up to the guard's station at the gate. Three hundred yards farther, past the cluster of administration buildings, they saw the entrance to the prison proper. Guard station, double fencing, barbed and razor wire. "How does somebody break out of this place?"

"Good question. That's what we're here to find out."

Juhle had called the warden's office on the way up to make arrangements for their visit—as a homicide inspector on an active case, especially one of this import, he had theoretical access just about anywhere he wanted to go—and they only spent a minute at the guard's station with their identification and signing in.

It was by now early afternoon on a Friday, and half of the parking lot off to their left was filled with the cars of other visitors who had come up the road with them—wives, girlfriends, children, lawyers. But Hunt had been directed to his right, to the administration building, and he parked in a visitor's space in front of it. The wind here whipped off the bay, cold and biting as they emerged from the car.

The warden, Gus Harron, projected a stern bureaucratic competence befitting someone who directed a business whose budget was over one hundred twenty million dollars a year. San Quentin housed over five thousand inmates, almost twice the capacity for which it had been built, and supported fifteen hundred or so combined guards and other staff. Harron wore a gray business suit, white shirt, dark gray tie. He carried a large frame that showed no sign of fat. Rimless eyeglasses seemed to intensify an already imperious countenance, but for all that, he came around his desk and shook hands pleasantly enough, then took a seat on a couch under one of his windows, bidding Juhle and Hunt to take the chairs that faced it.

"Did I get this right, inspector?" he began. "You're working on the Palmer homicide?"

"That's right. And Mr. Hunt's a private investigator who's been handling an investigation for one of his clients—a law firm named Piersall-Morton—that seems to have intersected my own at a couple of points." He paused. "Andrea Parisi works for Piersall."

Harron sat back, one leg crossed over the other, radiating the fact that the connection was intuitively clear. "And somehow both of your investigations are related to San Quentin?"

Juhle shifted slightly. "We don't know for certain, sir. We're interested in finding out as much as we can about the inmate who escaped out of here last Monday."

All amiability vanished from the warden's demeanor. "Arthur Mowery. He's the first escapee I've had in six years. You really need to contact the Department of Corrections personnel investigating that case. I can assure you, there'll be an exhaustive investigation and report into what happened."

"The papers had it that he went out to get a smoke and simply walked away." Juhle was treading lightly. "We were wondering if you had any more details."

Harron uncrossed his legs and leaned forward. "Look. I really don't want to talk about this. An escape is the worst thing that can happen to the warden of a prison, and now you want me to help you make it worse by connecting it to the murder of a federal judge."

"We don't know if it's connected," Juhle said. "If you can eliminate the possibility, we'd be grateful."

A long pause while Harron considered this. "All right," he said at last. "But how is Mowery even theoretically connected to Palmer's murder?"

"We've seen some articles on the possibility that the union might be using parolees on jobs outside."

"What kind of jobs?"

"Muscle. Extortion. Vandalism."

"Mowery was in for violating his parole," Hunt added. "His first time out, he was actually on the union payroll."

Harron's eyes were slits. "And what?"

"And Inspector Juhle here and myself thought it might be worth asking you if you'd heard anything about Mowery getting busted back here for failing to obey orders."

"What orders?"

Juhle shrugged. "Hitting Palmer, for example."

The slab of Harron's face had hardened down to rock. "Bullshit." Abruptly, he stood, walked over to his office door, opened it, and looked out. Then closed it again and came back to Juhle and Hunt and sat again. When he spoke, his voice was barely a whisper. "It couldn't happen. And even if it did, under your theory, Mowery wouldn't have been reported missing."

"Except he broke out," Hunt said. "And really went missing."

Juhle soft-pedaled. "We'd just like to know a few more details about the escape. Maybe there was an unexpected shift change among the guards. The guys who were supposed to protect him didn't get to his new guards in time . . ."

"All inmates must be in their cells at lockdown, inspector. There are no exceptions. If someone's not there, it gets reported immediately. As was the case here." He gave Juhle the hard eye, shook his head dismissively. "Listen. These people, inmates, they don't get out to do a job."

"We realize that, sir," Hunt said. "But until last weekend, Mowery had been out on parole."

"Okay. And?"

Juhle took it up. "And maybe he got violated because he refused to take a job."

Harron wasn't buying it. "In or out, these people are not contract labor, gentlemen. They're psychopaths. They don't keep agreements and they don't follow the rules. If they get out, they're gone until we find them. They never come back on their own."

Hunt knew that this was the obvious and correct response. It was also self-serving. But everyone in the room knew what was being left unsaid—that every prison had a bustling black market in tobacco, liquor, and dope; that sexual activity not only between inmates but between guards and inmates was not unknown; that "marriages" of convenience or protection or even love could create bonds as strong as anything on the outside, bonds that could make life in jail preferable to a life outside; that guards could beat inmates to death and never be called to account for it; that omerta—the code of silence—was the rule among the guards at every prison in the state.

Whatever crimes might be ongoing and abetted by some few venal guards—money laundering, prostitution, drug deals, murders—

the danger and boredom of the daily work and the degree of inter-dependence among these men guaranteed that no other guard would come forth to testify against any of their own. A bad guard was a bad guard, true, but he was a brother first. And you did not rat out your brother. That was the culture. Hunt, Juhle, and Harron all knew that Arthur Mowery's escape could have been arranged and executed with the collusion of some of the prison's guards.

Juhle said, "Nevertheless, at the moment, we've got no choice but to consider Mr. Mowery a person of interest to this investigation."

"Do what you want," Harron said. "But let me ask you this: In any of these articles you saw, was San Quentin in any way implicated?"

"No, sir. Corcoran, Avenal, Pelican Bay, Folsom, a few others, but not San Quentin."

"I'd like to think nothing like what you're proposing could happen on my watch."

"Yes, sir."

"We've already done our preliminary investigation, of course." He crossed to his desk, picked up a folder. His shoulders settled. He ran his whole hand across the top of his head. "I can't give you all of this, but what kind of details are you looking for?"

"You tell us," Juhle said.

Harron in his chair now held the folder open in front of him. He adjusted his glasses, but before looking down, his eyes came up, and he stared off into space. "Mowery's two previous parole violations are interesting in this context, aren't they?" Then he went back to the folder, flipped some pages, passed a computerized printout across the desk. Juhle and Hunt were up now, by the warden's desk.

"Written up three times for assault," Harron said. "Active AB"—the Aryan Brotherhood—"thought to be an enforcer. Connected to one fatal prison stabbing. No willing witnesses, so no prosecution. Five thousand dollars on his books. Probably bribery or extortion or both."

"So he's got money," Hunt said, "which means a connection on the outside."

Juhle went back to the sheet. "He apparently went straight for . . . eight years."

"Either that," Hunt said, "or his parole officer had a reason to stop violating him."

Juhle looked at the warden. "You don't have Mowery's lawyer in there, do you?"

Harron thumbed through some pages, found a business card clipped to one of them. "As of seven months ago, Jared E. Wilkins. The third, no less." He handed the card over.

Juhle took it, gave it a glance, held it up for Hunt. "Sacramento," he said.

"Does that mean something?" Harron asked.

"How does a San Francisco thug get hooked up with a Sacramento lawyer?" Hunt said. He took out his cell phone and, on a hunch, punched up the number on the card. "Mr. Wilkins, please," he said. "Sure, Jim Pine. Yeah, I know, I'm fighting a cold." Hunt closed the phone back up and handed it to Juhle. "Mowery's lawyer knows Pine."

Harron's mouth was stuck on open. Finally he got it to move. "If this goes anywhere, inspector," he said, "I'd appreciate a heads-up, just between us."

"If it goes anywhere, warden, the whole world's going to know about it. Who's Mowery's parole officer, who's busted him twice?"

For an answer, Harron found the page he wanted and under his breath said, "Son of a bitch." He took off his glasses and rubbed his eyes. "Phil Lamott."

"He means something to you," Juhle said.

The warden nodded. "I recognize the name. He started his career here, early nineties. As a guard."

25 /

They just got back to the car when Juhle's phone went off, and he picked it off his belt on the first beep, checked the number coming in, said, "Talk to me, Shiu. Make me happy."

But the call didn't produce that effect. After listening for less than a minute, shaking his head back and forth the whole time, he said, "I'm just leaving San Quentin with Wyatt Hunt. No, not the prison, Shiu. San Quentin, the burger joint. You don't know it? Out by the Cliff House. Awesome fries. Anyway, we might have something else maybe. But he can drop me back at the Hall. I'll tell you about it then."

"Let me guess," Hunt said when Juhle closed the phone. "The ballistics didn't match."

"I hate that guy," Juhle said.

On the rest of the drive back down to the city, Juhle made a couple more phone calls to verify that neither Andrea nor Arthur Mowery had turned up. No, to both.

After another lengthy phone call, during which Juhle asked a few questions but was mostly silent, he rang off. "That was Jeff Elliot. 'CityTalk'?" This was a popular *Chronicle* column that often dealt with the law and its practitioners.

"I know him well. What did he know?"

"Basically, everything. But I only asked him—you heard me—if he knew what it took to bring a guy in on parole violation? Give up? His parole officer says he's violated, period. Smoked a joint. Hung out with the wrong person. No warrant, no proof required. Is there any kind of hearing on this? Any moment with a judge or jury or lawyer?"

"I'm guessing no."

"You'd be right. So your violated parolee finally gets all the way back to prison and what happens?"

"They have a big welcome-back party?"

"Right. Balloons and everything. But after that, within thirty-five days he gets a hearing before a violation committee composed entirely of correctional officers, and guess what percentage of the time they uphold the violation?"

"A hundred and ten?"

"Close. Ninety-nine and a half. So then our guy gets up to a year *on the violation.* And this can be continued up to three years even if you're originally in on a one-year sentence. Can you appeal? Sure. It takes eight months and succeeds point oh-five percent of the time. One in two hundred."

"Was Elliot going to write a book on this or something?" Hunt asked.

"I hit him on a good day. He talked my ear off. I told you he knew everything. You want any more facts?"

"Does it have to be on the union? I'd like to know the depth of Lake Tahoe."

"Too deep to dive to the bottom. That's all you need to know. Here's your last real question, though. How many inmates in California prisons are there for violating parole? I'm talking percentages."

"Nineteen?"

"Fifty."

"That would be half."

"Correct."

"So more than nineteen percent?"

"Way more, Wyatt. Way more."

Juhle had to wait for Shiu, but Hunt had his own wheels and his own agenda, and he wasn't going to wait for anybody anymore, not when he felt they were getting this close. He finally dropped Juhle off at the Hall of Justice on Bryant, went around the corner and up to Mission and, doing his best imitation of Mickey Dade's driving techniques, turned left. The parole office for units 1–3 was six blocks down, and if Phil Lamott wasn't at that one, number 4 wasn't much farther away. It had gotten to midafternoon, between two thirty and three, now almost exactly forty-eight hours since he'd left Andrea at her house. Having worked within the city's bureaucracy for a good portion of his life, Hunt knew that there was a better than reasonable chance that parole officers, like his former CPS coworkers, would be at the office on Friday afternoons, getting their paperwork filled out before the weekend.

Close-up, Hunt put Lamott at about his own age. He wore his dirty-blond hair a bit long by police standards. He'd had bad acne at one time, and now tried to cover the scars, mostly unsuccessfully, with a short yet scraggly beard and wispy mustache. He was hunched over a dinosaur of a manual typewriter to the side of his cluttered desk, pecking away, filling in some official-looking form.

"Officer Lamott?"

His fingers stopped. His head turned. Hunt immediately recognized the expression from his days at CPS—don't let this be more work with only a couple of hours to go until the weekend. "Yeah. How can I help you?" No turn to face his visitor, no offered hand.

Hunt introduced himself, flashed his ID. The explanation of his involvement that Juhle had given to Warden Harron had been a good one for a sense of legitimacy, and he used it again. "I'm working with a law firm in town, Piersall-Morton, trying to locate one of their attorneys who's gone missing."

"Andrea Parisi," Lamott said. The story still big news.

"Right."

"What's she got to do with me?"

"Nothing. But she may have something to do with Arthur Mowery."

This got his attention. He abandoned his typewriter and swung around. "What do you mean?"

Hunt realized that in order to make any sense of the scenario they were pursuing, he'd have to give Lamott the same kind of in-depth explanation that he'd provided for Harron. This he wasn't prepared to do for any number of reasons, not the least of which was that any conspiracy theory involving CCPOA members more or less contemplated the involvement if not of Lamott himself, then of someone in an analogous position.

So he kept it simple, omitting any mention of the Palmer/Rosalier murders. "I mean the police are now considering him a person of interest in her disappearance."

"Arthur? Did he know her somehow?"

"I was hoping to get that from you. I'm assuming you're the one that violated him the two times he's gotten out."

"Yeah, that was me. Both times."

"What did he do?"

"The usual. He was loaded. He's a crackhead, but you probably knew that. What would he have . . . you're saying you think he abducted Parisi or something?"

"The police must think so. I got it from them."

"They're talking to private investigators nowadays?"

"I'm trying to locate her. They're trying to find him. We're cooperating."

"They give any reason? They have any evidence?"

"Not to me and, no, not that I know of."

Lamott pulled at one side of his mustache, then the other. He squeezed the meat of his lower lip. "So what's their interest based on? Is there a ransom note? Did he call from somewhere?"

Hunt feigned ignorance. He was asking his own questions. "I noticed he went about eight years between arrests?"

"He got married and straightened out for a while. He moved up to El Dorado Hills, someplace like that, evidently lived like a citizen until his wife left him a couple of years ago."

"Isn't that a little odd? A guy with his record? Especially with the violence. You'd expect a DV"—domestic violence—"complaint, wouldn't you? Something."

"Maybe not. People get better." Lamott shrugged. "It happens. Get off the dope, you're okay. But you're right, either way, Arthur's a violent guy."

"He's got an attempted murder by firearm on his sheet. Last time you picked him up—Saturday, wasn't it?—he had a gun on him, too. I understand he got into some shit in prison. You believe he really was straight for eight years?"

"Yeah, I do. More or less."

"You see him during that time?"

"A couple of times. Like I told you, he moved up by Sacramento, so he reported up there."

"And never got violated?"

"Apparently not."

"Until he got down here, and you hauled him in?"

"Right."

"After eight years?"

"What's your point?"

Hunt thought the point was obvious enough—Mowery had protection of some kind in Sacramento and got thrown to the wolves down here when he had stopped cooperating—but he didn't want to antagonize Lamott so that he wouldn't talk to him anymore. "I just find it curious," he said. Then he tacked. "So what'd he do? For work?"

"Mechanic. Mostly private planes."

"That's a little unusual, isn't it?"

"I don't know. He's got a pilot's license and knows airplanes pretty well. He's a pretty sharp guy, actually, unless he's strung out. But I go call on him Saturday and he's loaded, I've got no choice. I've got to violate him."

"He's got a pilot's license?" Hunt with visions of Mowery dropping Andrea miles out over the ocean.

"Suspended now. And of course no plane. Although that's a question."

"What is?"

Suddenly suspicion showed in the sallow face. "The cops didn't tell you this? They should know."

"I'm looking for her," Hunt repeated. "They're looking for him."

Apparently, this was good enough. "A small plane, a Cessna I think, got stolen out of Smith Ranch Airport on Monday night. It still hasn't turned up."

"Smith Ranch Airport? I don't know it."

"It's a private place. Small planes. Lots of tie-downs, no security to speak of. It's near San Rafael, and as a flier himself, Arthur definitely would have known about it. You want to know the truth, the whole airplane connection is where CDC's been concentrating their efforts to find him."

"And where is it? Smith Ranch?"

"I don't know exactly—maybe three, three and a half miles from San Quentin." Suddenly another thought struck Lamott with an almost visible force. "Maybe I don't remember, but Parisi hasn't been gone since Monday, has she? It's been that long?"

"No. Wednesday afternoon."

"Hmm. Well, not saying that Arthur definitely hot-wired and stole the plane, but if he did, and he certainly could have, he was long gone by then."

Down the street from the parole office, Hunt sat out in his car, trying to figure out what he had missed. And of course, as Lamott had said, it was still possible that Mowery had not stolen the Cessna at all. Or, for all Hunt knew, since Mowery was a flight mechanic, he might even have absconded with the plane out of Smith Ranch Airport, flown under everyone's radar to any one of the small private airports near the city, and committed all sorts of mayhem in San Francisco. But suddenly what had seemed almost too obvious only an hour before had become implausible if not impossible.

Lamott's reactions to Hunt's questions, or more precisely the lack of them, were instructive as well. Mention of one of his parolees had not sparked a trace of defensiveness, as it certainly would have if Lamott were involved in a conspiracy to break Mowery out of San Quentin so that he could assassinate a federal judge. Lamott appeared to be exactly what he was—a functionary in a civil service job that made few demands on his time or personal life. It was hard for Hunt to imagine the low-affect Lamott as any kind of player in the high drama and secrecy of the union's political arm. To this particular parole officer, Arthur Mowery was clearly just another one of the hundreds of mostly pathetic lowlifes he processed through the system again and again and again. Mowery may have had a controller among the parole officers in the Sacramento region, directing him in the union's mayhem, but Hunt couldn't put Lamott in the role.

Juhle had told him that half of California's prison population were parole offenders, but more than that, he remembered hearing that something like seventy percent of everybody out on parole in California got violated back in, which was twice the national average. Parole officers like Lamott weren't in the business of helping prisoners break out of jail, that was for sure. Not for any reason. The entire thrust of the CCPOA bureaucracy was to keep 'em in, keep the population up so there'd be more jails and more guards.

But all this left Hunt with a great hollowness. There had been a symmetry and even some elegance to the idea of the union as the solution to Andrea's disappearance. She and Palmer had both been involved with it on many levels. The judge's latest order was a great and immediate threat to the union's very survival. Andrea's clandestine research on the labor organization's apparent crimes furthering its political agenda may have been unearthed and exposed her to reprisal. But all of it, taken together, depended upon the belief that the union was engaged not just in systematic harassment but in actual premeditated contract murder.

And if that were the case, and Jim Pine had a war chest of many millions of dollars, which he did, then why would he use, at best, quasi-reliable parolees when he could simply pay professionals on the outside to do the same job more efficiently and with less possible downside? But if nothing else, Juhle had been adamant about one fact through all of their investigations: The Palmer/Rosalier murders didn't look like they'd been done by a professional.

That's what had led them to consider the parolee option in the first place. And now that theory, too, appeared to be fatally flawed.

Which left what?

Hunt pulled out his cell phone. He'd had it off all day and knew that if the damn thing rang right now as he was holding it, he wouldn't answer unless it was one of his gang. Thank God for caller ID. He had missed five more calls in the course of the day, though, and scanning down the list, he saw that they were all clients. Probably all at the very least frustrated with him; at the worst, furious.

Well, he couldn't help that. Not now. Not until this was over.

He'd have to get used to it.

Hunt closed up the phone, turned it off again, unclamped his jaw, threw the Cooper into gear, and pulled out into the street. Wisps of windswept fog condensed on his windshield and forced him to put his wipers on intermittent. He continued south and eventually pulled up half a block short of the Mission Street BART station, where he found a spot to park. Five minutes later, he was eating what he considered the biggest and best burrito in the city.

He kept coming back to Juhle's reluctance to accept the coincidence of Rosalier's presence at Palmer's when someone just happened to stop by to shoot him. Staci had always been there in the picture somehow, providing a tenuous link between Palmer and Andrea, but the CCPOA had always until now assumed a much greater prominence. Now, with all other options either discredited or disproved—it hadn't been the wife, it probably hadn't been Arthur Mowery. A professional in the employ of the union would have done a cleaner, more efficient job of the killings. Hunt could still give no credence to Juhle's early idea that Andrea herself committed the double homicide and then either ran or killed herself, and in any event, they'd tested her clothing and the weapons at her house and found no evidence to implicate her.

Itching to move, but with no place to go, Hunt sipped at his Coke, barely tasted the burrito.

Turning it all over, viewing it from every angle.

There were three victims. Start there.

If Hunt played Juhle's game and ruled out coincidence, these victims must all have been somehow related.

He sat indoors at a red plastic table. Too late for lunch, too early for dinner, there was only one other customer, a woman in her sixties or early seventies who was working on a bowl of *albondigas* a couple of tables down. Watching her, Hunt's mind flashed to Carol Manion of all people, whom he'd seen at Palmer's funeral that morning. Suddenly, it occurred to him that her association with the case, tangential at best, had always been because she'd made an appointment with Andrea Parisi. Parisi had been her connection, not Palmer. But now, apparently, if she'd been at his funeral, perhaps she'd known Palmer as well.

Trying to conjure up some sort of a relationship between Manion and Staci Rosalier to complete the trifecta got him nowhere except to scorn at himself for grasping at such feeble straws. But the exercise didn't seem completely futile as it led him to consider even the most peripheral dancers in this fandango.

Fairchild? Parisi's ex-lover, but no known connection to either Palmer or Rosalier.

Tombo? No. Nothing.

And both men alibied one another Monday night in any event.

Piersall?

Hunt stopped chewing, lowered his drink to the table. Piersall knew both Palmer and Parisi. Undoubtedly he'd eaten lunch at MoMo's at least once. Maybe he was a regular there. It was possible then that he'd met Staci Rosalier, which would make him the only person associated with all three victims. Also, Andrea had come to him about the imminent danger to the union represented by Palmer's order, and again with her concerns about the apparently criminal activities of the CCPOA. Beyond that, the Saint Francis Hotel was a short walk from his firm's offices on Montgomery. Might he have called Parisi from there on Wednesday afternoon and asked her to stop by the office . . . ?

Where what? Where he had Pine's people meet her as she parked in the downstairs garage and then drive her away?

Hunt closed his eyes, willing his brain to slow down, get a grip. This was what he and Juhle, too, for that matter, had been doing for more than two days now, building theories and scenarios out of possibilities plucked from thin air. He knew he could now spend the next hour checking to see where Piersall had been on Monday night, whether he'd left the office between two and three thirty on Wednesday afternoon. And even if Piersall hadn't hired it done, even if he'd done it himself, even if he couldn't account for any of those times, Hunt would still be back where he was now, with no evidence, no hint of proof.

But the tantalizing thought resurfaced. It was a fact that Piersall remained the only human being with a demonstrable connection to

Palmer and Parisi and quite possibly to Rosalier. With no other alternatives, Hunt asked himself, wasn't this worth pursuing, too? What did he have to lose?

He finished his Coke, wrapped up the remains of his burrito, and stood up. The old woman gave him a smile, and he patted his stomach and returned the smile, then walked behind her and dropped his garbage in the can by the door.

This neighborhood was usually the last place the fog hit in the city, and now it was thick and wet, so he knew it was going to be miserable everywhere else. He ran the short distance back to his car and, in the relative warmth inside it, pulled out his phone and called his office.

By the time Hunt got home, he had nothing left.

On his instructions, Tamara talked to Gary Piersall's private secretary and learned that her boss had been chairing a shareholders' meeting Monday night that had run through dinnertime until nearly eleven o'clock. All of Wednesday afternoon, Piersall had been with Pine and other union representatives and attorneys in the firm's conference room.

Tamara also told him that Craig had gotten his last two subpoenas served early, then gone to Ocean Avenue and found the place where Staci Rosalier had worked before MoMo's. It was called Royal Thai, and she'd been there for two years. It was her first job after graduating from high school in Pasadena, down in Southern California.

Juhle put the last nail in the coffin. Hunt had called him just after he left Lamott's to save him a trip to the parole office and to offer his revised opinion now on the likelihoood that Arthur Mowery had played any kind of role in either the Palmer/Rosalier murders or in Andrea's abduction. He'd just pulled into his warehouse, the door closing down behind him, when Juhle called him to say that it had been a long and fruitless day and now he was going home for the weekend, but Hunt might want to know that they'd just gotten word that the Cessna aircraft that had been reported missing from Smith Ranch Airport had been located, crashed in rugged terrain at seven thousand feet of elevation in the Tehachapi Mountains outside of Bakersfield. The pilot, not yet positively identified although the plane was, was assumed to be Arthur Mowery, who'd apparently been trying to make it to Mexico.

"I'm back to thinking she killed herself," Juhle said. "There's nothing else. You want to come by and have some dinner with us? You'd even get to watch me coach a Little League game first. I could call Connie. We wouldn't have to have pizza."

But Hunt had just eaten and didn't feel like company, certainly didn't feel like arguing with Juhle, who was welcome to think whatever he wanted. But for Hunt's part, he was certain that Andrea didn't kill herself, and that this was true because she hadn't killed Staci or Palmer. He took that as unshakable fact, immutable truth.

26 /

Hunt sat at the computer terminal, going through his e-mail. He had spam-blocking software but still the majority of his messages were from organizations or businesses he'd never heard of. There were a couple more Web site hits from people interested in his services and several others from law firms he'd already worked with. He forwarded all of the inquiries along to Tamara at the office on the chance that she didn't already have them—it was his fail-safe backup system.

Mickey's e-mail from yesterday gave him the street address of the Manion home, and his young runner had even gone the extra mile and dug up the private and unlisted residence telephone number, which Hunt no longer needed. Cursorily viewing the JPEG photos Mickey had attached, Hunt wasn't surprised to see that the house was huge and elegant. Terra-cotta, it could have been an Italianate castle overlooking the sea on the Amalfi coast. It must have had twenty rooms, but its most striking architectural feature was a bougainvillea-covered square tower. Mickey had expensive lenses and a good eye, and he'd shot the place from three or four different angles, maybe planning to use it as a model and build one just like it when he became a famous chef.

The last telephoto picture—catching Mrs. Manion and her son coming down the front walkway to what appeared to be a waiting limo—tapped into Hunt's continuing frustration. Hard times for the rich folks, he thought. And then, remembering the waterskiing death of the older son, immediately regretted the reaction. He was being petty.

This wasn't getting him anywhere. Nothing had gotten him anywhere. Somebody had killed Parisi just about right in front of him and gotten clean away with it. Hitting his keyboard nearly hard enough to break it, he logged off.

A few minutes later, having changed out of his work clothes into sweats and tennis shoes, he was back out in the warehouse side, standing at his free-throw line. He intended to shoot from there until he made ten in a row or wore himself out, whichever came first. He dribbled a time or two, stopped, dribbled once again, focusing on his target, narrowing it all down.

Setting himself, instead of taking a shot, he unleashed a straight hard pass—as hard as he could throw—at the backstop. The ball slammed into the top of the reinforced glass. The sound echoed loud and deep, a hollow gunshot, a hammer blow on an empty oil drum. The sound ricocheted off the walls around him.

He caught the return on the fly.

He gripped the ball again now with all of his strength. Stood stock-still. Then he threw it again. Same trajectory, same force. Same explosion of sound reverting to silence.

As he rode the wave, the wait between explosions became shorter. From one twenty-second interval, to once every ten seconds, then every five, then two. Throwing so hard he was grunting with the effort. Finally, shrinking uncounted minutes later, Hunt threw and caught the ball one last time. He was breathing hard, the muscles of his jaw cramped.

His body settled down. His breathing slowed.

Now he dribbled once again, set, and lobbed the ball in a high-arcing shot. It swished through the net, and he let it bounce its way off his court and away to a far corner.

It was 4:22 by the industrial clock over the backboard. He went back to his computer, turned it on again, and waited in a kind of suspension while it booted up. When the screen came on, he got back into his e-mail, brought up Mickey's photos of the Manions' house, and sat in front of the terminal for a very long time, trying to make sense of what his eyes were telling him, resisting the impulse to theorize ahead of facts this time.

Marginally satisfied, leaving the computer turned on, he stood up and walked as though in a trance inside to his living area. In his bedroom, he crossed to his closet, where he'd hung up his suit. In the jacket pocket, he grabbed his portable tape recorder and rewound it through the interview he'd had with Betsy Sobo that morning, then started playing it back from the beginning.

When he'd heard it twice, he went back to the bed and stood

over it for a long moment. Finally, sitting down, he reached for the telephone.

Wu must have been working at her desk. She picked up on the first ring. "This is Amy."

Without preamble, Hunt said, "What time did Carol Manion call Andrea's office to ask if she was coming to her meeting or not? After she'd missed it."

"Run that by me again, Wyatt, would you?"

"Carla said she got the message from Carol Manion on the answering machine the next morning. Isn't that right?"

"Yes, I think so."

"Okay, that means she must have called after Carla had gone home. Correct?"

"Unless Andrea had a direct line, and she called that. Are you getting somewhere, Wyatt? Tamara said you'd gone up to San Quentin . . ."

"No. That was a dead end. Now I'm trying to avoid another one. Carla will still be at work now, won't she?"

"Probably."

"I've got to go, then."

He hung up, Wu's absolutely logical objection echoing in his mind: *"Unless Andrea had a direct line, and she called that."* Hunt, as Juhle had earlier in the day, was beginning to wonder if he was still capable of rational thought. If Andrea had a direct line and Carol Manion had left her message on it between, say, three and five o'clock on Wednesday, then that would end this most remote line of inquiry, too.

But he had no choice. He watched as if from far above as his fingers punched in the Piersall-Morton number.

Then he was talking with Carla.

"No," she said as his heart sank yet again. "Mrs. Manion had Andrea's number, and it was on her machine, not mine."

"Do you know how she got Andrea's personal number?"

"I don't know. And it wasn't personal. It was just her direct line at the office. But a million ways. It was on her card. Or she met her somewhere and gave it to her. Anything."

"So you have no way of knowing what time she called?"

"Well, no, of course I do. It'll still be on the machine. I haven't erased anything this whole week, and it gives the time and date."

Hunt struggled to keep the urgency out of his voice. "Could I trouble you to run in and check that for me, Carla?"

She was gone for an eternity. Hunt, leaving his fingerprints on the receiver, could stand it no more and put her on speaker so he could pace.

Finally, finally: "Wyatt."

"I'm here."

"Seven seventeen, Wednesday, June first, except we already knew the date, didn't we?"

But Hunt had heard what he was hoping to hear. "Seven seventeen?"

"Right. I listened twice to make sure."

"And what time was their appointment scheduled for?"

"Three thirty. She mentioned it in the message."

"What else did she say? Would you mind calling me back from Andrea's office and playing it back for me?"

"Now?"

"Right now. I'll give you my number."

A minute later, Carla was back with him, and Hunt was listening to Carol Manion's voice on Andrea's answering machine. "Ms. Parisi, hello. This is Carol Manion. I was just wondering if you'd forgotten our three thirty appointment this afternoon or if perhaps I had the day wrong in my calendar. Would you give me a call back, please, and let me know? And maybe we can reschedule? Thank you."

"That's it," Carla said. "It sounds like a pretty normal call."

"You're right, it does." Hunt wasn't thinking about what the call sounded like. He was thinking about when it was made. "But listen, Carla. Would you mind not mentioning this discussion to anybody for a little while? Nobody at all."

"No, of course. If you say—"

"I do. Please. Now, is there any way you can connect me to Mike Eubanks? I think he's one of the partners. He's Betsy Sobo's group."

"Yes, he is. Sure. You want to hold a second?"

"I will. And Carla?"

"Yes."

"Between us, right? Nobody else."

"Nobody else," she said. "Okay, here goes. Hold on."

Mike Eubanks wasn't in.

Mr. Eubanks often went home early on Fridays. No, his secretary couldn't give Mr. Hunt his cell or home number, but she could try to reach him and have him get back to Mr. Hunt if it was important.

Hunt told her it was and took the phone with him out to the computer again, where he sat and stared at Mickey's JPEG picture of Carol Manion and her son Todd walking toward the limo parked in front of their house. He focused on the picture, on the slight anomaly that had at long last registered and struck him.

He'd seen Carol Manion in the flesh that morning, walking with her husband outside Saint Mary's Cathedral, on her way in to Judge Palmer's funeral. In that brief near encounter, he'd only had the time to form one impression, and that was of age. Not of debilitating old age, certainly, but not of anything resembling youth, either. Now the clear picture he was looking at confirmed that she appeared to be at least in her sixties.

He shifted his gaze to the boy. Could he be the link with Staci Rosalier that had always been missing in any consideration of Carol Manion in connection with the other two victims? He stared at Todd's face, nearly half in profile from this angle, and wearing a petulant frown. The salient feature of the fuzzy portrait that Staci had framed in her apartment was the boy's beaming smile, and so the similarity, if any, remained obscure. Aside from the coloring, stare and study as he might, Hunt could not say it was the same child or even if Todd Manion had any resemblance to Staci's brother at all.

But the question that had first grabbed Hunt's attention was not the boy's identity per se. It was the apparent age of the mother. Even if Hunt was ten years off on Carol Manion's age and she was only, say, in her mid-fifties (which he doubted), it was highly unlikely that she had borne a child eight years before.

Which meant that Todd was adopted.

This was Hunt's area of experience if not expertise, and he knew that if this were the case, it was decidedly unusual. It was relatively normal for a previously childless couple to adopt, and then go on to have natural children of their own. That had been the case in Hunt's own family—his mother apparently barren before they had adopted him, then giving birth to his four siblings in the next eight years.

But he knew that it was much more rare for a couple with a first or second natural child to want to add an adoptive brother or sister to the mix. Especially with an age gap of greater than ten years. Which is not to say it never happened. But when it did, the circumstances invited inquiry.

To say nothing of the reality that at this point, anything out of the ordinary that had even a tangential reference to Andrea was going to grab Hunt's attention and not let go until he'd wrung an explanation from it.

He sat unmoving in front of the computer screen, but he'd stopped seeing it. With all of his efforts so far, with all of his speculations, he was still left working with only one fact that might get him some traction: Carol Manion had called Andrea's office at 7:17.

Why would she call at that time? Why not at three forty-five or four while she would have been waiting for Parisi's imminent arrival at her home? To see perhaps if she needed directions to the house or if she'd gotten hung up with other business? Or even was stuck in traffic? Although that call would have been to Andrea's cell. Wouldn't it? Wouldn't she have had Andrea's cell number, too?

The telephone's ring startled him out of his reverie. "Wyatt Hunt."

"Mr. Hunt, Mike Eubanks. My office said it was important. What can I do for you?"

"I'm working under Gary Piersall's orders on the disappearance of Andrea Parisi." Not strictly true, but Hunt didn't care. It would get Eubanks's cooperation.

And it did. "Well, then, of course, anything."

"We're looking into the possibility that the matter she had planned to discuss with Betsy Sobo might be important in some way, but the two women never had that meeting. I talked to Betsy this morning and she didn't have much of an idea what Andrea wanted to talk about, other than in the most general terms. But she also said that Andrea had called you first and you'd referred her to Betsy."

"That's right. She wanted to talk about some custody issues, which is more Betsy's bailiwick, so I told Andrea she ought to call her."

"Custody? Was she more specific than that?"

Eubanks didn't respond for a few seconds. "She said she had a potential client with some custody issues that might be fairly complicated, so I told her that Betsy was our ace on that stuff."

"She said potential client?"

"Yes, I'm pretty sure of that."

"So it wouldn't have been the union?"

"The client? No, I didn't get that impression. I'd worked with her on some union matters before, general contract and benefit issues, but this was definitely different. Besides which . . ." He paused.

"What?"

An embarrassed chuckle. "Well, it was a joke Andrea and I had with one another. Whenever she called on union business, she'd start by saying, 'Start your engines, Mike.' "

"Start your engines?"

"It meant we were on billable time from the git-go. This call, though, my secretary told me it was Andrea on the line, I picked up and said, 'I'm revving 'em up,' and she said, 'Not this time I'm afraid.' So it wasn't the union. Is this what you wanted?"

"I'm not sure. It certainly doesn't hurt."

"Good." Then, "Mr. Hunt?"

"Yes?"

Eubanks hesitated. "Do you think there's any chance she's still alive?"

"No one's found her body yet." Hunt's next words came out before he'd thought about them. "Until it turns up, I'm going to choose to keep hoping."

"That's good to hear, especially since the rest of the goddamn world's already got her in the grave. I hope I was some help."

He was going to make a few calls right away, but it was closing in on five o'clock and there might be something on TV that he'd want to see first.

Hunt had bought his television so he could watch sports and the very occasional rented movie. He hadn't tuned in to a single regular network or even cable show in years. People he knew sometimes used to talk about *Seinfeld* or *Friends* and lately now *The Sopranos* or *Deadwood* or those reality-show stupidities. He didn't get it— maybe it was a habit he'd just never developed. Even if he had the downtime, which was rare enough, he would always prefer to do something active, keep the body or the brain engaged.

But now he had his set turned on to the news. For a new all-time low in tastelessness, he gave big points to the first channel that came on, with its picture of a smiling Andrea Parisi in the corner of the screen, the caption "Andrea Watch," and a continually scrolling digital display under it counting the hours, minutes, and even seconds that she had been missing. 50:06:47.

Counting from the phone call to her cell phone, three o'clock Wednesday.

Changing the station, he caught a moment of anchor gravitas: ". . . who refused to be identified confirmed a few minutes ago that Andrea Parisi is now being considered a possible suicide and is, quote, not an impossible suspect, unquote, in the shooting deaths last Monday of Federal Judge George Palmer and his alleged mistress Staci Rosalier. San Francisco police would neither confirm nor deny this characterization, but . . ."

Enough already.

Hunt flipped to Trial TV. Rich Tombo was doing his part of the Donolan wrap-up out in front of the Hall of Justice, just around the corner. It seemed as though it had been forever since this morning in the street outside the Piersall offices when Spencer Fairchild had accused Hunt of colluding with Andrea in concocting this elaborate publicity stunt. When Tombo finished with his analysis of the prosecution's day in court, he staggered even the cynical Hunt by starting to introduce the new woman who would be taking over for the departed Andrea Parisi and providing insight into the defense . . .

Hunt couldn't even look to find out who it was.

Back on network TV, the next station he tuned to had moved along to the inability of authorities to identify any Rosalier next of kin. They had been supplied with a copy of the out-of-focus photograph of Staci's brother, and now the boy smiled out at Hunt while the female anchor's voice urged anyone who recognized this boy to either call the police or the number at the bottom of the screen.

But suddenly Hunt didn't see the kid's face anymore.

He saw the shape and color of what he was standing in front of. It, too, was out of focus, in the background, but once seen, unmistakable. In a second or two, he was back at his computer. Mickey's pictures of the Manion castle. The terra-cotta tower, the bougainvillea. He checked the other shots of the house from different angles, even finding the place where he supposed Todd Manion must have been standing when the picture from Staci's condo had been taken.

Back to Mickey's shot of Carol Manion and her son, coming down to the limo. And something else, at the edge of that shot.

He went back through the pictures again. One straight on of the front elevation, then one of the tower on the right, the triple garages and wide driveway to the left of the entrance portico. Hunt stopped on this one, leaned in to the terminal, although he saw it clearly enough—on the driveway, gleaming in yesterday's bright sunlight, a black BMW Z4 convertible.

27 /

Hunt knew Juhle was off coaching Little League, and so called his cell phone, where he got voice mail: "Dev. The picture of Staci Rosalier's brother was taken in front of Carol Manion's house out in Seacliff. I don't know what this means exactly, but it's provocative as all hell to me. You might also want to see if there's a record of any phone calls between Palmer and Manion, office to office, home to home, anything. In any event, call me as soon as you get this. Go Hornets."

He next considered calling the Manion home, even going so far as to pick up the phone, but he stopped himself. What was he going to say? This was after all a family of extreme wealth and prominence with an exquisite sensitivity to privacy. They had a full-time publicist whose job it was to keep their name out of the newspapers except in preapproved fashion in the society or business pages. You didn't just call them up out of the blue on a Friday night, tell them you're a private investigator, and ask them questions about their son, their relationship—if any—with a murdered federal judge, his mistress, and a missing lawyer. As a homicide inspector, Juhle could perhaps make that kind of a call, but even he would be hamstrung again by their constant limitation in this entire affair: a lack of physical evidence of any kind. What was he going to hang his questions on?

And what did Hunt have, exactly? A completely legitimate phone call about an already scheduled appointment from a wealthy woman to her prospective attorney. A picture of a young boy probably taken in front of Carol Manion's house. A black convertible.

Yahoo.

Six hours ago, Hunt felt he'd had more on Arthur Mowery and

Jim Pine and even Gary Piersall, and the pursuit of those chimeras had wasted a lot of his time and gotten him precisely nowhere. He needed something real, something tangible and compelling that would at least supply Juhle with a wedge he could use to open some kind of an interrogation.

Since he was already at his computer, he got on the Net and Googled the enormous Manion hit list again, trying different combinations to narrow the field somewhat. When he combined Federal Judge George Palmer and Ward and Carol Manion, he found that the families must have known each other at least socially since they had attended a slew of the same fund-raising events in the city. He tried Staci Rosalier with Manion—zip—then with Todd Manion alone and got no hits with both, although Todd had nearly a thousand of his own, all but four of them mentioning one or both of this parents. The four independent listings were evidently captions from pictures of him without his parents that had appeared on one society page or another.

After fifteen minutes and no new leads, Hunt gave up the computer search. Something might be there among all the information on the Manions, but unless he had a more exact idea of what he was looking for—and he didn't—finding it would take forever. Like Mickey with his pictures of the Manions' home, he had to come at it from a different angle.

Before he left his place, Hunt changed again, out of his sweats into slacks, street shoes, a heavy black sweater.

A half dozen cars clogged the small circular driveway and the immediate curb space around Judge Palmer's home on Clay Street. He parked seven or eight houses away, got out of the Cooper, and walked along the fog-draped sidewalk, still unsure of exactly what he was going to do. All he knew was that he had to act, to do something, look under rocks, talk to someone, get out of his place and away from the temptation of doing legwork on his computer. If nothing else, now at least he had a focus, a general thrust to what he wanted to discover.

If the Manions had known Judge Palmer from their mutual charity events well enough to feel that they should attend his funeral, then the judge's wife might be a source of information, of facts, maybe even of evidence. Jeannette had buried her husband this afternoon. As Hunt had hoped and surmised might happen, people had come from the cemetery and gathered afterward at her home. It was as good an opportunity as he was going to get.

Hunt skirted the garden inside the low wall, cast an appreciative glance at the gently trickling fountain, mounted the steps, and rang the doorbell. Inside they obviously weren't doing the hokeypokey, but judging from the buzz and volume of the conversation he heard, the crowd was at least trying to enjoy itself.

A woman about Hunt's age opened the door, gave him a somewhat wary half smile as if she might have recognized him. "Can I help you?"

"I hope so. I was wondering if I might get a few words with Jeannette Palmer."

Immediately any trace of the smile vanished. "Are you a reporter?"

"No." Hunt reached for his identification. "I'm a private investigator . . ."

"I'm sorry," the woman said, "but this really isn't a good time, as you must know. My father's funeral was this morning, and my mother's really in no condition to talk to anybody right now. So if you'd like to call and make an appointment . . ." She backed up a step and started to close the door.

Hunt reacted without thought, put his hand out, his foot over the sill.

The woman looked down at the floor, at his arm holding back the door. "I'm closing the door now. I advise you to back off."

"Please." Hunt stayed where he was. "I'm not here to make trouble, I promise. But I've got an urgent situation that may literally be a matter of life and death."

She shook her head. "Don't you see? You've already made trouble. This is trouble, right now."

From behind her, Hunt heard a deep male voice. "Is everything okay here, Kathy?"

She turned back to the voice, opened the door another few inches. "This gentleman here says he's a private investigator and has to talk to Mom."

"What about?"

"I don't know. I told him it wasn't a good time, but he wouldn't go. He's blocking the door right now. He says it's a matter of life and death."

"Yeah? Let's see about that." Suddenly, the door was pulled opened from the inside. Hunt faced a scowling fullback in a dark suit with an amber drink in his hand. "Get the foot out of the house, pal. Right now. Then you've got ten seconds to tell me what's so important."

"I'm trying to locate Andrea Parisi."

"So are the police."

"Different reasons."

"Yeah? Well, last I heard, they're saying she killed my dad. So I'll go with theirs."

"They're wrong. She didn't. She herself may have been killed."

"By who?"

"The same person who killed your father." Hunt lowered his voice, though not his intensity. "I've got a lead in that case. I need to follow it. Do you want to catch up with whoever killed your father or not?"

Hunt could see he'd scored. The big man rocked back. He released a deep, shuddering breath. Setting his drink down by the door, he told his sister he'd only be a second, then stepped out onto the porch and closed the door behind him. "I'm Dave Palmer. What do you know?"

"I'm trying to get some information on the Manions. They were at your father's funeral this morning. I believe your father or mother must have known them."

"The Manions?" Hunt could see that the name came from about as far out in left field as it was possible to get. "You're talking the Manion Cellar Manions?"

"That's right." If Hunt wanted to keep Dave listening, he knew he had to talk fast. He stretched the truth of what he knew. "Staci Rosalier had a framed picture of the Manions' eight-year-old son in her condo. Todd. They've been showing it on TV tonight, and it'll be in the paper tomorrow. Staci told her friends that he was her brother."

Clearly, Staci Rosalier was a distasteful subject in this environment, but this was an unexpected development that overcame his qualms. "She was lying."

"That's possible, I suppose. But why would she do that?"

"I don't know. Maybe she was a liar as well as a whore. She wanted people, maybe even my dad, to believe she came from money? She had powerful connections? I don't know."

"She wasn't trying to impress my witness. Not like that, anyway."

But Dave still resisted the very idea. "So if she's Todd's sister, she was a Manion, too? I don't think so."

"I'm not sure about that either, to tell you the truth, the exact relationship. Maybe he was her stepbrother, or half brother. That's why I need to talk to someone who's maybe known them for a while. The Manions. Were they friends with your parents?"

"As you say, they knew each other. I don't know how close they were."

"It would help if I could find out."

He continued to wrestle with it. "Mom's not going to want to talk about Staci Rosalier. I guarantee you. She's not going to want to talk about any of this."

"I'll leave her out of it if I can. What I really want to know about is Todd."

"What's he been on TV for?"

"The police are trying to find Staci's next of kin."

"So, then, this is all out now, or will be soon enough. With the Manions."

"Maybe not," Hunt said. "It's not a great picture. And it might be a couple of years old."

Dave grabbed at another excuse to deny, his anger simmering at the surface, ready to boil over. "So you're saying the picture might not even be Todd?"

"No. *I'm* sure it's him."

"So the cops will have an ID by tomorrow the latest, right?"

"Possibly."

"And then they can go talk to the Manions and get anything they want and leave my mother out it."

"Yeah. They could. If the ID's convincing enough. But by then if the Manions have anything to hide, they'll have been warned. They could just deny that it's a picture of Todd. And if they need a better story, they'll have more time to come up with one. It might have gotten to there already."

"But you're talking the famous Manions. What could they possibly have to hide?"

"If there's any relationship at all between Staci Rosalier and themselves, it's got to be part of the investigation into your father's death. Don't you see that? And right now, it isn't. They are no part of it at all. All we have had so far is Carol Manion's appointment with Andrea Parisi—"

"Wait a minute. What?"

Hunt realized that in his haste, he'd left out a crucial link. Now he forged it in place. "So if there is a relationship—any relationship at all—between themselves and Staci, they've consciously kept that hidden so far. Don't you think they'd have to understand how important it is? Don't you find that pretty persuasive?" Hunt knew that it was, knew that he'd made all the pitch he could. He just didn't know if it would be enough. "Please," he said. "This is critically important. I'll leave Staci out of it entirely. I won't take five minutes of your mother's time."

The gatekeeper wrestled with himself. It wasn't yet dark, but a car with its lights on crawled by on the street out front. The fountain trickled into the pond. Inside the house, behind the closed door, a crest of women's laughter broke over the steady sea of conversation.

"Maybe. I'll ask," said the judge's son.

Nobody was going to leave Hunt alone with Jeannette Palmer.

She was flanked on the couch in the living room by her sister Vanessa and the daughter, Kathy, who had originally answered the door. The rest of what appeared to be perhaps twenty or so relatives and apparently a coterie of close friends congregated both here and in the kitchen and dining areas, but Hunt's first question to Mrs. Palmer killed the ambient noise in a rolling blackout throughout the house as though someone had thrown a switch.

"Carol Manion? Of course," Jeannette said. "We've known Ward and Carol for at least fifteen years. They were at the funeral this morning."

"Yes, I know." Hunt had pulled over and sat on an ottoman in front of the coffee table. "I was there, too, Mrs. Palmer. But I didn't notice that they had their son with them."

"Todd, you mean. No, that's right. I imagine he was in school. Funerals are no place for children, anyway."

"He's about eight now, isn't he?"

She paused, considered a moment. "Yes, I think so."

"So he's adopted?"

The question didn't slow her down at all. "Yes. He couldn't very well not be, could he? I think Carol's a year or two older than I am, and I'm sixty-two."

"Mrs. Palmer," Hunt said, "when the Manions adopted Todd, when they first brought him home, do you remember anybody remarking on the fact, the strangeness of it. I mean, Carol was fifty-six or fifty-seven, she already had a sixteen-year-old son. Cameron, right?"

"Yes. Cameron."

"So what on earth did she want with a new baby? She did bring Todd home as a newborn, right?"

"Oh, yes, very much so."

Hunt came forward expectantly. "Mrs. Palmer, did you think then or do you know now if Todd was actually Cameron's baby?"

Jeannette Palmer pursed her lips, then finally relaxed her mouth and nodded. "Cameron went away the summer before to a ski-racing camp. They brought Todd home in late April the next year. Not to be uncharitable, but it was a little bit hard not to draw that conclusion. Although, of course, no one ever said anything to them directly, not to Ward and Carol. And they never treated Todd differently or referred to him as anything but their own son."

28 /

Hunt wasn't far from the Little League field at the Presidio, so he swung by there to find that the evening's early games had all concluded almost an hour ago. Juhle and his family were nowhere to be found, probably out having a postgame meal at one of the city's five thousand eateries. But he tried calling Juhle's house first—you never knew, they might have just had their game and gone home for the first time in history.

But no, the streak was still secure.

He then tried Juhle's cell again, got the voice mail again. He left a much more specific message than the earlier one: "Todd Manion isn't Staci's brother. He's her son. You've got to talk to the Manions immediately, Dev. And bring your handcuffs. Call me."

But all pumped up, Hunt wasn't inclined to drive out to Juhle's house and wait until his friend got home with his family from wherever they'd gone out to eat. He had at least enough now to give Juhle leverage to start a meaningful discussion with Carol Manion.

But his problems with proof continued to plague him.

He knew that even if Todd was adopted, and even if Staci was his birth mother and Cameron the father, so what? If there was no record of any phone conversation or other contact between any of the principals—Carol Manion, Palmer, Andrea, and Staci—then the Manions could deny that they'd had anything to do with Staci since her arrival in San Francisco and stonewall Juhle forever. And with the banks of top lawyers they could afford to hire, they would.

At the very least, to make any headway Juhle would need proof that Staci was indeed Todd's mother. Cameron had died last summer at the age of twenty-four. Staci had been twenty-two. They would have been sixteen and fourteen, respectively. And they would have met while he was at ski camp. And the closest Hunt could come to that with Staci was in Pasadena, four years ago.

But at least it was someplace.

Hunt had learned in the people-finding business that quite often you started with the easiest, most obvious solution. Still parked in the lot by the Little League field, he punched up information for the Rose Bowl city and not really even bothering to hope, asked for Rosalier, first name unknown. Not exactly Smith, he was thinking. But then the operator said, "I have one listing," and he pushed his star key to get the number, which he scribbled on his pad while listening to the telephone ringing four hundred–odd miles to the south.

"Hello." A cultured woman's voice.

"Hello. Am I speaking to a Ms. or Mrs. Rosalier?"

"Yes, this is Mrs. Rosalier, but if this is a sales call, the dinner hour on Friday night really isn't—"

"Not a sales call! Promise. My name is Wyatt Hunt and I'm a private investigator working out of San Francisco. I'm trying to locate the relatives of a Staci Rosalier. It's really very urgent."

"*Staci Rosalier?*" The woman paused, her voice harsh when she spoke again. "Is this some sort of prank call? Some twisted joke? I'm going to hang up now."

"No! Please."

But it was too late. She was gone. Immediately, Hunt hit his redial button, heard a busy signal, hung up, and tried one more time with the same result. When after a couple of minutes he calmed down, he started his car and checked the time on the dashboard, still a few minutes short of eight o'clock. The sky was turning dark overhead. Maybe he should go out to the Royal Thai and check to see if Staci had left any references, pass Juhle's house on the way, see if he was home. Or would it be worthwhile, perhaps, after all, to drop in on the Manions?

As he was leaving the Presidio, he hit his redial button again. This time, much to his satisfaction, the phone rang. Pulling quickly to the side of the road, he shut off his engine, and waited.

When a man's voice said hello, Hunt answered with, "This isn't a prank call. Please don't hang up." He identified himself again and gave his phone number, telling the man he could call him back if he'd prefer. Repeating that it was an urgent matter.

The guy heard him out, then said, "We know who Staci Rosalier is. She's the girl who got killed with the judge up in San Francisco."

"That's right," Hunt said. "I told the woman who answered

before that we were trying to locate her relatives. I didn't mean to upset her."

"You have the same name as somebody who gets killed, people tend to tell you about it. It's made my wife a little uptight. She thought you were some weirdo. We don't know any Staci Rosalier personally."

In theory, that should have ended the call, but something about his answer struck Hunt. "I don't mean to be difficult, sir, but are you sure?"

"Of course I'm sure. What kind of question is that?"

"She would be twenty-two years old."

This time, the hesitation was lengthier. "That's what we read."

Now it was Hunt's turn to pause—if only for an instant. He didn't want to lose him. "You said you didn't know a Staci Rosalier personally. But it seemed that the name meant something to you."

He spoke away from the phone. Hunt heard, "No, it's okay, I got it. He seems all right." Then back to him. "It's just that, well, of course our last name is Rosalier. And we've got a daughter, Caitlin, who has just turned twenty-three."

Hunt had no idea where Mr. Rosalier was going with this, but he intended to let him keep talking. "And?"

"And her best friend in high school was named Staci. Staci Keilly. She basically lived here with us for Caitlin's senior year. We used to joke that she really should be in the family." The voice husked up a bit. "That's why when we heard about Staci Rosalier being the name of the woman shot with the judge—"

"Did you call the police?"

"No. We talked about it of course, but Staci Keilly really isn't Staci Rosalier. In the end, we decided it must just be a coincidence."

Except, Hunt thought, that Juhle was right. There were no coincidences in murder cases. And of course the Rosaliers didn't want to become involved in any trouble involving a murdered federal judge. "If you'll bear with me a minute, sir, do you have any idea where Staci Keilly is now? Have you heard from her recently?"

"No. Not in a couple of years, anyway. Caitlin went back East to college. Middlebury. She was always kind of a nerd and a great student, and Staci was more . . . well, she had kind of a different life. She was very pretty and popular, the way high school girls are, you know. Anyway, after Caitlin left for school, we stopped seeing Staci."

"What about her parents? Do they live in Pasadena?"

"I would imagine, yes. But we didn't know them. I gather the

home wasn't very . . . not much like ours. They didn't seem to care
how often Staci slept over here or how late she stayed. They weren't
exactly the walking advertisement for quality foster care."

Hunt felt an electric thrill that brought goose bumps to his arms.
"You're saying Staci was a foster child?"

"Right. I mean, we got all this information secondhand from
Caitlin, but the situation obviously wasn't very good. Which I suppose is why she hung out here." He went silent for a beat. "You
don't think the young woman up there . . . ?"

"Was your Staci Keilly? I don't have any idea. That would depend on whether you think it's possible that Staci didn't like her foster parents so much that she renounced their name and took yours."

"That sounds pretty extreme. But I just don't know. I've never
heard of anybody doing that. She might have." He cleared his
throat. "In which case she's dead, isn't she?"

As her father had said, Caitlin Rosalier was a nerd. Late springtime
Friday night, and she was in her apartment in Boston alone, reading. "My parents gave you this number? Really?"

"You could call your home and ask them, Caitlin. I could call
you back in three minutes."

"If you don't mind, I think I will. And if I decide to talk to you,
I'll call you back." Her mother's daughter, all right. She hung up.

Three or more long minutes later, she called, sounding as though
one of her parents, besides vouching for Hunt, had broken the bad
news. The voice was tremulous, subdued. "They said you want to
know a little more about Staci? I can't believe somebody killed her.
Who would ever have done that?"

"That's what I'm trying to find out, Caitlin. Your dad said the
Keillys were . . . well, maybe you could tell me what you know?"

"The main thing is I didn't know them too well. Just from what
Staci told me mostly."

"Which was what?"

"She didn't really like them, but also it didn't bother her too
much. She was used to it, I guess. It wasn't like a real home exactly."

Hunt had his own fairly well-formed ideas about some foster-
home environments, but every one was unique, and he needed to
know about Staci's experience. "How was it different?"

"Almost all ways. Except first, I guess, they adopted her." This
was unusual, Hunt knew. As a general rule, foster care was intended
to be short-term, with eventual placement either back with the orig-

inal or with adoptive parents. But only rarely did foster parents adopt any of their charges. "I think she was one of the first ones they took in, when she was like three or four."

"Do you know why she was in foster care in the first place?"

"I think—this sounds melodramatic, I know, but I think it's true—she was abandoned at birth. Then bounced around to a whole bunch of places when she was a baby. Evidently, she was pretty high-strung and colicky and cried a lot. In fact, that's what she used to call herself, the High-Maintenance Kid. Which she really wasn't, high maintenance, I mean, not when I knew her. Anyway, until she got placed with the Keillys, and they kept her."

"But there were other kids in the house?"

"Well, that was the thing. By the time Staci and I started hanging out, the foster-care thing was more like a business to her parents. Neither of them had other jobs and, you know, they get paid by the day and by the kid. So they'd just get kids delivered to the house by one of the agencies or another, then keep them a day or a few weeks, maybe a month . . ."

"Yeah, I know how it works," Hunt said.

"Okay, but what got to Staci was the change. Where suddenly, with all the coming and going, she didn't feel like they loved her or even wanted her as a daughter anymore. She'd caused them nothing but trouble and hadn't been worth it in the end. She wasn't bringing in any money. In fact, she was a drain on them."

"How had she caused them so much trouble?"

"That I don't know. She wouldn't talk about it. Just that she was the High-Maintenance Kid. But I gathered it was before they moved to Pasadena. Something must have happened, though, that changed the whole relationship, where suddenly they didn't think much of her anymore. Like they gave up on her because she was just too much trouble."

"When was that?"

"I think the end of her freshman year. I mean high school."

"And where did they live before that?"

"Fairfield, I think. That's in Northern California."

"I know. I'm calling from San Francisco." He paused for a second. "Caitlin," he said, "do you know if what happened is she got pregnant?"

She hesitated. "One day, we started talking about if we were going to get married and have kids someday. You know, the way you do when you're in high school with your friends. And she started crying. I mean really crying. And then when she finally stopped, I asked her what was the matter, and she said she just didn't want to talk about babies anymore. Never ever ever. Babies were just too painful to her."

"Why was that?"

"She had a baby once. They just took him away."

Hunt still sat parked within the bounds of the Presidio by the side of the street in his Cooper. He had one more stop to make on this bleak road if he wanted rock-solid certainty, and he had to have it. He consoled himself that he was actually performing a service for Juhle as well—locating Staci Rosalier's next of kin. The Keillys, too, were listed in Pasadena, and two minutes after he'd hung up with Caitlin Rosalier, he was speaking through the cacophony in the background—television, music, screaming children—to Kitty Keilly.

"I'm sorry. Who is this again, please?"

Hunt told her, then waited while she told him she had to get to someplace a little less noisy. Listening to her progress through her home—"Turn that thing down!" "Jason, put that away!" "No more food. I mean it, you!" "Damn damn damn!"—he got a decent sense of the environment from which Staci had fled and never looked back. A door slammed, and she was back with him. "There," she said at last. "I couldn't hear myself think in there. Now, Mr. Hunt, is it? You said you were a private investigator, calling about Staci?"

"I think so. Although I believe she changed her last name."

"Is she in trouble again? That girl was made for trouble. But I don't know how I can help you. We haven't seen hide nor hair of her for years now, since a few weeks after she graduated by some miracle. Not that that's not what you expect, of course, you been at this as long as we have. I mean, they have their own lives, and there's certainly no such thing as gratitude for the people who raised you. We've seen that enough, God knows. If she needs money, you best tell her she's barking up the wrong tree. But all right, what's she done now?"

"Before we get to that, ma'am,"—and the pain that Hunt would much rather avoid bringing to her—"I wonder if you would mind telling me about her baby."

The hesitation gave the lie away. "She didn't have no baby. Who are you working for?"

"At this point, I'm working for Staci, ma'am."

"Then why didn't she tell you about the baby, she wants to talk about it?"

"I thought you just said that she never had one."

A silence.

"She had a boy eight years ago, didn't she? The father was Cameron Manion."

"I'm not supposed to talk about this."

"Did the Manions pay you not to talk about it?"

She didn't respond.

"Mrs. Keilly?"

"She never had a baby. I told you."

"I think you've just told me she did."

"I don't want to hear any more about this." But she didn't hang up. Hunt waited. Finally, she spoke in a different, smaller voice. "Oh, God, what's happened?"

"It's not good, ma'am. I think you want to be sitting down." He gave her the news as delicately as he could. Envisioning her as ill-tempered, self-pitying, selfish, and ignorant, he nevertheless felt his heart go out to her when he heard the emptiness in her voice as she exhaled, "Oh."

When he finished, silence engulfed the line.

When Mrs. Keilly finally spoke, it was barely a whisper: "That rich old woman thought her boy was so great, so perfect. They were so far above all of us. And that my girl was trash. All of us were trash. She thought Staci got pregnant on purpose to get her hooks into them and their money."

"So what did they do?"

"Well, first, of course, they denied Cameron was the father. They said everybody knew that Staci was a slut and was sleeping with every boy in the camp."

"She was at Cameron's water-ski camp?"

A brittle laugh. "Are you kidding? We couldn't afford anything like that. She was a lifeguard at Berryessa, that was all. It was her summer job. Maybe we shouldn't have let her go up there alone, but it was supposedly an excellent camp for rich kids, and we trusted her. We didn't think . . . well, it doesn't matter what we thought."

"So then what?"

"Well, say this for the boy, he fessed up. Wouldn't hear no talk about Staci being with somebody else. That was his baby, their love child, and he was going to be a man and take care of it, and marry her, too. He loved her. Sixteen years old. The fool."

"So you—"

"Hold it. We didn't do anything. Nothing wrong, anyway. If

this was their precious boy's child, then the baby was *her* grand-child. . . ."

"You mean Carol Manion's?"

"That's who we're talking about, isn't it? Carol rich bitch fuck-ing Manion. Her son wasn't likely marrying any white trash. And she wasn't allowing no grandson of hers being raised in some trailer park. Oh, and the scandal. Don't forget the scandal. You know they never even came to see us, talk to us? Just sent their doctors and lawyers. Cutting their deal."

"With who? With Staci?"

She'd found her voice again, snappish, whining. "Staci didn't get to choose. She was fourteen years old, for God's sake. When she wouldn't sign the papers, we signed them for her. It was our deci-sion and best for the child, for everybody. There wasn't anything wrong with what we did."

"How much did they pay you?" Hunt asked. To leave your daughter's child with them so they could raise it as their own. And then to move your fourteen-year-old Staci—no doubt without any warning and perhaps with a deception tantamount to kidnapping—to another far-distant part of the state.

"It wasn't the money," she said.

But he knew that, of course, that's exactly what it had been.

29 /

Case or no case, Juhle had learned the hard way that you didn't take your cell phone to your kid's ball game if you didn't want to be disturbed. And tonight, since he was actually functioning as the Hornets' manager, the rule applied even more strictly. So he was truly unreachable, his pager and cell phone in his glove box.

Then, after the team's win and pizza with the family, his conscience got the better of him, and he drove them all over to the Malinoffs' place in Saint Francis Wood to visit Doug. He was still in bed, his leg encased to his thigh. Everybody signed the cast—Juhle wrote "Slide, dammit, slide!" and Connie had added under it, "But not on grass where the spikes can catch." And everybody had a chuckle. Then Juhle and Connie each had a couple of beers and hung out in the bedroom with the invalid and his wife, Liz, until the Giants game on the big screen was over while the six kids sat mesmerized by some animated feature film in the playroom.

Now it was a bit after ten, the kids were down in their own beds at home, and Juhle took off his sling and laid it over the bedpost, rotated his shoulder in a tight circle.

"Any progress at all?" Connie asked as she came in from the hallway.

"At least it's not frozen. I think I'm going to stop with the sling. And it's getting so I can pick up small objects in the other hand. It's slow, but every time it gets me down, I think of poor Doug stuck in his bed for the next few weeks with a spiral fracture and, call me cruel, but somehow I feel better."

"You are cruel."

"True. But in a friendly, kind of touchy-feely way. Was it just me or did you get the impression Doug was surprised we won tonight with me managing?"

"Surprised? His worldview went out of whack. Did you see his face when you told him you let the kids do their own batting order? With everybody in a position they'd never played before? I thought he'd have a heart attack."

"I probably set the team back a couple of years."

"No doubt about it." Without breaking stride, Connie walked up to him and put a finger on his chest. "I see you looking at your phone, inspector, and I must admonish you—do not turn it on. Don't even pick it up. I'm going to retire to the powder room for a minute and return in a state of natural splendor for which you should prepare yourself. You will need all of your energy, I warn you."

Connie was breathing deeply beside him most of an hour later when he left the bed, grabbed his phone and a robe, and walked out into his living room. Played his messages. Finally called Hunt. "You awake?"

"Full-time," Hunt said. "Where are you? You got my messages?"

"Home, and I just listened to them. You've been busy."

Hunt outlined it all briefly again, Juhle taking down names, approximate dates, telephone numbers.

"So it's all about this kid?" Juhle asked when he'd finished.

"Right. Carol Manion's been raising Todd as her own son since he was born, as Cameron's little brother, when he really is his natural son. It looks like the adoption wasn't even legal. They just paid off Staci's parents to get her out of the picture right after the birth."

"They admitted that?"

"As much as, Dev. But Staci doesn't learn to live with it. When she's eighteen, after high school, she moves up here, no doubt to just be close to her kid, and sometime after that finds Todd and from a distance takes the picture that everybody's seen now. After that, I don't know what happened exactly. Maybe she saw the good life this kid had, way better than anything she could offer him. Plus, she's still only a teenager. She's got to be intimidated by the Manions. But at least she's physically close to her son now. And Todd's got a mother who loves him, who he believes *is* his mother. Add to that, that Todd doesn't know Staci at all, never had. And he was, in fact, living with his natural father. Maybe she came to terms with all of it."

"Until Cameron died?"

"Right. I think that's what happened. Cameron died, Todd's real father. After that, somehow it wasn't the same. It didn't feel the same to Staci, Todd being raised by his grandmother alone. It wasn't fair and it wasn't right. Besides, by now—we're only talking last summer—Staci's life has changed pretty dramatically. She's not only four years older and a real adult, she's got a good job, she's living in this very nice condo. On top of that, she's intimate with Palmer, who not only has huge power, but who, it turns out, also knows the Manions. She's got leverage and even legal standing now. She can fight to get her baby back."

Juhle, going along with it. "So the judge gets her set up with Parisi."

"Not yet, I don't think," Hunt said. "He gives Andrea's card to Staci, okay, but before they get involved with a bunch of lawyers and it gets ugly, Palmer's the big negotiator with the ego to go with it, right? He can call Carol Manion, and everybody can talk it all out like civilized people. Plus, this makes him even more of a hero to Staci."

"So he invites her over to his place Monday night?"

"That's how I see it. It starts out a nice call from Palmer to Carol Manion, old friend to old friend. Come on over, and we'll talk about the situation, reach some amicable settlement. The judge mentions that he's extremely sensitive to Carol's privacy issues and so far has made sure that neither he nor Staci has mentioned a word about this to a soul in the world. All Staci wants is some time, some regular visitation with her baby."

"But . . ."

"Exactly. But Carol doesn't want an amicable settlement, she won't hear of any visitation. She's already lost Cameron within the last year. There is no way she's going to let this trailer-trash slut have anything to do with Todd, now her only son, and with the life she's given him. So when she comes over to the judge's on Monday night, she comes armed. She's ready to have the whole issue die right there with the judge and Staci."

"So where's Parisi come in?"

"I've given that some thought and think this works. Listen. We know that Carol didn't walk in firing. The judge was at his desk, right? With Staci over next to him. So they talked at least for a minute or two, maybe a lot longer. I figure Palmer told Carol that either he or Staci had talked to Andrea already, that she was going to be handling the visitation details, the documentation, something like that. So she called Andrea either that night or the next day and set up the Wednesday appointment."

"Uh-oh."

"What?"

"You were going fine up till then. Why would she have waited until Wednesday?"

"Maybe that was the first appointment Andrea had."

"But if we'd have identified Rosalier before then, Parisi would have seen the connection and come to the police."

"Maybe, but probably not. I don't think it necessarily means she would have said anything to anybody. She's a lawyer. Manion could have called, promised her a retainer to get them into an attorney-client relationship, then confessed the whole damn thing to her on Monday night, and she couldn't have breathed a word of it. Wouldn't have. Andrea could have met her thinking she was going to be doing her defense." After a minute of silence, Hunt said, "Dev?"

"Yeah, I'm here."

"I like it."

"Me, too."

"But we've still got no evidence."

"Right."

"Or sign of Andrea."

"Hey, Wyatt," Juhle said gently. "We may never get that. You understand?"

"I know. I'm not counting on it. The Manions aren't home, by the way."

"Did you go by there tonight?"

"Yeah."

"What for?"

"Maybe have a discussion with them."

Juhle took a breath. "I think we're getting into the realm of police work here, Wyatt. Maybe you've gotten us so close, I can start doing my job. You don't want to muddy those waters."

"Oh, okay."

"Where are you now?"

Hunt didn't answer right away. "Parked out in front of their place."

"Wyatt."

"I'm cool, Dev. Don't worry. I'm not going to do anything stupid."

"You're already doing something stupid. If Carol killed Andrea, it's a police matter."

"Of course. What else would it be?"

"It would be something you wanted to get out of Carol Manion on your own. Maybe some inkling that you'll be able to find Andrea?"

"No."

"What, then? Andrea's dead, Wyatt. Really. I'm sorry, but that's what it is. And I'd prefer it if you didn't even talk to any of the Manions, even if you get the chance. I mean it."

"Well, as I said, they're not home."

"Neither are you, and you should be."

"I will be soon."

"When, though, exactly?"

"When I'm done here."

When he hung up with Juhle, Hunt called Mickey Dade and tried to interest him in driving up to Napa, where he could find Manion Cellars, see if the proprietors were at their home up in wine country. Mickey showed little interest in this particular field trip. He'd already lost some taxi income running around for Hunt last night and earlier today. And now Friday was his busiest night with the cab, and he needed to make all the money he could if he wanted to get into his cooking class next week. Besides, Mickey told Hunt that he'd already been up in the area plenty of times and knew where Manion Cellars was. It wasn't like they were trying to hide the place, he said, since they'd gone to the trouble of building and staffing the visitors' tasting room and all. "If you can't find 'em, Wyatt, I'd consider a career change," he said. "I hear plumbing's got a lot going for it."

Hunt had gone up to the enormous Manion house when he'd first arrived and rang the doorbell, listened to its chimes peal and fade into the unseen vastness of the interior. For a while afterward, he'd sat in his car, hamstrung by ambivalence. He didn't know where the Manions were or if they were coming home here. And he wasn't really a hundred percent certain what he planned to do if they showed up and he got to talk with them.

But Hunt had come here on instinct, and now instinct stirred him again. He got out of his car and stood a moment, staring through the fog at the dark facade of the Manions' home. He crossed the street and started up the walkway to the front door but hadn't gone more than a third of the way when he heard the sounds of car doors opening and closing behind him. He turned, squinted against the sudden glare of a flashlight. Two men were advancing toward him.

"Hold it right there! San Francisco Police! Put your hands over your head!"

Instead, thinking it was either Juhle or some friends that he'd talked into hassling him for fun, Hunt spread his hands and started to take a step back toward them. "What are you . . . ?"

"I said over your head!"

"He's reaching . . . !"

Now suddenly in a rush they came at him, one of the guys hitting him high and hard, manhandling him backward, stunning him before he could even react.

"Jesus! Hey! What the . . . !"

Then they were both on him, complete professionals who knew how to take a man down in a hurry and had obviously done it many times before. One of them, getting Hunt's hands behind him as they rolled him over into the wet grass; the other, with a knee in his kidneys, one hand squeezing on the back of his neck while the other hand patted him down, found the gun tucked into his belt, freed it from its holster.

"Well, well, well," he heard. He looked up into Shiu's slightly puzzled features. Hunt's arms got jerked back nearly out of their sockets, and as the handcuffs snicked on one wrist, then the other, Shiu bound him from behind.

Hunt still had a knee on his spine, a hand at the back of his neck. Still struggling, he managed a few words. "Shiu, it's me, Wyatt Hunt. Knock it off. You're making a mistake!"

"You made the mistake," the other voice said, "when you didn't put your hands up."

Grunting against the pressure on his neck, Hunt spit out the words. "I've got a license for the gun," he said. "Check my wallet, back right."

"I know who you are," Shiu said. "Just calm down and we'll sort this out." But the pressure on his back and neck never let up. Hands plucked the wallet from his pocket, the flashlight's beam danced over the manicured lawn. For a few seconds, a chorus of heavy breathing framed the night, but no one spoke.

Shiu finally said, "What are you doing here, Hunt?"

The knee came off his back, the hand off his neck. His assailant straightened up quickly and backed away. The flashlight beam shined in Hunt's face.

He rolled onto his side, blinked against the light. "You want to undo these cuffs?"

"Not just yet," the voice said. "I asked you a question. What are you doing here?"

Hunt gave them an answer he thought they'd like. "I'm helping out Devin," he said.

It didn't go the way Hunt planned.

For whatever reason, most probably because Juhle had decided to get some uninterrupted sleep before he went in early on a Saturday morning, he had his phone unplugged when Shiu called to give him the news.

Shiu and Al Poggio, the other cop in on the bust, were part of a group of about a dozen homicide inspectors who put in serious off-duty time for the Manions. In a city where policemen augmented their salaries by serving as rent-a-cops for everything from sports events to business conventions, from fashion shows to grand openings, the best job going was this kind of private security work. And hence, it was reserved for the elite such as homicide and select other senior inspectors. Paying fifty dollars per hour, the duties were laughably light and typically included nothing more than several hours per shift of television viewing—closed circuit, cable, and network.

When Juhle didn't answer his telephone, neither Shiu nor Poggio were tempted to free Hunt from the cuffs. It was greatly to their advantage to show that they had responded to an actual threat to the client's security from time to time, and if that threat were exacerbated by the inherent danger of a concealed weapon, so much the better. The Manions were paying top dollar to keep their home safe, and if there was never a legitimate threat to that safety, they might be tempted to consider cutting back on their preparedness—and their security forces.

Under no circumstances were Shiu and Poggio going to let this incident end without an official report of some kind. Hunt's new Sig Sauer P232 was not the weapon listed on his concealed weapons permit, and that was all they needed. So they called for a squad car to pick up their suspect and take him back to the local station for questioning.

Shiu, of course, knew all about Hunt's involvement with Juhle, but he'd been very much on edge and chafing all day—in fact for the past several days—under Juhle's not-so-subtle ridicule. Telling him to exert his authority at the lab. Joking about the San Quentin hamburger stand. Not funny. Well, Shiu would see how funny Devin would think this was—Wyatt Hunt behind bars overnight. Trespassing. In possession of an unregistered weapon.

Shiu closed his phone and walked back to where Poggio stood with Hunt. "What we do is, if we're looking for something," Poggio was saying, "we get a warrant based on probable cause, signed by a judge. Maybe you've heard something about this? So given that, maybe you could tell us what you were doing?"

"I've been working on the Palmer/Rosalier case and I had some questions I wanted to ask the Manions," Hunt said. "I was out here in the area, anyway, and I figured I would see if they were home." He turned to Shiu. "You know I'm on this. Tell him."

Shiu shook his head. "I know you've been working with Dev, sure, but I don't know anything about what you're doing here, and Dev's not answering his phone, so it doesn't look like your lucky night. What *are* you doing here, since we're talking?"

"I wanted to have a word with the Manions."

Poggio chuckled. "That's good. Except, you notice, they don't seem to be home. So you just happened to be passing by and were going to knock on the door? This time of night?"

Hunt lifted his shoulders. "I wanted to see if any lights were on, maybe look in the garages."

Shiu said, "That's funny. We've got you on videotape an hour ago ringing the doorbell that time, too. And you've been parked here in the street since before that. You think they showed up while you were sitting out in front and maybe you just missed them?"

To which Hunt could make no response that wouldn't dig him in deeper.

In another minute or two, the squad car pulled up. As they finally unlocked the handcuffs, each man took one of Hunt's arms and together they stuffed him into the backseat, slamming the door locked behind him. Shiu pulled the driver aside. "You can write it up as a twelve-oh-twenty-five"—concealed weapon violation—"but don't send him downtown or he'll just bail out. Keep him at the station until the next shift shows up in another hour, then we'll be down to talk to him."

30 /

Mickey Dade was a serious food-and-wine guy. When Hunt had called him earlier in the night asking him to drive up to wine country, if he'd realized that this was the weekend of the Napa Wine Auction or, as they were calling it this year, Auction Napa Valley—the Holy Grail of American haute everything—he'd have told his boss he wouldn't have missed it for the world.

In celebration of the day, all of the great local restaurants were going to have special tasting menus, some available at prices affordable to the hoi polloi. There'd be grills set up in parking lots, world-class chefs roasting spring lamb and quail and asparagus, oysters and sausages and eggplant, the air redolent with herbs and mustard and smoke from vine cuttings.

So Mickey had made his three hundred and fourteen dollars, plus fifty-one in tips on his regular shift, which ended at two in the morning. Dropping his cab off at the dispatch house, he picked up his own used Camaro, and then, sick of fog and not remotely interested in sleep, he pointed the car north on 101 and took it over the Golden Gate Bridge, by JV's Salon in Mill Valley, then past Vanessa Waverly's home in Novato. Turning east on 37, he averaged eighty-two miles per hour until he got to the Napa/Sonoma turnoff at 121, then jammed it up over the Carneros grade and onto Highway 29 in just a little over twenty minutes. Forty-eight minutes, all told, a new personal best.

Once in the valley, under a clear and cool night sky, he took the Oakville Crossroads over to the Silverado Trail—the other north/south artery in the valley—and turned north. In a few miles, he pulled left off the road into the driveway for Manion Cellars, obvious and visible even in moonlight. In front of him, the château itself looked down from a small promontory. Off to either side, the vineyards traced sinuous lines over an undulating landscape. Slightly to his right and up ahead, the promontory fell off into more vineyards, but above them, he could make out the line of four newly excavated caves back into the limestone rock, the doors that Manion Cellars was using for its logo.

The gate to the estate was closed across the driveway, so Mickey backed out and proceeded north on the Silverado Trail up as far as Saint Helena and Howell Mountain Road, where he knew a few good hiding places, and here he parked on the side of a side street under a low canopy of oak. He carried a sleeping bag in his trunk for emergencies such as this, and within five minutes of setting his brake, he was sound asleep on the soft ground next to his car.

At five forty-five, Juhle got the paper from his front porch and brought it back to his kitchen table, where he laid it out next to his coffee. His shoulder had tightened up again overnight, but he'd made the decision to leave the sling at home, and he was going to stick with it. When his administrative miseries had concluded and they'd brought him back to work, Connie had given him as a present a device called, he thought—his French wasn't much—a *café filtre* that made coffee by filling a cylinder with very fine ground beans and hot water, and then pressing down on a strainer. It had been too painful to use since the burnout game he'd had with Malinoff, but this morning, in his new spirit of healing, as he forced the strainer through the black liquid, he realized that even the broken bones in his catching hand were truly on the mend.

The coffee was far thicker than anything he'd ever made at home, and he had developed a taste for the bitterness, albeit tempered with two teaspoons of sugar. Now he sipped, savored, opened the newspaper, looking for the picture of Staci's brother. Or was he, as Hunt now believed, Staci's son? Or was it a picture of Todd Manion, to whom Juhle had been cursorily introduced when he and Shiu had first interrogated Carol Manion earlier in the week?

Away on the Presidio Little League diamond, and then watching the Giants' game at the Malinoffs' last night, he'd missed the many times the photograph had been televised, and now he wanted to examine it again in light of Hunt's information.

He found the photo effortlessly enough, well positioned on the top of page five, but looking at it, he found himself disappointed and somewhat hard-pressed to place the face before him with that of the boy he'd shaken hands with a few days ago. In the first place, the fuzziness of the original photograph had been magnified by the half-tone reprint. Beyond that, the Todd Manion he'd met for only a few seconds was still clearly older than the smiling boy in this snapshot—indeed, neither he nor Shiu had remarked on any similarity between the two when they'd first come upon the picture in Rosalier's condo.

And, of course, this picture in the paper today was black and white, so even the so-called distinctive background—the terra-cotta tower of the Manion home—left him unconvinced. Studying the face in front of him now, Juhle realized he had little confidence that this would result in any kind of positive identification of Todd Manion from someone who knew him today.

And yet Hunt, starting with this premise, had apparently run a new quarry to ground. He'd unearthed another believable scenario for the deaths of Palmer and Rosalier, maybe even for the missing and presumed dead Andrea Parisi. As Juhle and Shiu had done originally with Jeannette Palmer, and as he and Hunt, working in concert yesterday, had done with Arthur Mowery, Jim Pine, and the CCPOA.

Juhle put his coffee mug down on the table and stared off into nothing. He did not underestimate the importance that this case might have on his career, for good or for ill. If he blew it by a false arrest, a bad arrest, or no arrest—all potential yet distinctly different kinds of failure—he could kiss away his chances to make Police Officer of the Year. And without that, he believed, his citation for heroism would always be tainted, his reputation forever clouded. On the other hand, success in this case would go a long way toward proving that Lanier's confidence in him had not been misplaced, that his reinstatement as an active homicide inspector had been justified.

He wanted it so badly it made his teeth ache. But now Hunt's latest path to his own salvation was starting to look like it meant an investigation into one of the wealthiest, most politically connected, philanthropic families in San Francisco. And why? Because they had adopted a child, perhaps their own grandchild, eight years before.

He recalled Lanier's words to him the last time they'd met in his office. Lanier did not want to hear about any suspects, especially in this case, and especially coming from Juhle, without evidence to back up the accusation. Juhle's gall rose at the memory of what this discussion had been when he'd been arguing that Andrea Parisi had killed the judge and his girlfriend, and then herself—a scenario that was still, from the facts in evidence, plausible.

Last night, both exhausted and exhilarated by the accumulation of facts Hunt was presenting, he had found that this new theory had taken on a lustrous quality. Shenanigans in high places, coverups, conspiracies, class warfare. It had all sounded so sexy, so right.

But here, now, as the first light of day outside revealed the thick, gray blanket that had wrapped itself around the city in its sleep, Juhle sneaked a last peek at the picture of Staci's brother/son. Or was it her nothing? A vision of a child she may or may not have lost.

Juhle realized that he and Shiu would have to make all the calls that Hunt had made last night. And even if everyone repeated their stories faithfully—nowhere near a certainty—he would then have to arrange for Mrs. Keilly to fly up and identify Staci as her daughter.

And only then, perhaps, could he begin to make a case against Carol Manion, if he were still so inclined. If she was already the child's adoptive mother and legal guardian, she wouldn't have needed to protect those rights. But if she'd simply bought the child from Staci's parents and had falsified or forged documents or even had no documents, then Staci might have had every right to reclaim her child. Carol Manion would be nothing more than a kidnapper. Juhle could envision no scenario more likely to provoke a woman of power and influence to do something hasty, not to say deadly.

Could it be that simple, that basic, that much a question of class and greed?

Yes, he decided. It could be.

But in a situation such as this one, every move had to be by the book. The smallest procedural flaw would render all of his efforts useless. Lawyers would be lined up to find ways to toss evidence, dismiss charges, slander the arresting officers.

He would have to take it slow. He had wanted a fast and right-eous arrest in this case more than he'd wanted to admit to himself. That desire had impaired his judgment at nearly every turn. He'd been flitting from theory to theory for the better part of this week, and each one had seemed workable until it became time to deliver any kind of proof.

So now here he was, up on Saturday at six o'clock. He'd already had his blast of caffeine, and he wasn't going back to sleep. He sipped more coffee, absently turning the pages of the newspaper. He paused briefly at the sports section, checked the no-surprise weather—morning and evening fog, partly cloudy afternoon, light winds, high of fifty-four in the city—and then his roaming stopped abruptly at the first page of the weekend insert.

And suddenly, he knew why the Manions hadn't been home last night while Hunt had waited outside their house for them. They were at Auction Napa Valley. As a matter of fact, they were profiled inside as one of the probable big bidders, as they'd been in years past. Nice, apparently recent picture of them, too, but alas, without Todd.

Juhle brewed himself another cup of coffee. He moved quietly back into his bedroom for his telephone, then walked back out to the living room window and gazed out into the gray. The paper had told him that Napa was expecting beautiful weather—no, perfect auction weather—today. Sunny, bright, highs in the mid-seventies. California was the land of the microclimate, and although Napa was only sixty miles or so from San Francisco, its weather was dramatically different and almost always better.

Checking his messages, he couldn't help but enjoy the midnight call from Shiu. So, against his advice, Hunt had stayed out in Seacliff after all and had reaped the rewards. It would be a riot, Juhle thought, if they'd actually put him in custody for a while. In the meantime, there was nothing Juhle could do now about his friend. If Hunt was still in jail, oh, well. Not Juhle's problem. Maybe they'd talk again after he'd slept off his long night. In any event, the entire incident could be worth months of abuse, and Juhle was tempted to call early, wake him up if he was home, and start on him right away.

But before he acted on that impulse, he thought he'd check in with the general-information desk to see if, contrary to his expectations, the skeleton staff that worked around the clock had received any calls on Staci's picture.

A surprisingly upbeat, wide-awake female voice greeted him with—if Juhle hadn't known this was impossible—what sounded like actual enthusiasm. "We've gotten seven calls since midnight, sir. And one so far from the paper this morning. Four of the callers identify him as the same person. A Todd Manion."

Juhle wasn't aware that any words escaped him in a whisper. "My God." Then, in his normal voice, "You've got names and addresses on these witnesses?"

"Of course."

"One of them wouldn't be Carol or Ward Manion, by any chance?"

"Just a minute. No. Who are they, the parents? The famous local Manions?"

"They might be."

"Why wouldn't they have called themselves?"

"That question occurred to me. Maybe they never saw the picture." Which Juhle supposed was possible if they'd been up partying in Napa all last night. It would be interesting, he thought, if they did call today when they eventually saw the paper. Or someone who knew them saw it and told them about it.

And more interesting if they did not.

Hanging up, all hesitance about calling due to the early hour banished now, he immediately punched in Shiu's automatic home number and listened to his partner's voice on his answering machine. He should have guessed that he would still be sleeping: Shiu had been hassling his pal Wyatt and hauling down his off-duty money at the Manions until after midnight. He left a message. Wrestling with the decision for about twenty seconds, he then called Shiu's cell number and again got told to leave a message. Next, he paged him and entered his own cell phone number as the callback.

He woke up Connie while he was putting on his clothes. "Hey," he said quietly.

"Hey. Isn't it Saturday?"

"Yep. Sorry to get you up. I want to ask you something."

She shifted, pulled herself up onto the pillows. "You're going in to work?"

"That's what I wanted to ask you about." He came over and sat on the edge of the bed. "Wyatt's latest theory on Palmer and Parisi looks like it just got some corroboration. We've had four calls identifying Rosalier's kid or brother or whatever he is. The picture? Any normal day, I go in and talk to some of the callers, see how sure they are, how reliable. Then I pull a warrant if I can tell a good enough story to a judge."

"Which you can."

He shrugged at the compliment, rested his hand on her thigh. "Here's the thing, though. Last night, this was just Wyatt with an idea. Today, if these witnesses are legitimate, there's some chance things will unravel fast."

"And you've got to be on top of it."

Another nod. "At the very least, I've got to see if I can make my suspect talk to me again before she gets lawyered up."

"It's a she again?"

"Oh, yeah. A definite she." He nodded. "Carol Manion."

Connie almost laughed. "No. Really."

"I'm not kidding." He rubbed his hand over her leg. "But I've been trying to tell myself to go slow, make sure I do everything by the book. If I screw this up—"

"How are you going to do that? Have you screwed up anything yet?"

"No. But I don't have much to show, either."

"But now you might?"

"Now I think I do."

"So what's the problem? Go get her."

"Just like that?"

"That's what you do, Dev. You play by the rules, okay. You don't cheat. But you get it done, don't you? You always get it done."

"So far. I've been lucky."

"Not just lucky. Good. Careful. By the book. But you don't have to do the book slow. That's never been your style. Slow would have gotten you dead last year, instead of being a hero." But she saw something in his face. "Hey, you, look at me. Don't you *dare* let those small and ugly people get inside of you, you hear me? You know what you did, what you had to do. You didn't second-guess yourself. You acted bravely and wisely and saved a lot of lives in the process."

"And lost one."

"No. Shane wasn't anything to do with you. He was gone before either of you moved. We've been over this, babe."

"I know." A silence settled. "I'm talking about the Manions, you know. If it's her and if it gets political again and I get squeezed—"

"If, if, if . . . we don't do *if*. Remember? If she's killed somebody, bring her down."

"Maybe three people."

"And you want my opinion should you go downtown?"

"I think I just got it."

She broke a smile, came forward with a kiss. "Don't walk," she said. "Run."

Mickey slept well and, undisturbed throughout the night, woke up a bit later than he'd imagined he would, as the last bit of ground fog was dissipating. He threw his sleeping bag back into the trunk and crossed half the valley again over to Saint Helena, where some small counter-style restaurants had already opened for breakfast. After cleaning up a little in the restroom, he went and sat alone at one of the six tables, each one dressed with a perfect orchid and a starched white cloth. He ordered his Peet's French Roast coffee, a Roblochon-and-chive omelette of Kelly Ranch organic eggs, with a side of Yukon Gold hash brown potatoes, house-made ancho-chili ketchup, and an Acme Bakery brioche. His waitress, Julia, was about twenty-eight years old, and when he first saw her, Mickey tried to remember when he might have heard about Julia Roberts going into waitress work, but the moment seemed to elude him.

She was nice, too.

After she'd refilled his coffee cup three times, he refused the fourth and leaned back in contentment, asking for the check.

"You're sure? Nothing else?"

"Well, there is one thing, if you don't mind."

"Sure. Anything."

"Maybe you can tell me why I live in San Francisco and not here."

"Oh, I love it down there."

"I do, too, but I love it here more."

"I know." She seemed to be floating in some ethereal place, completely unconcerned and unaware of the passage of time. Suddenly, but in no hurry, she looked all around her, taking in her elegant surroundings. "This place really is like nowhere else."

"Especially today."

She flashed a wicked smile. "Don't tell me you're going to the auction."

"Okay. I won't tell you that."

"But you are?"

"Actually, sadly, no."

"Well, that is sad, but if you were, I was going to hate you for a minute there."

"And now you don't have to. Do you work here all day?"

"Is that a line?"

"It could be. It might not be. If it was a line, would it offend you?"

"No."

"Okay, then, let's call it a line."

"That's sweet, but I've got a boyfriend." Her smile touched his heart as she told him she'd be right back with his check. He watched her with terrible longing as she waited on the other tables, as nice and efficient with each of them as she'd been with him. Maybe she was a robot, a Stepford wife in the making. But damn . . .

When she came back to him, she leaned over and confided in him as though they were old friends. "Don't look now," she said with quiet excitement, "but the grandparents and the boy at the front table? They are going to the auction."

"Who are they?"

"The Manions. Mega high rollers. Manion Cellars?" Mickey threw a quick glance toward them. "Out eating breakfast just like normal folks?"

"Actually, they come in here a lot."

"You think they're taking the kid to the auction?"

"Maybe not. But if they do, I doubt they'll let him bid."

But the Manions had paid their bill, and now they were getting up. Mickey, fighting sticker shock at the twenty-eight-dollar breakfast tab, decided he could make back some of it by going on the clock for Hunt. He left two twenties for Julia under his plate—might as well leave her with a good memory of him. At least he wasn't cheap.

He walked out onto the street, which now at a little after nine was beginning to come alive, although there was no sign of the Manions.

Which, he thought, was impossible. They'd only left the restaurant thirty or forty seconds before he had followed them out, and he'd seen them start off to the right. He didn't think they could have even made it to the nearest corner. They must have entered one of the adjacent shops, so he started strolling, window-shopping. Four doors up, an old-fashioned barber's pole slowed him down, then drew him inside.

"I just thought you'd want to know." Mickey was back in his car in Saint Helena, fresh from his own haircut.

"I do want to know," Hunt said. He hadn't gotten out of the holding cell until three thirty in the morning, Shiu and Poggio making his life unpleasant just because it was so darn much fun. They'd protected the lives of the good citizens of San Francisco by verifying Hunt's permit to carry a concealed weapon, by making sure that his PI license was valid, then graciously informing him that they were letting him off with a warning for carrying the wrong weapon on his permit. He felt that Shiu honestly expected him to say thank you.

Now at least he understood why Juhle hated him.

By the time he'd retrieved his car and gotten back home, it was close to five o'clock, and he'd crashed in his clothes for about four hours, until Mickey's call woke him up. "But," Hunt said, "I thought you weren't going up there."

"Yeah. I changed my mind." Mickey waxed poetic for a moment or two about the day's probable delights, including the breakfast he'd just eaten, which would have been worth its exorbitant price tag even if Julia Roberts hadn't been his waitress.

"Did you ask her out?"

"No. She's got a boyfriend."

"And also twins from what I hear."

"What? My waitress?"

"No. The real Julia, you fool. You want to tell me about the Manions?"

"Well, first off, the kid did not want the haircut, and I can't say I blame him. But the mom had made up her mind. By the way, is she really the mom? Julia thought she was his grandmother, and I have to say, that's more what she looks like."

"Well, she might be the grandmother, but she's also the mom."

"If you say so."

"I do. It's complicated. So, the haircut Todd didn't want? What about it?"

"They buzzed him clean. He was pissed. I would have been pissed, too. But she was, like, extremely uptight about it. It was going to happen."

"She needed to change his appearance. Today."

"Why?"

"So he wouldn't look like that picture you saw yesterday with me and Juhle. The kid."

"That was him?"

"That was him. So where are they now?"

"I don't know. I assume back home or off to the auction."

Hunt's voice reflected his disappointment. "You're not still with them?"

"That would have been a little obvious, don't you think? No. Since I was there, I stayed and got my own haircut. Just a trim, thanks."

"Mick."

"You want me to catch up with them again." Not a question.

"If you could."

"Are you coming up?"

"What do you think?"

31 /

From Hunt's descriptions, Juhle thought he'd have better luck with Caitlin Rosalier than with any of the other principals. Besides that, she lived in Boston, where it wasn't so early in the morning. The gods smiled, and she was home and seemed eager to talk with him.

The phone call she'd had last night had really bothered her and kept her awake most of the time since then. Yes, she would be fine with Juhle faxing her an autopsy photograph. "It's not too gross, is it?" She'd been really close to Staci once and now seemed to need some sense of closure if, in fact, her friend had been the victim. There was a copy shop on the corner, and she could go there and call Juhle back with the fax number, and he'd told her he would wait for her call.

Before it came, though, Juhle's partner got back to him with the news that he wasn't coming in on this weekend morning. Maybe Juhle didn't realize it, but Saturday was the LDS Sabbath, and Shiu had to attend services and do another shift at the Manions. Juhle would stay in touch and keep him informed, though. Right? Thank you very much. He could probably arrange to be in by early afternoon if it was a real emergency, but he didn't even want to commit to that until Juhle had something truly substantive and, in Shiu's words, "Remember, based on evidence, Dev."

Juhle hung up, said, "Asshole," and stared out through the fog at the freeway from his desk in the otherwise empty homicide detail.

For most of the next twenty minutes, he studied the forensics folder, laboring over the affidavit he would attach to the warrant he hoped to get on the Manions' two homes and their cars. At these locales, he would specifically be looking for the murder weapon or clothes that might be contaminated with blood or gunshot residue. From the cars, he hoped to get a hair or even a blood sample that would match Andrea Parisi's.

The evidence would not be as compelling since fingerprints lasted a long time, and perhaps Mrs. Manion had been to Palmer's home socially, but if he could get them, he'd like to find fingerprints indicating that Mrs. Manion had been in Judge Palmer's office. The rug in the judge's office, too, had yielded several different hair samples, and though any DNA or other sophisticated tests on these would be slow coming in, if they came up positive, they would help.

The telephone rang and he snatched at it. Caitlin, at last, with the fax number at her copy shop. He wrote it down, thanked her, told her to stay on the line if she could. He grabbed the best autopsy face photo of Staci Rosalier from the file and fed it into the detail's fax machine. By the time he was back at his desk, she was crying and he had his identification.

Still working on the affidavit for his warrant, Juhle looked up and broke a smile. "Look what the cat dragged in. Don't blame me for anything about last night. I told you to go home."

Hunt wasn't in much of a smiling mood himself. "Did you put them on me?"

"Give me a break, Wyatt. You did that to yourself. I even warned you. You find out anything for all your troubles?"

"Yeah. You're working with sociopaths."

"Hey, that's on the application. Get over it."

Hunt really hadn't come in to berate Juhle, and now he let it go, pointing at the folder. "They're up in Napa," he said.

"I know."

"How do you know that?"

"It was in the paper. Plus, you'll be pleased to hear that we've got four reasonably rock-solid IDs on Staci's picture. He's Todd Manion."

"He also got his hair cut this morning. Buzzed."

"Interesting. A little too late, as it turns out, but interesting." Juhle's head jerked up. "But wait a minute. How did you find that out?"

"Mickey's up there."

Juhle sat back, massaged his shoulder, apparently in real pain. When he spoke, he had his official voice on. "You've got to get out of this, Wyatt. I mean it. All the way out. And keep your guys out, too."

"Hold it. Let me frame an appropriate response." It took him about a second. "No, I don't think so."

"You obstruct this investigation at this point—"

"Hey!" Hunt pointed down at Juhle's face. "I'm the only rea-son you've got an investigation at this point."

Juhle remained calm. "Wyatt. It's moved beyond you. Caitlin Rosalier ID'd Staci about a half hour ago."

"I knew that *twelve* hours ago."

Juhle shook his head. "You didn't know it. You thought it. I proved it."

"And lost half a day while you were at it. And stopped me in my tracks in the process."

"That's because it *is* a process, my friend. Due process. Ring a bell? Sometimes it takes time to get it right."

"Sometimes you don't have the luxury of time. How about that?"

"This isn't one of those times."

"Except if it is, Dev. Except if it is."

Hunt's words brought Juhle up short. The fire went out of his voice. "You still think you're going to find Parisi alive, don't you?"

"Let's put it this way. I'm looking for Andrea. You're looking for a murderer. We can pretend there's no inherent conflict."

"Inherently, maybe not. But we'll be dancing close enough to one another we've got a pretty good chance we're going to trip each other up. And I need you to stay out of my way, Wyatt. I'm looking for a righteous arrest here before too long, and that whole process— *process* again—really is an orchestrated ballet. You've got to get it right or nobody applauds."

"I like to think I'm sensitive to that, Dev. But your arrest really is not my issue."

"You'll pardon me, though, if it's mine, huh?" But Juhle wasn't unaware of all of Hunt's contributions to his investigation so far. He'd basically built the case that now Juhle was trying to verify. And without any useful contributions from his true partner in homi-cide, Juhle was inclined to take whatever help he could get, so long as it didn't compromise his own endgame. He sat back in his chair, looked up at his friend. "So what are you here for?"

"I wanted to tell you about Napa and the haircut, make sure you were up to speed. I figure you're moving on your due process down here, am I right? Pulling warrants, whatever else you do. Get a team inside Manion's house and look around."

"A little of that, hopefully, yeah. So meanwhile, what are you doing?"

"Meanwhile, I think I'm in Napa."

"Doing what?"

"Shaking the sugar tree, seeing what falls out."

Juhle dropped his head for a minute, then looked back up and spoke in a reasonable tone. "If I asked you please not to talk to Carol Manion, could you restrain yourself? If you get her spooked and lawyered up by the time I talk to her, which I will soon, I'll have you tortured and then killed, and I mean it."

"I wasn't planning on talking to her, Dev. Even if she told me the truth, which she wouldn't, she couldn't tell me anything I don't already know."

"Except maybe where she dumped Parisi."

"That won't come out in an interview, Dev. She's not giving anything up voluntarily after all this."

"So how does it come out?"

"I'm working on that," Hunt said. "I find out, I'll let you know."

Still long before noon, and Juhle had his paperwork together as he stood in front of Judge Oscar Thomasino, on magistrate duty as he had been all week and obviously not particularly thrilled to be hassled at his home on a Saturday morning. Now the judge, in his street clothes, sat behind his desk in his office, the novel he'd been reading facedown on the blotter in front of him. "Refresh my memory, inspector," he was saying, "but wasn't it very recently that you and your partner came to me for a similar search warrant?"

"Yes, Your Honor. A couple of days ago."

"But it wasn't this same case, was it?"

"Yes, it was."

Thomasino's kindly face clouded under his wispy white hair. He removed his Ben Franklin eyeglasses and absentmindedly began to wipe them with a cloth he'd pulled from his desk drawer. "What were the results of that earlier search if I may ask?"

"We found some .22 caliber weapons in the woman's house, Your Honor, which we ran ballistics tests on. And some clothes, which we tested for GSR."

"And the results of those tests?"

"Negative."

"I see." Thomasino looked through his glasses, blew on them, then continued buffing the lenses. "And I presume you will be looking for positive tests this time on the same types of items—a gun, and clothes, and so on—if I sign this warrant?"

"Yes, Your Honor."

Thomasino put his glasses back on, threw Juhle a curveball. "Where is your partner today, inspector?"

"At church. Religious services. He's Mormon."

"Ah." The information gave the judge pause. "But you've been working this case together up until this time? You and Inspector . . ."

"Shiu."

"Yes, Shiu." He came forward a bit, elbows on his desk. "What I'm getting at, Inspector Juhle, is whether—this is just a question, so please don't take offense—whether your appearance here before me, without your partner, might indicate some lack of accord between you and Shiu about whether this warrant is supported by the evidence."

"No, Your Honor. I don't believe there's any lack of accord. Inspector Shiu has deeply held religious convictions and . . ."

Thomasino held up a hand. "Many of us do, inspector, many of us do. And yet I'm fairly certain that most of your fellow homicide inspectors, if they happened to be working on the extremely high-profile case of a murdered federal judge, might find it incumbent upon themselves to, say, cut Mass a little short or even miss it altogether if critical evidence suddenly came to light on a Sunday morning. Don't you think that might be the norm?"

"I do, Your Honor."

"Let me take it a little further, if you don't mind. Do you think your own partner, Inspector Shiu, would voluntarily miss the opportunity to take a more active role in what would no doubt be the most important, the most *significant* arrest in his entire career if he believed that you were close to a breakthrough in that case?"

"Normally, yes, he might, Your Honor. He would, I'm sure. But in this case . . ."

"Go on."

"Well, Inspector Shiu moonlights for the Manions. He's been with them for several years that I know of. I have often thought that it's not impossible he rose up as quickly as he did through the department and made it to homicide because of, shall I say, political influence."

"Friends of the Manions?"

"Just a pet theory," Juhle said.

"Not a nice one."

"No, Your Honor. But we were being frank."

"So you think he sees this warrant as some kind of conflict of interest?"

"I wouldn't go that far. Let's just say, he might feel uncomfortable having to explain to the Manions why he was part of having it served on them."

"And you think by the same token that he might be choosing to distance himself from an endeavor that he finds ill-conceived and which he also perceives might infuriate influential and powerful people without guaranteeing any success in the case. Inspector, people in your trade might call that a clue."

Juhle remained silent.

Thomasino nodded and sighed, an aggrieved expression flitting across his features. "Inspector," he said, "since we're being frank and off the record here, let me ask you something else, just between us. Do you feel that besides its natural importance, that there are people at the Hall and in the city at large who view this case as a kind of a test for you personally?"

The import of the question rocked Juhle, but he stood his ground. "Yes, Your Honor, I think I do. But I'm trying not to let that affect my handling of it." He pressed on in the face of Thomasino's skeptical look. "In the past few hours, Your Honor," he said, "I've learned irrefutably that Carol Manion's adopted child was the natural son of Staci Rosalier, the woman killed with Judge Palmer. Mrs. Manion has gone to great lengths over the past eight years to keep these facts hidden. To the extent that when I went to talk to her about this case just last week, she neglected to mention anything about it."

"Did you ask her about it?"

"No, Your Honor, but . . ."

"But you think she should have volunteered the information?"

"To me it's unimaginable that she didn't, Your Honor. Unimaginable. If only to say, 'I know this is an incredible coincidence, but I think you should know about it.' She couldn't have been unaware of it."

Thomasino considered, fingers templed at his lips. He looked down at the notes he'd scribbled while Juhle had been laying out the whole rather complex scenario. "I may have gotten some details wrong, inspector, and if so correct me. But as I understand it from the way you've outlined it to me here, Mrs. Manion adopted a baby from a Staci Keilly, isn't that so? And if so, why would the name

Staci Rosalier prompt her to mention her child to you? If you, in fact, even had *that* name on Tuesday afternoon when you spoke to her."

Juhle's face went slack. He felt a rush of blood draining from his head. Not that the basic fact of Todd's parentage was any longer in doubt—or at least, he didn't think so—but Carol Manion didn't necessarily know about Staci on Tuesday when he and Shiu had questioned her about her original appointment with Parisi.

The only way Carol could have known Staci's true relationship to her son was if, in fact, she had been confronted with it and killed her. But that was putting the cart before the horse. If she hadn't done that, and there was no evidence at all that she had, then all of her actions since—not mentioning Todd to him and Shiu, buzz-cutting Todd's hair because, after all, summer was coming on—had been blameless.

He also suddenly realized that even he and Shiu had been unable to identify Staci as either a Rosalier or a Keilly until late Tuesday night when they'd met up with Mary Mahoney in the morgue. And what, then, did this mean about the four identifications of Todd Manion this morning?

The judge was still looking over his templed fingers. "Are you all right, inspector? You don't look well."

"No. Fine, Your Honor. I've been taking some pain medication. I just got a little dizzy there for a minute."

Thomasino clearly wasn't so sure that was it, but he let it go and moved on. "So, bottom line, inspector, is that I'm a little bit leery to sign off on what amounts to an open-ended fishing expedition on one of the city's most prominent families. Especially given the fact that this would be the second nearly identical warrant on two different suspects that I'd have approved in about as many days. You can see where it might raise some eyebrows, huh? Where you and I both might be open to accusations of overreaching? Invading privacy without cause? In your case, even launching a desperate vendetta to deflect attention away from a stalled investigation?"

"Yes, Your Honor, although this is not . . ."

"Goes without saying, inspector, of course. No explanation necessary." Moving on again, adjusting his glasses, the judge lowered his gaze to the pages Juhle had placed in front of him and scanned over them. "Now what I might suggest, if I may, is you've got no privacy or probable-cause issues with the crime scene. You note here that you've got unidentified fingerprints, hair, and fabric fibers that have already been collected. If you can connect some of this to Mrs.

Manion, then okay, at least you've got some plausible reason to search her home to ask her to explain how they got there. If evidence rises to the level of probable cause, I'll entertain another request for a search warrant for her home at that time. Meanwhile," he looked up, offered his avuncular smile, "you might want to go home and sleep off some of that medication. It's Saturday, inspector. People aren't going to begrudge you a day off."

But Juhle, shaken, wasn't about to take the day off. There were other avenues under the great canopy of due process that he could take with impunity, and now he was going to be forced to explore them. Judge Thomasino may have been right that his request for a search warrant on Carol Manion's house was premature. But as a homicide inspector, Juhle was entitled to interrogate people when and as he saw fit, provided he could get them to talk to him.

Mrs. Manion may not have known on last Tuesday that Staci Rosalier was Staci Keilly, but the fact remained that it would be instructive, perhaps even conclusive, to see how she reacted when he confronted her with this fundamental truth. Juhle had a gut for witnesses—if they were lying, there were a million tells, and he could spot most of them. Then at least for himself, he would know. He would take the investigation from there and slowly, carefully build a case, over months if necessary, which the DA could prosecute and win against any army of high-priced lawyers.

If Carol Manion, in her wealth and hubris, had dared to kill a federal judge on his watch, Juhle would bring her down. And to do that—and right now while the questions he would ask her were all so clear!—what he had to do first was have a conversation with her.

32 /

In the wide and sun-splashed upstairs corridor of their château in Napa Valley, Carol Manion knocked on the door to her son's bedroom. "Todd."

No answer.

She knocked again. "Todd, please. Your mother wants to talk to you."

"I don't want to talk to her. I'm mad at her."

"Please don't be. I can't stand it when you're mad at me. Your hair will grow back, I promise."

"And meanwhile I look like a geek."

"You don't. You look like what you are, a handsome young man. Would you please open the door?"

"I don't want to."

"But I really need to talk to you."

"What about?"

"Todd. Not through the door, okay? Please. I'm saying please."

"I asked you please not to before you made him cut off my hair. Please, please, please." Punctuating the words by kicking at the door. "It wasn't fair."

"I know it wasn't. I'm sorry. Your father and I just thought it would be a good idea."

"Why?" In three syllables. "It wasn't hurting anything." But the knob turned, and the door came unlatched, although Todd didn't pull it open.

Carol gave it a gentle push.

Todd had crossed to the window seat that overlooked the vineyards, where he'd piled some blankets from his bed and now burrowed into them. Carol walked over and sat so that she felt the contours of his little body up against her. "Thanks for letting me in," she said. "You're a very good boy."

"Doesn't do me any good, though."

Carol Manion sighed. "Aren't you getting a little hot under there?"

The blankets moved as he shook his head no. "What did you need to talk to me about?"

Now was the time. She sighed again. "There's a picture in the paper this morning of a boy who looks like you. In fact, it might even be a picture of you that someone took from a long distance away a couple of years ago."

The head, teary-eyed but now curious, too, peeked out. "Why would somebody do that?"

"I don't know for sure, but in the paper it said that they found the picture in the room of somebody who was killed last week."

"Killed? You mean like really killed in real life? Not like on TV?"

"No. Really killed."

"Cool," Todd said.

"Well, it isn't really, Todd. It's really kind of scary. But, anyway, they thought if somebody could recognize the picture of the boy who looks like you that they might be able to find the relatives of the young woman who got killed. If you were related to her. Do you understand?"

"But I'm not."

"No, you're not. But your father and I don't know who took the picture or why. Or if it even has to do with you. We just want you to be safe."

"And that's why you cut my hair? Why didn't you tell me that before?"

"Because we didn't want to scare you."

"I wouldn't have been scared."

"No. Probably not, I know. But it scares your mother and father to think that somebody who got killed took a picture of you and kept it, and now the killer might know what you looked like. So we thought it would be smart to change that a little, for a while at least. You see? I really want you to understand."

"I think I do."

"Good. Because some people might come by and ask questions. Maybe even policemen. And I don't want you to worry."

"Why would I worry?"

"You shouldn't. That's what I'm saying, that there's nothing to worry about. We're just going to tell everybody it's not you. It might look a little like you, but we don't think it's you."

"In the picture, you mean?"

"Yes. And that way we just stay out of everything altogether. We don't get involved because we don't need to be. This doesn't have to do with us. I want you to understand that."

"But what if it is me? Can I see it? I bet I could tell."

"I bet you could, too. But the picture's not the most important thing, Todd. The most important thing is that we protect you. That you always know that you're safe, no matter what."

"I do know that, Mom."

"Because you are my only son, and I'm never going to let anything happen to you. Ever. Okay? Now how about if you come out from under those blankets and give your old mother a big hug?"

Ward Manion had the face of a Marlboro man gone corporate, and it wore a stern expression as he looked across the front seat at his wife. "I don't think I agree that that's a good idea at all. I wish you wouldn't have talked to the boy without discussing it with me first." Though Jay Leno wouldn't take the stage and the auction itself wouldn't formally begin until six o'clock, the Manions had been invited to an exclusive preview of some of the wine lots that would be up for bid, and they were driving the BMW with the top down on the Silverado Trail.

He glanced over at his wife, whom he thought was still a very handsome woman, albeit unconventionally so, with her strong jaw, deeply set and widely spaced gray eyes. She'd had her face lifted twice for lines and crow's feet, but the cheekbones needed no help and never would. "I agreed with the haircut," Ward said, "because what could it hurt? But I don't understand why you don't want to contact the police yourself. Say that it looks like Todd all right, but you don't know anything more about it, which is true."

"No. That's not true, Ward. Not from their perspective, and you know it. How can I tell them it does look like Todd and not mention that his birth mother's name was Staci?"

"It wasn't Staci Rosalier."

Carol waved that off. "So she changed it. Or maybe the slut had gotten herself married. Two or three times even."

Ward pursed his lips. To Carol, the girl who'd borne their son's, now their own, child, had always been and would always be "the slut." It bothered him, but he didn't suppose he was going to be able to do anything to change it now.

"And then what if it is her?" she asked. "Staci. Todd's birth mother."

He turned to her. "Well? We both agree that it might be. So what?"

"*So what* is that it then involves us, Ward. You and me and Todd. You know we weren't involved in killing anybody, but they'll just rake up all that history, look into Todd's adoption, everything. I know you remember how awful Staci's people were. I don't want to give them any excuse to get back into our lives."

He seemed vaguely amused at the idea, shaking his head at the absurdity of it.

"It's not funny, Ward. I told you George Palmer called me at home that last day. . . ."

"To ask us to a party, right?"

"Yes, but all they'll know—"

"Who are *they* now?"

"The police. All they'll know is that he made the call. What if they see it as a connection between us and that slut?"

"*What if? What if?* But while we're at it, using the slut word will not help you appear disinterested. The woman, after all, is a murder victim. She deserves a little sympathy."

"All right. But the point remains, I did hear from George, and then I did place a call to the Parisi woman. That's a lot of coincidence, a lot of interaction with people who are involved in this."

"Now that you mention it." Ward was still smiling. "If I didn't know better . . ."

"Don't you dare even tease!"

"Easy, girl," he said. "There's no call for that."

She took a beat, gathering herself. "It's far better if we simply stay out of it completely. If we say that the picture doesn't really look like Todd did at that age, that ends it."

"Carol." His own calm more than matched hers. "You're not exactly some prowling murderer, after all. I think we're both rather above all that, don't you? You're acting paranoid, and that isn't like you at all."

She shook her head. "I think you're underestimating how badly they want to bring us all down. We are rich and, therefore, evil. Just look at what we're doing today."

"And what exactly is that?"

"The auction."

"Giving six figures to charity? I fail to see the evil there."

"Paying criminal prices for wine, Ward. Flaunting it for those who don't have it. Paying seven thousand five hundred dollars just to buy tickets to bid. You don't seem to know how our kind of money affects some people, how we feed their envy."

"No, of course, I understand that. The worst crime a person can commit in some circles is to be successful. But people who think that way are always with us, and they should be none of our concern. They're far beneath us. Even our contempt."

"Until they smell that we've done something wrong, where they can bring us down. Look at Martha Stewart, in jail over a handful of peanuts. Michael Milken. All the CEOs."

"But we haven't done anything like any of them, Carol. I say if we acknowledge that the picture might be Todd, and that Staci might well have been his natural mother, we nip any inquiry in the bud. It's likely one of our acquaintances will have called the police, anyway, one of Todd's teachers, somebody. We're just pointing to ourselves as hiding something if we don't come forth." He put a large, gnarled hand on her thigh. "We don't want to appear to be hiding anything, Carol. We don't want to *be* hiding anything." He patted her leg. "I say we bring the matter up to one of our security people down in the city, who after all *are* the police, at our first opportunity. Tell them what we know. Answer their questions if they have any and ask them to be discreet as they've always been. Live with what little fallout there may be."

Carol turned away from him, then faced forward. Her mouth was set, her jaw clenched, the eyes hardened down. She snapped open a pair of sunglasses and put them on, looked at Ward as if she were about to say something, then thought better of it, and lapsed into a brooding silence.

Wine lovers mingled, schmoozed, grazed, and drank on a flawless gem of an afternoon in the elegant expanse of the Meadowood Resort. The croquet lawn/putting-green area was a sea of humanity. Woodsmoke hung in a fragrant cloud amidst the oaks and the pines. Celebrity chefs plied their wares on enormous open grills while equally famous winemakers freely poured their best libations into the Reidel crystal glasses of their colleagues and the other assembled guests—the sports heroes, movie stars, industry captains, and other notables from all over the world who shared both a love of all things grape and extravagant wealth.

The young couple chatting with the Manions were well dressed, articulate, charming, and obviously very much at home in the rarefied Napa culture. Making their acquaintance at one of the white wine tables under the enormous tent that shaded the first fairway at Meadowood, Ward Manion had taken the gentleman under his wing, and the two were now in deep conversation about the stunning recent popularity of Rhône-style varietals in California—syrah, mourvedre, carignane—and what it all meant to the local industry, which was so heavily invested in cabernet, chardonnay, pinot noir, and merlot. "Frankly, if you would have asked me to name the new hot varietal, say ten years ago," the young man named Jason was saying, "I wouldn't have even looked to the Rhône. My bet would have been on sangiovese."

Ward broke a satisfied smile. "Don't sell that idea short," he said. "I took that bet just about at that time." Ward was always happy to talk wine, especially in a setting like this one. "Now I've got nearly seven acres of sangiovese to blend with my cabernet."

"California Super Tuscan," Jason said. "Good way to go."

"It's hardly original," Ward said, "but it beats ripping out my good vines that are finally producing and guessing wrong on granache or some other damn thing."

The men clearly would be able to go on in this fascinating vein for a while, but even here and now on her second glass of chardonnay, Carol Manion seemed to be fighting herself to remain engaged, half-smiling in a vacant way, her mind clearly elsewhere, in a self-contained universe of her own.

At Carol's elbow, her own champagne in hand but untouched, Jason's young woman moved a step nearer to her and spoke in a confidential whisper. "It's really so wonderful to be here. It's our first time, and I must say we feel a bit like crashers, though. We shouldn't really be here at all technically, but we're kind of close to Thomas, and he got us in."

In this context, it went without saying, Thomas could only be Thomas Keller of the French Laundry, überchef of the valley if not, according to many, of the civilized world. "But if you happen to be lucky enough to get offered a couple of tickets on a fabulous day like this one, I say you go, *n'est-ce pas?*"

"*Oui. Sans doute.*" Carol dredged up a smile that for all of its weariness seemed genuine enough. "I'm sorry. I'm a little distracted. What did you say your name was?"

"Amy."

The well-bred society manners were kicking in, as Amy had

hoped and Hunt had assumed they would. Carol Manion, they both knew, spent a good deal of her time at charity events and benefit dinners. Social patter would come to her as easily as breathing, and now the very banality of it all offered an apparent respite from what they believed would be her overriding preoccupation.

"Well, Amy," she said, "it's very nice to meet you, even more so if you won't be in competition with us when the bidding begins."

Amy laughed appreciatively. "I don't think you have to worry about that. We're just regular working stiffs."

"Are you involved in the wine world? Your husband seems quite knowledgeable."

"Jason? Actually, we're not married until September. And it's not just wine, he's knowledgeable about everything. It's kind of a curse."

"I know what you mean. My Ward's a little like that, too. He sees something once, or hears about it, or reads it in a book, it's locked in his mind forever."

"That sounds like Jason, too. But we're not really involved at all in the wine business, except that we like to drink it." Wu shifted her footing, moving them both back, cutting them away from the two men. "In real life," she said, "we're both attorneys."

Carol Manion's mouth barely twitched, and so quickly that Wu would have missed it if she hadn't been watching closely. In an instant, the practiced smile had returned, but in that second or less, the older woman also seemed to lose half a step somehow, and a silence held between them, until Carol finally stammered, "I'm sorry?"

Amy saw no harm in hitting her with it again. "I said we were both attorneys." Chattering on. "We're both so lucky that we work in San Francisco. Jason's with the District Attorney, and I'm about five years now with a really good firm. I love the work, although people say such terrible things about us sometimes. All the lawyer jokes, you know. But I find that my colleagues are generally way much nicer than most people think. In fact," as though she just remembered it, "it's so funny that Jason and I should have run into you of all people here, because I think we have a mutual friend." Wu's face fell, and it wasn't an act. "Or had, I should say, until this week. Andrea Parisi?"

The surface of Carol Manion's glass of wine shimmered as though a tiny temblor was shaking the ground under their feet. "Andrea . . . yes, the television-anchor person?"

"And one of your own lawyers, wasn't she? If I'm not mistaken. Am I?"

"No, no. Although we never actually met. I just . . . well, it's such a tragedy, what's happened. I mean, they still haven't found her yet, have they?"

"No. But I don't think anybody's holding out much hope on that account anymore. It's the worst thing. She was such a great person. We were really good friends." Amy was somewhat surprised to feel real tears begin to form in her eyes. "Oh, I'm sorry. I don't want to put a pall on a nice day like this. But you and she . . . I really was under the impression that you knew her well, too. If she was going out to your house . . ."

"No! She never did that."

"Well, that's right. I knew that. I talked to her just after you called her from the Saint Francis and suggested you meet at her office. She was worried it might mean that you were getting cold feet."

"About what?"

"Her representing you."

"But she wasn't representing me. She was . . ." Abruptly, she stopped as another thought struck her. "Did you say she called you?"

"Uh-huh. Just after she talked to you. She and I were supposed to have dinner together out in the Avenues that night, and we decided to move it to downtown since that's where we'd both be working. God, was that just last Wednesday? It seems like forever ago." As though she'd just realized it, Wu said, "But if you've never met her, that means she must have missed her meeting with you, too."

Carol Manion's eyes took on a furtive cast. In a quick pass, they scanned the length and breadth of the tented area, then came back to Wu. "Yes. I mean, no, I never did meet with her. I," she paused, stuttered, "I had to cancel at the last minute."

"That's a shame," Wu said. "I'm sure you would have liked her. I can't believe she's gone. She was just terrific . . . a terrific person."

"Yes, well . . ." Unsteadily, Carol Manion moved a few steps forward, toward her husband. "I'm sure I would have. Now if you'll excuse me, I think it's getting to be time for us to start looking at these lots. It was very nice talking with you. Ward."

Brandt and Wu went and made themselves invisible behind the flap of the tent and watched them as they walked off, Carol leaning heavily onto her husband's arm.

"Nice guy," Brandt said. "Ward."

"She's not. She's a killer."

"You think so?"

"I'd bet my life on it, Jason. I thought she was going to pass out when I mentioned Andrea. She didn't deny the call from the Saint Francis, which is huge. I honestly thought she was going to be sick. I know it shook her up."

"That was the goal."

"No, the goal was to get her upset enough to leave early."

"But not too early. Devin's got to have time to get up here."

Wu checked her watch. "He's had two hours already. He'll make it."

"He'd better," Brandt said. "Check it out."

The Manions had stopped in their progress toward their place at the bidding tables, and now Carol had one palm against her husband's chest and the other pressed against her own left breast. Her posture implored. Wearing an unmistakable expression of frustration and anger, Ward looked at the ceiling of the tent for a moment. He took his wife's wineglass and with an exaggerated calm placed it, along with his own, on the nearest table. Then the two of them began walking toward their nearest exit.

"It's happening," Brandt said.

Wu nodded with a grim satisfaction. "Looks like."

33 /

Tamara and Craig held their wineglasses up above eye level, intently peering into the half inch of red liquid. "What are we looking for?" Craig whispered.

"I don't know for sure," Tamara said. "Redness?"

"I see it."

There were three pourers—two men and a woman—at the Manion Cellars tasting room. All of them were young, knowledgeable, enthusiastic. The person who'd poured their wine was a twenty-something would-be matinee idol named Warren, and he waited expectantly for reactions among the dozen people at the bar in front of him before he continued with his spiel.

"First I'm sure you'll all notice the amazing clarity, a deep ruby with a just a hint of amber, or even brick, at the edges. That's natural with an older vintage such as this one, especially with the sangiovese. You'll see this a lot with old chiantis, which I'm sure you all know is the same grape. As you swirl, I think you'll pick up the highlights of the deeper ruby red that tends to characterize this varietal in its youth. And then, as the wine settles back into the bottom of the bowl, check out the incredibly beautiful legs . . ."

Craig backed a step away from the bar, stole a glance downward. "He's right about your legs," he whispered to Tamara, "but how can he see them from where he is?"

She elbowed him in the ribs, took a small sip, spit it out into the bucket provided, and put her glass down. Warren was rattling on about volatility and alcohol and structure and what to look for, what sensory information to register, when the wine passed the lips and the actual tasting began.

Tamara leaned over to Craig, spoke in her own stage whisper. "No offense, but give me a margarita any day."

"I hear you." Craig didn't even bother to taste this particular wine. He'd already tried sips from three or four other bottles, and the education hadn't had much impact on his initial reaction. He and Tamara didn't much care for the stuff. Either that or they just didn't get it. Who cared if the color was ruby or if it was more garnet? What difference did it make? Was color a flavor component? It all tasted pretty much the same to him, in spite of all this talk about forward fruit with a firm backbone of tannins, of cassis (whatever that was), and currant, perhaps with chocolate and tobacco and saddle-leather notes.

Tobacco? Saddle leather? As opposed to baseball-glove leather? Did Warren think people wanted to taste horse and cigar in what they drank?

Not Craig. Not Tamara. If they were drinking, pour something cold with a kick. If Craig wanted a citrus overtone, he'd suck a lime, thanks.

But this morning they had gotten Wyatt Hunt's urgent call and driven up here with him on his last chance, critical and perhaps even dangerous business, and under orders to draw no attention to themselves, they both feigned the kind of interest they were seeing all around them from their fellow tasters.

Warren was going on. "And now if you'd all like to leave your glasses here, the next part of the tour involves a bit of a climb up to our new caves, but I think you'll see it's worth it. We're incredibly excited about our storage capacity now, almost fifteen thousand barrels, about half-and-half new and old oak, which the limestone holds at a constant temperature and humidity which is the . . ."—blah and the blah, blah—"so if you'd all like to follow me." He led the way out the side of the tasting room and onto an uphill path that met a semi-paved road that swung right around the edge of the promontory and out of sight.

Their own path continued a bit farther uphill and took them, as promised, to the new caves which, Craig had to admit, were impressive. Extending for seemingly hundreds of feet back into the solid white rock and lined to the high ceiling on both sides with barrel upon barrel of wine, the caves were a complex labyrinth cut into the core of the limestone hill.

And apparently it remained a work in progress. At regular intervals, unfinished wings fingered off into blackness. The four primary arteries—one leading in from each of the doors—terminated at a vast, dimly lit, double-wide main chamber that in the next few years would come to house a comprehensive wine museum named Fine Art of the Grape, which the Manions hoped would become a valley destination in its own right. Here also was a private dining area and even a stage for drama and musical productions—the acoustics, their guide assured them, were perfect.

Warren and fourteen of the sixteen visitors on this morning's tour gathered around the artist's rendering in the center of the chamber that indicated what the space would eventually look like when all the work was finished.

Two of the visitors disappeared into darkness.

"Manion Cellars. Can I help you?"

"Hi. This is Andy with the Oakville Grocery. Is this the kitchen?"

"No. I'm sorry. You got the tasting room, and we're jamming."

"Okay. Sorry to bother you. Would you mind connecting me to the kitchen, please?"

"I can't do that. This is the public line. We don't connect to the house."

"Perfect. You mind giving me that number?"

"Sorry again. I'm not supposed to give that out."

"Jeez. Who am I talking to?"

"Natasha."

"Well, look, Natasha, I got a problem. Carol Manion called here for something like sixty people coming by the house up there after the auction, and we've got her very expensive and rather particular order all together, but I need to talk to the kitchen to see what we've got to have completely cooked here and what you guys can handle up there. But this number here we're talking on; this is the number Carol gave us."

"I believe it. She is so distracted lately."

"Who isn't? It's nuts week here, too. Anyway, if we're not there on time and with everything cooked just so, the fallout from the explosion is going to render our lovely valley uninhabitable for the next two hundred years, and then where will you and I be? So could you please, just this once, give out the home number? I promise I'll burn it up, and then swallow the ashes twice as soon as I'm done with it."

Natasha gave a little chuckle. "Once ought to be enough, Andy. Hold on a sec. Okay, you ready?" She gave it to him.

* * *

"That was too easy," Mickey said. "It can't be that easy."

"Sometimes it is." Hunt wasn't in a joking mood. He had the Manions' phone number, and that's what he'd needed, and now he had his cell phone back at his ear, on with Juhle.

"What is this place?" Devin asked him. "Disneyland? The Epcot Center? I didn't know they made this many cars all told in history, and they're all here right now. I haven't moved a mile in fifteen minutes."

"Where are you now?"

"In traffic."

"I guessed that. You've got to get out of it. I just got word from Amy and Jason. Carol Manion all but admitted she made the call from the Saint Francis."

"What's that mean? All but admitted."

"Didn't deny. Amy mentioned it specifically."

"If that's true," Juhle said, "it may be our first real break."

"It might be," Hunt admitted. "But you've got to hustle. Carol and Ward are on their way home."

"They'll be in this parking lot, too."

"Yeah, but coming from the other direction, and maybe a lot faster. Where are you now?"

"On some freeway somewhere. Twenty-nine."

"Are you through the town of Napa?"

"I think so."

"Okay. You're going to make it. Take your next right."

"Any right? You don't even know where I am."

"You're north of Napa, I don't care. Take your first right, and every chance you get keep going right, toward those hills you see out your passenger window. Got it? The next big road you'll hit is the Silverado Trail, where you'll hang a left. I'm on it now, and the traffic's moving both directions. You'll see Quintessa Vineyards on your left—it's huge, you can't miss it, slow down. Manion Cellars is next on your left, but Mick's got his green Camaro parked on the right side of the road a few hundred feet up, and that's where you'll find us. You shouldn't be another ten, fifteen minutes, which ought to do it."

"Do what?"

"Get you here before they get home."

"And why is that important?"

"Maybe it isn't. But since you wanted to talk to her, anyway, humor me, all right? I'm delivering her to you. Maybe badly shaken up and maybe ready to break."

"In spite of your promise that you weren't going to talk to her."

"I never did."

"But you got her shaken up. How did that happen?"

"Magic. I'll tell you the secret later, but for now, your job is to drive, okay? I know you're a cop and it flies in the face of your every belief, but speed if you have to."

"Fat chance," Juhle said.

Juhle drove up the winding driveway, past the "Open to the Public" tasting room and its parking area and continued uphill until he stopped and pushed the button on the box by the wrought-iron gate that straddled the private road. Identifying himself as a police inspector with the San Francisco homicide detail, he waited another five minutes or so until a young man in a dark suit appeared, let himself out of the compound area through another gate in the fence, and came to Juhle's driver's window to verify the credentials.

"But I'm afraid you may have driven up here for nothing. They're not home right now."

"That's all right. I'll wait if you don't mind."

"It might be a while. They're down at the auction."

"What auction?"

"Auction Napa Valley."

"Sorry. I don't know it."

The guy didn't know if he believed Juhle, but he said, "Well, it's a big event up here, and it's been known to go late, with parties afterward."

"Are you telling me you're not letting me come up?"

Long pause. "Sir, you can come up the drive, but I can't let you into the house without explicit instructions from the Manions."

Flashing a smile, Juhle nodded. "Thanks, then. I'll take my chances."

The security guard punched a code into the box, the gate opened, and Juhle drove through. The road climbed steeply for fifty feet and then forked immediately as it leveled slightly, one lane going off to the right, winding through vines, before it disappeared around the side of the promontory. Juhle waited at the fork until the man who'd let him through got to the car. "You want a lift to the top?"

"Sure, thanks. It's farther than it looks from the road."

"Left or right."

"Left."

They drove in silence over another rise, dipped to the right in front of the new caves with their impressively carved heavy oaken doors, climbed a last time and leveled off on a large, gravel-strewn circular parking area with a working fountain in the center and bounded by olive trees in front of the ornate structure of the château itself. Juhle passed two parked dark SUVs and an old Honda Civic and continued around the circumference until he caught up with some shade and stopped within it, telling his passenger that he'd wait in the car.

"It really could be some time."

"If I get stir-crazy, I'll walk around. How's that?"

"Your call, sir, but please don't leave this area in the front of the house." He walked around the car and paused by Juhle's window. "Excuse me, but it just occurred to me. You're with homicide? Is this bad news? I mean, for the family? I do have a number to reach them, but only in an absolute emergency."

"Just routine." Juhle offered nothing else.

After a second or two, the young man shrugged and walked away.

Juhle sat in the car with the window down for a short while, enjoying the warmth and the sunshine. From his vantage point up here, he could see for miles in both directions up and down the valley. The green of the budding vines against the reddish soil, the jagged peaks studded with granite on the eastern slope, the cerulean cloudless sky with a lone turkey vulture circling in a thermal. It was a stunning panorama.

Closer in, he noticed that while the traffic wasn't exactly thin on the Silverado Trail below him, it was moving. If Hunt was correct in his assumptions—and he had been so far—Carol and Ward wouldn't be long.

It eventually got too hot in his seat, so he opened the door, slid out, and walked to the front edge of the parking area where the promontory fell off steeply below him. Here, with the foreground up close, the view wasn't as magical. With something of an effort given the grandeur of the rest of the setting, he reminded himself that vineyards, after all, were basically just farms that grew grapes as their crop.

And, indeed, in a little hollow to the side of the new caves, Juhle caught the jarring note of a truly dilapidated ancient redwood barn surrounded by what seemed to be an inordinate amount of rusting old farm tools, as well as some of the newer heavy machinery that had obviously been used in the recent excavations, gradings, and plantings—a couple of tractors, backhoes and rotary hoes, huge bits and drill parts, shovels and spades, mattocks and rakes. Some were glinting in the sun; most had fallen into hopeless, permanent disrepair. The land itself around the cave entrances was still scratched and stripped of its soil, the bare limestone shining like animal bones in the bright sunshine.

But he'd come here for a specific purpose, and much to his satisfaction, Juhle saw that he wasn't going to have the time to take any more inventory of the château and surrounding grounds up here. Just below him, a black BMW Z4 convertible crested the rise beyond the gate.

Juhle backed up a couple of steps until he was lost to the view of the car's passengers. By the time they cleared the promontory and broke onto the olive-shaded area where he'd been waiting, he'd put on his sunglasses and was walking toward them, his badge extended in front of him, his face locked down into impassivity.

His footfalls crunching noisily on the gravel of the parking surface, Juhle walked directly to Carol's side of the car, spoke before it had rolled to a complete stop. "Mrs. Manion? Inspector Juhle from San Francisco homicide. You might remember me. If you could spare some time, I'd like to have a few more words with you."

34 /

"I must insist," Ward said. "As you can see, this really isn't a good time, inspector. My wife is really feeling quite ill. We just had to leave the auction preview because of it, and I assure you we would not have done that if it wasn't quite serious."

The two men stood face-to-face in the circular, vaulted marble foyer. The fact that they'd acquiesced to this point and in essence invited Juhle inside the château represented a colossal logistical error on the Manions' part—if they'd made him stay outside, he would have needed a warrant to enter without their express permission, but once he'd been admitted, it would be a lot tougher psychologically to kick him out.

As soon as they'd come inside, Carol, in the attitude of someone overcome by heat, had collapsed into one of the wing chairs along the walls. Now she rested an elbow on the arm of the chair and, eyes closed, supported her forehead with the first two fingers of her right hand. Juhle's unexpected presence, appearing out of the blinding whiteness of the afternoon, had dealt her the day's second psychic blow and rocked her.

This had been Hunt's intention, the crux of his plan, and clearly it was working.

Juhle kept up the pressure. "Mr. Manion, I've driven all the way up here from San Francisco to ask your wife just a very few questions after which I'll be on my way. But I'm in the middle of the murder investigation of a federal judge, and it's critical that I have your wife's statement. If you'd like to take a few minutes to get her a glass of water or freshen up a bit, that would be fine, but this is really very urgent."

Ward Manion looked down at his wife, over to Juhle. "This is intolerable. I'm going to call my lawyer."

"By all means," Juhle said. "That's your right. But if you've got nothing to hide, the easiest thing might be to just answer my questions."

Manion raised his voice. "Nothing to hide? This is preposterous! You get out of this house right now. You can't talk to us like this . . ."

But Carol suddenly got to her feet, came up from behind her husband, and touched his arm. "Ward."

He whirled, nearly knocking her over. "Carol, sit back down. I've got this . . ."

"No. No, it's all right. I'll talk to him. I don't need a lawyer. As you know, we haven't done anything wrong."

"No, of course, we haven't. But all this is so . . . so wrong. They're treating you like a common criminal, barging in like this . . ." Ward shook his head in disgust. He came back to Juhle. "This is absurd. What do you want to know?"

"What do you want to ask me?" Mrs. Manion said.

Juhle got out his portable tape recorder, turned it on, and put it on the umbrella stand next to the front door. "When was the last time you spoke to George Palmer?"

She sighed heavily, threw a weary glance at her husband, and sank back into her armchair. Finally she raised her eyes to Juhle. "On last Monday afternoon. He called me at my house to invite me to a party."

It went on for nearly a half hour. It all came out—the long-ago relationship between Staci Keilly and her natural son Cameron, the connection between Staci Rosalier and Palmer, the photograph, her son Todd's true identity. To everything, her answers were straightforward and unambiguous. She admitted to the incredible coincidence factor. But she really hadn't known who Staci Rosalier was. She'd never heard the name before it had been in the press last Wednesday. If the victim's name had been Staci Keilly, of course, she would have notified the authorities. As to the photograph, naturally she'd noticed some similarity between the boy in the picture and her son Todd, but given the fact that she knew she'd never met this Staci woman—and why would this strange person have a picture of Todd?—she wrote it off as another in what was turning out to be a bizarre string of coincidences. But for the record, she didn't think the other boy looked exactly like Todd, anyway.

Finally, Juhle brought it around to Andrea Parisi, and Carol again said that she'd already told him about her original telephone call to Andrea, the invitation to be the celebrity emcee at the Library Foundation benefit, the appointment that Parisi had never kept. What was the problem?

Juhle hammered at the apparent discrepancies: Why did she wait *three hours* before calling Parisi's office after the time of the meeting when Parisi hadn't shown up? Why didn't she call while she would have been waiting in frustration? Why had Parisi told colleagues at her law firm that their meeting was going to concern custody issues? Given that, did Carol expect Juhle to believe that Mrs. Manion and Staci, Palmer, and Parisi were not already involved in negotiations over the child to whom they both had a claim?

And yet she denied it. With a gathering calm and growing disdain.

As they continued to spar, Juhle could feel the air between them grow thick and putrid. Though his understanding of exactly what had happened and why seemed to shock her, she grew more imperturbable as the interrogation went on.

Finally, Juhle got to the phone call. "Mrs. Manion. You talked to one of our witnesses not two hours ago, and you didn't deny that you called Ms. Parisi on Wednesday afternoon from the Saint Francis Hotel to change your appointment to her office downtown."

The accusation—and with it the knowledge that Juhle had obviously spoken to the young woman who'd chatted her up in the tent at Meadowood—drew new blood. The facade gave, cracked, came back together. "That's just not true, inspector. I wasn't there."

"You told our witness you were."

"I did not. She's either mistaken, or she's a liar."

Juhle didn't miss a beat. "How do you know it's a *she*?"

"I don't really know, inspector. It had to be a *he* or a *she*, didn't it? I picked one at random. Do you have other witnesses who say they actually saw me at the Saint Francis?"

"We'll find them."

"I doubt you will, inspector. I very much doubt you will. Because I wasn't there. I was at home waiting for Ms. Parisi."

At last, Ward could endure it no longer. "Aren't we just about to the end here, sergeant? If you haven't gotten what you came here for by now, don't you agree it's probably not going to be forthcoming? Obviously, my wife has some inadvertent connection to all these tragic events, but to assume as you appear to that she played even the most minor role in any of them is patently absurd."

Part of Hunt's plan had been for Juhle to deliver the message to Carol that she hadn't fooled anyone. The truth was out there. People knew what she had done. He had done that. But he couldn't pass up at least taking a shot at getting her to confess.

He went into a crouch to put himself at her eye level, his elbows resting on his thighs and his fingers linked in front of him. He spoke from his heart. "Mrs. Manion," he said. "You're an intelligent woman. I think you must intuitively understand that it's only a matter of time before this will destroy you. You're not a bad person. You snapped under an unexpected threat to your son's future and your life together and then tried to cover up what you'd done. But you're not the kind of person who will be able to live with yourself, knowing what it is you've done, that you've killed innocent people. You don't want your son to have to live with all the ways this will change you. And you know it will. It already has."

From her expression, he thought for just a moment that he had her.

"It can be over right now," he said. "You can end it all right here."

She seemed to be considering what he'd said. Drawing a breath in sharply, she pursed her lips and blinked rapidly several times. At last, she cocked her head to one side and brought her open hand down over her mouth. Her back went straight in the chair. "Todd is my son, and he is innocent. He loves me."

And Juhle knew that he had lost.

"I am his mother," she went on. "I would never let any harm come to him. I will protect him. I am his mother," she repeated.

Juhle, sickened and depleted, pulled himself up to his feet. "As a matter of fact," he said, "you're not even that."

35 /

Hunt's base camp was up a side road that began a few hundred feet north of the Manions' driveway and wound up the western slope facing the château. It was a place Mickey knew of—he'd come up here a few times with female companions to make out—where a turnout that coincided with a break in the topography gave them an unimpeded look and more importantly walkie-talkie access across to the valley, the promontory, and to the California oaks, which grew amid the boulders at the very crest of the ridge beyond the Manions' roof.

On a line, they were less than a half mile from the main house.

Hunt's Cooper and Mickey's Camaro, both excessively visible on the Silverado Trail, were parked on the shoulder of the road. Jason, back from the Meadowood, had parked his purple PT Cruiser well up the street, so that the random Napa County cop, should one appear, wouldn't become suspicious.

Amy and Jason, Hunt and Mickey stood in a tight group in a patch of shade. Juhle had been in the house across the way for about a half hour, and the small talk in the clearing had gotten smaller and smaller until finally it had disappeared altogether. Suddenly, Mickey, who hadn't taken his eyes off the château the whole time, said, "Happening."

Hunt lifted his binoculars and was watching as Juhle appeared at the front door on his way out. His body language alone told the story, affirmed when nobody accompanied him out.

Juhle got to his car door and opened it, Hunt lowered the binoculars, got his telephone off his belt, and handed it to Wu.

"You ready?"

She'd been game all along. Though her task was simple and

straightforward enough, she and Wyatt had discussed it in some detail, and now she took the phone without any hesitation. Still, she did have a question. "You're sure you don't want to wait until Devin gets up here?"

"I'm sure," Hunt said. "Whatever else happened with Dev and her, you can bet he delivered the message, so we hit her now when it's still in her craw, before she can digest it. And I'm damn sure Dev doesn't want to see this next part. He won't even want to hear about it."

Mickey said, "The dude's in this far, Wyatt, he's following your lead, he ought to get over it."

Hunt shrugged. "Yeah, well, it's his job. Everything he's done up to now, it's in his little manual of what he's allowed to do. As we all know, he's got these due-process issues, which fortunately I don't have to worry about."

"Yeah, but for the record, Amy and I are officers of the court, too. In fact, last time I looked I was a DA." Jason, all nerves now, wasn't complaining, just stating a fact. "So Wyatt's idea that we don't talk about it, that might be a good thing to remember when this is over."

Amy put a calming hand on his arm. "Understood. I think everybody gets that, Jason. Let's get this done. Wyatt, what's the number?"

Hunt gave it to her, and she punched it in, the three men standing around her in various attitudes of tension. Hunt, arms crossed, the muscles in his jaw working. Mickey shifting from foot to foot. Jason, hands in his pockets, high color in his face, although his dark eyes were hooded, almost brooding; he chewed at the inside of his lower lip. Nobody said a word.

Amy affected being cool, but her eyes darted from the trees to the sky to the men around her while she waited for the first ring and gave away the state of her nerves. A breeze freshened and blew some of her hair across her face, and almost angrily, she brushed it away. Suddenly, with an audible sigh of relief, she nodded. "Ringing," she whispered.

Then she nodded. Someone had picked up.

"May I please speak to Carol Manion?" Wu's eyes were closed in concentration. "Yes, I understand that," she said, "but this is an emergency. I need to speak with her personally." Another pause. "That won't be possible. Would you please ask? It's actually really urgent. Yes." And finally, the coup. "Tell her it's Staci Rosalier."

Wu's knuckles were white on the cell phone. She opened her

eyes, caught Hunt's steely gaze, and nodded again imperceptibly. Carol was coming to the phone.

When it came, the voice was far from the refined contralto Wu had noted at the auction preview. Everything that had happened to Carol Manion today, first with Amy and then evidently with Juhle, had as Hunt predicted finally managed to erode the surface veneer of control and sophistication. The voice rode a wave of dread now that broke and churned in her throat. "Who is this?"

Hunt had told Amy to get right to it, not to give her a chance to hang up. Wu spoke in measured, even tones. "It's Staci Rosalier, Carol. Staci Keilly. Todd's mother."

"Who is this? Is this the police again? This is pure harassment."

"It's not the police, Carol. You know it's not the police."

"Who is it, then? What do you want?"

"I want my son back. But it's too late for that. I'll settle for Andrea Parisi."

"I'm hanging up."

"I'll leave you alone if you lead me to Andrea."

"I don't know what you're talking about."

"Yes, you do, Carol. Don't make me threaten you. I don't want to take Todd and force you to trade, but I will if I have to."

Now through the line, Carol came across in a clear panic. Wu heard her yelling back through the house. "Todd! Todd! Where are you? Come in here. I need to see you. *Right now!*" She ended in a shriek.

Other noises sounded in the background. Male. Concerned.

Now, back into the phone, no mistaking it, Carol's fear bled out and over into her voice. "He's here. He's fine."

"I know that. I'd never hurt my own son. But I would take him from you."

"Tell me who you are!"

"I've told you that. Where is Andrea?"

"I said I don't know! I don't know."

"All right," Wu said. "I've warned you. Look out your back windows. I'll call back in exactly five minutes."

In the dining room off the kitchen at the château, Carol stood holding the phone, breathing hard, her face gone pale. Ward had come in with the earlier screams, followed by Todd along with the security guard who'd admitted Juhle earlier, and Todd's nanny. Now the four of them hovered in the doorway.

Looking at the phone as though surprised that she still held it, she put it down into its receiver and turned back to the rest of them. "Oh, Todd," she said, moving toward him, arms extended. "My baby. Are you all right? Tell me you're all right."

"I'm fine, Mom. I'm good. Are you okay?"

She was down at his level, hugging him tightly. "I'm good," she said, but her voice broke. Her shoulders heaved and then heaved again. She tried to stifle a desperate sob.

"Carol." Ward was down next to her. "What's this about? Talk to me."

But instead she gathered herself, stood, and faced the guard. "Has anyone been here to the house today besides Inspector Juhle?"

"No, ma'am."

"You're sure?" Her voice snapped at him. "*Don't look at Todd! I want your answer.* Was anybody here?"

Stunned by the violence of the outburst, the guard backed up a step. "No, ma'am. I'm sure. Nobody."

Ward reached out his hand. "Carol . . ."

She held up a warning finger to her husband, came back at the guard. "When we drove up, he was outside. Juhle. Had he been out there alone for long?"

"No, ma'am. A minute, two minutes at the most, before you got here. I watched him the whole time."

"What did he do?"

"He sat in his car for a minute, no more, then got out and walked to where the driveway drops off."

"And what did he do there?"

"It seemed like he was looking at the view."

"And that's all? He never went around the back."

"No, ma'am, he didn't have time for anything like that. You and Mr. Manion arrived about a minute later. Almost immediately, in fact."

She whirled around to the nanny. "And you've been with Todd all day, too?"

"*Si, sénora. Toda el dia.*"

She turned to her son. "Todd? Is that true. All day?"

The boy, now frightened by his mother's madness, moved a step away toward his nanny. "Mo-om."

Ward came over and put his arm around his wife, dismissing the others with an impatient wave, wanting to get her away. He walked with her a few steps into the living room, whose enormous west-facing windows featured full-length white drapes now drawn against the afternoon sun. "Who was that on the telephone now that's got you so upset? Is it more of this, this police business?" He reached after her as she moved away. "Carol? Please . . ."

She had reached where the drapes met in the center of the windows and now threw them open with enough violence that one of them ripped at the runners above. Then, stepping back as if stung, her hands to her mouth, she whimpered through her fingers.

In silver paint on the glass, backward so they could be read from inside, someone had spray-painted the capital letters: T-O-D-D.

"Hello." Mrs. Manion's voice now barely audible in the cell phone, laced with panic but still managing to maintain a tenuous control.

"Don't interrupt. You can send everyone else away," Wu said, using the exact, carefully rehearsed lines they'd agreed upon. "No one else has to be involved. This is about Andrea now, not about you. We'll be watching."

Amy had gone pale, her hand shaking as she handed the phone back to Hunt—it had grown hot to the touch. "God!" she said, blowing out with each breath. "Oh, my God."

Jason put his arm around her. "You okay?"

She shook her head no. Blew out again. "Shit. Shit shit shit. That was horrible."

"It was awesome," Mick said.

"I think I might be sick."

"Here." Jason lowered her to the ground, sat with his arms around her.

Hunt went down on a knee, lifted her chin with his finger. "That was perfect, Ames," he said. "You did good."

She nodded, her breath still coming hard, and Jason looked across to Hunt. "So what do we do now?" he asked.

"Now, you guys—Amy and Jason—you take off. You've both done plenty. You get caught in any part of this, your jobs are at least severely compromised if not over. You've got too much to lose."

"Like you guys don't," Jason said.

Hunt waved away the objection. "I've changed jobs before. It didn't kill me. I can always do something else. And Devin's a big boy who's here because he wants to be. Everybody else—Mick, Tammy, Craig—they're on the payroll. I'm sure they'll get a huge bonus."

Mick perked right up. "How big?" he asked.

"Huge," Hunt said, "unprecedented." He went back to Amy and Jason. "But you guys are volunteers who've done some great work, and now you've got to get out of here and go home. I mean it."

"And what are you all going to do?" Amy asked.

Hunt said. "The rest of us, we play this way."

Juhle and Hunt had been together at the base camp for three hours since Amy's call to Carol. Now Mickey was back in his car, parked again where the road cut into the Silverado Trail, where he would be ready to tail the Manions should all of them, including Carol, come off their mountain by car and try to make some kind of getaway.

Juhle hung up from the "I'm going to be late" call to his wife and walked over to where Hunt, his binoculars mounted on a tripod in front of him, half-leaned against the hood of his Cooper. "How long you gonna give this?" he asked.

Hunt looked at his watch, at the declining sun, at the château, finally at his friend. "As long as it takes," he said. "You want, go on home. I'll call you from wherever we find Andrea. You can come out then and get famous."

"You still think this is going to work?"

"I don't know."

"It's taking a while."

"I figured it would. She's got some choices to make. She could come clean to Ward—or mostly clean, enough to get him to cooperate with her. Either that or convince him and everybody else in the house that she can handle whatever it is herself, that she's not having a breakdown. If that's her choice, then she's got to get rid of them, send them out to dinner, say she's got a headache, something. Whatever it is, it's going to take some time."

"If somebody writes one of my kid's name on my windows, I call the cops."

"I know, but she won't do that."

"What if she calls in twenty private security guards or even Shiu, for Christ's sake. Wouldn't that be a fine kettle of fish?"

"What if . . ." Hunt looked over at the house. There'd been no activity in or around it since Wu's phone calls. "She's not going to any kind of police, Dev. If she was going that way, they'd already be here. You guys are all the enemy now. Even Shiu. He might moonlight for her, but I've got to believe he's your partner first, a homicide cop investigating a couple of murders which, p.s., it looks an awful lot like she committed."

"He might just come on for double overtime."

"Unlikely."

"And you don't think Ward will call the cops, either?"

Hunt shook his head. "He might want to, but she'll talk him out of it. It's her problem and she's motivated. I hope I've made her realize that giving us Andrea is her only out. That's all we want."

"Not quite," Juhle said. "I, for example, want to put cuffs on her."

"I left that part out. And if you weren't here, that wouldn't be my issue, as I've said all along."

"You'd let her walk on the murders?" Juhle asked.

Hunt shrugged. "I want Andrea." He deadpanned his friend. The discussion was over. Picking up his walkie-talkie, he pushed the button. "You guys still good?"

Chiurco's voice crackled back up at him. "*Affirmativo, mon capitaine,* but nothing since the curtains. Except we did see a rattlesnake. Big old sucker."

"How about you catch it and go set it loose in the house? That'll scare her out."

Tamara's voice carried out of the speaker. "No way, Wyatt."

"That was more or less in the order of a joke, Tam."

"I'm laughing," she said.

"Good. Call if you get lonely." Hunt rang off, turned to Juhle. "Really, you don't have to stick around. We can handle it. Besides, it might not happen."

It was Juhle's turn to take a beat, check out the château, note the time.

"Really," Hunt said.

"Maybe I'll just hang a few more minutes. Take my chances."

It was within three weeks of the longest day of the year, but the Coast Range cut off the direct sun in the lower parts of the valley by a little after six. By quarter to seven, the shadow had moved up to the base camp, and Juhle put on the jacket he wore every day in San Francisco.

"Here we go," Hunt said.

Juhle came up next to him, squinting into the shadows, as Hunt straightened up off his car's hood, grabbed his walkie-talkie, and buzzed his troops, telling Mickey down on the lower road that people were coming out of the house into the parking area in front. He should hit his ignition and be ready to roll.

"How many we talking about?"

"Hold on." Hunt put a steadying hand on one leg of the tripod and leaned down into the binoculars. He had his night visions in the trunk of the Cooper, but it wasn't really quite twilight yet, and he hadn't changed over to them. "Some guy in a dark suit with the kid and a woman. I don't know if it's Carol. Can you get her, Craig? Over."

"No. We're blocked by the house."

Hunt followed the little procession as they made their way over to one of the SUVs. "Do we know how many people were in the house? The Manions, the kid, the security guy. Anybody else?"

"The kid's got a nanny," Craig said. "We saw her upstairs through the windows."

"So five. Five."

"Sounds right," Mickey said.

The man in the suit got into the car while the boy and the woman got into the backseat from the far door, now outside of Hunt's vision. In the evening stillness, even from across the distance, Hunt picked up the faint echoes of the car's ignition kicking in. It rolled forward, pulled up, and stopped right at the front door, blocking most of it. Hunt saw the house's door open and close. He had a sense of movement, but that was all it was. "Mick," he said, "they're coming down. I don't know if everybody got in the car, but you'd better follow and find out."

"Roger. On it." Three minutes later, Mick checked in again. "Tinted windows, Wyatt. I can't see in."

Hunt resisted the urge to swear. "All right. Which way are they headed?"

"North."

"So not back to the city?"

"Probably not. Maybe food in the valley."

"Let's hope. Okay, stay with 'em. Call when you know who's with them."

"Check."

Twenty minutes later, Chiurco's voice, albeit quietly, rasped through the speaker. "Wyatt, you got me? The back door just opened."

"You on night vision?"

"Yeah."

The sky directly overhead was still blue, but by now the shadows from the Coast Range had engulfed the entire landscape up to the peaks behind Hunt's lookout. True dusk wasn't ten minutes away. Hunt had changed over to his Night Scout binoculars, but they were useless since he had no view of the back of the house.

Hunt didn't need any visual equipment, though, to see the blade of light that swept across the ridge behind the château, then swung back higher in among the oaks and boulders, where Tamara and Craig had been hiding all afternoon. Hunt saw no trace of them in the light's beam, a good sign that nobody else could see them, either.

He hoped. "Lay low," he whispered.

The beam of light disappeared altogether, only to return in about twenty seconds from the same spot and following the same trajectory. Chiurco's voice, barely audible now: "Trying to flush us."

"Got you. Hang back. Can you tell who it was?"

"An older woman, I'd say. It must be Carol, huh? Now she's back inside."

Glued to his binoculars now, Hunt realized that he'd made a tactical error. With Mickey now gone with his walkie-talkie, he could not leave his own vantage point at the base camp and keep the front door under surveillance at the same time. There would have to be a gap. When they started driving down to the house, they would not know whether Carol was driving or walking to some location on her property. Everything depended on their ability to follow wherever she might lead them, and while she was out of their sight, they might lose her. He pointed this out to Juhle.

"So what do we do? You want me to go down first?"

"Same problem. No communication," Hunt said. But then suddenly the point became moot. "Damn. Here she is." He spoke into his walkie-talkie. "She's out the front door, Craig. Can you get her in vision?"

"Not fast. We're starting down. Coming around your right side."

"Got it. Be quick if you can. But she's got her flashlight, and looks like something in the other hand. Maybe a gun, Craig. Watch out."

"We're watching."

Next to Hunt, Juhle whispered. "Where's she going? If she gets near her car, we've got to haul ass!"

"We've got to wait, Dev. We've got to wait. If she doesn't get in a car, we've got her."

They could see the flashlight crossing behind the fountain. "Come on, Carol," Hunt said. "Don't get in the car. Don't get in the car!"

"We've got to get down there." Juhle, caught up in the urgency, opened the passenger door to the Cooper. "We've got to move, Wyatt. Now! We're going to lose her!"

As the flashlight's beam now crossed in front of the other SUV down in the château's parking area, Hunt realized that she wasn't going to be driving anywhere. He grabbed his tripod, threw it into his backseat, and picked up his one pair of Vipers, his night-vision goggles. Running around to the driver's door, he handed the goggles to Juhle as he slid in behind the wheel. "Don't drop those," he said. He started the car, threw it into gear, swung a U-turn, and peeled out in a hail of dust and gravel.

36 /

From the time Hunt hit the gas on the downhill, it took the Cooper seventy-eight seconds to get to the driveway turnoff up to Manion Cellars. After the right turn, Hunt doused his headlights, took his Vipers from Juhle, and pulled them down over his eyes into place. Getting his bearings with the night-vision lenses, he drove slowly and hoped quietly up toward the gate that crossed the driveway.

He whispered into his walkie-talkie. "Craig? You got her?"

"No. But there's an old barn down to my right, where there might have been a light when I first got here. But it's gone now."

"Where are you?"

"Pretty far up, still. I didn't want her to hear our chatter. I'm by the road that runs around the back of the hill, where the caves are."

Juhle said to make sure whether he was above or below the barn, and Craig said he was still above.

Hunt turned in his seat. "Where's this barn?" he asked Juhle. "You know it?"

"Yeah. If you go up in front of the new caves, it's in a little hollow on the right. Lots of junk laying on the ground all around it."

Back into his walkie-talkie. "Craig. Where's Tam?"

"Up above with the binoculars. How about you?"

"Me and Dev are just at the gate."

"You guys ought to split up."

"That's the call. I'm going to send Dev around up the trail you're on." Hunt had seen this clearly enough from the base camp. The unpaved road wound around behind the base of the promontory and continued up until it disappeared behind the château. "You start coming down slow. He'll be coming up. Meet up in back of the barn and wait there. If she comes out, don't let her see you, and don't stop her. Let her do whatever she's doing."

"What about you?"

"I'm going past the caves in the front."

"So she's in the barn?"

"I guess that's the working theory. Now we've got to shut down the chatter."

"Okay," Craig whispered. "I'm out."

Hunt clicked off his walkie-talkie and dropped it on the floor beneath his feet. Shading the light with his hand, he flicked on and off his small, industrial-strength flashlight, and put it in his jacket pocket. Both men in the car reached for their door handles, but Hunt grabbed Juhle by the sleeve, stopping him. "Dead quiet, Dev. Easy open, no close. Let it happen. And if this goes south, take off immediately. You were never here."

Hunt crossed around his car and, crouching, followed Juhle for the first fifty feet or so, until he came to the trail on his left that led up to the new caves from the tasting room below. As soon as he left the pavement of the road, he became aware of the gravel crunching under his feet, each footfall magnified in the stillness of the night.

He had to slow to a near crawl, each step now an eternity. Clearing the first rise, he came out into the relative openness of the entrance to the cave area. The staff had closed the huge doors of the caves for the night, but Hunt double-checked each one and found them all to be solid and immovable. When he cleared the entrance to the fourth cave, he recrossed the path to get a better angle on the hollow that enclosed the barn.

Juhle was right. The foreground was littered with tools and equipment. Without the night-vision goggles, Hunt stood no chance at all of getting to the barn, much less inside it, without making a racket. Even with them, though, he would be picking over the ground by inches.

In the eerie green glow, he took a step and then another, trying to keep one eye on the obstacles ahead and the other on the barn, for any sign of light from within. Between each step, he would stop and wait, listening. He heard no sound.

It was a large, two-story, three-sided structure, built into the westernmost wall of the promontory. He'd made it through the no-man's-land out front, and now directly in front of him, the door to the barn hung halfway open. If she were behind it, waiting for him . . .

He could not let himself think about that.

He listened. He listened.

He drew his gun.

Stepping through the opening into the barn, he ducked and whirled around. Something moved in the periphery of his vision, and he jerked back to see a large green-glowing rat scurrying into a pile of straw and out of sight. Taking a shaken breath, he turned again, all the way around now. Six stalls lined the side wall, a partially open tack room stood in the corner off the back door.

And then he saw it.

In the promontory wall, another door to apparently another cave. Of course, he thought. How had it never occurred to him before? If there were new caves, then it stood to reason there must have been old caves.

Or at least one old cave, now abandoned, unvisited, locked up.

He crossed to the door, which was in fact not locked up like the others, but stood a few inches ajar. A faint cold breeze emanated from within, and Hunt pulled the massive door—it was at least four inches thick—a few more inches toward him.

He stepped inside.

Even with the night-vision goggles, it was difficult to see—the glasses didn't shed any light of their own, only magnified the ambient light that was present, and here in the cave there wasn't much to magnify. He put his hand to the wall and took another tentative, silent step, and another. After about thirty steps, the cave bent to the left slightly, then sharply back to the right. He had to negotiate several old wine barrels that lay on their sides against the walls of the cave. Hunt continued pushing himself forward until he could go no farther.

The night goggles were useless this far in. There was no light left to magnify. Hunt lifted the goggles and turned on his flashlight, surprised to encounter another door completely blocking his way, seemingly built into the stone walls of the cave. Behind him, in the vast echoing darkness, an unmistakable creak resounded in the confines of the cave. He barely had time to begin to turn when the creak was followed by a muted and terrifying percussion.

It could have been nothing other than what it was—the door to the cave slamming shut.

*   *   *

Though it wasn't loud, it was the first sound Andrea Parisi had heard since the solid door had closed behind her however many days ago. She was lying on her back on the stone just inside the door—in fact her side was pressed up against the door. She was nearly paralyzed by hunger and thirst, and at first, she imagined that she'd dreamed the sound in her present altered state. Most of what was left of her mind had come to believe that she was not really there anymore. None of this was real, and even if it was, it could not go on for much longer. Perhaps she was already dead.

But there had been a definite sound. Close enough for her to hear it.

She tried to turn herself to the side, to face the door and call out, but her muscles wouldn't obey her to let her move at all, and her throat was so dry, it couldn't be coaxed into sound.

But if there had been a sound, that meant that someone might be out there. She might still be saved, still have a life before her.

She had to try again.

She tried to concentrate, fought to draw air into her dry and empty chest.

This time the sound, when it came from her, had no form. No words. An inchoate moan that dissipated almost as it sounded in her chill grave and left her exhausted, her throat burning.

And yet she gathered the last bit of reserve she could muster and threw it out again into the darkness that had become her world and her hell.

And there it was again! Without question, another sound through the door, and someone knocking on it. And her name!

Andrea.

From the bottom of a deep well, someone was calling her name.

Hunt had no time to give in to the terror that threatened to consume him. After all, he told himself, Craig, Juhle, and Tamara were close by, just outside on the property. But they all were waiting for his instructions and would be unlikely to move in after he had specifically instructed them to let Carol alone and let her lead them to Andrea.

Which she had done.

Even Juhle, he realized, would be reluctant to move at this point. Juhle did not know that Andrea was locked behind the second door in this cave—only Hunt knew that—and without knowing about Andrea, Juhle had no more cause to arrest Carol Manion than he'd had earlier in the day. To say nothing of the fact that Juhle had moved himself completely out of bounds by coming onto her property. He was, in fact, trespassing. If anyone connected him to any of the more unorthodox if not to say illegal elements of Hunt's plan, it would cost him not just this case, but his precious job.

Hunt had made his way back to the door at the cave's opening inside the barn to verify that the noise was what it had sounded like. Yes, that door to the outside was closed now. Locked, solid, immovable.

But then he'd returned to where he'd been, and through that second door had heard Andrea's strangled cry. Pounding at the unyielding door, he called out to answer her, but the sound seemed to be swallowed up by its own echo.

And after the one response, nothing.

He shone his flashlight again over the wood of the door. The faintness of the sound from the inside could only mean that the door was extremely thick. It was also framed with heavy beams, which in turn were set into seamless concrete, built into the cave walls.

Hunt sank to the floor and pounded over and over at the door, but the sound didn't carry at all. It was as if the door itself were made of solid rock. "Andrea!" he called again. "Andrea, can you hear me?"

Deafening silence.

"We're getting you out of here," he whispered.

The words themselves seemed to galvanize him. Getting to his feet, he held a hand up over his head, feeling for movement in the air. When he'd been standing out in the barn at the cave's entrance, he'd felt a distinct breeze coming from within the cavern. This could only mean that air was getting into the cave from the outside, from another way in.

Again he tried the door to the very inner chamber where Andrea was locked in, and again he couldn't budge it. Shining his light around the edges, he realized that the seal was at least nearly, or perhaps perfectly, hermetic. No air, or very little air—certainly not enough to cause a breeze—was coming through. This was not bad news. It meant that the moving air he'd felt at the mouth of the cave originated somewhere within his own chamber and not behind that door.

Hunt began walking back toward the front of the cave, shining his light on the walls and the roof, making sure he covered every inch of surface. With the door in the barn closed, there was no breeze blowing in the cave now, either. He tried to remember if he'd felt the source of the breeze as he'd made his way in while the front door had still been open, but he'd been concentrating on what might have been in front of him, on where he placed his feet, on who might have been waiting there in ambush.

The source of the breeze had never entered his consciousness.

Where the cave turned sharply left going back toward the entrance, he noticed a fissure high in the rock as it began to curve to form the roof. No more than eighteen inches at its widest point, and perhaps five feet from tapered end to tapered end, it disappeared into blackness. Standing directly under it, Hunt reached his hand up and strained to get some sense of fresh air coming in through it.

But he felt nothing.

From where Hunt stood below it, even standing across the cave by the opposite wall, he couldn't make out how far back the hole went. It might go all the way to the outside, it might gradually narrow to nothing, it might stop after three feet. There was no way to tell. And at first it wasn't clear why it would matter, anyway. Even if it did mark a possible opening to the outside, he estimated that the fissure itself was at least four feet above his extended reach.

It was impossible.

He kept on looking along the cave's walls, past the barrels, making it all the way to the front door again. That door, too, had been cleanly carved into the limestone. The narrow fissure, ten feet off the ground back where the cave hooked left, was the only possibility. There was no sign of any other outlet. He let himself down to the floor, his back against the door to the barn. Turning off his flashlight, he collected himself in the blackness and tried to concentrate.

And thought of the barrels.

Midway back again, and laying his flashlight on the ground, he dislodged one of the heavy empty barrels from its wooden rack and rolled it back to the spot underneath the fissure.

It wasn't going to be enough.

Hoisting himself up to stand on the barrel, he still could not reach the bottom edge of the crack in the limestone. He was short of it by a foot or more.

Getting down off the barrel, he retrieved his light, and shone it again into the opening, trying to get a better idea of how far it extended. He still couldn't see back into it more than a few feet. Changing his focus, he scanned the beam over the lower edge of the hole. Jagged, sharp-edged, and clearly defined, the ledge appeared to be a natural fault in the solid rock, but he knew that if he tried to jump and grab a handhold and it gave under his weight, or simply crumbled, he would be looking at, best case, a bad fall. Perhaps a broken bone or worse.

But there was no other choice.

He used his night goggles to prop the flashlight on the ground in such a way that its beam centered on the fissure's opening. Boosting himself back up onto the barrel, he studied the place where he'd have to grab, tried to visualize the next exertions—flush against the wall, pulling himself up enough to get his shoulders in, elbowing his way inside, swinging his feet up, hoping there was room to hold him. And that the fissure didn't end in another wall of rock, somewhere back in the heart of the promontory.

Thinking about it wasn't going to help.

He jumped.

Utter blackness.

Hunt should have brought his night goggles. Or his flashlight, although he had needed its beam to illuminate the fissure's mouth. He should have used his gun instead of the precious goggles to prop the light up; his useless gun now snug in its holster against his lower back.

He could do nothing but continue to crawl forward on his belly, inch by inch, feeling in front of him for the outcroppings in the narrow space that had twice already closed down enough over him to cut into his head; the liquid he felt now dripping down his forehead and into his blinded eyes tasted like blood. His hands, he knew, were shredded and bleeding, too.

Ahead of him the passage narrowed and narrowed some more. When he'd begun, there'd been enough clearance to pull himself along on his elbows, to kick with his knees as he'd learned in boot camp. Now, though, after an interminable climb, he felt the walls closing in on both top and bottom—against his chest, nearly flush against his back, his gun catching with almost every movement. He couldn't even begin to turn over, wasn't sure if he could back up now if he wanted to. Pushing himself forward, arms outstretched, scrabbling with his feet, he found himself, finally, nearly wedged into the solid rock.

If it got any tighter, he couldn't go any farther in either direction. He'd already been crawling for many, many minutes, had covered at least a couple of hundred feet. If he got stuck, he would die here, buried in the mountain.

His arm now at full extension, he reached again in front of him, feeling for the stone above and below. His shoulders ground into the rock on both sides of this, his third and worst constriction.

But if he could force himself through it, it seemed to widen again on the other side. Top to bottom, side to side.

His bloody fingers grabbed at the stone. They tried to pull him forward, and the rock crumbled under his hands. Seeking some leverage from behind, he dug in his feet, forced a shoulder forward, gained all of an inch, no more. Finally, with an inhuman cry that he never heard, he pushed with everything he had and cleared the wedge.

Somewhere ahead of him, he caught the first faint scent of fresh air. He pulled himself forward toward it. Ahead the quality of the darkness seemed different. Focusing on that, he pulled again and felt the eroded earth give slightly around him. He saw a pinpoint of light and recognized it for what it was.

A star.

37 /

Hunt rolled out onto a very steep hillside dotted with low shrub and coarse spring grass. The rest of it seemed to be a kind of slippery schist of broken-up limestone and dry dirt. A bright half-moon had risen on the horizon. About a hundred feet below him in its light, Hunt could see an unpaved road that ran in the cut, where the promontory's steeper slope met the tended vineyard beneath it. There was no question in his mind that this was the road that Juhle had taken when they'd split up, and that several hundred feet farther along by the barn was where he had been planning to meet up with Chiurco.

He wiped the blood off his face, off his hands onto his pants and shirtsleeves. He started downhill, keeping low, using the cover of the shrubbery whenever he could, just in case. For all he knew, and had to assume, Mrs. Manion was armed and obviously at least competent enough as a strategist to have been nearly able to eliminate him from tonight's equation.

Because of Amy's phone calls to her, she would certainly have known that she was dealing with more than one adversary, and she might already have disabled one or all of his troops. It would not do to be careless now.

So he forced himself to move slowly and with great care. Even so, every five or six steps brought a small landslide of the unpacked dirt and rock that comprised the face of the slope. Twice, Hunt slid as he stepped and loosened what felt and sounded like an avalance of earth under him. Moving next from shrub to shrub to avoid further slides, he made it down finally to the road, where he turned to his left. He unholstered his gun, racked a round, then keeping low, broke into what he hoped was a silent enough jog.

It wasn't far—a few hundred yards uphill—to the crossroads where Juhle and Chiurco were to have met, and Hunt stood in the middle of the road, where a driveway broke off and led to the barn off to his left. Hunt, paralyzed, standing tall here where the roads met, where Juhle and Chiurco couldn't miss him, held his breath and tried to listen to the sounds of the night over the beating of his heart.

Where were his guys? And on the other side of the barn, where was Tamara?

Automatically, he glanced at his watch, although it told him nothing. He realized that he had almost no idea of how much time had passed since he'd left Juhle—maybe as much as an hour. Certainly no less than forty-five minutes.

But whatever it had been, his men weren't where he thought they'd meet up or where they were supposed to have been waiting for him. Which meant that something else had gone wrong. Or Devin and Craig had given up on him and forced something. And if that were the case, judging from the silence, it was already over.

He turned back to the barn and stared at its looming form. Moving to one side, then another, he tried to get an angle through its ancient redwood planks. Were there places he could actually see through the structure? Did he just imagine it or was there a dim light out in the junkyard beyond it on the other side?

Now, without his goggles, without his flashlight, he had to depend upon the moon, but as he advanced on the barn, the promontory's shadow engulfed the road, and again he was in darkness. But here, because of the contrast, he could see that he hadn't been mistaken. Someone had turned on some kind of a light, perhaps over the barn door on the other side.

He kept moving forward, slowly, quietly. Now into the barn, stall by stall, letting his vision grow accustomed to the space. The front door wasn't completely closed, and a thin shaft of weak yellow light drifted through the crack.

And then, so faintly he couldn't at first place where it came from, he heard a man's voice. He waited, patient now, unwilling to expose himself until he was completely certain about what was transpiring out there. At last, he came around the low wall of the last stall and crossed the no-man's-land of open space in the center of the barn, coming to rest in the shadow still far back behind the door.

Now a woman's voice. Sharp and imperious, although the words were still indistinct. It definitely wasn't Tamara, but Hunt didn't imagine that Carol Manion would use that tone to Juhle. So who did that leave?

He moved to his left and forward toward the door. Quietly, quietly. The gun flat down against his side. One more step, and then he finally could see Juhle, obviously still alive and even well, sitting with his arms behind him, next to Chiurco on the edge of an empty trough in the middle of the junk-strewn foreyard. A great relief flooded him, and he even dropped his guard and took another step toward the door—now as the whole scene opened in front of him.

Shiu was here, too!

Juhle must have relented and called him earlier while they'd been killing time at the base camp and told him he'd probably want to come up after all. Obviously, Juhle wanting to let him in on the arrest, covering his sorry partner's ass, when it might otherwise look bad for Shiu, who looked as though he hadn't wanted to investigate the people for whom he'd done so much security work.

Shiu's presence hadn't been part of Hunt's original plan, but not much this night seemed to be working out in textbook style. Besides, Dev was always such an incorrigibly good guy, and if calling Shiu up without telling Hunt had been an element in making the plan work, he wasn't going to complain about it.

Shiu was standing in front of a rusted-out old tractor, next to Carol Manion, his own gun drawn.

An instant before he got to the door and stepped out into the open, something about the arrangement of the characters stopped Hunt in his tracks. His eyes darted back to Juhle—*with his arms behind him.*

He looked more closely, caught a glint of metal.

Christ! Juhle was handcuffed.

Which could only mean that Shiu . . .

Shiu?

"What's your girlfriend's name again?" Shiu raised his gun to Craig Chiurco's face.

"Tamara."

"Call her."

"She's not here," Chiurco said.

"Juhle said she was."

"I was mistaken," Juhle said.

"Shut up, Devin. I'm talking to your friend here."

"Juhle's telling the truth, sir. He was wrong. She went out the back way, when he was coming up."

"Then that's going to turn out very badly for you, I'm afraid."

Carol Manion spoke up. "Mr. Shiu, please don't . . ."

"Not now, Mrs. Manion." Shiu never took his eyes off Juhle, but he was talking to Carol. "If you hadn't panicked and taken Parisi, we wouldn't even be here. But no, you had to talk to her and find out what she knew, didn't you? And that's what's screwed it all up. Don't you understand that? If you'd left it all up to me, none of this would have happened. So don't tell me how we're getting out of this. Right now it's a work in progress and I'm making the calls."

"So what'd she do with Parisi?" Juhle asked. "Is she dead?"

"Probably," Shiu said, "by now." He came back to Chiurco. "Call your girlfriend."

Craig took a shallow breath and swallowed. "I told you. She's not here."

Shiu took a fast step forward, sighted along his barrel, and pulled the trigger—a huge blast that echoed across the valley. Craig let out a muffled scream and dropped to the ground. "Tamara!" Shiu called out. "That was a warning. The next one's in your boyfriend's head. I need to see you right now."

With a cry, Tamara broke from around the far side of the château, running into the light toward them. "Craig!"

Shiu turned his gun quickly to Juhle to make sure he still had his attention, then turned again to Chiurco. Stepping back, he made room to let Tamara get up next to Craig. He was getting himself back up, his face spooked and his hand over his right ear.

"You didn't have to do that, Mr. Shiu." Carol Manion, used to giving orders, spoke in that sharp tone of hers. "She would have come out eventually."

"We don't have *eventually*, Mrs. Manion. We've got now, and she *is* out now, so let's call the way I did it a success."

"Enjoy it while you can," Juhle said. "Would that be your first? Success, I mean?"

"Why, no, Devin. Since you mention it, locking you up with your own handcuffs ranks right up there. Or is it the thought of shooting you with your own gun here?" Shiu gave his head a disappointed wag. "What? No clever comeback? I don't know why, but I keep expecting you to come up with something pithy, suitable to the occasion. I'm beginning to think you just don't have the imagination for it."

"Considering the source, that's a compliment. And speaking of imagination, what do you plan to do now? Have you given that any thought, you fucking moron? You think you'll be able to get away with killing us all?" Juhle took a chance on the ongoing dynamic between Shiu and Carol Manion. He turned to her. "What did he mean, you took Parisi, and she's *probably* dead by now? You didn't have him take care of that like you did the judge and Staci? I'm assuming you paid him to do them."

Shiu raised the gun again. "Shut up, Devin."

But Juhle had had guns pointed at him before. The current threat left him so unfazed that he actually produced a chuckle. "Or what, Shiu? Or you'll shoot me here where I sit. I don't think so. I'd bleed all over the place, and even you should know that will leave traces. In some jurisdictions, most of the homicide cops are competent."

Carol Manion crossed her arms over her chest, worry now written all over her face. "Mr. Shiu, he's right. We can't . . ."

"That's enough! I'm thinking."

Juhle kept his eyes on the matriarch. "Listen to those gears try to turn," he said. "It's a little painful to watch, isn't it?" Then, the truth dawning, Juhle said, "You put Parisi in the cave where you've locked up Hunt."

"I didn't want to kill her," Mrs. Manion said. "I couldn't shoot anybody."

"No. I don't suppose you could," Juhle said.

"With George and that slut . . . they were going to try to take my Todd, and suddenly, there was no other solution but Mr. Shiu . . . but I, I didn't plan for Ms. Parisi. And Mr. Shiu couldn't . . . he was working. It was the middle of the day."

"So you went and picked her up in her garage and drove her up here?"

Carol nodded. "She wanted to come. I told her I was impressed with her from the television and wanted her to do some legal work for us, for the winery, that she just had to see it. I didn't want to hurt her. I never did hurt her. She just needed to go away." She looked over toward the old rickety structure. "We're knocking down the barn this week, you know? Cleaning up the whole area. Ward wants to plant an organic-herb garden. And stucco over the old cave, of course. The thing is just an eyesore."

"That's enough!" Shiu said. "Everybody on your feet."

"I don't think so," Juhle said. "It goes down out here or not at all."

"All right, then, if that's how it has to be, it goes down here." He raised the weapon.

Next to Shiu, Carol Manion brought a hand up to her face. "No! You can't do that."

In the barn, Hunt saw he'd run out of time. He raised his own weapon, extended his arm, drawing a bead on Shiu.

But out in the yard, in her panic taking a step toward Shiu's prisoners, Carol Manion got herself to where she was blocking Hunt's line of sight. He couldn't squeeze off a round at Shiu. She was in the way.

But something was happening with Shiu out of his vision, and Mrs. Manion took another step, reaching out toward him, and yelled, "You can't do this!"

Hunt heard Shiu's voice. "I've had enough of you."

A tremendous explosion ripped the air. Hunt saw Carol Manion's arms fly out to her sides as she staggered backward and then collapsed into the dirt on her back. Tamara screamed. But in the time, an instant really, that Hunt took his eyes off the place where Carol Manion had fallen, Shiu had moved again, this time behind Juhle, blocked again, his gun extended.

Hunt had to move *right now* if he was to have a chance.

In his haste to get to one side, no time to decide or to waste, trying to keep his eye on Shiu and get a shot at him—Hunt wasn't thinking about all the farming tools and debris littering the barn's floor that he'd up to now been so careful to avoid—his foot kicked something metallic, and in the otherwise dead silence outside, he might as well have set off a cherry bomb.

With no hesitation at the noise, Shiu turned and fired twice at the narrow opening in the barn's door. The bullets hit wood on either side of the gap. He fired another couple of rounds on the heels of the first.

No return fire came from the barn.

Juhle's hands were locked behind him, but in the seconds of distraction from the gunshots, he managed to get to his feet and direct a vicious karate kick at Shiu's gun hand, hitting the weapon and sending it skittering along the dirt.

"Craig! Tam!" he yelled. "Get it."

But Shiu threw an elbow into Juhle's face, knocking him backward over the trough, then spun and kicked at the same time, catching Chiurco as he broke from where he'd been sitting and sending him sprawling into Tamara's path. She, too, went down. Shiu looked around for a length of a heartbeat, got his bearings, turned and dove for the gun.

Now, finally, Hunt had a clear shot, albeit at a moving target, and he came up into the door shooting. Two shots, four shots. All misses. He saw the dirt kick up on all sides around his target. Shiu, on the ground and rolling, got to Juhle's gun and, on his stomach, fully extended, got off two more shots at the barn door. On the first one, Hunt cried out. Shiu then turned and fired once in the direction of his prisoners to slow down any thought of their own attack.

His gun clicked empty. It clicked again, and Shiu swore, then dropped it as he rolled again, going for cover behind the back wheel of the tractor.

"Wyatt!" Juhle called. "He's out of ammo! Wyatt!"

"I'm down, Dev. I'm hit!"

Huddled behind the trough with both Juhle and Chiurco, Tamara was the first to find her wits and move. "Stay down, babe," she said as she broke around the trough at a dead run. Juhle's gun was on the ground five feet in front of the tractor, and she dove, somersaulted, and came up with it, tossing it back behind her to her boyfriend. "Craig! Devin's got ammunition! Use it!"

But she'd barely gotten the words out when Shiu hit her from behind at the knees, and she went down hard. In the seconds of respite he'd earned himself behind the tractor, Shiu had wrestled his own gun from his holster. Now he pulled Tamara up by the hair with his gun hand, then locked his other arm around her neck, pushed the barrel of his weapon into her temple. "That's it! It's over! Give it up!"

When he got no response, he fired in rapid succession twice into the air, then screamed out, "The next shot kills her! The next shot kills her! I'm not bluffing! Throw the guns on the ground and come on out! Everybody! *Move* or she dies now!"

Chiurco only paused for an instant before throwing Juhle's gun out over the trough. He and Juhle shared a look. They had no choice. They got to their feet.

In a fluid and unexpected move, Shiu leaned down and scooped up Juhle's gun. Keeping his own weapon pressed tight up against Tamara's head, with his other hand, he released the automatic's magazine and almost before it had fallen to the ground, he'd rammed a fresh magazine of his own into place in the handle of Juhle's gun. Tamara couldn't see what was happening and didn't react fast enough—and now Shiu had his own gun reholstered, and Juhle's loaded weapon at her head.

"Okay, now, you two," he said. "Over by the barn door." Then, raising his voice, "You in the barn! Hunt! Throw out the gun."

A silence.

"Hunt! I'm counting to three, and she dies. One . . ."

"I don't have it. You shot it away. It's somewhere back in the dark."

This slowed Shiu down for a beat, but he recovered quickly enough. "I need to see you. Get out here."

"I'm on the ground."

"Then crawl. Hands out front. Any sign of a gun and everybody dies, understand? The girl first. You other two, move aside. Let him out."

The only sound was the slow drag of Hunt's body as he pulled it across the last few feet over the floor of the barn. When he started to come into view, it appeared as if he'd been hit twice on the left side. His left arm hung apparently useless behind a bloody left leg, as he pulled himself forward with his good right side into the light. His face was still a smeared mess of dried and fresh blood. His right hand, scratching against the floor as he pulled himself along, left a bloody trail in the ancient dirt.

When his body was a little more than halfway out of the barn, Hunt was breathing hard with the pain and exertion. He stopped and looked up. "You can't do this, Shiu."

"No? What's it look like I'm doing?"

"You'll never sell it."

"No? Funny, I think I will," Shiu said. "After all, it was Devin's gun that shot poor Mrs. Manion. I'm afraid it will look like Inspector Juhle got himself in another firefight—he's known for that, you know. And then he found a reason to shoot you and your people, too. Maybe you double-crossed him somehow. When I came up here after the Manions called me, after all of your threats to their family today, I saw what was happening and tried to stop it. In the end, I had to shoot my partner in self-defense, but unfortunately not in time to save the other victims. I think it works out just fine."

"Except for one thing."

"What's that?"

Hunt paused, making sure that his body was primed to react. "You didn't rack a round on the last reload." As he said the words, Hunt pulled his left hand out from where he'd been keeping his own gun hidden behind his leg.

Shiu's double take took only a fraction of a second before he pulled the trigger on Juhle's Glock behind Tamara's head.

The dry click still hung in the air as Hunt was swinging his own gun up as fast as he could. In one movement, he steadied his left wrist with his right hand and squeezed off one shot.

It hit Shiu high in the forehead.

Juhle's gun went flying as the bullet knocked Shiu backpedaling until he rammed up against the tractor and sank to the ground.

Tamara, too, had collapsed in a heap, and Chiurco had run to her, but Juhle was already moving beyond them, getting to Shiu where he slumped, kicking his shoulder hard so that he fell to one side. Hunt, limping, was right behind him and pulled Shiu's gun out of his holster.

Taking a gasp of breath, he reached over and put a finger to Shiu's neck, leaving it there for a long moment. Then he stood up and faced his friend.

"I don't think he's going to make it," he said.

"Yeah, but enough about him," Juhle said. "Get me out of these goddamned handcuffs."

38 /

Hunt never used the crutches they gave him at the ER. The bullet had creased the top of his thigh. It gave him a scar he'd be able to brag about for the rest of his life in certain company, but the actual damage, while painful enough and spectacular in terms of blood loss, was never life threatening, although he was going to be limping for a while. His disregard for Juhle's due process in the execution of his plan, though, gave him enough bureaucratic headaches for the next couple of weeks to make up for any physical pain he might have missed due to the wound.

The Napa County DA acknowledged Hunt's role in closing the Palmer matter and in saving the life of Andrea Parisi. Nevertheless, he was not initially inclined to overlook the extra-legal methods against one of the area's most prominent citizens—vandalism, trespassing—that Hunt had employed to get his results. The DA also didn't appreciate Hunt's still sloppy CCW paperwork, especially since it was the gun in question that had fired the shot that killed Shiu.

In the end, though, Juhle's statement about the unfolding of the night's events in combination with Ward Manion's reluctance to pursue prosecution—he just wanted the nightmare to be over—persuaded the DA that he didn't need to file any charges against what was, after all, a satisfactory conclusion to an extremely unusual, difficult, even tragic situation; though the DA did make it clear to Hunt that the next time he came to the wine country to work, he'd be well advised to avoid anything like the methods he'd employed against the Manions. And if his CCW wasn't current, the DA would flat out bust him for it.

But between the rehab on his leg, the visits to Parisi first at the hospital and then at her home during her recovery, and the resolution of all the legal issues hanging fire up in Napa, his business took a serious hit during the first weeks of the summer. The notoriety he had acquired because of Palmer and Parisi did not compensate for the lack of time he could actually spend on billable work, and so he, Craig, Tamara, and Mickey spent virtually all of their time through early July out in the field or in the office, catching up.

It was some measure that his life had at last reverted to near normalcy when he found time to meet Juhle for the first time in a month at Ploof, a French restaurant specializing in mussels, for lunch. It was Bastille Day, a Thursday, and Belden Alley was decked out front to back with the tricolor. A bright summer sun shone directly overhead, the temperature hovered in the mid-seventies.

Juhle sat alone at an outside table under a Campari umbrella, nursing a clear drink with bubbles and ice. He gave no sign that he'd noticed Hunt's approach until he said, "You've still got that sympathy-limp thing going?"

Hunt pulled out his chair and sat down in it. "You want, I'll shoot you in the leg, and you can have one, too. Except I might miss and hit your kneecap by mistake."

"Nobody would believe it was a mistake. Not after the shot that took out Shiu. Which had to be as lucky as the one I got all the heat for. I still can't get over it."

"That wasn't luck, Dev. As you should know better than anybody, hand-eye is my thing. I had him all the way. What are you drinking?"

"Club soda."

"Walking on the wild side."

Juhle shrugged. "I'm on duty. I don't drink on duty. It's one of the perks of the job. But you go ahead."

"I think I will. I've got a few hours for a nice change. Maybe I'll walk home after lunch and take a nap."

"You're still walking everywhere?"

"Mostly, or taking Mickey's cab. I can't work the damn clutch yet in the Cooper." The waiter came up, and Hunt ordered a glass of beaujolais. Both men were having variations on the mussels' theme. Hunt watched the waiter walk away. "So," he came back to his friend, "you said there was news."

"Some." Juhle sipped his club soda. "I thought you'd want to know, we closed Palmer this morning. Officially."

"I wasn't really worried about it. It had to happen sometime."

"Maybe, but it's good to have it done. I mean rock solid, which it wasn't ever going to be until we found out a few things we didn't know."

"Such as?"

"Such as the gun, the murder weapon. The idiot didn't even toss it when he was done."

"Where'd you find it?"

"In a storage unit he rented out by his apartment, where he also kept his Beemer convertible." The waiter was back with Hunt's wine, and Juhle went silent until he'd moved away again. He leaned in across the table and lowered his voice. "Along with the cash."

"Cash?"

"A box of it. Same storage unit. Ninety-seven thousand, eight hundred dollars."

"So she paid him a hundred grand. I was wondering about the going rate."

"Yeah, but remember, it was a two-fer. Plus, you could probably do it a little cheaper if one of the hits wasn't a federal judge."

Hunt tasted his wine, took in the sun-dappled al fresco dining area. "You want to tell me something?"

"Like what? You used to be better-looking?"

"You used to be cleverer. Tell me something else."

"All right. What?"

"Andrea told me Mrs. Manion said it all came down that Monday afternoon after the judge called her to set up the meeting at his house. So my question is this: How do you hire somebody to kill two people on no notice? Like, 'Oh, by the way, Mr. Shiu, after you pick up the laundry, would you mind dropping by Judge Palmer's house and shooting him and his girlfriend?' I don't see how that happens."

Juhle held up a finger. "Aha! This is cool. I haven't told you about this?"

"I guess not."

"She'd felt him out before. Ward gave this to us. Evidently they'd had a problem at the house last year, some whack job deciding they owed him money or at least they needed to give him a bunch because they had so much of it. Anyway, he came onto the property here in the city a couple of times, and as you yourself have seen, their security can be pretty persuasive."

"At least."

Juhle nodded. "So they busted him and sent him on his way, but he showed up again, so they busted him again, and then again. The guy seemed basically harmless, but he was turning into a real nuisance. So one time when Ward's gone, out traveling again, the guy comes up while Carol's pulling out of the driveway, taking Todd to school. And he kind of goes off on the kid. Why does he deserve everything he's got? And so on. But evidently it got personal and pretty threatening, and Carol decided she wanted him taken care of."

"Tell me Shiu killed him."

"Can't do it, because he didn't. But what he did do was beat the living shit out of the guy and leave him in a Dumpster downtown. Out of uniform, random homeless beating, right? No record of any of it, of course, but Ward noticed the guy wasn't around anymore when he got home, and asked Carol about it. And she told him. So after Ward got over the worst of the shock last month, he remembered it and told us."

"She pay him?"

"Ten grand. Ward himself paid it out as a Christmas bonus. But the bottom line is it worked. The guy never came back."

"I can't blame him. That kind of rudeness, I don't think I would have, either."

Their waiter arrived with the food, and for a few minutes, they chowed into the succulent shellfish—garlic, cream, wine, parsley. Killer.

After a few minutes of bliss, Hunt took a break from the food. "So how's Todd?"

"Hanging in there, I guess. He's with Ward and his nanny."

"And how old's Ward?"

"I don't know. Seventy? Seventy-one?"

"Christ. The poor kid."

"The poor *rich* kid, Wyatt. I wouldn't lose any sleep over him. He'll be well taken care of, don't worry."

Hunt put down his fork. "Not to sound too sensitive or anything, Dev, but he won't be loved, and that's kind of the main thing, you know?"

Juhle was picking the meat out of the mussels, using one of his earlier shells. He popped his latest morsel and chewed for a moment. "Yeah, but so few of us are," he said, "present company excluded, of course." After a minute, he shrugged. "He'll get over it, Wyatt. Most people do."

"Except the ones who don't."

Juhle considered, swallowed, drank some club soda. "Right," he said, "except for them."

* * *

Wes Farrell's T-shirt read, THIS IS WHAT A FEMINIST LOOKS LIKE. His girlfriend Sam Duncan wore one saying, ANGER MANAGEMENT CLASSES PISS ME OFF. Neither was wearing theirs under work garb but right out loud and proud of it. It was that kind of day—yet another rare warm one, a Saturday in late July.

And it was that kind of party at Hunt's warehouse.

The celebration was over the announcement that Devin Juhle had been named San Francisco Police Officer of the Year. He'd had his formal dinner with the police brass, his family, and a roomful of his fellow lawmen at Gino & Carlo's in North Beach last weekend, but this party was different.

Hunt had a barbecue going in the alley out the back door and a pony keg of Gordon Biersch on ice in the kitchen sink. The garage door to the front of the place was all the way up. The warehouse itself had been rocking for over an hour now with everything from the Beatles and Rolling Stones to Tom Petty, Toby Keith, Jimmy Buffett, Ray Charles. Juhle and his two boys, Eric and Brendan, were playing basketball on the inside court with Mickey, Jason, and Craig. The people Hunt worked with every day as well as the other ex officio Hunt Club members—Sam, Wes, Jason, and Amy—were all in attendance, as well as Juhle's wife, Connie, of course, and their daughter Alexa.

Hunt was turning sausages and flipping burgers as Connie—pert and pretty in a yellow sundress—sidled up to him. "So where's the famous Andrea Parisi?" she asked. "I thought I was finally going to get to meet her in person."

"I don't know. To tell you the truth I thought she'd be here by now. She's probably just running late with work."

"On a Saturday?"

Hunt smiled, shook his head. "I don't know if you realized, Con, but lawyers don't differentiate between days of the week. They just work all the time. Saturday, Tuesday night, four in the morning, you name it, they're working." He gestured back inside. "Even Wes, Amy, Jason, those guys in there. They're working right now, I guarantee it."

"I'm glad I didn't decide to do that."

"Me, too. But Andrea did."

Connie hesitated. "And you like her? She likes you?"

"Well, I saved her life after all, so she's kind of obligated to be at least nice to me. But, hey, here you go. You can ask her yourself."

Andrea Parisi, accompanied by Richard Tombo, appeared at the head of the alley. In espadrilles, culottes, and a sleeveless tangerine T-shirt, she looked impossibly desirable even from a distance. As they got closer, Hunt realized that even close-up she showed little if any of the effects of her eighty hours without food or fluids. Her hair gleamed in the sun; her face had regained its color.

Connie turned back to Hunt, gave him an approving nod. "Okay, then," she said.

They made the introductions, then Hunt went inside and brought out a beer in a plastic cup for Tombo and a glass of white wine for Andrea. They made small talk, while Hunt attended to the grill. The first round was about ready, and Connie went inside to make the announcement to the rest of the guests.

Hunt moved some of the food around and smiled at the latest arrivals. "Burger, sausage, tri-tip, potato salad, and condiments inside. We've got it all. What are you both having?"

Tombo, as if on cue, said, "I'm having a bathroom run. Back in a flash."

Leaving Andrea alone with him, wearing a look he couldn't read. "Still time for rare if you decide quick," he said. But then, at her pained expression, he stopped fiddling at the grill. "Are you all right?" he asked.

"Fine," she said. She sipped some of her wine. "When you're done serving here, though, can we talk for a minute?"

"Sure."

"This is a little awkward," she said.

He'd delivered his platter of food inside and now was back out in the alley with her, halfway down to the street, away from his back door and his friends.

"I can handle awkward. What's up?"

"Well." She took a breath. "The truth is, Wyatt, I've got an offer."

"Offers are good."

"Sometimes they are. This is one of those times." Speaking more quickly now, wanting to get it all out in a hurry, she went on, "You know how everything was, I mean with the Trial TV people, before I got . . . before I disappeared? I mean, Spencer wasn't going to be able to help me. It wasn't going to happen."

"Right."

"Well, this is . . . I mean, you couldn't plan something like this, but when I was gone, missing . . . you know this, I kind of became a story."

"No 'kind of' about it. You were hot."

"I was hot," she admitted with a rueful look. "And then when it turned out I'd been kidnapped and then getting rescued the way I did . . . the way that *you* did, I mean . . . all of that, you know. Then all the interviews and stories."

Hunt had something of a vague recollection. *Time, Newsweek,* CNN. Basically, everywhere—he'd been a small part of the frenzy himself. He decided to make it easier for her. "They want you now."

She couldn't quite hide the pride in her small smile as she nodded. "Yes. Yes, they do. Without doing anything myself to make it happen, it seems now I've got name recognition."

Hunt forced his own brave smile. He brought a finger up and touched her cheek. "And pretty-face recognition."

"Maybe even that," she said, "if you can believe it."

"Oh, I believe that all right. So have you told your boss here yet?"

"Gary? Well, that's the other thing. Things at work, at Piersall, have been . . . well, I've told you a little about this. It seems Gary has come to think I might have been personally involved with Judge Palmer. . . ."

"That's all right, Andrea. I don't need . . ."

"No." Her eyes bored into his, signaling her complete honesty, begging him to believe her because she was being so sincere. "But I just need to tell you that I would never have done that. It would have been completely unethical. We were working on huge cases together, Judge Palmer and me, millions and millions of dollars, and anything personal between us would have jeopardized every single case we touched."

"Okay," Hunt said, his heart tightening in his chest. For an instant, he considered telling her that it didn't matter. People weren't perfect; everybody made mistakes. It wasn't his place to judge her. What hurt him now was that she felt she had to lie to him, that perhaps it was okay, even noble, to lie to him if it would keep his vision of her intact.

As though he had ever wanted the vision.

He'd wanted the person.

And now that person irrevocably was someone who could look him in the eye and not tell him the truth. Because though he might never be able to prove if she had had her rumored affair with Judge Palmer, he knew that her denying it now with these rehearsed lines was a lie. And now suddenly what might have been had become what never could be.

She was going on. "Gary said that even a hint of that suspicion, any sign at all, and Jim Pine would fire the whole firm. All of our work for them would be suspect, subject to appeal or lawsuits, worthless." She drew a breath. "Anyway, I don't know if there's any more law work for me in this town anymore. For what it's worth, Gary seemed to recognize that. The severance package was pretty good."

Hunt forced another smile. "So it's all worked out?"

"Yes, except for . . ." She paused. "Well, that you and I never really had a chance to . . ."

Gently, he raised a hand and pressed two fingers against her lips. "Don't worry about you and me," he said. "You're a star, Andrea. Go be a star."

She nodded, sighed, smiled up at him. "I knew you'd understand, Wyatt."

"I do. Completely." One last attempt at a smile. "So when are you going?"

"Can you believe it? They want me Monday. I fly out tomorrow."

Hunt was sitting on the cooler in the alley, hands around a plastic cup full of beer as Connie came out the back door. "Can I take a minute with Mr. Hunt?" she asked.

"You can take an hour if you want, although Devin might be upset."

"No. He likes me to spend time with other guys. He says it always makes him look so much better by comparison."

Hunt had to grin. "He's one of a kind, all right."

"He's not all wrong, not most of the time, anyway."

Hunt put an arm around her. "If you're flirting with me, you've got a half an hour to cut it out."

"I'll time it," she said. Looking back over her shoulder, making sure they were out of earshot, she said, "I just want to tell you, seriously, how grateful I am—we all are—to you. And how proud."

He turned to look at her. "What for?"

"Well, maybe it slipped your mind in the crush of events, Wyatt, but while you were getting all the fame and glory for finding Andrea Parisi, the important thing to me is that you also saved my man's life. He knows you did, too."

"I didn't—"

"Don't go all modest on me, Wyatt. It's unbecoming. You saved his life. You saved all their lives. I will never be able to thank you enough, nor will the kids, and they don't even have any kind of real understanding of it yet."

"Not being modest, Con, but it was really just circumstances. It could have gone another way, and he would have saved me. I mean, he's not the cop of the year for nothing."

"No. I know that. But he also wouldn't be the cop of the year if something hadn't got him back into being who he is."

"I think that might have been a little bit you, too."

She nodded. "Acknowledged, but you lit the fire under him. You made it happen. I think you saved more than his life, Wyatt. You brought him back to who he is."

"Well, he's a great guy."

"Yes, and he always has been, although sometimes he forgets it. But when *he* does, he's got me to remind him. You. I don't think you get reminded often enough that you're pretty special yourself. So I thought I'd take a minute and tell you." She put her hand on his arm. "Do you hear me?"

Hunt let out a breath. "I hear you. Thank you."

"You're welcome." Connie leaned into him briefly and then stood up and looked back behind her. "Okay," she said. "Where did she go? I didn't get to say ten words to her."

"Who?"

" 'Who?' he asks. The famous Andrea Parisi? Perhaps your girl-friend, not that I'm asking."

Hunt tried to keep it light. "She had to leave. She got a new job in New York and starts on Monday."

"In New York. But what about you?"

"What about me? I'm fine."

"You're not. You liked her. You liked her a lot."

But he shook his head. "I never really knew her, Con, except that she was beautiful and smart and fun and nice."

"Well, my friend, that doesn't sound all bad. Some people, they look for those things in people they date."

"They're good qualities, I admit, as far as they go."

"But they don't go far enough? Is that it?"

Hunt considered for a second. "That's a nice way to put it," he said. As he turned to Connie, this time his smile was genuine. "It's for the best, Con. I really think it's for the best."

ACKNOWLEDGMENTS

My first and most important acknowledgment is to my mate, friend, partner, and muse Lisa Sawyer. Without a solid and happy home front, nothing creative is possible for me, and Lisa's strength, good sense, and fundamental joy in life makes her the best lifelong companion imaginable. Contributing mightily to our domestic tranquility as well as to the tone of these books, our son Jack Sawyer Lescroart remains constant in his role as best pal, jokester, plot checker, general all-around mensch.

Also close to home, my longtime collaborator Al Giannini has once again walked the walk with me from the earliest stages of this effort. His take on the most labyrinthine inner workings of the legal community, his encyclopedic knowledge of both the law and of human nature, and his creative instincts have been part and parcel of the underpinnings of every one of my San Francisco books, and my debt to him cannot be overstated. For thirty or so years, Andy Jalakas worked in child protective services in New York, and many of his experiences led me to the backstory for this novel's lead character. At Andy's suggestion, I also read and drew from a powerful and important book, Marc Parent's *Turning Stones: My Days and Nights with Children at Risk*. I also tip my hat in thanks to David Corbett, a very, very fine writer and former private investigator, who was very generous with his time, expertise, and insight. My assistant, Anita Boone, continues in her role as majordomo, efficiency expert, fact checker, and general right-hand person. She's a terrific help and perhaps the world's most patient human being, especially around sometimes angst-ridden writers.

Over the past several years, my Internet correspondence has assumed an important role in helping me communicate directly with my readers, some of whom have recommended concepts that might be fun to explore. Before I even began to think about *The Hunt Club*, one of my correspondents, Joe Phelan, recommended that I take a look at the California Correctional Peace Officers Association (the CCPOA), or prison guards' union. That suggestion came to play a central role in this book, and I'm grateful to Joe for all of his references. That said, I reiterate that though the CCPOA material in the book is based on actual facts and occurrences, this is a work of fiction, and I took substantial liberties with both the organizational structure and leadership of the union. (I love hearing from my readers and can be contacted through my Web site, www.johnlescroart.com.)

For technical advice on various topics, I'd like to thank San Francisco Police Officer Shawn Ryan for the chilling details of his own firefight; my friend Peter J. Diedrich, Esq., for the odd, obscure legal nugget that helps to season this narrative; and Frank Seidl for his wide-ranging knowledge of Napa County and the wine industry, which much to my delight I've finally had an opportunity to exploit. Karen Hlavacek is an incredible proofreader whom I can't thank enough.

This book, to say the least, did not write itself. In fact, in the early stages, it sometimes felt as though it would never get truly started. But helping me out of the blocks were my two great friends who also happen to toil in these fields of words—John Poswall and Max Byrd.

Carole Baron, though no longer at the helm at Dutton, has been a guiding force and cheerleader for my work from the very beginning, and she contributed mightily to the original concept here. Day to day, my editor, Mitch Hoffman, has kept the process on its course with several interim readings (and astute comments). Don Matheson, perennial best man, provides my regular gumption fix, without which the pages would pile up far too slowly and would be far less fun to write.

Several characters in this book owe their names (although no physical or personality traits, which are all fictional) to individuals whose contributions to various charities have been especially generous. These people (and their respective charities) include Doug Malinoff, Yolo County Court Appointed Special Advocates (CASA); Sue Kutschkau, Cal State Fullerton Foundation; and Betsy Sobo, the

American Repertory Ballet. Lastly, I am extremely grateful as always to my agent, Barney Karpfinger, who embraced the perhaps risky idea of this book from its conception and helped to keep the seed alive until it came to fruition.

ABOUT THE AUTHOR

John Lescroart is the author of sixteen previous novels, including *The Motive*, *The Second Chair*, *The First Law*, *The Oath*, *The Hearing*, and *Nothing But the Truth*. He lives with his wife and two children in Northern California.